Guardian

Aisling Trilogy, Book 1

Carole Cummings

This is a work of fiction. Names, characters, places, and incidents either are the product of the author's imagination or are used fictitiously, and any resemblance to actual persons, living or dead, business establishments, events, or locales is entirely coincidental.

Guardian Aisling Trilogy Book 1

Interior layout and design by P.D. Singer

Cover content is for illustrative purposes only and any person depicted on the cover is a model.

Maps created using a template courtesy of freefantasymaps.org

Print ISBN: 978-1-62622-090-4

First Edition published 2010 by Prizm Books

Second Edition published 2015 DSP Publications

Third Edition published 2020

Rocky Ridge Books
Box 6922
Broomfield, CO 80021

For Julia

Cynewisan
(The Commonwealth)
The Guild
Riocht
(The Dominion)
Old Bridge
Lind
The Bounds
Chester
Green Basin
Putnam
Kenley
Dudley

GLOSSARY

Æledfýres

(āel-et-fēr-es) God of fire. Brother of the Father. One of what are known as the old gods. Also referred to as dearg-dur or daeva.

Ǽlíf

(āel-if) Given name of the Mother; literally translated as "eternal."

Aire

(ə-rā) Literally translated as "danger."

Aisling

(ä-ēsh-ling) Literally translated as "dream." In Ríocht's culture the Aisling is also referred to as the Chosen, a holy figure who is called on once a year to ask the Father for His favor and blessings, and then convey those blessings onto the people.

Brethren

A band of priests cast out of the Guild and reformed as a more fanatical sect dedicated to the Father.

Brionglóid

(briŋg-lòid) Given name of the Father; literally translated as "dream."

Célnes

(sāl-nəs) Goddess of the wind. Sister of the Mother. One of what are known as the old gods, or the gods of the Four Corners.

Chester

A midsized city south of Lind.

Chosen

See Aisling.

Cildtrog

A holy place in Lind; literally translated as "cradle."

Cliabhán

(klē-ə-bän) Cradle.

Coimirceoir

(kim-ȯl-ēk-āȯrr) Literally translated as "guardian."

Commonwealth

See Cynewísan.

Cynewísan

(kin-ə-wiss-än) Also referred to as the Commonwealth. A conglomeration of united provinces with a democratic government overseen by their elected Elders. Bordered to the north and east by Ríocht.

Daeva

Vampire.

Dearg-dur

Incubus; soul-eater.

Deartháireacha

(dē-ath-air-rēch-ə) Brothers.

Díepe

(dē-əp-ā) Goddess of water. Sister of the Mother. One of what are known as the old gods, or the gods of the Four Corners.

Dudley

A small village south of Putnam.

Ealdordéman

(al-dȯr-de-mȯn) Chief judge.

Eorðbúgigend

(ē-ərthpā-gēg-ānd) God of the earth. Brother of the Father. One of what are known as the old gods, or the gods of the Four Corners.

Father

The patron deity of Ríocht. God of music, harmony of the seasons, beauty, the stars, and dreams.

Fæðme

(fa-äm-ə) Womb.

First Tongue

The language of the old gods and the first clans.

Flównysse

(flō-win-üss-e) A major river that runs a southeasterly course from the mountains on Lind's northern border.

Foreládtéowes

(făr-eläd-tā-äw-es) Chief; leader.

Gníomhaire

(gə-nēv-əm-h'er) Literally translated as "agent."

Guild

The governing body of Ríocht.

Lind

A province of Cynewísan known for its Old Ones, a governing assembly of magic users and healers. Its denizens are devoted to the Mother and are highly secretive, keeping themselves as isolated from the rest of the Commonwealth as is possible. It sits in the northeast corner of Cynewísan. Ríocht sits at its northern and eastern borders.

Mother

The patron deity of Cynewísan. Goddess of cultivating, reaping, comfort, nurturing, protection, and war.

North Tongue

Native language of Ríocht.

Old Bridge

A tiny hamlet in northern Cynewísan, northwest of Putnam.

Putnam

A major city in the mideastern region of Cynewísan (also referred to the Commonwealth).

Ríocht

(rē-äkht) Also referred to as the Dominion. A highly religious and patriarchal country governed by priests sworn to the Father, their patron deity. Bordered to the west and south by Cynewísan.

Wæpenbora

(wap-en-bär-ȯ) Weapon-bearer; warrior-knight.

Wæterþéotan

(wat-er-thă-ät-an) Conduit; floodgate.

Weardas

(we-ȯrd-ȯs) Watchmen; guards; ones who stand post.

Guardian

CHAPTER 1

"This one's yours, Brayden."

Dallin watched the leather folio skid across the desk and come to rest with a smart *slap* against his mug. Coffee slopped over the rim, and he scowled. Elmar stood grinning at the chief's elbow, snorting wolfishly. Dallin ignored him. He'd never liked Elmar.

Lips pursed, Dallin wicked up his lamp and tipped a nod to Jagger. "Chief." Swiping coffee from its flyleaf, Dallin opened the folio. "What's this, and why's it mine?"

"You're good at this sort of thing," Elmar supplied, still with that arsy grin. Dallin wondered what that grin would look like with a few less teeth. "That is, it's within your purview of interest, I should say." A waggle of thin eyebrows beneath a lank fringe of greasy brown hair. "A pretty little piece too, innit, Chief?"

Jagger rolled his eyes with a slight clench of teeth, then

turned on Elmar. "Have you got that request to the Ambassador finished yet?"

Elmar's grin finally fled. As did he. "Right away, Chief" was all he said as he scarpered.

Jagger watched the back of him with a sour grimace. "That's the sort as gets shot by his own in the army." Dallin covered his smirk as the chief turned back to him and waved a hand to the folio. "Witness," he said. "There was murder done at the Kymberly last night."

Dallin snapped his glance up. "*Murder?*" He stared. He'd lived in Putnam for more than twenty years, been a constable for nigh on ten of them, and yet, even after two tours in the cavalry and all the violence inherent therein, murder in the more civilized Putnam still gave him a mild shock. Dallin focused on the few sheaves of paper inside the folio. "And at the Kymberly, by the Mother." He shot another glance at the chief. "Was it robbery?" The significance abruptly caught up with him, and his heart did a bit of a flip. "Not Ramsford?"

Medeme Ramsford—respectable proprietor of the respectable Kymberly, onetime companion, and best friend in the long years since.

The chief shook his head. "Master Ramsford is unscathed, but for p'raps a few bruised knuckles." He shrugged at Dallin's quizzical look. "He had to pull the brigand off the victim, and the brigand didn't want to let go."

"Bloody damn." Dallin sighed in relief. "Is this the man, then?" He held up the prisoner profile. "There isn't much here."

"And I wouldn't make bank on what is," Jagger told him. "That's the witness—or the instigator, depending on what you manage to wring from him." A frown from Dallin got another shrug from the chief, this one a little uncomfortable. "It would seem that the fight started over who would keep company with this...." He took the paper and scanned it quickly, then handed it back. "This Calder."

A prostitute. Bloody hell. Dallin slumped. *Now* he understood Elmar's sly digs.

"And you want me to slap him around a bit." His voice was flat, but he couldn't keep his jaw from tightening. He'd thought that was finished, at least between himself and Jagger. "I never touched the woman, damn it, and I won't be used as some sort of ogre to scare the whores into—"

"I want you to *question* him because I don't fancy letting Elmar or Payton at him. Have I ever done else to make you think otherwise?"

The chief stared, gaze level and hard, until Dallin's hackles smoothed again and he glanced away. "You have not, sir," he said, chastened. In fact, he'd asked Dallin the question once, and when Dallin had testified that—as little as even he'd believed it—the woman had bounced her own head off the table before screeching her accusations, Jagger had merely nodded, accepted Dallin's word, and signed off personally on all the reports. Dallin supposed it wasn't Jagger's fault the other smarmy gits wouldn't let it go. Payton had bloody *congratulated* him. Slimy little shit. Dallin cleared his throat. "My apologies."

Jagger accepted this with a small nod. "It isn't like it was before." His mouth set in a thin, bitter line. "These men aren't veterans of Aldrich's army like you and me—honor is something they talk about, not something they know, and it's only got worse since Wheeler took command. People view this truce as a victory and affirmation that Wheeler's ways are the right ones, not the capitulation it really is, and all the while, we become more and more like our enemy every day. Men like us are getting steadily pushed out of positions of rank and authority to make way for the types who would as soon pull a few fingernails as ask a simple question." He shook himself with a surly snort. "Which is neither here nor there at the moment, but the bottom line is that as long as I am in charge here, we do things the old way—our way.

"Here is this Calder's statement, and those of the other witnesses." He slid more papers at Dallin. "The truth is, even had I not already decided as much, Ramsford asked that I assign you. He says you've been a friend to him, and he's concerned for the... lad." He cleared his throat. "And in truth, I'm not sure I trust any other with this witness. This man, this... this *boy*... I can't tell." The chief looked away. "I'll say no more. Ask your own questions, draw your own conclusions, then report them to me."

"But... wait—witness, not suspect?" Dallin lifted his gaze from the papers. "We have the murderer in custody, yes? So why did we bring this man in? Did no one interview him at the scene?"

"I interviewed him at the scene. I decided the... situation required further enlightenment."

Dallin shrugged. "As you wish. But I'm not sure I understand what I'm to do with him. All these statements seem to say the same thing. One man killed another—one is on a slab, and one is in a cell. What exactly am I meant to wring from this one?"

Jagger sighed, pulled out the chair opposite the desk, and lowered himself into it tiredly. There were circles under his bloodshot eyes, and his skin was pallid gray. He must have been dragged from his bed for this some hours ago. He leaned into the desk and folded his hands atop it.

"The victim and the assailant were both Dominionites."

Dallin's stomach gave a little flip. "That's...." He pushed a low whistle between his teeth.

"It is," Jagger agreed. "The talks in Penley go bad enough as it is. The last thing Cynewísan needs is to give the Dominion an excuse to make them go worse. If I can help it, Putnam will not be giving them that excuse." His big hands opened. "I'm sending a courier with a request to their ambassador for instructions on what they... *suggest* we do with this Orman."

"The suspect." When Jagger nodded confirmation, Dallin smirked. "May I suggest Corliss for courier duty?"

"You may. She's due for a day away from the brood, I imagine—an overnight will be good for her. Anyway, she's likely the only one I can trust not to get drunk and start a fight at the inn."

Dallin loosed a mild snort as he flipped through the papers. "I wouldn't take that bet."

"A good subordinate allows his chief an illusion or two."

"All right, then." Dallin peered down at the papers, all innocence. "In that case I'll let you believe I made the suggestion because Corliss is the better rider, and not because I'll be chuckling myself to sleep tonight, imagining the looks on a bunch of Dominionites' faces when they receive that request from a woman's hand."

"Ha!" Jagger sat back with a dreamy look in his eye. "A woman in *trousers*, no less. I think I'd pay to see that. Devious bugger, you are." He grinned when Dallin gave him a modest little flourish of his hand. "Even if you weren't so good at your job, I think I'd keep you about for sheer comic relief."

Dallin took the gruff, left-handed compliment with a shrug and a stifled grin.

Jagger snorted, then turned serious again. "I'll want your report ready for the afternoon's post. I mean to send it on to their ambassador and ours, plus copies of everything we have to the Elders in Penley. I want them there with the morning post so Corliss can bring back…." He sighed. "Whatever word they choose to send with her."

"Don't suppose I could pull courier duty and let Corliss take the statement?"

"No, but it was a nice try. We need to go by the letter on this, no mistakes. The scrap is said to have started over this Calder person, and I'm not satisfied he's been truthful thus far. I would know all I can before I send those reports." Jagger shifted uncomfortably. "There was talk of conjuring."

"There's always talk of conjuring."

"True. Still, two of the other witnesses—including Ramsford himself—said the victim, if you can call him such, and the assailant both seemed tranced, and this Orman accused as much during his interrogation."

"Don't they all," Dallin muttered. "Do you believe it?"

Jagger sighed, weary, and rubbed at his stubbled chin. "As you say, they all claim witchery when caught. Still, I've met the man, and I must admit to… entertaining the possibility."

Dallin looked again at the scant information he'd been provided. "His papers look legal."

"They also say he's from Lind," Jagger told him. "And if that man is from Lind, or even from Cynewísan, I'll don petticoats and ask you for a dance come Turning Night."

Ah. Lind. Better and better. Shaking his head, Dallin tucked the page back into the folio and flipped it closed. "Never place a bet on which you have no intention of making good, sir."

"Not unless you're dead certain." Jagger stood and turned to quit the room. "You'll see."

Dallin had never liked coming down to the gaol wing of the constabulary, set dark and dank in the basement of the great building where justice ground its wheels above and in the light of day. It was dim and moldy, the only light the oily flicker of smoky gas lamps set in sconces too few and far apart. And even though the interrogation rooms were set more toward the center of the cellars, at least fifty feet down and around the corner of the wide corridor to the left, still Dallin wrinkled his nose at the smells that breathed from the cell wing, permeating every pore of stone and brick: piss and vomit, stale liquor and fear, rancid heat from new fires built on the bones of the old. Death leached in somehow, snaking its darkling spice into brick and mortar, and Dallin shook his head at himself. They'd not lost one down here in seven years, and that had been the old caretaker who'd tripped over his own wash bucket and broke his tosspot neck. No angry ghosts. Still, Dallin couldn't help the slight shudder as he slipped his holster from his hips and handed it over to the bailiff.

Beldon turned the book on the table with his wide, callused hands and handed Dallin a pen. "Sign in."

Dallin bent to comply but couldn't help a sideways glance as Beldon looped the belt around the holster, eyeing the cool metal inside it with greedy appreciation. "From Booker's in Wedgewood," Dallin offered. "A pretty sum, but it comes with proof and papers from Oxnaford."

"And it sings?"

"True and sweet as a virgin lass on her wedding night."

Beldon snorted. "Your witness is in there." He jerked his head toward the heavy wooden door in the center of the stone corridor. "You'd best step along. Payton didn't wait for you."

Dallin frowned. "Payton? What's—"

"He's the one signed him in," Beldon cut in. "Couldn't've stopped him had I wanted to."

The discomfort in Beldon's glance gave Dallin pause. "You wanted to?"

Beldon sat back as he slid Dallin's revolver carefully from hand to hand. "He spoke of having another go at the 'poof enchanter.'" He said it with a disapproving curl of his mouth but hitched his shoulders in a *What do you want from me?* shrug when Dallin glared. "His words," Beldon said. "But I wasn't keen on the way he said 'em. The lad was already bruised a bit going in, but...." Another shrug. "I made sure Payton knew someone would be counting them on his way back out. I've bent my ear, but so far I've heard nothing to move me down the hall."

Dallin merely nodded and tightened his jaw. He only just remembered to offer a curt "Thank you" over his shoulder as he made his way down the corridor.

He was almost hoping to surprise Payton in midblow or something when he swung the door open. He liked Payton only a little more than he liked Elmar. Both men were rather too fond of the more sordid aspects of their jobs than was decent; both men looked upon their constant striving to earn the responsibility of carrying a sidearm as a goal and a right to be had rather than the somber, ofttimes distasteful duty it was. But Payton was merely lounging on one of the wooden chairs, his handsome face smiling easily, perfect white teeth bright even in the dim of the lamps.

"Ah, Brayden, I wondered when you'd spoil my little chat." Payton waved over the table. "You've not met this—" He cleared his throat with a shrug that was a bit exaggerated, but still theatrically elegant. "*—gentleman.*" The inflection made it all too clear that the intent was in direct opposition to the word itself.

Dallin said nothing, only pointed his gaze toward the huddled figure on the other side of the table. Dark hair worn long to his shoulders, but clean and kempt, hid the man's face, and he had yet to look up. The shoulders were hunched, an attempt at smallness, perhaps, but Dallin could see that the build was lean and lanky. Height was not readily apparent, but the hands that stuck out from the ends of sleeves too long and loose were long-fingered, red and roughened with new chafing and calluses. The posture was one of resigned defeat, but there was nothing abject about it. Dallin sensed a hum beneath it all, an alert watchfulness that belied the weary set of the shoulders and hang of the head.

"Says his name's Calder." Payton tipped his chair onto its back legs with a laconic smile. "What was that first name again, Calder?"

"Wilfred" was the soft answer. "Wil." The voice was quiet,

nearly gentle, so why did Dallin get the impression the name had been shoved out from between clenched teeth?

"Mm." Payton peered up at Dallin. "Wilfred Calder. Wil. From Lind." He rolled his eyes. "Wilfred Calder, this is Constable Brayden. He's to be your new friend, because frankly, you've bored me." The chair thumped as Payton stood and moved aside to let Dallin have it. "I've got nothing from him we don't already know. You handle it, Brayden." The tone had changed from pleasant and conversational to cool disregard. "P'raps you speak the same language."

Dallin let the slur go, but not the insolence. "Since it's my case," he said levelly, "I suggest you should not have been questioning a witness without my presence to begin with." He kept his voice even but allowed a slight edge of menace into the tone. "See that it doesn't happen again."

Payton's cool look turned sour. A glare he couldn't possibly back up kept wanting to stretch at his face, but to his credit he kept his expression to mere calculation. Dallin let him look. Dallin had rank and seniority, his size, and Jagger's ear; Payton had what passed for charm, his looks, and Elmar for a friend. Dallin gave him a moment to draw his own conclusions.

Thwarted, Payton turned his ire on the witness. "Wake up there, Calder, and give the constable his due *respect*." The word curled up in sarcastic mockery. Dallin ignored Payton's bit of a smirk but took a step forward when Payton gave a light cuff to the witness's ear. "Look up and greet your new friend—he's likely the only one you'll have here."

Calder flinched away from the blow but shot a murderous glare up at Payton. Dallin only just kept from snorting. It died in his throat when the man turned his head and leveled his gaze with Dallin's.

It was like looking inside a liquid pool of verdigris, deep and dense, murky depths shifting with swirls of sage and emerald. Almost as though the black ink spots of the pupils lay buoyant, gently poised atop a shifting well of malachite. Not just looking at Dallin, but *seeing* him—seeing him profoundly, and into depths Dallin himself had never plumbed.

I know you, he thought, grasping at a purling wisp of recognition that slipped through the saner fingers of reason. *No. No, I don't, but... why does it feel like I should?*

The face should have been pale, but layers of sunburn flaked about the nose, one atop the other, and a thin swarm of new freckles flecked the high cheekbones, as though the man had spent his life locked up in a dark room and had only recently got his first bite of the sun—and the sun had bitten him back. The features were sharp and angular, too thin and too young, but the eyes took all youth and buried it beneath darkling depths of years and sorrows this man could not possibly have lived. Dark circles bloomed beneath green eyes, and a bruise flowered and purpled along the right cheekbone, swept up past the temple and into black hair. None of it served to mar the comely features; none of it took away the sheer beauty.

Disturbed and disoriented, Dallin tried to pull his gaze away—couldn't.

Is this what those men saw just before they'd come to blows? Was this witchcraft, as they'd claimed? Or merely the animal reaction of men confronted with something they'd never seen before and perhaps wanted to possess? A reaction, Dallin was dismayed to find, to which he himself didn't seem immune.

Stop looking at me, stop seeing *me.*

Dallin shook his head, opened his mouth—a greeting, an introduction, he didn't know, just *something* to shock him out of his own absurd stupor—but he was suddenly, embarrassingly mute. He rubbed at his eyes to cover it.

The movement brought Calder to action—he leaped from his chair, stumbled a bit as he backed over it, and then pressed his back to the far wall. Payton was instantly on alert. He took a step, but Dallin shot a hand out and held him back.

Calder was taller than he'd thought, Dallin realized with the small part of his normally analytical mind that was still working. Wider too.

He was only trying to make himself small, unthreatening. Remember that later—you might need it.

Payton was the first to recover, shrugging out of Dallin's grip. "Sit down, sir." He took a step forward, request and warning both.

"*Aire,*" Calder breathed, eyes locked to Dallin, disregarding Payton completely and vibrating now as though his bones would shake loose. "*Gníomhaire!*"

Payton snorted. "Oh, you're from Lind, all right." Disgusted now, he stepped around the table to right the chair. "I asked you to sit down, Mister Calder. I won't ask again."

Calder only kept staring, didn't even seem to hear. "*Guardian.*" He spat the word like it tasted bad.

They all three stared—Dallin and Calder at each other, Payton shifting his glance between them. The fear and betrayal in Calder's eyes mystified Dallin. People reacted to his size; it was a natural thing, double takes and instinctive backward twitches. Dallin had been used to it since before he'd sprouted his first patchy bit of beard. In the line of work he'd chosen—or had chosen him, depending on how one looked at it—it was sometimes a handy tool. Useful, and therefore useable. Still, this seemed a bit extreme. *What have I ever done to you?* he wanted to ask, and only just kept himself from actually voicing the question out loud. Instead he stood silent, staring into eyes that seemed to swallow his sense, set him swaying.

Bewitched. Calder wasn't beautiful, Dallin decided. Those oracles he had for eyes just made one think he was. Even the fear was beguiling.

Dallin was still staring, trying not to feel so off, and only came back to himself when Payton cleared his throat.

"You will agree, Constable, that the witness has turned hostile and presents a danger to himself and the constabulary officers." Payton held out his hand. "May I have your manacles, please?"

The benevolent, sympathetic part of Dallin's mind registered the flare of panic in Calder's eyes at the prospect of restraint. The rational part of it understood immediately the advantage of that fear.

Dallin tore his gaze away from Calder, blinking, then stared down at Payton's open hand. Reluctance swept him.

Dallin could break Calder in half if he really wanted to. Shackles were hardly necessary. Anyway, the anticipatory gleam in Payton's eye filled Dallin with vague disgust. He almost refused just for the pleasure of spiking the smarmy git. Still, it would take hours of steady pressure to get the same level of discomfort the mere threat of confinement had brought. Dallin calculated that carrying out the threat would ramp up that discomfort and save them all some time and trouble, perhaps trip this Calder into anxious confession before lunchtime. And considering the raised hackles at the back of Dallin's neck, the swarming sense that something was going on right beneath his sight but not where he could see it with his eyes, magic seemed all too likely at the moment.

He handed over the shackles, their wide cuffs etched with charms and suppression spells. Dallin had always thought those engravings a silly pretension—now he only hoped the engraver hadn't been asleep on the job.

The snap of the metal over his wrists seemed to pull Calder back to the room. His eyes widened, gaze turning bright with dread for a moment, before it deliberately dulled and sank to the floor. His shoulders hunched again, and he bowed his head. A perfect imitation of submission, but Dallin had no delusions. The calculation in his lack of resistance as Payton all but threw Calder into the chair and the limp defeat of his posture all but screamed buried defiance, calm cunning.

"Well, that was the most excitement I've seen in months." The light in Payton's eyes and the near pant as he breathed reminded Dallin again why he didn't like this man. "I think perhaps I'll stay after all."

"No." Dallin's voice was calmer than he'd expected it to be, but his nerve endings were jittering, keeping the hairs at the back of his neck at rigid attention. "I don't think you will." He ignored Payton's glare, merely stepped to the door, hauled it open, and stared, expectant. He'd like to think the flat look was a handy reminder that if Payton didn't do as he was bid, Dallin could very well make him.

It worked. Payton loosed a small growl under his breath, then lifted his chin, straightened his coat, and swanned to the door. He shot a sour sneer over his shoulder. "Don't think I won't—"

"You're not leaving me in here alone with *him*, are you?"

It was shaky, high-pitched, and frantic. Payton and Dallin both turned back to Calder, manacled hands clenched atop the table now, the dull look of defeat forgotten in new panic. Dallin could hardly credit it. He knew his size was intimidating, but this man looked at him as though he'd done murder right in front of him—as though he knew him and had cause to fear him.

It was unnerving. Dallin didn't *get* unnerved.

"Out," Dallin said to Payton, and when Payton didn't move fast enough, Dallin let go of the door and let its weight swing it home. Payton didn't yelp, but his arms windmilled a bit as he pulled them hastily through the steadily narrowing doorway. Dallin allowed himself a small smirk before turning back to the... he kept wanting to think of this Calder as a prisoner and had to remind himself he was merely a witness, manacles notwithstanding.

Dallin shook his head and pulled in a long steadying breath, then pushed it out slowly. Calmly, moving deliberately so as not to alarm again, he lowered himself into the empty chair, took up the folio, and splayed it open.

"These papers name you Wilfred Calder. Do you hold to the claim?"

Calder's green eyes narrowed in confusion and suspicion. A slow nod was all Dallin got by way of answer. Dallin sighed. This would go hard—he could tell already. He mentally waved good-bye to another cup of coffee, and probably his lunch, and prepared himself for a long morning.

"They further claim that you are from Lind." This time Dallin peered up, openly skeptical.

Calder's gaze dropped and shifted to the table. "I've done no wrong." His voice was soft again, but with threads of rebellious bravado. "Do you intend to keep me prisoner here, or…?"

"You are not a prisoner." Dallin pointedly didn't look when Calder's hands shifted on the table, deliberately dragging the small chain across the surface. "You were witness to foul murder, and a statement is needed."

"I've given my statement—twice. I saw a man who introduced himself as Orman beat another who introduced himself as Palmer to death. May I go now?"

Dallin nearly smirked, mildly amused at the cornered audacity. "I'm told they fought over who would keep company with you."

Calder's mouth screwed up in an uneasy scowl. "I encouraged no such contest. Nor did I want it."

First hit.

"So, they *did* quarrel over you."

Calder's eyes closed, and his head sank lower. Dallin could almost hear the inner *shit, shit, shit* at the accidental confession.

"Did they argue over price, one trying to outbid the other?"

A clench of the teeth this time. "I am no doxy."

And there's another.

"A witch, then?"

Calder snorted as though he'd expected the accusation. "Magic is illegal, but for those registered and sanctioned to practice by the Commonwealth."

"I know the law, thank you."

"As do I."

"Then you know that failing to register is a minor infraction, and you'd not be likely to spend even a fortnight in gaol—*if* you confess."

It wasn't a lie. Failure to register was a small violation. Practicing magic without license, however, was decidedly not. And magicking with criminal intent was another matter altogether. Dallin had every intention of sharing those bits of information —*after* he got whatever confession there was to be had.

Calder's head was still down, so Dallin couldn't see his face, but he saw the jaw set rigid. "Men would see witchery where there is only vice. I cannot be blamed for another's lack of control."

"Vice, then, as you will. So, you accepted attentions from one and not the other."

"I accepted nothing!"

Dallin let the slight roll of his eyes speak his doubt. "Do you say you didn't intend to sleep with either man, or that you didn't intend to charge them for it?"

Calder's long fingers curled in, fisted, knuckles turning yellow-white. Heavy, pinioned silence.

"Prostitution has not been a hanging offense for decades," Dallin ventured quietly. "A fine the first time, nothing more. If you cooperate, I can see there's not even that, but I must—"

"I do not sleep with men for *money*." It was almost a hiss.

Dallin lifted an eyebrow. The same mark, and hit harder this time. He went for a third. "What do you sleep with them for?"

"Why?" The sudden smile was coy and cold. "Interested?"

Not at all the wrath and loss of control he'd hoped for. "And if I were?"

The smile slid away. Calder looked down again. "You like to play with people, don't you, Guardian? Makes you feel powerful, I expect." He lifted his hands, chain jinking and jangling. "You already have all the power. Why do you prolong this? Can we just get on and have an end?"

Dallin resisted a puzzled frown. "All right—tell me who you really are, and I'll see what I can do."

The defeat was back again, real this time—Dallin could read it in the slope of the shoulders, the desperate grasping of the hands as Calder pushed his fingers into his hair and groaned, small and helpless. The body language was speaking volumes, but actual information was apparently going to have to be dug out from between verbal feints and weaves.

A livid scar drew his gaze, jagging around Calder's left wrist and over the back of his hand to the knuckles, lumping the skin into tight pink puckers. Dallin noted it but put it aside.

"Just do it and get it over," Calder whispered. "I'm tired and I can't do this anymore. Stop playing, *Gníomhaire*, and just do it."

"Why do you call me that?"

"Because it is what you are. We should call things by their proper names, shouldn't we, you and I? Now, of all times."

Annoyed now, Dallin allowed a tolerant sigh. "I am Brayden, First Constable of the Province of Putnam." He dipped his head in a small, ironic imitation of a respectful bow. "I suppose 'guardian' is a more delicate term than some would choose, but what is the other? Are you swearing at me? Or are you speaking in tongues? That in itself is enough cause for an accusation of magicking."

Slowly, Calder lifted his head. Eyes that too obviously held back tears blinked across the table—curiosity, disbelief, and... something Dallin couldn't name. Hope?

"You don't...." Whisper-quiet, but not as shaky. Calder's eyes narrowed again, and he tilted his head. "Guardian?"

"Brayden," Dallin repeated patiently. "*Constable* Brayden." He leaned in, a bit of concern now leaching through the irritation. Calder was far too pale beneath his unfortunate overdose of sun, and his eyes looked unfocused. "Are you well? Do you need rest, water?"

"Am I... well?" Calder stared like he was looking for something, trying to dig into Dallin's head and pick apart what he found there.

Dallin stared back, wondering why he'd thought this man beautiful. Handsome, surely, in an angular sort of way, but nothing to stop one's breath, nothing to merit a fight to the death for the honor of his company. The green eyes weren't even all that spectacular, now that Dallin really looked up close—they were fine, certainly, clear and deep as forest pine, and unusual in one with hair dark enough to be called black—but still merely green. Perhaps there *had* been some kind of enchantment involved.

Abruptly, Calder shook his head, squared his shoulders, and leaned into the table. "Stable help."

Dallin blinked. "Sorry?"

"I work in the stables of Ramsford's inn—*with* my back and not on it."

It was said with conviction and an earnest gaze. Dallin noted it and once again curved smoothly along with the sudden turn in conversation.

"You don't look like you'd be much help in a stable."

It wasn't meant as an insult—Calder was nothing like to the sort. Not broad enough by half, for one, and not rough enough about the edges.

"I've no doubt I don't look like I can do a lot of the things I can do. Looks can deceive."

"No doubt," Dallin muttered. "For instance, you don't look like you're from Lind."

That brought a slight twitch, quickly covered. "Oh? And what do those from Lind look like, then?"

"Fair-haired, for one. Without exception." Dallin noted the aborted reach toward dark hair. His smirk was entirely inward. "Like me, for two. I am from Lind. They grow them a bit bigger there." He waited a moment for a reaction; when he didn't get one, he went on, "Hill folk. Clannish. They don't breed outside their own, and I'd venture to say that if there was a black-haired child born among them, he'd be strangled for a witch with his own cord before he'd drawn his first breath. The green eyes wouldn't've helped. Superstitious lot, Linders."

"Another man might seize upon the opportunity to point out the dangers of choosing constables from such inbreeders," Calder observed mildly. He peered sideways at Dallin, looking for reaction.

Dallin didn't give him one. He shrugged. "And your accent isn't right. Oh, it's very good, understand, but it's off around the edges. Too flat on the vowels and not enough roll in the hard consonants."

A moment of quiet as Calder looked down with a flush, then shifted a steady look back up at Dallin. "Perhaps I am a bastard, a shameful get on my poor mother by a black-haired brigand, and so we were forced to move about, never staying in one place very long for fear we'd be harried, possibly even stoned for witches by ignorant, inbred villagers."

Dallin hid a smile at the bold diversion, and he mentally conceded the point. Very clever. And not a little bit twisty.

"Perhaps," Dallin agreed. "And perhaps you are not who you say you are, and these papers are forgeries."

Calder didn't answer, instead asking, "Would you take these off, please?" He held up his hands. "You see I pose no threat."

The manacles all too obviously bothered him—even more than being questioned about complicity in a murder, even more than being here, alone, for all intents and purposes locked in a room with a man twice his size, despite his controlled panic when he'd practically begged Payton to stay. Dallin indeed saw no threat from this man, but the advantage in keeping Calder on edge was becoming more and more apparent. Anyway, there was the matter of those suppression spells, and considering what had happened when he'd arrived, Dallin didn't mind admitting he'd just as soon leave the cuffs right where they were.

"You seemed to pose no threat when I walked in, until...." Dallin opened his hand.

"A mistake." Calder dipped his head, once again the picture of meek submission. "A foolish error. I thought.... I apologize."

"That rather stuck in your throat, didn't it?" Dallin tilted his head. "You thought what?"

Calder shrugged. "You are a very large man. You frightened me." He smiled, tentative, then bent his neck again. Shrewd surrender, sweet and treacherous—a bullet in the soft, pulpy belly of a berry.

All right, so far they'd gone through anger and outrage, and now it had moved on to seduction. Resignation and weary surrender should be next.

It was slightly repulsive, watching Calder work his way through the routine like an actor in a play, and Dallin wasn't sure he knew why he was almost disappointed. Not as challenging as he'd thought, perhaps, or....

You were impressed for a little while there. You thought he was above it, somehow. Why would you think that? This man is neck-deep in lies, trying to use his eyes and clumsy wiles to dig himself out from beneath them. Why do you hesitate to beat him at the game he chose?

No, not lies, not really—avoiding lies, stopping just short of them, as though it was some kind of morality code—but refusing to wade into truths too, skirting them with deflections, answering questions with questions, oblique accusations, righteous defenses. Calder hadn't actually said he was from Lind, but he'd let the papers speak the lie for him, and each denial of more unseemly implications had the ring of truth to Dallin's ears. Dallin would wager that every word Calder had spoken was a truth of some sort. It was breaking the code of those truths and maneuvering Calder into the things he wasn't saying that would be tricky.

Dallin sat back in his chair, relaxing his pose. "Are you easily frightened?" He made his voice soft, a potential paramour expressing concern.

Calder looked down, demure as he slipped one shoulder up in a small shrug. Dallin didn't miss the sinuous shift of the collarbone beneath smooth skin revealed by the pull of the half-laced shirt—didn't miss the fact that it had the appearance of calculated deliberation.

Calder's hands came up with a *tink* of metal, long fingers pushing black hair from eyes gone soft and distant. "I'm frightened only by those things over which I have no control." A rosy little flush softened the fine spray of freckles over Calder's cheeks. "Some have begged for the opportunity to bind me. Others have threatened it, even tried it, with no regard for my wants or fears. And now...."

Dallin tilted his head, encouraging. "Now?"

"Well." Calder's smile turned gently ironic. "Now you don't have to beg, do you?"

The insult was clear and not wholly unexpected. Nonetheless, Dallin's jaw tightened. "A slattern's trick. You won't find me so easily gamed."

The soft acquiescence fled beneath a hot spark of anger. "I tell you, I am no—"

"Then stop playing at one!"

"You ask questions, I answer them—isn't that how this game is supposed to go? And now I am maligned, *again*, because I play by your rules! If I've misunderstood them, do tell, so I can make sure my next step is well within your strategy."

Edging on anger now, Dallin clenched his teeth. "What did you say to those men?"

Calder loosed a soft groan of weary frustration. "I said *No*, and *Leave me alone*, and was given a solid blow to the head for my trouble. Will there be charges for assault as well as murder? Or is the constabulary indifferent to crimes against someone like me?"

"Someone like you." Dallin leaned in. "Tell me first what you are so I can decide the proper course."

"You don't even know what *you* are. Why would you believe anything *I* would tell you?"

That one gave Dallin pause. "What does that mean?"

Calder sighed. "Nothing. I'm... upset. I don't know what I'm saying."

Dallin didn't believe that one for a second—every word that came out of this man's mouth was calculated. "You've not answered my question."

Calder was silent for a long moment, staring at his hands as his fingers picked at each other. Slowly he looked up, his expression fatigued but bold.

"You would make me a depraved conjurer because you want to think me a depraved conjurer. You think I look the part so you'll fit me into it, no matter what I say." He dropped his gaze and furthered softly, "Only remember that I could make of you a monster by the same logic."

Enough. The man didn't seem to know what a straight answer was.

Dallin snatched up the identification papers and waved them under Calder's nose. "Who are you, *really*?"

Calder shifted an anxious glance to the papers. "They are legal and in order."

Another not-lie/not-truth. Dallin allowed his voice to rise in volume and deepen in timbre, threatening. "Where did you get them? How much did you pay for them, and who sold them to you?"

"I've done no wrong!" Calder snapped, all pretense of calm regard or soft compliance gone. "I suffered attentions I *did not* want and find myself accused because of it! I had nothing to do with those two men—"

"Those two men tried to beat each other to death in order to give you those attentions, one succeeded, and now you evade my questions and play at seduction! Who are you and how did you drive sane men to murder?"

"How d'you know they even *were* sane?"

"Did you try to play them against each other?"

"No! I never even—"

"Cast a spell, then?"

"I'm not a witch, I wouldn't even know *how* to—"

"Did you spurn one in favor of the other?"

"I was *trying* to spurn both, I didn't—"

"Did you look at them the way you looked at me before?"

"I wasn't—" Calder clenched his teeth, fisted his hands. "You see seduction because you *want* to see it, because you think you merit it! You assume I caused men to attack one another for the same reason you assume I'd even *want* you, when all you've done is try to bully and intimidate me, and then you look at me like you just found me on the bottom of your boot and call me things no man would suffer without a call to duel! You do these things because you can, because your size and your authority permit it, but I'd *love* to hear the questions you'd ask if I were your size and you were mine!"

His anger was contagious—Dallin found his blood rising and his heart tripping up in rhythm. "*Where* did you get the papers?"

"From the same place all citizens of Lind get theirs!"

Dallin growled and pounded his fist on the table, trying not to feel too much satisfaction when it made Calder jump and some of the color fade from his cheeks. "Why do you keep this up, when you *know* I've twigged? They're forgeries—

you're as much from Lind as I am a third nipple on the Mother's left tit."

Calder's glower was scathing. He sat forward, jaw twitching. "Prove it," he snarled. "You have legal verification of my identity, and I have given my statement as witness and fulfilled my obligation as a citizen of the Commonwealth. Unless you can prove those papers a forgery, you can't keep me here." He pushed his hands at Dallin. "Let me go."

"What did you call me when I walked in?"

Calder glared, teeth grinding. With a long breath, he swallowed and looked away. "I don't remember."

A blatant lie this time—the first one, Dallin was fairly certain, since he'd come into the room. Dallin noted the change in demeanor—from anger and defense to quiet anxiety—and silently congratulated himself on hitting another mark. He'd throw himself a party when he figured out exactly what it was.

"You called me by a name, like you thought you knew me."

"Nonsense muttering," Calder murmured, subdued. "I was frightened."

"Of my size." Dallin lifted an eyebrow. "It sounded like the North Tongue."

A small twitch. It appeared there were marks all over the place. Perhaps if Dallin kept stumbling blind, he'd hit the right one.

"How would I know the North Tongue?" Calder wanted to know.

"You see my point."

"I see that you've bound me and held me against my will when you have no cause for either. *I* was very nearly a victim. Would you have been so dedicated in your questioning of those two *gentlemen* if it were me lying on a slab?" Calder's hands flopped on the table again. "Please." Real entreaty this time, quiet and near desperate. "I've done no harm to anyone, and I want to leave now."

Not quite a break, but at least a crack.

"How long have you been in the province? Why have I never seen you before?"

Calder slumped. "Perhaps you don't get out much," he muttered. "I expect that'll be my fault soon as well."

"How *long*—"

"*Three weeks!*"

"And where were you before that?"

"I don't.... Why won't you just...? I've done no wrong. Why are you doing this?"

"Tell me who you are."

"You have my papers. Please." Calder scrubbed at his face, then peered at Dallin with a look of raw appeal. "You said I was not a prisoner. I have answered your questions. I have told you everything I can tell you." Once again, he held his hands out. "Please. Either arrest me or let me go. I don't even care which anymore."

Of all the faces he'd seen this man don this morning, Dallin thought perhaps this was the true one: exhausted and miserable, saw-toothed terror blurring about the periphery. Pity rose, softening the hard edges of suspicion. Dallin didn't believe for a moment that this man was Wilfred Calder from Lind. But he also didn't believe he'd enchanted anyone into murder.

So what was he hiding, what was he hiding *from*, and why was he so afraid?

Dallin was only slightly moved, his pity tucked back behind

duty and then hidden beneath the hard set of his face. Almost everyone brought behind these doors was pitiable in some form, whether hard-bitten villain or truly innocent victim, and long experience had taught him that most people hovered somewhere in between the two. Treating one like the other and alternating his approach—sympathizing, then victimizing—served to unbalance and confuse.

This man was not confused. Unbalanced, certainly, and agitated beyond the point many others had fallen into tearful confession, but no sobbing declarations hovered at his tongue, no indignant justifications. Instead he all but obsessed over those manacles, begging not for his life or forgiveness or anything so trite and unseemly as reprieve—he begged instead for release from the cold metal about his wrists, so fixedly that Dallin began to wonder if the discomfort they achieved had not somehow balanced out against his favor rather than in it.

He peered at the shackles, at the pink, knobby scar on the left wrist. Newish and thick, and reaching halfway about the blue-veined wrist, with the uneven healing marks of botched care and badly treated infection.

Looks like someone who's spent his life locked up in a dark room, Dallin had thought when he'd first seen Calder. Now Dallin thought perhaps he'd been all too close to the mark. This man had been someone's prisoner before. It was no wonder the restraints unnerved him so.

"Where did you get that scar?"

Calder's hands curled into loose fists, withdrew. A slack shrug was all Dallin got for an answer.

"Who thought you so dangerous as to bind you? Have you been arrested before?"

Calder shook his head slowly. "No."

"Then what did you do to merit shackling?"

A low chuckle, dark and bleak and maybe even a little bit crazed. "An offense almost as heinous as what I did this time." Calder looked up, fixed a defiant stare on Dallin, and gave him the ruins of a desolate smile. "I had the audacity to exist."

Rebellion and despair, obstinate mutiny and raw panic. Too many things clawed for domination in Calder's gaze, and Dallin would swear that every one of them was a cryptic truth in a language he didn't know how to read. This wasn't about what happened at the Kymberly last night. Whatever this was, it made the Kymberly's events small and unremarkable.

"You," Dallin said quietly, "are in very deep trouble."

Calder laughed, pure bitter irony, and rolled his eyes. "Nothing gets by you, does it?"

"No, not from me, not even from the constabulary, and it's no small trouble, I judge. You're hiding from something. No," Dallin said more slowly when Calder twitched, "some*one*." There—a slight wince and flinch. Dallin lowered his voice, spilled salt into the wound. "And you're terrified."

"If I were," Calder answered, soft and resigned, "that would make you terribly cruel for tormenting a man already tormented." He peered up at Dallin, eyes brimming wet now and once again gone glittering, liquid malachite in the sooty light of the lamps. "Are you a cruel man, Constable Brayden?"

The tears were no ruse, and the question no idle inquiry. Dallin sat back, eyes locked to Calder's, absently pleased that the stare didn't have its former effect. "It is possible," Dallin ventured finally, "that I could help you, if you would but trust me."

“Perhaps you could if I did. But since we find ourselves, quite literally, on opposite sides of the table....” Calder stretched out his arms so his hands splayed on the table, palms up. “Please. Let me go.”

Dallin didn’t. Not at first, at any rate. It took another several hours before he admitted he would not learn Calder’s secrets, that whatever it was Calder was running from, the fear of it was much greater than any bluff of incarcerated horror Dallin could impose. He’d found out all he was going to, as far as Calder’s involvement with the grisly murder was concerned, and believed every definitive statement denying that involvement. Whatever secrets Calder kept, they had nothing to do with any guilt or complicity in the events at the Kymberly last night—of that, at least, Dallin was certain.

He propped the door open when he finally quit the room, and left the key to the manacles with Beldon. He was too tired to go through the mechanics of discharge, and for reasons he didn’t want to think about, he had no desire to witness the relief when those shackles finally came off. One of the perks of rank and seniority was the right to delegate, and today Dallin used it.

“And tell him not to leave Putnam,” he told Beldon as he headed back upstairs.

He slow-stepped it to Jagger’s office, informed him of his conclusions and the release of the witness, then wrote his report and handed it off to Payton with a bit of scorn he couldn’t help and an order to ink two copies. “Keep his papers,” Dallin instructed. “He’s not to leave Putnam anyway, so he won’t need them, and I want to send to Lind for verification before I release them."

Orders given and details seen to, Dallin left, but not for his longed-for lunch. Anyway, it would be suppertime in a few hours.

"Ah, *there's* the lad!" Portly and florid, with an ever-present tranquil smile, Manning was of the firm belief that *healthy* meant one could survive a months-long famine.

Dallin was only too happy to indulge him. He grinned with a small bow, then handed over the sack of sweets without fuss or flourish. "Crystalled honey with peppermint zest," he told his once-tutor. "It sounds odd, but you'll like it."

"I've no doubt." Manning shooed Dallin into his private office. "You've a look of business about you." He frowned and sighed. "*Must* you carry that thing in here?" He gave Dallin's holster a bit of a glare, gesturing him to the shabby little couch as he plopped into a chair by the fire. He wasted no time in digging into the sack and sampling its contents.

"I'm still on duty, I'm afraid, so yes, I must. Sorry."

Manning conceded with a roll of his eyes, though he was concentrating more on the candy in his mouth than any mild indignation. "Anyway, a fine bribe you've brought me in recompense." He rolled his hand. "Well, get on, then, spit it out."

Dallin scooted closer to the small stove in the corner and held his hands out to warm them. "I need a translation. The North Tongue, I think, or at least that's what it sounded like."

"The North Tongue, eh?" Manning's knobbled fingers

stroked at his rounded chin as his brown eyes went unfocused—already thinking about where to start looking, Dallin had no doubt. "A text, a song...?"

Dallin shook his head. "A word. Two words, actually. Although...." He frowned. "Now that I think about it, one might have been part of the other. It had the same sound, at least."

Manning pished with another roll of his eyes. "Hardly a challenge," he chided. "You've got it written down? Give it here." Dallin dug into his breast pocket and retrieved a small wax tablet. He handed it over. "You've done it phonetically," Manning said, squinting. "See here, the 'guneev' would be g-n-i-o-m-h—'io' is usually 'ee' and 'mh' is usually 'v.'" His eyebrows beetled. "This 'uh-ray' you've got is likely 'h-a-i-r-e'—silent 'h,' you know, and since 'ai' is 'uh' and 're' is 'ray'...."

"That was the first one," Dallin put in, "that 'uh-ray' one. Is it perhaps a shortened version of the other?"

Manning shook his head, still squinting at the impressions in the wax. "Likely not. The language is too complex for a translation to be that simple, and not much for contractions and simplifications." He stood, distracted and distant. Dallin recognized the look as Manning's version of concentration. "Wander about," Manning told him vaguely, "shan't be long," then left Dallin to his own devices while he went to find the pieces of the puzzle and fit them into their proper places.

Dallin smiled and willingly obeyed, idling out into the great main chamber and eyeing the various shelves and their contents.

The library had been one of his favorite places when he'd first come to Putnam. Lind didn't believe in the written word, its histories handed down and entrusted only to verse and song, and so Dallin hadn't known how to read then. Quiet was what he'd craved, and dim seclusion, and Manning's library had opened its dusty arms and given it to him. Almost as tall already at twelve as most of the adults around him, people didn't give Dallin the wide berth normally afforded the mourning, as though they assumed that because he looked almost adult, he shouldn't *feel* like a child. The library had been the place he could come and live his grief in private quietude, watch the skirmishes behind his eyes over and over again until they lost their brilliant edges, hear his mother's voice in his ears, stern and forceful, as she dragged him onto the back of the cart and shoved him into the arms of a stranger, promising she loved him, promising she'd find him.

He'd loved the smells before he'd learned to love the ink and parchment that made them—that latter a love that hadn't come easily for him. Twelve and angry and stricken, he hadn't understood why anyone would treat ancient lumps of paper with such caution and tender care when there were flesh-and-bone people dying under flintlock and blade, old men watching sons blown to pieces right in front of them for nothing more than being alive and wanting to stay that way, mothers sending their children away and then turning 'round with a stiff back and set chin to face their fates at the edge of a sword or the end of a noose.

Manning had understood. Picture books first, slid quietly and unobtrusively to the elbow of the scraggy, too-tall youth kipping with his shaggy head on the table. Then books with words that looked like nothing so much as chicken scratch in between the pictures, month by month the pictures growing farther and farther apart, until the words finally outweighed the images and Dallin couldn't make a story out of the pictures anymore. Frustrated beyond reason, he'd drawn himself to his full height, aimed all his preadolescent thwarted rage and angry grief at his torturer, and demanded that Manning tell him what the damned letters meant. Manning only smiled—an annoying, knowing little thing—said he wouldn't tell him but teach him, and set to right then and there.

More of a guardian than the man who'd agreed to temporarily foster the too-big, too-angry young Linder, Manning patiently sat through the boy's quiet tirades and frustrated *trying* until he hit upon a flash of brilliance.

"Think of it as a code," he'd told Dallin.

Dallin knew codes. Three chirps of the lark and the faint snicker of a squirrel meant *Get down and hide, don't move, don't breathe*; a trilling whistle in two short bursts gave the *all clear*. The long curl of the horn singing the war song meant *Get your swords and hide your children*, only that one hadn't sounded in time when it mattered. Dallin knew codes before he'd known speech.

These codes, though—these codes handed Dallin the world in Manning's serenely gruff voice. The strange characters finally stopped looking so much like a drunken bird had tripped in paint and gone toddling across the page, and instead took on pattern and meaning and the bright, crisp lines of *discovery*. Every second not spent apprenticing in his foster parents' shop was thence spent reading—if not at the library itself, then in his own small bedroom, poring over whatever books Manning had seen fit to lend him.

Writing came next, then cartography and maths, along with gentle hints and prodding about hair length and hygiene. Dallin had once thought he might like to be a scribe, maybe even one day work for Manning, spending his days breathing in the must of the books and learning about the world through his fingers. Manning would never trust Dallin with the task of copying, though, and eventually disabused him of the wistful adolescent notion, saying with a kind smile that ham hands did not make for delicate work. Dallin didn't take offense. By the time he was sixteen and old enough to join the army, he didn't have to just line up and make his mark for the privilege of being a moving target in the infantry—between Manning's scholarly tutoring and Tanner's patient instruction in carbine and steel, Dallin tested well enough to qualify for the cavalry.

He owed more to Manning than just the gratitude of a student to his unpaid tutor. Childless by choice, the Tanners had been shelter, even if the barest definition of the word, but Dallin had never blamed them for the dearth of warmth. They'd volunteered, after all, to take in a refugee until his mother came to collect him. They'd never agreed to finish raising a leviathan of a foster son when she was finally listed among the dead. Still, there had never been even a question or a scarce hint of turning him out, and he was grateful to them. To Tanner and his wife, Dallin owed respect and thanks for having fed him and boarded him and taught him a trade, even if they'd shrugged helplessly and uncomfortably and looked the other way when he needed something more. To Manning, Dallin owed *life*.

"See here."

Dallin was startled out of his somewhat maudlin reverie by Manning standing at his elbow, head bent over a book butterflied between his thick, surprisingly deft hands and muttering under his breath.

"*Aire*, there's no question, there's only the one meaning," he said, more to himself than to Dallin. He peered up, brow creased and eyes bright. "How did you say you heard these words?"

"I didn't, actually."

Manning gave him a sour look. "I don't want your professional secrets, boy. I need to know." Slightly snappish, the teacher chastising the recalcitrant student. Dallin couldn't help the little grin, which only made Manning roll his eyes. "*Aire* has only the one meaning, as I said—it means danger. Easy enough to understand when faced with you in a dark alley, I imagine." Manning sniffed, then riffled some pages. "The other, this *Gníomhaire*... the possible meanings are nearly a page long. I must have some context to decide the proper one."

Dallin kept his grin, though he dipped his head in respectful acquiescence. "A witness," he admitted. "And not a terribly... cooperative one."

"Ah," said Manning with a sly tilt of his mouth. "Intimidating the citizens again, are you, great lummox?"

"Well, you'd think so, but he didn't even give me a chance. Came over all frightened rabbit the moment I walked in, and started spitting those words at me like they were poison."

"It's not a wonder," he muttered with a teasing smirk. With a sideways glance up and down the length of Dallin, Manning sniffed again and turned his eyes back to the book, once again all business. "Most of these translations boil down to an agent of some kind, an emissary, perhaps—varying types, none of which seem to fit you or the situation, although I suppose a general definition of an agent would suit a constable." He frowned. "Did he perhaps think you some sort of spy?"

"Can't imagine for what." Dallin tilted his head. "None of

them mean 'guardian' or something of the kind?"

Manning's head jerked back. "Guardian?" His eyes narrowed. "Did he name you Guardian as well?"

"Well, yes." Dallin shrugged. "Several times. I didn't think it a terribly inaccurate description of a constable, though it seemed an odd one. I thought perhaps one of those other words would work out to be a translation of it, but... now I've no idea what the bugger was getting at."

Manning was silent, staring. Once again, Dallin could almost see him carding back through his memory. "*Gníomhaire* can also mean 'intermediary.'" Manning paused, noting Dallin's blank look, and smiled. "Middleman, perhaps—some sort of go-between." Gone vague again, Manning stared off into space. "Only those two, then, not *saoi*, or *aingeal*, or—?" He stopped, blinked. "Not *Weblic*, perchance? Though *Weblicne* might do better, I suppose—you said he was distressed...." He shook his head, annoyed. "No, no, North Tongue, so that would be.... *Coimirceoir*? *Aisling-brídín*, perhaps?"

Aisling.

Why did that ping a small echo in the back of Dallin's mind?

Dallin frowned. "No, just the two I told you. Why?"

"Amuse yourself," Manning said, then abruptly whisked away again.

Dallin blinked after him, watching him rummage about a far shelf for a moment before he straightened, said "Ah!" and swept into his office. There was a bit of banging and shuffling before Manning reemerged, somewhat red-faced and excited. "It's likely nothing," he was saying, to himself again, "but sometimes one and one don't necessarily equal two, they equal twelve instead, and there have been whispers. This would be considered sacrilegious contraband over the border, and you'd likely be hanged for even laying eyes on it, but... well. We're not over the border." Manning shoved the book at Dallin. "I shouldn't let you have this—you've not returned the other two yet—but it's too much of a coincidence." He laughed, somewhat wondering. "I'll be damned if you don't look the part. Don't know why it never occurred to me before, but... well, you were such a clumsy, angry lad, and I didn't.... Anyway, you came straight from the bloody heart of giant country, so I expect I never...." He trailed off, eyeing Dallin with a critical gaze.

"What part?" Dallin wanted to know. "Never what?"

Manning only kept staring for a moment before he frowned and asked, "What did this witness look like?"

"Why should that matter?"

"Tut-tut, ever the suspicious lawman." Manning pursed his lips. "It was the eyes, wasn't it?"

Dallin jolted. "How did you know that?"

"Mm," said Manning. "You know what the Chosen is, yes?"

"The... yes," Dallin answered, bewildered.

"It's been rumored for... well, for longer than I can remember, that the Dominion's Chosen is actually the Aisling of legend. Though why he should be frightened at the sight of you instead of overjoyed, I haven't a clue." Manning tapped at his lip, staring off into space again. "Curious."

Dallin rolled his eyes. "Dominionite religious rot, and what's it to do with... well, with anything? And what's this ash... thing... whatever?"

"Aisling. And I'll not do your homework for you." Manning pointed at the book. "Read that, and then we'll talk."

Dallin scowled. "Why've you come over all cryptic all of a sudden?"

"Because I won't be the one to talk you into believing something I'm not sure I believe myself," Manning told him. "You came to me for a mere translation, but take along a bit of advice, if you will. Call it recompense for the sweets." He tapped a meaty, ink-stained finger to the pliable cover of the book, the script in his own hand. "Read it," Manning said. "And don't let that witness out of your sight. He may be in a great deal of trouble."

"*That*," Dallin grumbled, "I already knew."

He headed back along the flagstone path that led to the constabulary just after dusk, foul-tempered from lack of coffee and an empty stomach. He'd almost taken the damnable book straight home, but he had yet to go over Orman's statement with anything resembling scrutiny, and he wanted to talk to the man too. Jagger was more than skilled in interrogation—Dallin didn't doubt he'd made a thorough affair of it—and certainly had more years on the job than Dallin did. Still, there was a reason the chief called his first constable in when information was hard in coming. And anyway, Jagger had handed the case over to Dallin, all of it, so digging through the debris was now his job. Despite the morning having drawn a veritable blank from Calder, Dallin's instincts usually managed to drag new details from otherwise dry wells. He hoped whatever this Orman might have to say could shed some new light on the puzzle that went by the name of Wilfred Calder.

The pleasant almost-warmth of the day had disappeared with the sun. Dallin wished he'd thought to snatch up his greatcoat when last he'd left the constabulary. Now he peered pensively at the mishmash of cottages and small houses that stumbled alongside the road, scattered in no particular order as though some giant child had been playing knucklebones and got called away to supper in the middle of a game. The cordial flickering radiance of gas lamps and hearth fires spilled through the slats of closed shutters, the chill of the gloaming all the more dismal for their teasing warmth. Dallin tucked deeper into his surcoat, scuffed a bootheel along the flagstones, and pretended not to hear the lonely sound it made in the quiet of the falling night.

This street fair swarmed with activity during the day, carts and portable stalls crowding the small thoroughfare to near choking, hawkers making a cheerful competition of the racket. More than once, Dallin had found himself holding back a growl and rolling his eyes as he tried to politely work his way around various lollygaggers. At night, though, it could be a lonesome place.

A lone dame was selling spiced lamb cubes on a stick, roasted over an open pit in front of a small but respectable butcher's shop—probably hoping to unload the last of what hadn't sold during the day, Dallin suspected. The smell hit him square in the belly. He stopped and bought one to eat along the way to tide him over. In deference to his livery, the woman tried to push a discount on him. Dallin noted the neat and subtle mending of her plain tunic, the gauntness of her cheeks, and the unhealthy pallor to her skin. There was the smell of death about her, faint but encroaching steadily. Dallin politely accepted her offer—*One does not reward pride with pity*; he'd read that somewhere—though he handed her an extra few billets as gratuity to make up for the loss.

The woman smiled demurely with a dip of her head. "Shall I scry for you, Guardian?"

Dallin jolted. "*What* did you just call me?" It was sharp, the tone heavily laced with accusation, but he was too unnerved to care.

The woman blinked up at him, startled. "I called you 'sir,'" she answered carefully. "I said, 'Thank you, sir.'"

"Lie!" Dallin wanted to accuse. But he peered at the woman closely and saw no lies in her frightened face, only anxiety and confusion and likely some sincere regret that she hadn't closed up and gone inside five minutes ago before the crazy man happened along. He was jumping at shadows, hearing things, and scaring a sick old woman in the bargain. What the bloody *fuck* was wrong with him?

Dallin rubbed at his eyes. "I'm sorry," he said, as sincere as he could make it. "I've had a long day, and I thought.... I'm sorry."

The woman accepted this with a small nod, but she wouldn't look at him now. "The Mother's blessings upon your path, sir," she said softly.

Dallin tried to smile another apology as he swept her a respectful bow. "And on yours, mistress," he answered and turned off, the fragrant meat in his hand somehow not even the least bit tempting now. He waited until the woman's little fire was no longer visible behind him, then chucked the stick of lamb into the weeds beside the road.

Shaking off his odd little go at insanity, he stepped along

with purpose. He'd do what needed to be done at the constabulary and then head to the Kymberly; he'd take supper there to make up for having missed lunch and the lamb he'd just discarded, and perhaps spy on Calder while he was at it. Anyway, he wanted to go over a few things from Ramsford's statement with him too. And perhaps punch him in the mouth for having requested Dallin on this bloody case.

By the time Dallin got back to the constabulary, the bailiff's shift had changed. Instead of Beldon, Dallin met—what was his name again? Woodrow, that was it—just making himself comfortable, propping his feet up on the wide desk and stretching out for a long, boring evening. Big, like all the bailiffs, wide-shouldered and thick-armed, but none of it could take away from the round youth in his face, the bit of naïveté still left in his ingenuous gaze.

When that gaze landed on Dallin, Woodrow choked almost comically. He sprang to his feet. "Constable Brayden!" He gulped and stood like someone had just rammed a poker up his arse. "I was... I just...." His pale, sweaty fingers flicked about the hem of his blue surcoat, curled around it, then clenched tight. "I'm only just back from supper, you see, and I—"

"Ask for my sidearm, Woodrow," Dallin cut in, trying not to let the amusement into his voice.

Woodrow twitched. "Er... sorry?"

"The first thing you do when a constable comes down here is to ask for his weapon," Dallin told him. "Then you record it in your book there"—he pointed—"to prove that no arms have crossed the threshold on your watch."

"Yes, sir. I did know that, sir, I would've done, it's...." Woodrow trailed off into miserable silence.

Dallin took pity. "Your first week, innit?"

Woodrow gave a loose bobble of his auburn head, face so bright beneath his sea of freckles it almost competed for color with his hair. "First night on duty by myself, sir."

Dallin nodded back, considerably less bobbleish. "You're doing fine." He tried to make it reassuring rather than amused. "Here." He handed over his sidearm. "Careful with that, it's new and I'm rather fond of it."

"Y-yes, sir."

"And don't call everyone *sir*," Dallin advised brusquely. "It'll only remind them you're new and green, and they'll fob off all the disagreeable tasks to you. And for pity's sake, don't ever let a prisoner or witness see you blush and stammer like this. They see a weakness, and your size won't make a damned bit of difference—they'll have you spitted and cooked before you even remember your first defensive stance."

Another bobble. "Yes, s—Brayden. Um. Right."

Dallin allowed a smile. "Good. Now, if you please, I want to see the prisoner Orman in whatever room you've available."

"Um...." Woodrow shifted uncomfortably. "It'll do you little good, s—Brayden. The chief's been down to see him this afternoon with some toff-nosed Dominion stick. The prisoner was well enough when they went in, but came out gibbering. Chief sent for the physick and then the shaman, but...." He shrugged. "No one could make heads nor tails, and then he just up and turned mute." He shot a nervous glance to all points before leaning in and lowering his voice. "Looked like magicking to my eyes, and I reckon that Dominion blackguard done the work right under the chief's nose."

Dallin was silent for a moment, trying to parse that, before he jerked a nod and said, "I suggest you speak to no one else about what you *reckon*, Woodrow. Gossip can be a deadly thing." He narrowed a hard stare, satisfied when Woodrow flushed and nodded. "I'll see this man in his cell, then," Dallin went on. "Sign me in and take me to him."

Dallin found Jagger in his office, head in hands.

"I was just about to send Seward to find you." Jagger leaned back and flung his pen down. "I spent a rather… interesting afternoon with Ambassador Einín's man."

If he hadn't already been aware of today's odd happenings, Jagger's grimace alone would have been enough to tell Dallin the meeting hadn't gone well—at least from Jagger's end. "So I hear. I've just been down to Orman's cell." Dallin flung out a hand. "What the deuce *happened*? Surely he wasn't like that when you brought him in?"

"Oh no, not by a long stretch."

"And how'd the Dominion get here so quickly? I would have thought we wouldn't have to deal with them for another day, at least. And in person. Have they spies we don't know about?"

"Not so far as I can tell."

Dallin chewed his lip. "Was this ambassador's lackey on the road already or something, then? Did Corliss go for nothing?"

"Depends on your perspective, I guess. Corliss didn't get her overnight away after all, though." Jagger shook his head with a long brooding sigh. "She tells me the ambassador had his offices hopping thirty seconds after my request left her hand. Wouldn't wait for a post, but insisted she escort his man back here straightaway." He frowned. "Oddly, the man was all ready and saddled up, like he was waiting for her."

Dallin frowned too. "Well, what happened? Surely they found no fault—"

"Oh, painfully polite, this one, and careful to thank us for a job well done, but... I don't know. There was something behind the man's eyes I didn't like. I don't know what happened downstairs. I swear I saw nothing strange, not even a twitch of a finger, but one look at this Síofra fellow—that's the ambassador's emissary—one look at him, and Orman fell to blubbering and gibbering." Jagger shifted in obvious unease. "I don't mind telling you, it made my skin want to crawl right off my bones."

"Woodrow says conjuring."

Jagger waved that away impatiently. "Woodrow's just wet out of the fields and thinks an eclipse is conjuring. Although I won't deny the possibility. That's what shamans are for, and they at least got Orman to shut up."

"So well that he's gone mute! And if there's anything going on behind that blank stare, it's—"

"Not the doing of the shaman," Jagger assured him. "The sense went out of the man the moment we stepped into the room—I saw it happen." He wrinkled his nose as though he smelled something foul. "Like the mere set of the man's beady little ferret eyes did Orman in." Dallin was uncomfortably reminded of his own reaction when he'd first laid eyes on Calder. He blinked it away when Jagger went on, "You'll just have to use the statement I squeaked out of him, I expect. Fairly cut and dry, at any rate. He admitted to everything. Several times."

Dallin found his teeth clenching. "It's all a little neat,

innit?" He didn't like any of it. A growing sense of alarm and suspicion was vibrating unpleasantly over his skin.

Jagger only shrugged. "Anyway, you'll like this—that Síofra, he doesn't want Orman back. Says he committed a crime against Cynewísan and should pay whatever price Cynewísan demands. He was especially careful to point out that, should Cynewísan's price be blood, the Dominion—oh, do pardon me, *Ríocht*—would not be displeased."

"It'll make things a bit easier, I expect," Dallin offered grudgingly.

"Likely. But that wasn't the whole of it." Jagger peered up at Dallin, sardonic. "He wants Calder."

Dallin's teeth clenched again. "I *knew* it." With effort he turned a growl into an annoyed sigh on its way out of his throat. "What's he done?"

"That's the thing. Apparently nothing, or at least nothing they'll admit to. You see, if he's wanted for a crime, according to the latest treaty, the extradition would have to go through the Citadel in Penley. A quorum would have to view all the evidence and decide whether or not they want to let them take him. It would take months." Jagger's mouth lifted in a sour smirk. "On the other hand, if he were, say, their Chosen, and he'd gone and run away from home...."

Dallin's legs almost went out from under him. "You're joking."

"I wish I were." Jagger ran a hand through his thinning hair. "In truth I'm surprised they even told us as much. Shifty lot, they are. Although I expect they've nothing to worry about—we've no way to verify any of it. No one lays eyes on this Chosen but for once a year, and then it's from the Guild's turrets. He could be anyone." He growled. "This... honesty, cooperation, polite compliance, whatever it is—it isn't like them. I don't trust them, especially not after what happened downstairs. If Calder's a criminal, why not just take the time to extradite him? And if he's this Chosen, why tell us? Apparently even their own people don't know he's missing."

"There's... yes," Dallin agreed slowly. "You'd think they'd just kidnap him and have done." It wasn't as though it hadn't happened before. They were a little too good at the sneakier bits of diplomacy.

Damn. Dallin had known there was trouble hanging over Calder's head like a black cloud, but *this*....

"That's more their method, yes, and I expect they might've done," Jagger said wearily. "Except when I sent Corliss out to Ramsford's to collect him, he'd already hied off."

It just kept getting worse. Dallin shook his head. "Gone?"

"Gone. And word from our ambassador is that we are to use any means necessary to find the man and deliver him safely into Einín's hands. Or Síofra's hands, more like, seeing as how he's gone and dug in at the Kymberly and looks to be staying until he's got his Chosen back. I'm sorry you missed him. I would've liked to know if you saw something I couldn't, because I can't for the life of me figure out how one such as him managed a position as powerful as his. Eager, pompous little shit, him. All hot and bothered, beady little eyes agleam. I swear I thought he was going to mess his trousers, right up until Corliss got back to say Calder'd flown. *Then* he showed his colors, all imperious and officious." Jagger blew out a breath between clenched teeth. "Little *shit*. I don't like it, but we've no choice. It seems the progress of the talks in Penley depends entirely upon our ability to bend over and smile—or so that axe-faced, thin-necked, squawky ambassador's weasel would have me believe, and our man backs him." Jagger's head dropped back into his hands, the same pose as when Dallin had walked in. "Who'd've thought the peace of our little corner of the world would hinge on that skinny little catamite."

"I don't think he was," Dallin murmured absently, then wondered why he'd said it and shut his mouth.

Jagger didn't call him on it, though, only looked up and shrugged. "Didn't even wait for the purse he was owed, says Ramsford. Two weeks' pay due him tomorrow, but from what we can figure, directly after he was released from here, he skulked back to the Kymberly's stables, snapped up whatever was his, and took to his feet." He waved a hand. "Lucky for us he didn't steal one of the horses, so he'll be on foot. Ramsford was very insistent that we record somewhere that he took nothing that wasn't his and left without a two-week purse that was."

"Brilliant," Dallin muttered. "An honest skiver. I suppose they want us to—" He stopped, closed his eyes, and groaned. "Oh *no*."

"Oh yes," Jagger said. "Your case, your man. And keep this closer than close—no one's to know who this man is but you and me. The extradition papers are on Elmar's desk. As soon as you find him, he's Putnam's property and your responsibility until you get him back here and hand him over to the Guild." He gave Dallin a tired shrug and a rueful grimace. "You'd best get along before the trail runs cold."

CHAPTER 2

Putnam had been a mistake. Almost as big a mistake as Old Bridge had been, and Old Bridge had nearly cost him... well. Old Bridge had nearly cost him everything.

One day he would learn to ignore his instincts, no matter the pull on his mind and sanity. They seemed to be a little too intent on his destruction, even more so than—

Wil gritted his teeth and tightened his grip on the strap of his pack. No good could come of letting his mind wander there, so he slapped it in its cage and closed a lock on it. He hunched down into his thin, scraggy coat and walked on, mouth set in a hard, grim line and eyes to the ground. The chill had already worked its steady way into his bones, and exhaustion kept whispering treachery in the guise of reason—*rest, close your eyes, only for a moment*—but he locked that away too. There weren't nearly enough miles between him and Putnam yet.

A lawman. Wil snorted, soft and bitter, and rolled his eyes.

A *lawman*, for pity's sake. How... *predictable* that the *Coimirceoir* would choose a mask of righteousness and safety.

If it's so predictable, why were you so eager to stumble into the trap?

He growled.

Stumble. *Ha!* He'd all but run into it, blindly following his feet, giving himself over to the pull as though his heart were whispering cryptic suicide to his mind, and he'd been too stupid or desperate—likely both—to notice his own betrayal.

Perhaps he really did want to die.

His eyes stung, and he blinked.

He didn't want to die. He *didn't*. He only wanted... save him, he didn't even *know*. Just not *this*.

Hunger and weariness and fear—they welcomed him back like old friends. Two weeks this time, one of the longer stretches in memory, of a full belly instead of a gnawing pit of emptiness that sapped strength and will and even thought when it got bad enough. An actual bed, with *blankets*, not hard ground and fending off snakes and rodents for the best place to lie up for a night. People who actually spoke to him and looked at him when they did it, with kindness and the closest he'd probably ever come to respect, and not with a predatory gleam in their eyes and murder behind them.

One second of panic, one momentary loss of control, and all of it gone. Just... *gone*. A wisp of smoke, water sluicing through his grasping fingers. Damn it, he *knew* better. Perhaps it wouldn't have hurt so much if he hadn't almost talked himself into believing it could last this time.

An owl blatted a mocking cry and whizzed past his ear, its dinner still squeaking a helpless agony in razor talons. Wil jumped, brushing at his ear, and shivered. He decided it probably wasn't the good omen he would have once thought it.

Pausing, he peered to all points around him, then strained his ears and listened. He hadn't been paying attention for who knew how long, and anyone could've been creeping up behind him. His mind conjured blond hair and dark eyes boring into his soul from behind the camouflage of a kind, handsome face.

It is possible that I could help you, if you would but trust me.

Ha.

Ha bloody *ha.*

Help. What a laugh.

Anyway, what the bloody *hell* was the *Gníomhaire* doing in Putnam? Why wasn't he in Lind where he belonged? Bastard. And the great oaf probably believed what he was saying too. And would go on believing it until... what?

Wil stopped, frowned. How could he not know? How could he be what he was, born to a destiny as dark as his, and *not know*?

He shivered and glanced at the moon to gauge the time. He started walking again. Two more hours until sunrise. Best he find somewhere to hole up before then. The thickness of the wood was diminishing, and hearth smoke was more frequent on the air now. He was closing in on a more populated area, and the chances of running into some random traveler or hunter—or worse, a not so random traveler or hunter—were growing steadily higher. He'd have to chance a market or go begging at a farmstead soon, if he didn't want to starve, but coming up on someone in the dark—or having someone come up on him—was too great a risk, and he didn't dare travel by day.

An inn, he decided. His flight from Putnam had taken him

through the fens that skirted the north of the city, and the rank, moldy stench still clung to his boots and trousers. He'd just about kill for a hot bath but would settle for a stream or rain barrel to wash his clothes. And filling his water skin would be helpful too—only a few mouthfuls sloshed around in its near-empty bladder, and the scent of rain was notably absent from the night air. All good and well for sleeping, but not for growing thirst.

He'd been able to snatch up very little when he'd fled. He'd made it last for six days now, and that was pushing it, but it hadn't been much and it wouldn't last much longer. *He* wouldn't last much longer. Trekking cross country with only three sausages, a crumbled handful of cheese, and two apples for fuel wasn't enough for even a day, and his body was starting to feel the lack. Game was almost nonexistent, and he didn't have time to stop and hunt at any rate. Anyway, he'd left his sling behind at Ramsford's. Idiot. He *deserved* to starve to death for that one.

Frost had set in early this year, so there wasn't even a stray patch of wild onions to scrounge through. The only good thing, to Wil's mind, about the fast-approaching winter was that it meant the nights were longer and he could cover more distance. Which wasn't going to be a whole lot of help if he didn't find at least some water soon.

A rivulet—even a puddle, for that matter—would be a blessing, but he judged an inn the more preferable alternative, if he could find one. His lips were cracked and dry, his gums were sore, and he'd stopped pissing two days ago—he was starting to really worry and almost ready to chance a city center, should he happen upon one, though that was hardly likely out in the middle of nowhere as he apparently was. A small village would do, and an inn would do better. Head down, eyes to the ground, gold between his fingers—if he wasn't forced to actually speak to anyone, and he didn't linger, he might slip through unnoticed.

He dug into his trouser pocket, fingered the few gilders and billets he had left. Shook his head on a snarl. Damn it, two more days and that pocket would've been much more encouraging. *Two more days.* The timing of it all nearly broke his heart.

"Fuck you, *Constable* Brayden," he muttered, teeth clenched. And *fuck you*, Palmer and Orman too, while he was at it.

The loss of his papers was going to be a serious problem, but he'd managed before. It was an unbelievably lucky stroke of chance that he'd come away from his encounter with the *Coimirceoir* still alive—so incredibly lucky that he still almost couldn't believe it had been as easy as it had been, even for the terror—so the loss of the papers was a small thing, comparatively speaking.

Still, the loss of the name was a blow. It was the first one he'd ever had, and he'd let himself get attached to it in the few years he'd borrowed it. It was the one thing he could read, that name, and he'd liked the look of it on those papers, the clean black strokes on the cream-colored parchment, once he'd learned what those strokes said. *Peaceful river*, or something like that, that's what the name meant. He'd often let himself imagine that he'd end up there one day—whatever quiet place Wilfred Calder's parents had named him for—staring down into slow churning water and not having to listen for the sound of footsteps behind him, not having to look over his shoulder every ten seconds. Not *running*.

His hands clenched into fists on the straps of his pack, and his jaw tightened again. Damn them. Damn them all. Tears of rage crowded his eyes, burned beneath his brow, and he stubbornly blinked them back.

The rage was what kept him going sometimes, he thought. The injustice, the unfairness, and his seeming inability to buckle to either. *Mutinous little badger*, that's what Síofra used to call him with a mix of disgust and that repulsive greed in his narrow, pointy face, and Wil supposed the name fit well enough. It explained the black joy that had moved through him when Síofra had snarled those words from between bloody teeth, clots and rivulets of scarlet sliding from a broken nose. Wil had paid for that one, a price that still set him shuddering when he let himself remember, but he'd laughed through the agony until it sounded too much like screaming, so he'd stopped. Anyway, *mutinous little badger* was probably a more accurate name than *peaceful river*, but he liked the sound of the latter better.

In the end, neither name was his to keep, so he supposed it didn't matter. Though until he found a new one, he'd hang on to *Wil*, at least. It was, after all, the only way he knew how to refer to himself.

"Myself." He laughed a little, sardonic. "I wonder what that is?"

It was another two days before he came upon a village—nothing more than a hamlet, really. Small wooden cottages with waxed parchment tacked to the windows to keep out the approaching winter winds, the occasional sod-roofed hut, grubby children drudging about the dirt courtyards in weary semblance of play. They stared at him as he approached, goodwives' brooms stopping in midsweep and hard looks from thin, weathered men, faces set wary and harsh, careworn features shadowed stark in every angle beneath the weak autumn sun. Almost all of them were armed—daggers and short swords at their belts.

Wil kept his head down, only darting quick sideways glances from beneath his fringe. *Hunch in, make yourself small and unthreatening, keep your head down, and keep walking.* The state of his clothes and hair probably spoke his poverty—no point in robbing him—and the lack of any obvious weapon, he hoped, spoke his lack of threat. No one need know about the little dirk in his boot—at least, not if they left him alone.

He passed an old woman stirring something fragrant and spicy in a small cauldron in her kitchen dooryard. The smell made Wil's belly growl and flop about a bit in his empty gut, and he couldn't help the desperate glance he gave the steaming pot. The woman merely gave him a guarded perusal, frowned, opened her mouth as though she meant to say something.... She caught herself just in time and closed her eyes with a slight shudder, then turned her head and deliberately looked away. Wil looked down at his boots and kept walking.

When he'd woken that morning, the unmistakable ring of mallet to metal, butting up against the otherwise smudgy gray stillness, had announced a forge less than a mile distant. He'd followed the sound without much thought. Now it was deafeningly absent as grimy, besweated, and leather-aproned men gathered at the open doors of the dilapidated building and watched him shuffle past.

He'd spotted the grange hall as he'd spied from the ridge rimming the outskirts of the tiny village, and he headed there, risking daylight for want of an alternative. It wouldn't do to come strolling down after dark, not in this sort of forgotten, misbegotten hollow, and he no longer had a choice. It was either take his chances here, or give up and starve to death in the woods.

No store to speak of, not here, but the grange looked like the most prosperous and promising place to try his luck, and they might sell him some bread, at least. If he was lucky, they had some vegetables laid up they might be willing to part with. Harvest was only a month over, after all. Barter would do better in a place like this, but he had nothing with which he could part. He'd have to hope the grange wardens did enough trade with the outside world that the few coins he had in his pocket would be worth something to them. The presence of the smithy added to that hope.

Three voices came from inside the hall, two deep-timbered and one somewhat higher and younger, and all with the thick country accent that made everything they said sound lilting and musical. When he'd come to this country, Wil had loved the sound of the language first, and he'd never got tired of listening to people speak it, regardless of whether they were welcoming him to a village or running him out of it. He brushed it away and made his careful way past the public well and up the two steps that led into the grange.

Strange, how even something so simple as a wooden floor beneath his feet could make his throat go tight and those idiotic tears rise to the backs of his eyes. Wil stepped through the open door of the hall, slid his back to the frame, and dipped his head lower, waiting to be noticed.

It didn't take long. The talk of scarce game and a lucky harvest tapered quickly into expectant silence. Wil could feel three sets of eyes on him, boring past his thin coat and dirty shirt and right through his skin. He shivered.

"You'll pardon," he said quietly, gave a respectful tug to his fringe, and bobbed his head. "I've had a difficult road, and more to go. I'd hoped I might replenish my supplies here and p'raps get directions to an inn."

Silence greeted this. Wil chanced a quick glance up. Father, son, and grandson, he guessed, for three identical sets of hard blue eyes stared warily from faces aged by seasons that sat harsh on their weathered brows. Brown hair, curling at the collars of coats almost as threadbare as his own, and great callused hands, palms rough and red and knuckles gnarled too soon. Like looking at the same man caught frozen in three different stages of his life, and none of them easy.

The din from the forge resumed outside. Wil had no idea why it relieved him so, but he nearly sagged with it.

"What kind of supplies are ye lookin' for?" the eldest asked slowly, the rough brace of his voice in contrast to the almost friendly tilt of the tone.

"Meat, if you have it," Wil answered, paused at the resigned snorts, then pressed, "bread if you don't, and potatoes." It was just as well that meat seemed unlikely. He hadn't dared a fire yet, and potatoes were just as filling raw as cooked. "And water. An extra skin, if you've got one."

Silence again. Wil kept his eyes to the rough grain of the wood floor, but he could almost see the three men looking at each other, speaking silently through raised eyebrows and facial twitches—a language that only three men who shared blood and years could know. After a moment, the youngest turned and made his way across the wide hall and into what Wil guessed was the larder.

"No fresh meat 'til the slaughter," the middle one said, his thick voice still cautious but a little less wary around the edges. "There's a handful of deer jerky I could part with. Bread and potatoes we can do with ease, and we can likely scrounge up a water skin, but I'll want to know how ye plan on paying first."

Fair enough. Wil dug three billets from his pocket and held them out in the palm of his hand. "Two for the food," he said, "the other for the water skin, and I'd like to fill it at your well."

This was where it would go wrong, if it was going to, and he could never tell until he was in the moment which way it would go. Either they were honest men and would take fair payment and let him buy his goods and go, or the sight of the coins would make them wonder how much more he had in that pocket. His gaze remained downcast, but he watched every move from beneath his lashes, waiting for a start or sudden step, his body tense and ready to rabbit through the open door at his back if he had to.

But there was only a shrug from the eldest and a wave of a big hand toward the yard. "Water's free, son. For three billets, I can give you the water skin, the jerky, two loaves of black bread, and as many potatoes as you can carry."

Wil's heart gave a relieved little lurch. He could probably carry at least a score comfortably.

"Unless you'd rather half potatoes and half apples," the man went on. "The Mother was generous, bless Her."

Relieved almost beyond sense, Wil let a low sigh loose from a chest gone far too tight. "I would." He chanced a quick glance up and a smile. "Thank you."

It was a mistake. The man's gaze caught on Wil's, and all kindness vanished.

Wil quickly looked down again and held his breath. The too-abrupt turn from watery relief to a startling immersion inside the confused, nebulous fear of a stranger, the bewildering slide of his own guarded hope into someone else's blurry panic; it was too much, catching him in the chest like a hammer blow. The younger man felt it too—Wil could tell by the stiff stillness. And beneath it all, that *want* crept out from the men, that greed they didn't even know they possessed for something they didn't even know they wanted, a spider skulking on a sticky gossamer thread from their hearts and into his. The rhythmic strike of metal on metal from the smithy was now more distant in Wil's ears than it had been when he'd stood a mile away this morning and wondered if it was worth the risk. And then a grinding scrape and a grating curse, and that stopped too.

Silence.

A splinter in his brain. Unformed thoughts that weren't his own, brilliant colors melting like wax and dripping through his soul, then hardening into pebbles and pelting over his senses in scattershot patterns that bruised the mind.

"Do I know you, boy?" the older man asked slowly.

Do I know you?

Do you know me?

How many times had that same question been put to him in different forms?

I won't hurt you.

Give it to me.

Let me take it.

I want it, you have it, give it to me, giveitgiveitgiveit—

Wil clenched his teeth and tried to breathe deeply, but his chest was too tight.

"No, you don't know me," he managed.

He didn't trust himself to speak more, only hunched down, shook his head, and slowly leaned onto his right leg, readying for a sprint. It was the hunger and exhaustion doing it, he knew, breaking his concentration, weakening the barriers. A decent night's sleep and a full belly, that was all he needed, and then he'd have the strength to beat it all back, lock it away. Last time it had been the fear, roiling in a black cloud over his senses, reaching out all around him and choking him as Orman closed in, and by the time Palmer had snuck up behind him, it had been too late—he'd already lost his grip on it. All he could do was weave the thread between the two of them and step back.

They'd meant to kill him, he'd told himself, or at least one of them had, and what Palmer wanted didn't bear thinking about. They were not good men, there hadn't been a good intention between them, and it was their own natures that had been their undoing.

And yet what was he supposed to do now? These *were* good men. He could feel it, he could see it, and they were kin. What was he supposed to do if father turned on son? How was he going to tell himself—

"Found it, Da!"

Wil jumped, and he only just kept himself from screaming and bolting through the door as the other two jumped as well. But they made no move toward him, only turned toward the youngest man with identical blank, confused expressions as they watched him cross the hall from the back room.

He held up a dusty water skin and jiggled it above his head. "'Twas under the empty feed sacks on the back shelf." He paused with a tilt of his head. "Everything all right?"

The quiet had a physical weight to it, pushing down on Wil's shoulders and constricting his chest. Fight or flight—he couldn't tell which, wished someone would move, speak, do *something* so the heaviness would either crush him or let him go.

Then the old man merely cleared his throat and said, "Well done, Brayden."

Brayden?

Wil nearly choked again and flashed a terrified glance to the young man.

Kindred. A trick. *They knew.* How could Wil have been so incredibly stupid as to walk into the same trap *twice*?

But the young man only gave his grandfather a sideways smile and a nod, obviously pleased by the small bit of praise.

Wil closed his eyes and leaned against the doorframe. His knees felt weak. Stupid, stupid, *stupid*—it was a common enough name, whether given name or surname, and none of these men could possibly be confused with that behemoth of a constable who'd stared Wil down with eyes that knew and didn't know at the same time. For all Wil knew, the man hadn't even said what Wil had thought he'd said, and Wil's overtaxed mind was just playing cruel tricks on him. He was too hungry, too tired, jumping at shadows he was inventing out of so much nothing.

"Are you all right, boy?" That was the father.

"Thank you. I'm very tired." Wil nodded toward the water

skin. "If you'll let me have that, I'll fill my skins while you ready the rest of my purchases." He took a wobbly step toward the young man and held out his coins, trying to tame the jitters that were coursing through every limb, but he couldn't. He allowed the coins to be plucked from his fingers and replaced with the water skin. Glad to be able to breathe again, Wil turned and made himself walk normally through the door and out to the well.

He hadn't noticed how warm the grange hall was until he was back outside it. His breath oozed heavily from his chest in thick plumes, and the weak sun bit into his eyes with a white, high-pitched drone. He concentrated on the ripple and pull of the muscles in his arms and shoulders as he primed the well's pump, the icy brace of the water that spilled down his throat as he drank deeply from the spigot and then over his fingers as he filled the water skins.

They were watching him, all of them. He could feel it like knives between his shoulder blades, pressing, seeking, and he was too raw and open to tether it, clamp it down. He looked down at the muddy water puddling around his knees beside the pump and realized, with a dull sense of weary anger, that he couldn't bring himself to care. *Let them look.*

Reckless, he stoppered the water skins and put them aside, then sucked in a deep breath before he plunged his head under the spigot and let icy water sluice over his scalp. It was *cold*, so cold it drilled a sharp ache behind his eyes, spearing down his nape and backbone, but the pain was a welcome thing. Fear was so exhausting, and this... this merely hurt. Hurt, he could stand. If he wasn't so tired, he'd've stripped naked and washed every bit of filth from his aching body. Let them watch, what did it matter, at least then he'd be clean.

Sputtering, Wil let go of the pump handle and flung his hair back, collar soaked through and hands red, frozen lumps on the ends of his arms. His fingers were numb, but he drove them through his tangled hair, squeezing out as much water as he could into the mud. There'd be icicles dangling from the ends soon, but at least his scalp wasn't so itchy now. Blowing and gasping, Wil made to mop the water from his face with the dirty sleeve of his coat, thought better, and merely swiped at his eyes with his cold hands.

"Which way were you headed?" came from behind him.

Wil didn't jump this time, only turned calmly to see the grandfather standing behind him, holding out a sack. The coarse fabric of it was darkened in spots with drops of water. Wil let his gaze drift up, noting the same on the sleeve and breast of the man's coat. The man had been standing behind him for a while. A dark little chuckle lurked at the back of Wil's throat, manic and drained, but he choked it down.

"West" was all he said.

The man nodded and hooked his chin to the left. "There's an inn over to Dudley. Ten leagues due west. Take the road out through the village, then turn south a little ways 'til you see the dairy on your right. There's a trail through the tree brake—a little hard to make out, so you'll have to look for it. Pick that up and follow 'til it peters out, then just keep on west and you'll find it." He paused to peer up at the sky. "If you keep on steady, you're like to make it before sundown tomorrow."

"Thank you," Wil mumbled. Hands shaking only a little now, he rechecked the stoppers on the water skins and stored them carefully in his pack. Sliding his arms through the straps, he stood, straightened, reached out, and took the offered sack. He swung it over his shoulder without checking its contents; if they'd shorted him, they'd shorted him, but he somehow doubted it.

"You don't look well, son," the man told him. "No meat on your bones, and you look like you en't slept in a while. And you oughtn't to be haring off in this cold with a wet head." A pause, then softer, "If you need it, there's a bit of space in the storeroom for a pallet. My wife en't the best cook, but her supper's hot, at least."

It was a sorry state for a man to find himself in when the least little show of kindness rose pathetic tears to his eyes. And what wouldn't Wil give for that gesture to come from something real? But *oh*, he was tempted. One night of warmth, one hot meal, and he *needed* it....

giveitgiveitgiveit

Wil jammed his thumb and forefinger into his eye sockets, pressed—*hard*—and called to his mind's eye the bewildered craving on the man's face not five minutes ago, the vicious animal light in the eyes of Palmer and Orman, and more before them. He shook his head.

"No." He scrubbed a hand over his damp face and shifted his burden on his back. "Thank you, but I have to go."

The man nodded slowly. "As you will." He shifted uncomfortably, then reached out a hand but pulled it away when Wil flinched back. The man turned his hand palm up and said quietly, "My apologies, young sir, it's only...." The hand dropped away, the man's voice falling to an unsteady whisper. "I think... I think I dreamed of you."

It was the tone—the complete absence of pride or guile.

giveitgiveitgiveit

With a tiny, strangled gasp, Wil jerked a nod, turned, and headed out of the dirty little village.

He didn't look at the villagers still standing in their yards staring, and he didn't look back once he'd passed them. Only kept his head down, eyes to the ground.

He didn't hear the chime of the forge again until he was at least a mile gone.

Sleeping is dreaming, and dreaming sleep, and he can tell the difference now, but what does it matter? It's all the same—grazing thought and fantasy, reaching out to touch secrets he doesn't want to know because he can't make himself stop. It's his design, his purpose, and he can't go against his own pattern. Except he doesn't know what his pattern is, *so he keeps butting up against its limits, bloodying himself, because it's all he knows of who he is.*

The dark shape at his shoulder hovers as it has always done, silent and watching. It used to unnerve him, but he's learned to accept the weight of the invisible stare, has learned to pretend it's a nightmare phantasm made of smoke and mist, but now he knows its true shape. He tries to ignore it now, concentrates on his work.

Weave this strand into that one, truss reverie into truth, truth into reverie, then step back and guide the threads into a tapestry to please Father. Tiny strands of brilliant color blossom, and he weaves them into the like threads, binding them; others go to dark-

ness between his fingers, and he carefully plucks them loose from the weave. A coil here, a wispy whorl there, then delicately pick away at the snarls, tame the strands, and slip them into their true design. Wend nightmare into fancy, guide fancy into hope, then watch as the waking world shreds the tapestry, rending warp from carefully woven weft, and unwinds the threads to be mended again.

He tries not to hate them for it, but he does a little bit anyway.

He tries not to hate Father too, but he's usually just as unsuccessful.

Blood entwines the threads of delusion, his *blood, and still he keeps lacingplaitingweaving, still they call to him, wanting more, always* more, *and oh, he's* so tired.

"I can't," he whispers, tears falling into the plaits and binding with the blood from his shaking fingers. "I can't, I can't, I'm too tired, leave me alone!"

They never do, and he never stops, begs Father to take it all away, but Father smiles from dreams, tells him, "Mother has given you a gift, for She loves you so."

The dark shape at his shoulder curls itself into focus and for the first time gives itself a face: wide and tall, handsome and dark-eyed, hair like gold curling about the ears and nape. The face gives nothing away, the countenance calm beneath his anxious regard, dark eyes assessing, asking silent questions he can't answer.

"One cannot be reborn without returning to the Womb." Father yawns. "All patterns must have a warp to their weft." Then He turns His face away, unites His song to the night, and sleeps deeper.

"I want no gift," he whispers, daring to peer over his shoulder as his fingers fly among the threads. "It frightens me." He pauses with a frown. "Who is Mother?"

Father doesn't answer him, and then Father isn't there anymore. He is alone, always alone, friendless and defenseless, heart as raw as his abraded fingertips, with only the silent, brooding Watcher at his back.

"I have no mother," he whispers to no one.

Stranded in stillness, abandoned, he bows his head, takes threads in his bleeding fingers, cools them with his tears. Keeps weaving.

The inn was a small one, but it seemed to make up for its lack of bulk with an abundance of light and noise. Nestled at the edge of the woods skirting a village Wil hadn't seen yet, it dead-ended a hardpack road that curled from its front yard and up a slight incline to disappear into more trees. He'd heard the music from at least two miles away, string and flute twining with the awakening songs of the stars, only this music was earthy and viscerally alive.

Skulking behind the wide bole of a pine, Wil made himself look, take in the details, and assess the risk before hurrying into the warmth he could almost taste, body vibrating for the want of it. Two stories and very well kept. If a semiprosperous man were unlucky enough to find himself in this part of the world, this was the inn he would seek. Likewise, if a local were looking for an evening of song and safe companionship, he'd pay the extra coin for beer from these taps in exchange for the dependable sanctuary.

It was a respectable establishment. Not at all the sort of place Wil would normally chance, nor did he doubt it would stretch his already screaming purse strings. Still, of any of those still attempting to follow his trail, who among them would think to look for him here?

Smoke poured from the chimney in the center of the main roof, white and thick against the cold slate of the evening; a fire was likely stoked high and hot in the center of the common room. A great cauldron bubbled in the yard, a plump maid stirring whatever heavenly concoction was simmering within it. Indulgent, she shooed away the occasional drunk who staggered from the inn and out into the yard. Slurred compliments and grinning propositions were cheerfully laughed off with a flip of her apron. A covered pit smoldered beside her, the man tending it keeping a watchful eye on the play going on alongside him. He looked amused but sardonic, and Wil guessed that he was either the girl's companion or wanted to be.

The common room must be crowded—the back doors were propped open and at least a score of the patrons had spilled out onto the lantern-strewn yard and brightly lit porch with mugs in hand. A fiddler had followed, keeping rhythm to the rousing melody of pipe and lute still playing inside. Rough wooden tables and benches had been set in the yard, and those who'd wandered out of the warmth inside made use of them—some eating a late supper purchased from the girl at the cauldron, some merely sipping from their mugs and engaging in quiet conversation beneath the night sky.

A small outbuilding caught Wil's eye, set back from the inn, past the pump house and the small stable and toward the trees that ringed the yard. He sighed. A privy. Which meant that, despite the deceptive promise of the pump house, there was no indoor plumbing. Ah well—beggars and all that. He almost dismissed it before the shape and set of the little building made him look more closely, squinting past the soft glow of the lanterns and into the darkness. It was ramshackle and slightly dilapidated, but mud cemented the joints of the timbers, and the roof was shingled in rusted tin rather than the thatching atop the inn itself. Smoke curled from a small metal chimney there as well, and Wil gave a wistful little bleat of delight. Not a privy—a *bathhouse*. His eyes nearly watered.

He'd found an abandoned stable this morning, stone foundations standing like the broken teeth of some long forgotten forest god and covered in moss and lichen. What was left of its interior had been heavy with the musty stench of mildew and rot, but it offered some bit of shelter from the cold, so he'd chased spiders out of the corners and slept there. The weather was turning sharply toward winter, and he'd dared a small fire, nearly smokeless for the abundance of dust-dry kindling just lying around on the floor of the wood. Good thing, because the smoking tip of a stick worked far better on ticks than merely plucking them.

He supposed the cold could be called a blessing in a way—at least it kept the fleas hibernating. He hadn't dared to take his boots off since he'd fled Putnam—he never knew when he might have to get up and run—and the feel of his crusty stockings scraping at the increasingly raw skin of his feet had been almost more of a misery than the cold. One water skin was still halfway full, and he hadn't yet touched the other, so he'd used it to wash the stockings and his feet. Horribly extravagant, considering, but the slime of the fens still moldered in his boots, and he wouldn't be able to walk at all if he let his feet develop the rot.

Wistful, Wil watched the smoke curl up from the narrow chimney of the bathhouse, already imagining the exquisite burn and sting of hot water against his filthy skin. He checked the yard once more, found no one who appeared to be watching for anyone in particular, and made his cautious way down the low slope. Head down, eyes to the ground, gold between his fingers.

Stepping gingerly, careful, Wil angled his approach toward the cauldron. He wasn't as hungry as he'd been, but the smell was a low ache anyway—if not in his belly, then in the part of his heart that longed for the small normalcy of cooked food and clean trenchers from which to eat it.

The girl was prettier than he'd thought from farther away—red hair, thick and bright, pulled back from her clear brow and tamed beneath a blue scarf tied tight around her head. She was plump and healthy-looking, with a generous bosom that made Wil wonder what it might be like to lay his head on her breast and let her short, nimble fingers stroke his hair until he fell into a happy, dreamless sleep. She smiled as he approached, eyes sparking on a cheerful gaze with only a quick dart over the state of his filth. She kept her smile warm and expectant, but Wil could feel the man's gaze sharpen over her shoulder, alert for threat. Wil did his best not to offer any reason to pounce. The man was almost as skinny as Wil, but he looked strung-steel strong.

"You look like you've seen better days," the girl said kindly.

Have I? Wil thought. He couldn't remember. "I...." The

man was unnerving him with his hard stare, so Wil swallowed and focused on the girl's encouraging smile. "I want a bath."

"I'll say you do." Wil must have flushed, because her smile turned apologetic. "Now there, that's all right. Don't mind me. I've a foot that won't keep out my mouth, en't I, Tom?"

The man tending the pit—Tom—gave a noncommittal grunt, poking at the coals with a long rod of iron. "Spit out the foot, Miri, and ask the...." Tom glanced up and raked a skeptical glance from Wil's matted hair to his cracked, muddy boots. "Ask the lad how he plans to pay, first. Let one more skive off, and Garson'll have that foot of yours off to kick my arse with."

The girl—Miri—rolled her eyes and gave Wil a sideways little grin. "Tom thinks he's the boss of me," she confided with a wink, though she made no effort to lower her voice. "He'll learn better come spring, once that binding cord goes about our hands."

Another grunt from Tom. "You say that like I en't learned it already."

"There you go, Miri!" someone called from the yard. "You've got 'im fasted already, and it en't nothing to do with his hand."

A jovial smattering of laughter rippled, and then someone else piped in, "Aye, Miri, open up that apron pocket of your'n and let the lad have his balls back for a tick, why don't you!"

More laughter rolled across the yard, warm and jolly. Wil found himself grinning, glancing over his shoulder to the small, ebullient crowd in the yard. They were an odd mix of the common and borderline lordly, their various states of wealth or lack of it apparently mattering little here. It was freezing, but none of them seemed to mind, and the longer Wil stood here, the less he minded it himself.

"Shut it over there, Ridley Miller, or the next mug I hand you'll be filled with more than just beer," Tom grumbled, but Wil could see the cheerful cast of his glance and the tilt of a stifled grin. The hint of a smile made his hard-set face look almost boyish, but the long dagger at his belt, the hilt notched and worn with use, warned otherwise. He peered back at Wil, considerably softer now. "Can you pay?".

"I can." Wil frowned. "That is, I'm sure I've enough for a bath." He looked back at Miri. "A bath—hot water and soap—a bowl of whatever that is you're stirring there, and...." He considered the state of his right trouser pocket. "Perhaps a room, if I've enough left."

Miri was still smiling, but it slid a bit into a sympathetic grimace. "Room and board for a night, plus a bath, will run you three gilders." Rueful, she nodded when Wil's shoulders drooped. It would clean him out, with maybe a few billets left over, and there was no way in the world he could linger about looking for work. "Tell you what," Miri went on, "for one gilder, you can have the bath and the stew, and if you keep out of sight—"

"Miri," Tom cut in, a warning rumble beneath the tone.

"Hush, you," Miri snapped over her shoulder. "What Garson don't know won't piss him off. When's the last time he hauled that great arse of his out to the stables?" Tom subsided with a roll of his eyes and a shake of his head, rather proving the earlier jibes about who wore the stones in this budding little family, but he glared dangerously into the yard when several snickers drifted from their small audience. Miri must have noted it too, because she kindly lowered her voice when she turned back to Wil. "I can't fill up a new bath for you—you'll have to make do with what's there from the last one—but it ought to still be warm, at least, and soap's included."

"No, it en't," Tom muttered, but he only kept poking at the coals of the pit when Miri ignored him.

Wil looked down, pushed a hand into his pocket, and toyed at the coins. "I wouldn't want to get you into trouble," he said quietly, a little surprised by the truth in it. Only this morning, burning ticks from an arm and a thigh with a malicious little snarl, he'd thought he'd be willing to push someone over a cliff for a dip in a half-frozen pond. Now, knowing he would be paying for probably only about half of what he was actually getting, shame overwhelmed greed. "How much for just the bath?" Bathing in someone else's filth wasn't exactly a pleasing notion, but it was better than walking around in his own.

Miri only peered at him, her kind eyes assessing. Still smiling, she let the paddle rest against the side of the cauldron and told Tom, "Lend an eye for a moment, won't you? Don't let it scald the bottom." She turned toward the bathhouse and gestured for Wil to follow. With one last glance at Tom, Wil did.

"That's Tom's place over there." Miri pointed out a neat little shack past the small paddock and next the stables as they walked. She'd set rather a brisk pace, and Wil had to pay attention to his footing so he wouldn't trip in the dark. "It'll be ours once we're bound." Wil smiled at the proprietary glint in her girlish grin. "'Tenny rate, Tom doubles as hostler, so there's no one as would know if someone were to make a quiet nest in the stables in the night." She winked over her shoulder at Wil; he gave her a quick grin in return. "Here we are, then," Miri said cheerfully, swung the door of the bathhouse open, and gestured him through.

The heat of the little room slammed Wil in the face like a thick, soft wall. It took a moment for his lungs to adjust, the air heavy with moisture and blessed, blessed heat. The fragrance of cedar and soap hit his nostrils, their clean scent blundering into the stench coming from his own body, making it sharper and more pungent. Again, he felt those damnable tears crowding his eyes, a quick moment of mourning for how low he'd come, but he shoved it away. If he'd learned nothing else over the past few years, he'd learned that one who managed few pleasures should snatch at the ones offered and be grateful. Peering around, breathing in the clean steam, he was.

Slender slats of wood lined the walls—not the mud-mortared boards he'd seen from the outside. This little bathhouse must have been double-walled, the interior boards fitted tight together and snugged so close no draft wended its way from the chill outside. Red clay tiles lined the floor, sloping gently to an open drain in the center of the close little room. A thin stain of rust ran to it from three dripping spigots on the wall opposite the door, but that was the only blemish Wil could spot in the whole of the room. Otherwise, it was a haven of cleanliness and civilization.

Three large wooden tubs took up the rest of the space, their sides darkened and smoothed from years of constant use. Only one was full, its water only a little gray, Wil noted—a far cry from what it would likely be when he got through with it. A hearth took up the entire east side of the room, its fire blazing high and bright; five oversized coppers hung from hooks over it, the tick of the heating metal dulled by the crackling of the coals.

Miri stepped smartly over to the fire, slid a blackened mitt over her hand, and lifted a copper from its hook. Wil stepped back as she breezed past him, and with a wink, she poured the hot water from the kettle into the tub.

"I won't tell if you won't." She smirked as she took a key from her apron, stepped past Wil again, and unlocked a cupboard by the door. "One bath sheet and one cake of soap," Miri said, stacking both on the small table beside the tub. As if by habit, her hand fell upon a straight razor, but then she paused and peered over her shoulder with a frown. "Why don't you need a shave?" No suspicion, only ingenuous curiosity. She tilted her head. "How old are you?"

"Old enough," Wil said, probably a little too quickly—definitely a little too tightly. How was he supposed to answer that? *I have no idea how old I am, but I know I'm old enough to grow a beard, and yet I don't, and I have no idea why that is either. There's a lot about me I don't know, and too much I do know, and a lot you probably don't want to know, so we'll both be better off if you just don't ask.* He took a breath, offered an apologetic smile, and rubbed at his beardless chin. "It just... I'm not one of those rugged sorts blessed with a thick growth." He did his best to make his smirk look winsomely philosophical. "Sometimes I have to find other ways to prove my, um...." He trailed off, embarrassed.

Miri snorted. "Not sure I'd call it a blessing, and you look like you do just fine." She rubbed her cheek. "I think Tom's could cut through leather sometimes."

Wil flashed a nervous grin. "It's just as well, then."

Dropping the shaving supplies and closing the cupboard, Miri gave Wil another quick assessing glance. "Have you got a change of clothes?"

You mean besides the one I meant to buy with the money I'd earned at Ramsford's before I got run out of Putnam? The thought came with not a little bit of venom. Wil said nothing, only flushed some and looked away.

"Right, then." Miri sighed. "You're not supposed to wash clothes in here, but if you've not got enough for a room and a meal, I imagine you've not got enough to have what you've got on laundered, neither." She tutted. "Just don't be washing 'em in the tub 'til you're out of it, or you'll be more dirty getting out than going in."

Wil gave a guilty little start. He'd just been wondering if he could get away with exactly that, and how ungrateful and unappreciative it would be of him if he did. He shifted, embarrassed. "I won't—"

"Well, you should," Miri cut in. "If you don't, that gilder that's so dearly spent will be so much wasted coin. And it won't make no difference, anyhow. Two to a bath is the limit. I'd be emptying the tub when you're through at any rate." She tactfully didn't mention that she'd have to empty the tub after him even if he weren't the second to use it. "You can hang them by the fire to dry. Don't worry, the fire's high so it shouldn't take too long, and I doubt there'll be much more business for the baths tonight." Her expression took on that benign look of sympathy again. "I'll have to ask for the money now."

Wil only blinked at her for a moment, then shook his head, said, "Oh!" and dug into his pocket. He handed her one of his three remaining gilders. She'd never answered him about how much it was for just the bath, but now that he was here with the water calling to him, he thought she could ask him to empty his pockets and he'd probably do it.

"That should do you for now," Miri told him, "unless you can think of something else?"

Wil shook his head, mute. He couldn't think of a single thing he wanted more right now than for this kind young woman to leave so he could strip off and dive in. Perhaps she sensed this, because her smirk broadened and she gave him another of those knowing winks, then let herself out without further comment.

He wasted no time. His pack dropped to the floor with a *thunk* that reminded him vaguely that he'd likely now have several bruised apples, but he couldn't give the thought enough room in his brain to care. His boots and clothes made a stiff pile on the floor. He kept it close to the tub. Meager as it was, it was all he had, and he'd been robbed in the bath once before.

A brass plate hung on the wall opposite the foot of the tub, so he supposed it was inevitable that he caught a glimpse of himself. He'd lost the light tan that the string of sunburns had left behind. Now he was pale and drawn, with sunken eyes beneath a wild tangle of longish dark hair that was glossy when it was clean but dull and unhealthy-looking now. Haggard and bedraggled, with new bruises over old scars and a sad exhaustion in his eyes that gave even him a twinge. No wonder Miri had felt sorry for him. The thought made him blush.

"At least I got all the ticks." Clenching his jaw, Wil shook his head and stepped into the tub.

The water wasn't hot, but it was warm and sluiced gloriously against his skin. It couldn't have been better if it were made of rose petals and silk. A groan loosed itself from his chest as he sank in to his collarbones. He dipped his head under first, lying back beneath the water and stretching out as best he could so only the knobs of his knees broke the surface. It was bliss.

Baths hadn't always had this effect on him. He'd taken them for granted once. Three years ago, "dirty" had an entirely different meaning to him; he snorted grimly at the fool he'd been, small bubbles leaking from his nostrils to pop in tiny, silent explosions on the surface of the water. Simple pleasures had never really been simple for him—he'd had so few of them, and he hadn't really known the difference until the *Dearthåireacha* had clumsily and inadvertently opened his eyes, showing him that what he'd thought of as life had only a passing acquaintance with reality. Still, baths had been daily and routine, before.... Well. Before.

He sat up, blew water from his mouth and nose, and reached for the soap. Hair first. He'd likely have to wash that at least twice. He ought to cut it. The people of the Commonwealth wore their hair short by comparison, and he'd seen few others with hair as dark as his. That constable had been right—Wil stood out. Granted, less so in a big city like Putnam, but standing out at all was never a good thing for someone in his position.

A quick knock at the door gave his heart a bit of a jolt, and he reached down instinctively toward his boot and the small blade secreted inside it. It was only Miri, that little grin tugging at her mouth as she barged through the door with a tray in her hand, a bowl of the pottage she'd been cooking and two thick slices of brown bread slathered with butter balanced at either side of a tall mug. She closed the door quickly, ghosts of steam escaping past her and sucking back a cold whorl of night's breath that slid over Wil's skin. He pulled his arm back in and dipped it beneath the water.

"Well, glory be, at least there's one man in the world who doesn't shriek like a lass when one walks in on him." Miri moved the bath sheet from the table next the tub and slid the tray there instead. "Honestly, the way some men jump and cover the jewels, you'd think they had something I en't seen before, and probably better stuff at that."

Wil frowned, peered down. He hadn't felt self-conscious before, but now he wasn't so sure.

"The beer's a bit watery." Miri snapped out the bath sheet and draped it over a hook behind Wil's head. "But the stew is good and hot. I thought you might like to have a bite while you soak."

She had such a kind practicality about her. Between that and the bath and the rich smell of the stew, Wil suspected he might be falling in love. Either that or he was drunk on pleasure.

"I haven't paid for it," Wil reminded her.

"Course you have. One gilder for a bath and a meal." Miri peered at the soap Wil hadn't rinsed from his hair yet. "You'd best dry that by the fire while you wait for your clothes to dry. You oughtn't to be ramming about in the cold with a wet head. Have you got a comb?"

A slight smile tugged at Wil's mouth, and he nodded. Two days ago a kind old man had said almost exactly that—yet with Miri, nothing dark or worrisome lurked beneath the concern. He was in better shape now than he'd been when he passed through the little village, due mostly to the generous supplies his three billets had bought him, and he'd let himself sleep a little more since then, too. If he kept himself away from the edges of starvation and exhaustion—*and let's don't forget fear*, he thought with a slight clench of teeth—he could almost pass for a normal person without having to concentrate so hard on keeping such a tight leash on what roiled about within. It was when he lost his concentration that things went wrong.

"All right, then," Miri said, all pragmatic cheer. "You ought to have the place to yourself 'til I come back in a few hours to close up. Buy yourself a beer in the common room when you're dry and dressed, if you've got enough left, and sit by the fire 'til Garson calls last orders. Tom will have checked the stables by then." That last she said with a conspiratory little waggle of her eyebrows. "Hang your bath sheet up on that rack by the fire when you're through, eh?" And with that, Miri tipped Wil one last wink before she let herself out again.

The waft of cold from the door prickled at Wil's soapy scalp and raised gooseflesh on his arms, but he barely felt it. He dunked his head beneath the water again, watched as murky trails of soap tendriled from it, and smiled.

Funny how the cold didn't seem to bother him when he stepped back out into it. His collar was still damp and the waistband of his trousers was already soaking through his shirt, but he didn't feel any of it. Clean and warm and relatively dry, and smelling of soap instead of dirt, Wil stepped back out into the yard with a happy sigh. The stew and bread had filled his belly almost to the point of lethargy as he'd lounged in the tub, and the beer, combined with the heat of the fire as he'd sat beside it and waited for his clothes to dry, had sent him into a light doze right there in the bathhouse. He'd have to watch himself in the common room; it wouldn't do to fall asleep there.

He spotted Miri on his way through to the yard, where she was chivvying Tom as he scrubbed out the cauldron, but she stopped as he sauntered by, peering up at him with a grin and a teasing whistle. "*Cor*, look how pretty he is under all that!" She gave Tom a bit of a nudge with her elbow.

Tom huffed what Wil guessed was his usual grunt, nodded a bit, and went back to his work. The pit was empty, Wil noted, and the coals had already been raked thin and buried in the ash to die. Whatever had been cooking in it must have been the main course in the common room while he'd been dozing and drying. Wil was pleased to note his stomach didn't give so much as a disappointed grumble at having missed it.

"Thank you, Miss Miri," he said sincerely, pausing just out of the way of Tom's thrashing elbows. "I can't...." He shook his head, unable to find words. "You've no idea—"

"Course she does." Tom's voice was less prickly than Wil had heard it yet. "Why d'you think she's such a bloody pushover?"

Miri scowled and flung a wet cloth at his head but couldn't cover a smile when Tom merely ducked and smirked. "Ignore him. Everyone does."

Wil dipped a half bow. "Thank you," he said again. "It meant everything." And since there was really nothing else he could add, he merely turned and headed for the front of the inn.

He would've liked to have gone right to the stable and sleep, he was so relaxed, but though Miri definitely seemed the one in charge, Wil saw no point in causing unnecessary discord. Miri's intent had been crystal clear, and Tom's disapproval of it equally so—but it would be easier for Tom to turn a blind eye if there was nothing for him to see.

Supper evidently over, the crowd inside had thinned, some having apparently gone to their rented rooms and others to their homes, so the spillover out to the yard had spilled back in. Wil recognized one of the men who'd bantered with Tom, now draped over the bar and trying to drunkenly proposition a middle-aged woman who looked like she wanted nothing to do with whatever the man's no doubt clumsy offer might be. Wil only ducked his head and moved toward the scattering of tables and chairs arranged around the central hearth.

Oil lamps burned smoky and low, adding a slight tangy fog to the air that stung his nose. A one-legged man was just tossing a coin onto a table in front of the plump, worn chair he was vacating. Wil eased around behind him and slipped into the chair as soon as the man had gained his crutch and taken two lurching steps away from it. Not only would his wait be comfortable, tucked away in a nice dark little niche as he was, but the man had left behind a mug and a trencher with the leavings of his supper. If Wil was very lucky, anyone who might notice would think he was already a paying customer, and he wouldn't have to spend unnecessary coin on a watery beer he didn't want.

The fiddler and the flautist had apparently packed it in, but the man with the lute still sat on a stool in the far corner, dreamily strumming to the lulling babble of the crowd. The barkeep—Garson, Wil assumed—let out a braying laugh and slapped his hand on the bar as those around him broke into a jovial argument over something Wil didn't catch.

It was... nice. Wil was sleepy but no longer exhausted. The din around him would have been grating to his nerves another time, but now it had a strange sort of comfort to it, and he sank into the cushions of the chair, absently marveling at its depth and softness. He hadn't felt this good since his third night in Putnam. Nothing else seemed terribly important.

He dozed, though he tried very hard not to, jerking himself awake several times when the sounds of the crowd would briefly swell or when his own inner alerts would tiredly sputter to momentary life. The breeze from the open doors curled in, tendriling the night's chill around his feet to stir him, and he blinked and snuffled and tried to sit a little straighter.

Miri came in, flirting and joking her way through the small crowd between the door and the bar. Her bright eyes gave the room an assessing glance, paused on Wil briefly, squinted, but then passed on. She hadn't seen him in his dim-lit little nook. *That's all right*, Wil thought with a drowsy smile as he sank deeper into the cushions. *Being invisible isn't such a bad thing.* Maybe a short kip wouldn't be such a bad thing either.

"Lovely girl, her."

It was the accent that made him freeze, made his heart lurch and his dinner turn rancid in his stomach. The thudding of his heart in his ears drowned out the merry sounds of the crowd—laughter, music, the *clink* of stoneware and glass. All of it faded into thudding silence as Wil slowly turned his head, gaze slamming headlong into eyes cold and blue and hard as tempered steel.

"You."

He nearly choked on it. If it made a sound, Wil didn't hear it, but the man gave him a sloe-eyed smile and shrugged.

Wil had never seen the man before, but he recognized him immediately—the series of small round tattoos on the upper right cheekbone told Wil all he needed to know. Blue-eyed and dark-haired, easy smile flashing teeth that shone white against clear, fair skin. Another time Wil might have thought him handsome.

"You had to know we'd catch up to you one day, Aisling."

Slowly Wil slid his hand under the table and reached down to his boot. The man sighed, shook his head—then, quick as a snake, snatched Wil's wrist in strong fingers, twisted.

Wil kept himself from crying out. "That isn't my name," he snarled and tried to jerk his arm out of the man's grip—couldn't.

"It is the only one I need," the man replied calmly.

Too late, Wil darted his glance around the room looking for help or escape. Another man he didn't recognize stared at him from the doorway, the hard set of his face almost comical beneath the huge black bushy brows. Wil wasn't laughing—the man's arms were folded across his chest, and his coat was pulled back far enough from his hip to let Wil see the butt of his gun angling from its holster.

Wil almost wept. Fear and frustration lumped in his throat, and his heart slammed against his breastbone. He would almost have rathered Síofra. At least Síofra only wanted him dead.

Wil licked lips gone abruptly dry. "How did you find me?"

The crushing grip on Wil's wrist tightened. "You left a bit of a mess behind you in Putnam," the man told him. "Palmer managed a message before you saw to him."

"I didn't 'see to him,' he was—"

"He was Brethren, which makes him better than blood to

me, you filthy little *puke*, and you saw to it he met his end at the hands of Guild scum—after everything they did to you."

Wil's lip curled on a sneer. "And what you and your 'Brothers' *wanted* to do was so much better?"

The man's eyes went dark, glittering, and his grip on Wil's wrist twisted down so hard Wil thought it might snap. "*Never* make that comparison again," the man seethed.

Rage colored his words, turned his false accent thick and slurred. True Believers, Wil thought with mounting panic, were always the scariest. His heart sank down to the floor. He wasn't going to get out of this with fast talk or wheedling, and certainly not with anything as practical as reason.

"And let me give you a small word of advice, now that it doesn't matter anymore," the man went on, teeth clenched tight on a snarl. "When you stop to ask directions, don't then go exactly where you've said you would be." Another derisive snort and a shake of the head. "You make a piss-poor fugitive, you know. And you only leave those who've been kind to you behind to pay for your stupidity."

Wil's stomach dropped. "What did you do?"

"Only what you forced me to." The man shook his head and gave a mocking little *tsk*. "That's two villages burned behind you now, Aisling, and how many dead on your conscience? How many more innocents will it take?"

"The men in Old Bridge were not *innocent*. And it wasn't me who—"

"The men in Old Bridge were my *Dearthráireacha*, as was Palmer." The man's grip ratcheted down yet more cruelly. "I ought to kill you right here for what you did."

Wil fought a gasp as fresh pain shot through his hand and

up his arm. His fingers were going numb, and a burning ache was turning his muscles useless. It didn't matter to this man that Wil hadn't been the one to set the blaze; it didn't matter that what happened in Old Bridge had happened because those men hadn't had a clue what they were playing with and they'd made their own end. The only thing that mattered to this man was his *purpose*, and to such a degree that he'd been insane with it long before Old Bridge had even happened.

Rage built, and Wil tried to think past the fiery agony splintering up his arm. He dug down and looked for courage in the frozen hollow of his gut, sucked in a shaky breath, and gritted his teeth.

"You might as well do." It came out too thin, like a wheeze. "It doesn't matter. I can't give it to you."

"You mean you won't."

Wil only glared, mouth twitching with a suppressed grimace of pain.

The man's smile curled, cruel and alarmingly smug. "You're right, it doesn't matter—we know how to take it now."

Dread beyond words rose in Wil, but no real surprise—there were just as many spies inside the Guild as there were without. It had only been a matter of time before the Brethren acquired the piece of the puzzle they'd been missing three years ago. And unlike the Guild, they didn't have the luxury of simply replacing him. They needed him alive, and they were willing to destroy entire villages to keep their purpose—their very existence—an enigma. Wil managed to keep the shocked tears at bay and focused on the one tool he had left.

He sucked in a harsh breath so his voice wouldn't shake. "You won't kill me—you can't—and I won't go quietly. If you try to drag me out of here, I'll kick and scream and shout to the rafters that I'm being kidnapped."

The man shrugged again. "Then my man at the door will shoot your little ginger friend and whoever else gets in the way. How many more dead will you leave behind you like a grisly scattering of breadcrumbs for me to follow?"

Wil's gaze darted to Miri, who was washing mugs and dishes behind the bar now, still flirting and laughing good-naturedly with the patrons.

What do you care, you don't even know her, and her death will be a lot kinder than your life if you let this happen. They can't kill you, they can't, *there is no threat to you but what you let them make.*

His eyes watered, and his throat locked up.

But the threat wasn't to me.

Well, then. All the better.

Wil shut his eyes and willed away the burning behind them. The faces of the three men at the grange drifted into eerie focus, kind beneath their confusion, guileless beneath the suspicion. Miri's smiling face came next, dropping him a smirking wink, just before a smoking hole opened in the middle of her forehead.

Another in a regrettable string of necessary sacrifices. That's all.

I can't. She was so kind, and for no reason except that she wanted to help a bedraggled stranger to whom she owed nothing. I can't.

The air stirred around him, hot and cloying, and he clamped his free hand to the arm of the chair.

Then the choice is easy, if you'll let yourself see it.

There is *no choice!*

A small, brooding laugh scattered through him, something pale and putrid that lived its life in the perpetual twilight of the shadowed corners of his mind he didn't allow himself to see.

Isn't there? Do you really think they'll leave anyone here alive anyway? Haven't they proven already how talented they are at covering their tracks? You've only the one choice, and they've already made it for you.

Dark light in his heart, throbbing a sickening rhythm through his veins and spiking out to pulse in every nerve ending. Like an obscene benediction.

So obvious. So simple. So... perfect.

I've never done it on purpose. I don't know how.

So, then. Let them take you to another Old Bridge.

Wil snarled, frantic and desperate. He didn't allow himself to think or pause, just peered up, locking his gaze on Eyebrows at the door.

Nothing more than a white buzz at first as the man stared back. Alien thoughts and emotions pattered inside Wil's head, rippling out like the first drops of rain on the unbroken surface of a sleeping lake. Instinct told him to pull himself back when the first familiar wave of craving broke over him, but he kept his gaze steady, heart pounding with a bizarre, almost thrilling anguish.

Threads of blinding light and color slid through his senses, eldritch and transient as fireflies in a lazy summer breeze. He snatched for them, grasped them with his mind's eye, stretched them from one edge of consciousness and toward another. Found the thread of another and reached.

Then *pushed.*

Wil turned his mind from the unpleasant nausea that engulfed him, turned his mind from everything but the eyes staring back at him. An abstract, near-sensual queasiness moved through him when the man's gaze took on the familiar confusion, eyes going wider, dimming.

Come to me, help me now, and I'll hand you what you think you want to keep you from taking what I can't give you.

Some part of him vaguely heard a curse in the North Tongue and then "There'll be none of that" right next to his ear. Wil was jerked back to himself with a soul-tearing abruptness that rocked his mind and threw it back at him with a bone-jarring *thump*.

It took a moment for Wil to register the fact that his face hurt, the pain in his mouth so exquisite it was like a red throb swathing his entire head. His nose was dripping, and he reached up to swipe at it, stared, stupidly amazed as his fingers came back red with blood.

Bastard slammed my head into the table.

Dazed, he tried again for the knife, tried to stand. A hand knotted through his hair, and his head was driving into the table again.

"Try it again and I *will* kill you." Growled into his ear, but Wil barely heard it. His blood was too loud and his head was all-over knives.

Someone was hauling him to his feet, dragging him toward the door. He dug in his heels, twisted, tried to yell, but a fist slammed into his belly, then his back and kidneys—they just kept coming—and the intended shout emerged as nothing more than a thin wheeze. Everything was far away and spinning.

Eyebrows was suddenly there, and hard fingers dug into

Wil's arms, held him upright, and pulled him through the crowd. He couldn't keep his head from lolling like a rag doll's. Yanked to the side, out of one grip and into another, low snarls vibrating through his head, but he couldn't make out what anyone was saying. Yanked again, and he was caught between them. Strong hands gripped each arm, pulled him like a wishbone. And all the while, the door kept getting closer.

No one's going to stop them, he thought numbly. *They think I'm drunk and my friends are carrying me home. I guess I'm going quietly after all.*

He tried to laugh at the irony; it came out as a whimpering sob. He could hear the toes of his boots scraping across the rough wood floor, loud in his ears, and his own panting breaths, but nothing else. His knees were water, and his head was a pulsing soap bubble.

"Help." He choked on it as blood from his nose dripped down the back of his throat. "Someone...."

Some mutinous part of him noted they almost had him to the door, knew that once he crossed that threshold it was over—over for good this time, because they wouldn't make the same mistakes they did last time.

His arms weren't free, but his hands were. He made a clumsy lunge to the side, twisted, and scrabbled at the gun hanging from the holster on Eyebrows's hip, amazed when his fingers closed over the smooth butt—even more amazed when he yanked and it came free in his hand. Too bad he had no idea what to do with it, except perhaps point it in the right direction and hope. Although it was heavier than he'd expected—it would at least make a handy blunt instrument if he could get himself loose.

A shout in the North Tongue rang Wil's eardrums, but he could neither tell who said it, nor what it was, heard only thunder in his head and his own breathless scream in his ears as his hand was crushed around the butt of the gun and his fingers were wrenched back. He tried to scream again as pain shot up his wrist and he felt the sickening crunch of breaking bone, but someone's arm locked around his throat and squeezed.

His ruined hand was still trying to clutch at the gun, frantic and scratching, but at least one finger was broken and the others had gone numb and clumsy, and the wholeness of his wrist was now in serious question. His lungs seized up as he tried to claw air in through the searing blockage in his throat. He abandoned his weak grasp on the gun and reached instead to claw at the arm around his neck. It was like iron, curled around and cutting off air and thought. Steadily, reason and sense began to slip away. Darkness crowded in, spangling at the edge of his vision.

Not a bad way to go, Wil supposed dully. Sort of peaceful, really, once you got used to it.

Through a muffled haze, he heard a scream and the thunderous boom of a gunshot, then another, and Wil was being propelled face-first into the doorjamb. He hit with a breathless grunt, forehead and cheekbone slamming into too-solid wood, reawakening the blinding pain still thudding in his head from its forced meeting with the table. Air burned into his chest in a searing rush, tangy with the acrid taste of gunpowder, as his lungs mindlessly wrenched breath in and then forced it back out in wheezes and harsh barking coughs.

With a crazed, choked little giggle, Wil focused on a great jagged splinter of wood jutting from the doorframe that had just missed skewering his left eye. Some still-coherent part of his mind registered the newness of it, the greenish blond of the wood beneath the stain and lacquer, and knew the small explosion of timber and paint had come from a bullet tearing through it; the less-than-coherent part thought it all vaguely hilarious.

"Lucky me," Wil snickered, garbled through bleeding lips, drunk on pain and murky shock. His eyes fell shut as his whole body turned to a loose assembly of jittering nerves strung together by agony.

Still cackling quietly, Wil slid down the wall and into darkness.

CHAPTER 3

Three... no, four of them. *Damn it.* Propping themselves in the shadows of trees or ducking behind the tables strewn beneath the faltering gutter of the lanterns. One of them was even flattened to the ground, nothing but a smear of slightly more substantial gloom beneath the shadow thrown by the stable into the paddock. *Idiot.* You couldn't get a good firing stance like that.

He supposed it could have been worse—there could have been forty. And they could have been competent. All of them had taken point, their eyes and ears trained on the door of the inn, and not one of them had bothered to give even a cursory glance behind them in the time he'd been watching.

Dallin's mouth curled into a dark little smirk.

Seriously. *Idiots.*

Dallin withdrew a score of yards, quietly doffing his pack and his crossbow. The rifle he might need, but it also had a tendency to get in the way with close work, so he reluctantly unslung it from his shoulder and left it. New revolver, old revolver, short sword, and... dagger. He really needed to make the time to find a belt sheath or something for that. Carrying it around in his boot was annoying and not terribly safe for one's sock. Or ankle. Maybe when he got back home. And Mother's tits, wouldn't *home* sit really well just now.

Except now there were these guys.

They weren't the law. They weren't smart enough for that. Dallin knew because he'd been following them as they'd followed Calder.

And then there'd been Kenley.

Dallin took the two in the trees first—carefully, quietly, and one at a time. The first fell so quickly beneath the butt of his gun that Dallin feared he might have hit him too hard and accidentally killed him. Which. Oh well. He hadn't, though, so restraint it was. The only rope he'd brought with him, he expected to need, and the cuffs too, for Calder, so Dallin removed the man's holster, took his gun, and trussed him with the belt.

The second must have sensed him somehow, because he turned just before Dallin got into position, obviously expecting a compatriot, since he actually started to smile a greeting before Dallin dropped him too. If the bugger hadn't turned, Dallin wouldn't've lost his angle and had to whack him twice. Served him right, anyway. Dallin bound that one in the same manner as the first and moved on.

He paused to take stock. He'd been following what he was fairly certain were six men, and here were only four accounted for. Dallin could see one hovering about the open back door of the inn—safely distracted and in turn distracting Calder, if Dallin was lucky—and assumed the other was inside where Dallin couldn't see him, but he wanted to make sure of their numbers before he walked into anything. Anyway, he *really* wanted to know what this little posse was doing on Calder's trail in the first place, and why they'd felt it necessary to spread carnage in their clumsy wake to eliminate witnesses. Then again, he might have just answered his own question.

Except the bigger question was *why*? Why go to all this trouble for some skinny little troublemaking runaway who was, so far as Dallin knew, merely a figurehead and easily replaced? And especially after Ríocht's ambassador had gone to such lengths to drag Cynewísan into the search. Having read the little fairy tale Manning had given him, Dallin could *almost* understand why they wanted him back—religious fanatics, in Dallin's experience, could see perfect reason in the most unreasonable things—but Calder couldn't possibly have this much import. Something else was very wrong.

Not Dominion spies—they weren't nearly good enough. Although, now that he'd got a look at them—albeit a very quick look in the dark—he was rethinking that assessment. All of them were dark-haired with light complexions. Though clearly and undeniably from the North and likely candidates for agents, the fact that they rather stood out here made them useless as spies. The fact that the two he'd taken out in the trees had no papers added to the suspicion rather than dismissed it.

Dallin shook his head. He'd find out from one of them.

The man with the best hiding place was, by dubious

default, apparently the smartest among them, which wasn't saying much. Still, Dallin's curiosity and patience had both reached their limits, and he wanted that one able to answer his questions, so he'd prefer to save him for last.

Though, truly, the *best* man for answers was likely Calder himself. Dallin would have to deal with these others first.

The moon was new and too bright for Dallin's liking, but it was hiding behind a scrim of cloud at the moment. Not exactly a circumstance he could control, and he was loath to expose himself in the light of the yard. He decided to keep trusting his instincts and went for the man by the paddock first, keeping a wary eye on the other as he sidled through the shadows. This one was flat to the ground, so no convenient angles of assault presented themselves. Dallin would have to kill him quick and quiet and hope he was right that this one was just a lackey. The paperwork when he got back to Putnam would be a bitch, and Jagger would sigh wearily at him and roll his eyes, but really—what choice did Dallin have? It was the man's own fault for being so incompetent.

His luck was improving—the horses had got bored and wandered out farther into the paddock. He'd have to do this one with all speed, so he would be away and back into the shadows before they got curious again or started making noise when they smelled the blood. Because there would, Dallin knew, be a lot of blood.

The muffled *whoof* of breath when Dallin fell on the man's back was the only sound. Dallin's weight and position made struggle impossible as he covered the man's mouth with one hand and the dagger in the other found its mark, severing the man's jugular in one clean plunge-and-sweep. Dallin waited until there were no more twitches before rolling off and wiping his hands and weapon on the grass and the man's coat.

Damn it, no papers on this one either. Dallin breathed a silent growl as he started to work his way back the way he'd come. It was either risk the pockets of weak lantern light and the moon, or make his way around the front of the inn and approach the last one from behind. Time was pressing, so risk it was.

It took him longer this time to work his way around the yard, setting his boots softly in the grass and testing his steps for unseen twigs or other alarms before resting his weight for the next. Closer now, Dallin could make out posture and stance and the way the man held his gun. He crouched in the dark with a discipline Dallin recognized—former military. Likely one of those wily little recon ferrets the Commonwealth's infantry so despised. He held his weapon as one used to the heft and shape, and his body as one who remained alert and on watch. Unlike the others, this one had obviously been well trained.

Not well trained enough, though—Dallin was perhaps four strides from the man when he noted the telltale tensing of the shoulders, the firming of the fingers about the gun. Dallin caught the man's arm in midswing, aimed the barrel of the gun at the ground, and jammed the web of his palm between the gun's hammer and firing pin. Some part of him knew the pain was exquisite, but most of him was battle-removed and coolly distant. Teeth gritted, Dallin yanked the gun from the man's hand and flung it harmless into the grass. A hammer blow to the belly nearly brought the man to his knees, all his air whoofing silently from his lungs. Easy. Dallin gave him no time to regain his breath—spun him about, slipped his arm about the man's neck, and lifted him off his feet.

"Fight me and I'll kill you," Dallin whispered calmly. "Make a noise and I'll kill you. Tell me a lie and I'll kill you." The man stilled, but the coiled tension remained. Dallin loosened his arm just enough for the man to drag a breath in. "Why do you follow Calder?"

The man tried to shake his head—couldn't. "I know no Calder."

Dallin thought that likely enough, since Calder obviously wasn't *Calder* anyway. Though Dallin had a very difficult time believing these men had been following someone all this time without learning the alias under which he was traveling.

"All right, then," Dallin agreed, "why do you follow the man you're following?"

A quick spurt of energy from the man spent itself quickly when Dallin cut off his air again. The restrained thrashing of his limbs tapered into weak spasms before Dallin let the man have another breath. It was raspy and not deep enough, but Dallin didn't need him comfortable—he needed him fearing for his life and willing to try to talk himself out of his predicament.

"*Why* do you follow the man you follow?" Dallin asked again, this time through clenched teeth. "Why is he so important, and what do you want with him?"

"They said you would come." It was snarled, breathless, and a withering little laugh crept up from the man's constricted throat. "You are no Guardian. You refused the call, but there are hundreds more who have not."

The last bit was choked and garbled, and more so than

could be explained by Dallin's arm around the man's throat. Sickening wet strangling sounds rose from the man as his body arched against Dallin's chest, stiff and rigid. Cursing, Dallin lowered the man to the grass and flipped him to his back. A light froth oozed out the side of the man's mouth, eerily blue in the weak moonlight, and his eyes bled exaltation and triumph. A ragged, truncated breath dragged through a grimace that was trying to be a grin, macabre in its rapture, and he pushed out a throttled cough, a fine film of blood and spittle flecking Dallin's cheek. Dimming eyes held Dallin's, narrowed in victory.

"*Hundreds*," the man gasped before his whole body seized, stiffened, and went limp, head dropping heavily to the side.

Dallin slowly sat down in the grass and kicked the man's gun a little farther away. Throttling more useless curses, he pushed his fingers to the vein beneath the man's jaw, though he knew there would be no pulse. The stupid bugger had managed to poison himself somehow. Dallin moved his fingers from the man's neck to his mouth and dipped them in to feel about, ignoring the repugnant pool of froth that was still foaming lightly. He found what he was looking for immediately—a small, paper-thin capsule of tin, bitten through. He'd heard about such things in the army, but he'd never actually seen one used. Surgically inserted in the soft tissues inside the mouth, so one would have to actually bite through one's own flesh to activate the capsule. He hadn't really believed it before. He did now.

Perfunctorily he checked this one for papers too, not at all surprised when he didn't find any. The clan marks on his cheek were something, at least. Dallin stared at the pattern a moment, wondering where he'd seen it before, before peering once more up at the moon. The tattoos were interesting—and possibly significant, if he could figure out why they twitched at his memory—but not the answer he was looking for. Although if things didn't start going in his favor soon, it might be the only answer he was going to get.

He stood, swore quietly, and only just restrained himself from kicking the corpse.

Damn it. *Damn* it.

He surveyed the yard with a quick, circuitous glance, tried to gauge the amount of time he'd been faffing about out here, and couldn't. He hadn't been prepared for someone to take his own life, certainly not while Dallin was holding onto him, and he had no shame in admitting that it threw him. He pulled himself together. The ones he'd left unconscious could stir any moment, and he hadn't gagged them—and who knew what must be going on inside the inn. He peered over his shoulder. The man who'd been at the door earlier was gone, and even as Dallin noted it, the noise and soft strumming of a lute stopped abruptly.

Something was happening. And here Dallin was, cursing at corpses.

Forcing a calm he no longer felt, Dallin drew his gun and then walked quietly to the porch of the common room.

And right to the edge of chaos.

It took a moment for Dallin to understand what he was seeing. All eyes in the room were nearly vacant, glancing toward the only people still moving and then quickly caroming off again as though dreaming upright and open-eyed. It was like they'd all simply stopped in the middle of whatever they'd been doing to fall into a waking torpor—all except the three men who stood grappling not five feet in front of him.

Dallin had dealt with the reality of magic his entire life, knew that many practiced it and many more tried, knew that more often than not what some claimed as magic was likely something more akin to mundane coincidence. He'd actually seen magic exactly once and been thoroughly unimpressed. Until now.

"Bloody fuck," Dallin breathed, running his thumb against the reality of the smooth, burnished wood in his palm, if for nothing else than to assure himself that at least *he* was awake. The little group lurched and stumbled. "Bloody *fuck*," Dallin said again when he recognized Calder dangling from the grip of the smaller man. Calder's face was bloodied and his eyes were beginning to bulge and dull from lack of air. It was like a repeat of what had happened at the Kymberly—the two men were obviously fighting over possession of Calder, snarling and cursing at each other in another language, what Dallin could see of their eyes enraged and near insane.

Dallin stepped through the door and to the side and put his back to the wall. Giving the rest of the room a quick scan, he lifted his arm and aimed at the largest of the group.

"Hold!" he shouted.

They didn't. There was a scream from across the room and then two reports, one right after another, neither from Dallin's gun. The man he'd been aiming at crumpled to the floor, the misfire whizzing past Dallin so close he heard it whistle before it exploded into the wood of the doorframe, spraying his shoulder and cheek in a rain of splinters. Another went off and he ducked down and farther to his side, taking inadequate cover behind the first thing available—a stray barstool that had somehow wandered several feet from the bar itself—in time to watch Calder hurtle past him and crunch headlong into the doorframe. He crumpled too, and Dallin dismissed him for the moment, his attention on the last one standing.

The gun the group had been fighting over was now in the man's hand. He peered down at it as though dazed, blinked, then gripped it tight. Combat-cool again, Dallin didn't even register the swing of the man's arm, didn't feel his own arm tighten or his fingers close, didn't hear himself shout "Hold!" a second time. The man was aiming into a small cluster of people huddled behind the bar. He didn't so much as twitch at Dallin's command, only smiled, that same look of crazed triumph in his eyes Dallin had seen in the man outside.

Dallin sighted down, then squeezed the trigger gently, and again—right shoulder, left thigh—and watched as the bullets thumped into the man, rocking his body from one side to the other. The gun the man was holding flew out of his hand to skid across the rough pine floorboards, coming to rest under an overstuffed chair by the fire. Dallin made a mental note to retrieve it after he'd assessed the immediate damage.

All three were now on the floor, the big one and Calder lying very still, but Dallin could see that Calder was at least still breathing. The other didn't appear so lucky—too still, with a grisly flap of scalp peeled back to expose the pulp of his skull and what Dallin was fairly certain was a mash of brains and bone—so Dallin concentrated on the one he'd shot himself, who was moaning and thrashing weakly in a spreading puddle of blood. Dallin quickly checked the door, then stood and put his head cautiously around the frame to peer out into the moonlit night. No movement from the yard, but he reminded himself not to put his back to the door just in case he'd missed one out there.

He focused back on the inn's common room, too many frightened and confused faces blinking back at him as though he were some bogey they'd just been dreaming about and now they were caught wondering how he'd managed to follow them from nightmare. No gasping shrieks, no stampede toward the door—their silence was unnatural and unnerving.

There was talk of conjuring, Jagger had told him. *The assailant seemed tranced.*

Dallin shook himself. "Who is the law here?" No one answered, only kept blinking at him, so he scanned the room again, found alert intelligence in the eyes of a young woman behind the bar, and addressed his question directly to her. "Have you a local constable?"

She nodded, wide-eyed, then turned to bark at a scrap of a lad behind her, who blinked himself into some kind of focus, turned without a word, and disappeared out the front door—hopefully to find whomever represented law and order in this place and bring him or her along. Dallin wished he'd had a chance to ask the boy to fetch a physick before he'd bolted, but no help for that now.

Dallin shook his head and brought himself back to the matters at hand, trying to decide which was more pressing. He crouched, turned Calder over carefully, somehow not at all surprised to see he was battered and bloodied and thoroughly unconscious, but the pulse was steady beneath Dallin's fingertips. Keeping a sideways eye on him, Dallin made his way over to the one he'd shot. He cursed. Colorfully. He'd been aiming to disarm and cripple the man, but his second shot had hit inside the thigh instead of outside, and bright red blood pulsed and spurted from the wound in a way Dallin recognized all too well. There would be perhaps one minute, maybe two, for questions. If Dallin wanted answers, he'd best stop inadvertently killing suspects.

He leaned over into the man's line of sight and slapped lightly at his cheek—same damned tattoo—until dull blue eyes fluttered and tried to focus.

"Who are you?" Dallin demanded.

The eyes cleared abruptly, sharpened, and the man looked up at Dallin with a calm that was almost beatific. "So. You have come." He gave Dallin a smile that made his skin crawl. "The Aisling is recalled." He reached up with a shaking hand as if to stroke Dallin's cheek. Dallin flinched back, but the man only widened his smile and dropped his arm limply to the floor. "He belongs to the Brethren now. You will not have him, Guardian—you have already failed."

Dallin nearly growled in frustration. Damn it, he *really* wished people would stop calling him that.

"Failed at what? What brethren? What are you talking about?" The man's eyes closed. Dallin took hold of his lapels and shook him. "Who are you? What do you want?"

"I am... a failure." Black eyelashes fluttered again, slid back halfway to reveal eyes once again gone cloudy and dim. "But for the fact that I did not abandon my charge," the man whispered through a cruel little smile, "I am you."

A long, whispered sigh left his throat, eyes fixed to Dallin's in a last smirking smile. Dallin didn't need to check for a pulse to know the man was dead, but he did anyway before he pulled back and sat on the floor with yet another curse.

What the bloody *hell* did *that* mean?

What the bloody hell did that *mean*?

"*Shit*," Dallin growled, set the safety on his gun, and gave his head a shake.

He crawled across to Calder, gave him a quick once-over, then blew out a long breath and peered about. The patrons of the inn were still staring silently, but thankfully they seemed to have come back to themselves. Their gazes met Dallin's with awareness behind them and no small amount of fear mixed with morbid curiosity.

"Is anyone here a healer?" Dallin asked.

No one answered at first, but some of them turned to scan their fellows, apparently looking for the familiar face of one of the local healers. A soft murmur bloomed and several heads shook.

"Is he dead?"

The bold voice came from behind the bar, a hint of nervous challenge in the tone. Dallin looked toward it and found the redheaded woman who'd caught his attention before. There was a man behind her now, tugging on her elbow and attempting to shush her. She ignored him as she pulled away from his grasp, her bright eyes flicking from Dallin to the splayed body of Calder beside him, a bit of accusation flaring behind her gaze.

Dallin met it, focused on her alone. "No," he answered steadily. "Not yet, at any rate. D'you know him?"

Her eyes narrowed. "Why?" Defiant.

"*Miri*," the skinny man hissed.

She ignored him again. "What's your business with him?"

She—Miri, apparently—pushed past the man and another great burly fellow Dallin guessed was the owner of the inn. A few servers had huddled behind the bar, and Miri bullied them out of the way to step out several paces toward Dallin. "Who are you?" She jerked her chin toward the two dead on the floor. "Who are they, and what business have ye with the lad?"

Brash and bossy and protective as a mother hen—she reminded him of Corliss, right down to the hair. The girl would've made an excellent sergeant.

"My name is Brayden." Dallin kept his demeanor calm and matter-of-fact. "I am a constable from the city of Putnam, and my business is not for public ears." He shot a quick, pointed glance around the room.

Miri's mouth pursed down, disapproving and suspicious, her own glance moving keenly over Dallin's travel-stained getup and lack of surcoat. She said nothing, only raised a skeptical eyebrow.

Dallin sighed, reached a blood-stained hand into his breast pocket, withdrew his badge, and held it up. "Now, if this satisfies you," he said as he tucked it back into his coat, "I should appreciate it very much if you could send someone to find a healer or physick to see to this fellow here." He leaned over Calder, lifting one eyelid and then the other; the pupils were even and reacted normally. "It doesn't look like he's been addled, but he's had at least one good knock...." Dallin swept his hands over Calder's limbs and shook his head. Nothing but skin and bones. "I don't *think* he's broken anything but for perhaps a few fingers, but I'm no healer." His touch was as gentle as he could make it as he slid his fingers over the soft bone and cartilage of Calder's throat, already purpling with bruises. Bloody damn, what was it about this man that brought out the animal in people? "No damage I can feel, but this needs looking at too."

Dallin turned back to Miri. "Have you got rooms?" He shot another quick glance over the crowd, all of them still staring but now muttering to one another and beginning to mill about. "I'll need to take this one to someplace more...." He almost said *secure* but decided on "private." He thought about shackling Calder now, while he couldn't make a fuss over it—but this Miri was the only one so far who seemed as though she might be helpful, and Dallin doubted he'd keep her precarious, grudging tolerance by slapping manacles on an unconscious man to whom she was obviously somewhat attached. "There are others in the yard," Dallin said. "I'll want a few volunteers to collect them."

That woke up the big man behind the bar. "Collect them *how*?"

"Two have been incapacitated," Dallin answered. "Two others have been... more incapacitated."

The gazes of both the man and Miri were narrowed and dismayed, but Miri's took on indignant anger as she stalked toward Dallin. She knelt to run chapped but gentle fingers over Calder's brow, then his hand before turning a glare up at Dallin.

"Why'n't ye see to *that* mess," she growled with a jerk of her chin toward the two dead men, "and I'll see to this one." She dismissed Dallin with a flip of her bright hair and turned toward the innkeep. "Garson, I'll need some o' that boneset and willow bark you've got squirreled. Ackley, fill a basin and find me some rags—*clean* ones—and bring them here. Tom, make yourself useful and come over here. He's got two fingers broke and two dislocated. We'd best pop 'em back afore he wakes." She shook her head. "The whole hand'll need splinting." She looked back at Dallin. "*If* you please," she said evenly, with another barbed glance to the men leaking brains and blood all over the floor of the common room.

Under any other circumstances, Dallin would've bristled and stomped her. Now he only barely suppressed a chuckle. Sergeant, hell—she'd've made a damn fine general.

The lad she'd ordered to bring a basin hovered, and the one Miri had called Tom knelt by her side.

Dallin stood and stepped back to give them room. "He might try to run when he wakes."

"Well, then, I expect you'll just have to keep a good eye on him, won't you?" Miri snapped. "Lad'll be lucky to walk, and this one's worried about running," she muttered with a sharp scowl. "Hold that arm, Tom, and watch the wrist—looks wrenched, if nothing else."

Dallin sighed and thought about reminding her that *he* hadn't done the damage, but only turned back to the innkeep. "I'd like at least four strong men. The two in the yard will need to stay until your constable gets here, but the two up on the ridge may be stirring by now. Do what you must, but I need at least one of them able to talk. And have someone bar that other entrance. No one in or out until I say so."

And hopefully Dallin could get this mess into some sort of order before the local law arrived to bollix everything even worse than it was.

"What about"—the innkeep peered at the two on the floor, winced, and waved a hand—"that?"

Dallin looked down too, grimacing at one and then the

other. He ran a hand through his hair. "I'm afraid they stay there and wait for your constable along with the rest of us."

"En't got a constable," the man said. "Got a sheriff."

"Whatever." Dallin only just kept from rolling his eyes. "Either way, I need no one to touch them, and I need everyone to stay where they are. I need to know what happened here, and your sheriff will want witnesses."

The man's expression turned distant and worried. He shook his head. "It's the oddest thing. It's all like a dream. I think I saw...." His eyes went vague, and his face screwed up in thought. "I *think*... but...."

Dallin glanced around at the patrons, noting slow nods of agreement and that same murky thoughtfulness. *Tranced*, Jagger's voice kept saying in the back of his brain, but he pushed the unease away with a firm hand. All of its own, his hand stole behind him, fingers slipping over the engraved spells on the shackles hanging from his belt. Glares from protective women or no, those were going on as soon as Calder's wrist was tended to.

A breathless shriek came from behind him. Dallin spun, gun instinctively coming up and to the ready, turning in time to see the woman pop the second finger back into its joint. Calder's eyes were wide-open now, but hazy and confused, filled with pain. Scared and bewildered, he tried to pull away from Tom's grip, tried to retreat and curl in, but Tom held firm while Miri shushed with soft sounds of comfort.

"There now," she murmured. "The worst is done." A soothing smile curled her mouth.

Calder seemed to focus on it, because he relaxed a little. "Miss Miri," he whispered, "I'm sorry, I didn't mean—"

"Hush," Miri told him before Dallin could stop her. He would have liked to have heard exactly what it was Calder hadn't meant. Miri placed a gentle hand along Calder's cheek, kept his gaze on hers, and spoke to him directly. "Those men are gone now, no worries." Her hand went to Calder's wrist, fingers prodding gently, pausing at each hiss and flinch. "Not broken," she assured him. She leaned over to retrieve a washrag from the basin and wring it out. "It'll need wrapping for a few weeks, no doubt."

She looked up with a scowl toward the bar. "Garson, where's that bloody boneset?" Her tone was all at once sharp and commanding until she peered back down at Calder, gaze and voice instantly softer as she brought the rag to his chin and began blotting at the blood. "You can let go of that arm now, Tom."

Tom did, scooting back a bit, but he shot a wary glance toward Dallin and then back again to Miri as he slipped his hand around the hilt of the knife at his belt and stayed close. His gaze on Calder was cagey even as Miri patted Tom's knee reassuringly.

Smiling, Miri nodded at Calder. "Let's have a look at your teeth, lad." Calder did as he was told like an obedient puppy, opening his mouth and allowing Miri to gingerly prod with the tip of her finger, though he closed his eyes and winced at the obvious pain she was causing. "Nothing loose, thank the Mother. You've nice teeth—it'd be a shame to lose any of 'em. You're lucky your nose en't broke." Calder sighed when Miri withdrew and dipped the rag into the basin again to rinse it, her nose scrunching up a bit as the water turned pink and cloudy. "I keep calling you 'lad,' but I never asked your name."

Dallin's attention sharpened at that, though he made no move to impose himself just yet. It looked like this Miri was going to get more answers than Dallin was, and with a lot less effort. He stood where he was, just out of Calder's line of sight.

"You didn't," Calder agreed softly with something that was trying to be a smile. He lifted his chin a little so Miri could get the blood that had run down his neck. "I thought that was very polite of you."

Miri smirked, eyebrow cocked as she leaned again to rinse the rag. "And is that your polite way of saying you don't want to tell me?"

"What's your name, boy?" Tom growled.

"*Tom*," Miri warned, but Tom shook his head.

"There's been murder tonight on his account, girl, and I'll at least have his name!"

"Murder?" Calder stiffened, and for the first time, dragged himself up, slowly and with lots of wincing. He cast his glance about to take in his surroundings—

Spotted Dallin.

"*Fuck!*"

He flinched so hard he fell back into Tom, didn't pause when Tom reached out—either to steady him or keep him from bolting, Dallin couldn't tell and had no time to ponder. Calder was rolling, then lurching up and throwing himself out the open door before Dallin could leap past the two blocking his way.

Calder was fast but unsteady. He stumbled, nearly falling down the two steps of the porch before he grabbed hold of one of the porch posts and catapulted his way around it. Dallin didn't bother with the steps, vaulting the porch banister instead and landing just over an arm's reach from Calder. Dallin threw himself forward, arms outstretched, and shoved at the small of Calder's back. A low grunt and then a desperate wail came loose as Calder flew sideways into the side of the inn. He curled on impact, rolled on the ground, then snarled. It was pure luck that the sputtering light from the porch hit the blade and warned Dallin, else he might well have thrown himself at Calder and ended up gutted for his trouble.

Dallin leveled his gun at Calder's chest and said, "Drop it. I'm meant to bring you back alive, but I'm getting closer and closer to working up the proper reasons I'll need for bringing back a corpse."

Calder laughed—*laughed*—crazed and hopeless, and crab-walked one-armed until his back was to the wall, face pulled back in a ghoulish mockery of a tooth-baring grin. "*Alive.*" He laughed again, the hollow sound of it grinding into the thin, cold air like nails on a slate.

"Stay *back*!" he snarled and raised the knife when Dallin took a step toward him. Dallin paused, eyes narrowed, and took another step, mostly to see what reaction he would get. It wasn't one he was expecting. Instead of waving the knife or even trying to throw it and wing him, Calder raised it to his own throat, the rusted tip of it resting just heavy enough to dimple the thin, bruised skin over his jugular. "Don't think I won't," Calder whispered frantically, voice wobbly and hand shaking.

It threw Dallin. This was getting more out of control with every second, and there was no way to threaten a man who was willing to cut his own throat.

Slowly, Dallin made a show of securing the safety on his gun again before he pointedly crouched to lay it carefully in the grass behind him and out of Calder's immediate reach. Both hands empty in front of him, Dallin inched a little closer to Calder than he'd been a moment ago. Calder didn't seem to notice, only kept staring at him, shaking, eyes trying to bore into him and mouth working between a snarl and a sob.

"Why doesn't it work on you?" Calder angrily swatted a tear from his cheek with his bad hand, cowering back as though trying to burrow his way into the wood. "I... it *worked,* it.... Damn it, *why won't it work?*"

Dallin almost asked what wouldn't work, but he remembered too well the blank stares of the inn patrons, the crazed rage in the men who'd tried to kill each other. *Tranced,* Jagger's voice said again, and Dallin shook his head, spreading his hands palm up.

He's trying to do to me what he did to them. And it isn't working.

One small piece of luck in this night of insanity.

"Perhaps because a Guardian is meant to guard," Dallin offered softly, smoothly. He slid in and leaned a tiny bit closer. "Isn't that what you called me? Guardian?" He tried a soft smile. "I wouldn't be much good if I fell to swooning every time you looked at me, would I?"

"Don't... don't *play* with me." Small and shaky, but alive with wrath. Another tear tracked down Calder's cheek, and his face twisted in misery. "Please," he whispered. "I won't... I only wanted...." He shook his head as he slid himself up the wall until he was on his feet, the tip of the little knife pressing harder so a thin rivulet of scarlet trickled down his throat. He didn't seem to notice it. "I *can't,* it hurts too much, and it *never stops,* they just keep wanting *more,* and I *can't.* Please."

Dallin could feel his eyebrows climbing up his forehead.

This was... far more than a simple case of running away from home. Far more than even Dallin's most cynical suspicions. Calder was genuinely terrified, so terrified that plunging a knife into his own throat seemed the better alternative, and after what he'd seen tonight and the long days preceding, Dallin wasn't sure he blamed him.

Dallin got slowly to his feet, keeping his hands open and unthreatening. "What happened to you?" he asked quietly. "Why are you so afraid?"

A quick jerk of Calder's head widened the small wound at his throat. Still he didn't notice. He edged his back along the wall, a single half step to the side.

"I can help you, if you'll tell me," Dallin said.

"Don't you *know*?" Calder wailed. "How are you here if *you don't know*?"

Dallin took another cautious step. "I need you to tell me." He made his voice as smooth and gentle as he could. "You called me Guardian. So did those men in there, so perhaps that's what I am. I killed them, you know." He paused as Calder frowned and sucked in a sharp breath. Well, one of them he'd killed accidentally, but no need to get into unnecessary details. "You see?" Dallin went on, "I've already helped you. Let me keep helping you. Put the knife down and tell me why you're running. Tell me why you *have* to run, because I see now that you *do* have to run." He reached out slowly, hand open. "I understand that now, but I don't understand why, and I need you to tell me."

"If I tell you," Calder croaked, gaze tracking Dallin's hand keenly and then skittering back up to his eyes, body tense and ready to bolt, "you'll want it too. Or you'll want me just as dead. Or both."

A low murmur was coming from behind Dallin. Calder's eyes shot over Dallin's shoulder, and he winced. Dallin spared a flicker of a glance behind him, catching a flash of red hair out the corner of his eye before nailing his gaze back to Calder.

"Stay back," Dallin ordered over his shoulder, gaze on Calder.

But Calder's eyes misted with remorse and apology. "Miri." It was a sorrowful whisper as Calder shook his head, then finally, *finally* took his eyes off Dallin. "I'm sor—"

Dallin lunged in, got hold of Calder's wrist, and jerked the knife away, squeezing until Calder loosed a sharp cry and dropped it. Calder yanked himself free, but Dallin latched onto his collar, jerked him around, firmed his grip.

Catching sight of Miri in his peripheral vision along with the rest of the small crowd that had gathered behind her, Dallin turned, met her startled gaze with a fierce one of his own, and shouted, "*Get back inside*," restraining a grunt as an elbow landed a blow just below his ribs. "All of you," Dallin snarled, "inside—*now*!" vaguely satisfied when they obeyed and he could return his full attention to Calder.

"Settle down," Dallin said more calmly. "I can help, just —Ow, *fuck*!"

The man was a bloody eel, arms and legs snaking, torso curling and stretching, and all the while, foul invective leaked from his mouth, just as liquid and shocking as the blood that oozed from the wound on his throat. His mouth and nose were both beginning to bleed again, spattering over cheek and chin, near black on the pale skin in the uncertain light. Hazed eyes glared fiercely at Dallin from behind bruises and contusions that should have laid him out already but failed to damp the roil of emotions behind them.

Dallin had seen so many faces looking out from those eyes—frightened, clever, coy, hunted—but this glamour was new, this face of rage and desperation and a terror so deep and real that Dallin had to fight pity. He dragged a foot around and behind Calder's calf, crooked his knee, then *pulled*. Calder yelped as they toppled, gave a cry when his back slammed to ground, but didn't stop moving.

A fist came up and hammered into Dallin's right eye, and then fingernails raked his cheekbone, a searing path across Dallin's temple to his ear. Not an eel, then—a bloody rabid ferret.

Dallin throttled back a snarl, reached blind, caught one bony wrist, then two, and slammed them both to the grass. He tried to mind the injured right one, but Calder was making care extremely difficult at the moment. A furious, ragged, animal cry burst from Calder when he realized he was caught, and he bucked as he tried to draw up a knee. Dallin was faster. He swung his body from the hip and rammed his whole weight down. A loose, heavy expulsion of wind flew from Calder, and then a pained gasp, but the frantic resistance, though not as fierce now, kept up.

Damn it, he was nothing but skin and bones, and beaten nearly to a pulp already—he shouldn't be this hard to pin down—but it took every ounce of Dallin's strength and weight to keep leverage.

"Stop, damn you! I'm trying to *help* you!"

Dallin drew back, then hurled himself down again. The sound he drew forth this time was closer to a whine than a growl. Calder's twisting abated as he tried to catch his breath, but the struggle went on—just enough to keep Dallin off balance. Dallin gritted his teeth, then reluctantly tightened his grip around Calder's injured wrist. A breathless, watery scream this time as Dallin squeezed, feeling joint and tendon shift between his fingers. Calder tried one more arch, one more twist, before his eyes jammed shut, his teeth bared. He slumped. *Finally.*

Dallin relaxed his fingers, allowing bone and skin back into their proper places, but otherwise kept his hold. He was glad he hadn't had to grind the broken fingers, but he would do, if it came to it, because this one wasn't through yet, Dallin had no doubt. Spring-coiled tension ran like a dammed river. Defeated, there was no doubt, but there was no surrender in Calder—there was only waiting and calculation and a rebuilding of breath and strength.

"D'you have a death wish, boy?" Dallin spat, voice coarse and clotted with residual anger and adrenaline.

Calder huffed out a thin chuckle, weary and strange. He shook his head, and sucked in as much air as he could with Dallin's weight resting heavily on his chest.

"I have a *life* wish as deep as the sea." He dragged in another wheezing breath before he opened his eyes. "And fate sends me the last righteous man in all the land. What luck." The tone was cutting and sarcastic, but Dallin was relieved to see that sanity was back in Calder's gaze. But then it narrowed. *Glittered.* The muscles in Calder's forearms tensed and pulsed in Dallin's grip. Calder's lips pulled back in a feral snarl. "And I am no *boy.*"

Like a striking snake, Calder's head came up, mouth

fastening on to Dallin's, followed by a slow, rolling arch of his hips. Assault on two fronts, and both of them surprise attacks. There was no sense, no reason to the kiss, if "kiss" it could be called—more an attempted seduction of the mouth, tongue curling and swiping, teeth latching on with just enough pressure to spark reaction, then letting go. Dallin jerked back—blood, copper-salt and tangy on his tongue.

"What the *fuck?*"

Calder only purred, vibrating from his chest and right through Dallin's, the wanton curl of it both near nauseating and disturbingly sensual. "I can give you what you want," he murmured, low and throaty. He pushed up, tried a provocative twist of his hips, but couldn't quite manage it. "I *saw* you wanting me all the way back in Putnam. Did you think I wouldn't know?"

Dallin thanked every star in the sky that he was too surprised and repulsed for the sort of mindless reaction that kind of attention to the stones usually produced. Calder must have mistaken his confusion for weakness, because he smiled, the split in his lip opening again with the pressure and beginning to ooze down his chin.

"Tell me what you want." It was breathy and sly. "Anything you want, any dirty, filthy little thing you've ever dreamed, it's yours, just let go of my hands and I'll do it, any—"

"*Damn* you," Dallin hissed, "you are testing *every* scrap of sympathy I own." He gritted his teeth and tightened his grip on Calder's wrists again, dug his fingers into the wounded one until the soft promises rose in pitch to a garbled whine and then a scream. Dallin wrenched himself back and up and jerked Calder up with him, twisting both of Calder's arms behind his back and hauling him in tight, chest to chest. Staggering to his feet, Dallin yanked Calder's hands up between his shoulder blades. Another scream, more pained this time, as Calder arched and twitched.

"I can do this too," Calder wheezed as he curved his back and clenched his teeth to hold back a gasp. He grimaced, desperation and pain acid-etched into the lines of it, yet the smirk still tried for seduction.

Dallin wrenched again, trying to dislodge the smile. Another flinch and a sharp "*Ah!*" was all he got for his trouble.

"I see now." Calder was breathing hard, in pain, but the smile wouldn't uncurl, the limbs wouldn't stop twisting. "You like it rough, you like to hear me scream, you like to *hurt*." A single nod of the dark head caught russet and jet from the lamplight, shadows making planes on the rawboned face, gilding angles. "I can do that too, anything you want, and I won't tell anyone, only let me go, let me—"

"Don't give me whore's tricks," Dallin snapped. "Isn't *anything* beneath you?"

"Think you're too much the man for me, then?" A breathless, mocking snort this time. "Have you ever done anything with your cock besides threaten? Swing it about to scare the lads and—*Ah!*"

That last as Dallin tightened his grip once more, just to get Calder to *shut up*, then heaved and jerked until Calder was off his feet, dangling, toes knocking into Dallin's shins. "Shut your filthy mouth," Dallin grated. "The more you spew filth, the more inclined I am to shoot you instead of help you."

"*Help.*" They were nose to nose, Calder's face only an inch from Dallin's, contorted in fear and rage, all invitation gone now, green eyes spitting out poison. "Why don't you use your cock instead of your fists for your 'help,' *Watcher*?" He spat it. "You know you want to, and it would save us both some bruising."

Dallin wanted to help, he really did, surprised himself by the honesty of the thought, but Calder was making it nigh impossible to cling to even a thread of charity. He'd run the gamut of nearly every dark emotion that existed in the past five minutes and was doing his damnedest to drag Dallin along with him, when all Dallin wanted in the world was for Calder to shut his damned mouth before Dallin snapped and finished the job the other two had started.

With more strength than was necessary, Dallin flung Calder back and away, shoving him into the wall. Calder hit hard enough to rattle the boards, head slamming back with a *thump* that made even Dallin flinch a little. Dazed, Calder tottered but kept his balance, vague eyes already darting, seeking an escape his body couldn't possibly pay out. Dallin closed in again, cutting off any chance, however slim. One arm buttressed to Calder's heaving chest, Dallin reached to his belt for the manacles.

"*Now* I understand why men turn to animals around you." It came out as a growl as he slipped the cuff around Calder's left wrist.

Calder didn't even appear to realize what it was until the metal snapped home. The dull *click* seemed to drive right into his chest, and his eyes cleared all at once. He jerked, tried for a quick dodge and twist, but Dallin was ready for it. He slammed his shoulder into Calder's ribs, flipped him, then shoved him face-first into the wall to shackle his wrists behind his back.

Dallin couldn't even be careful of the injured wrist anymore. Inexplicably, that fact alone drove Dallin's fury up another few notches, and he had to really try to choke it down this time.

"Stop fighting, damn it, I'm *trying* not to hurt you!"

And even then, Calder didn't stop, wouldn't stop... seemed perhaps he *couldn't* stop. A low feral cry wrenched from his throat, and he jerked, kicked, writhing like a pinned snake against the wall. The strength in him astounded Dallin anew as he leaned in with his shoulder and shoved up with all his weight to keep from being flung backward.

"It's done!" Dallin took hold of Calder's shoulders, flipped him again, and drove his back into the wall once, twice, only just managing to pull his strength at the last second, noting with both satisfaction and dismay that Calder's head thumped hard the second time. The anger and fear in the wild eyes dulled with the concussion until Calder finally slumped, knees loosening and feet sliding out from under him. Dallin guided him as he slid down the wall, vague gaze seeking until it found Dallin and latched on.

"I can get you money." It was warbled, bleak now, the wild hope of potential escape finally guttering. "I'll... you can even watch." Dallin tried to be revolted as what Calder was offering sank home, but all he could seem to muster was pity. Calder pulled at the shackles, wincing when the chain jingled and the metal bit into his wrist. "Please." Choked and wavering. "Please, you can tell them I ran, tell them... tell them you had to kill me, tell them—"

"I'm sorry." Dallin's voice was thicker than it should be, so he swallowed. "Unless you can tell me what you've got yourself into, I've no choice but to take you back to Putnam." And why was Dallin suddenly feeling like nothing more than a heartless bully? "Whatever this is, it's gone too far, and I have to...." Damn it, Dallin *hated* it when his heart started getting in the way of his job. "The Guild has demanded your return, and too much hinges on Cynewísan's cooperation. I've no choice. Anyway, I've a feeling you're safer with me right now than with anyone else I can think of, regardless of...." He waved a hand and looked away.

It was almost as though he was trying to convince himself. And deliberately not thinking about the fact that trying to "help" Calder and get him under control had been nearly as violent as what had apparently gone on before Dallin had walked into the inn. Every bullying husband he'd ever had the pleasure to arrest recited the same mantra, like it was some sort of secret handshake by which all tyrants recognized each other—*I didn't want to do it, she made me*—and now Dallin's thoughts seemed all too similar.

"The Guild...." Calder snorted, mirthless and bleak. "You're to take me back to the Guild?" The tears were back, dripping down and mixing with the blood. "They mean to kill me." Toneless, the voice of a man already dead. The change from the wild fury with which Calder had fought only a moment ago to this broken creature, weeping silently and pleading with a stranger... it was unnerving.

"You are the Chosen." There was a little too much sympathy in Dallin's tone for his liking. He set his jaw. "I won't pretend to know all of your strange religion, but I know some, and I know what the Chosen is, and you're going to have to convince me of your claim. Like it or not, you're stuck with me—I'm your only hope—and unless you tell me what this is about, you *have* no hope and back to Ríocht you go." He was pretty sure that was a lie—right now Dallin could find nothing within himself that indicated he'd be willing to hand this man over to the Dominion, regardless of any number of repercussions he could think of, and he had no idea what to make of that. Still, with everything that had happened since he'd left Putnam.... "I believe you're in danger. I'd thought at first you were just a spoilt runaway, but there's more here, and I don't know what it is, and unless you *tell* me what it is...."

Dallin let the rest hang there, unspoken threat.

Calder breathed out a weary laugh. "Spoilt." He thumped his head back and closed his eyes. "I have no religion," he muttered, strangely hollow. "But you're right about one thing, Constable—you know fuck all about it." His eyes snapped open, the venom seeping back into his gaze as he leveled it at Dallin. "And when you meet your end, and you stand before your Mother-goddess as She asks you why you knowingly sent a man to his death, what will you tell Her? That it was your task?"

"I don't know that I *am* sending you to your death. I've seen enough to give me pause, but lying comes too easily to you, and drama like a second skin. Except I don't think you're lying, and there's too much you're not telling me. I've no idea what to believe and not nearly enough evidence to sway me one way or the other. I *can*not simply take your word when you've lied to me since the moment I met you, and you're too damned good at it—you change faces as a snake changes skins."

"Look at me," Calder demanded, "and tell me you see lies."

Dallin did look. He stared for a moment, trying to find pretense, and couldn't. He shook his head. "Why would they want to kill their own Chosen?"

A wry smile this time, and a look very near pity. "Because I am not *their* Chosen." Calder turned his head and spat out a sticky stream of saliva and blood. He wiped his mouth on his shoulder. "I am merely in their way."

"How? In their way of what?"

Calder peered at Dallin for another long moment, indecision warring with distrust, hope against fatalism. On the cusp. Dallin had seen it so many times in hundreds of different faces, and his heart picked up pace in anticipation of pending confession.

But Calder only slumped and bowed his head. "I'm thirsty, and my head hurts."

Dallin sighed, ran a hand through his hair, and let it drop. For now. "I'm not surprised." He reached out. "Here, let me—" He paused when Calder flinched. The cursing was only on the inside this time as Dallin softened his voice to say, "I'm going to help you up, and then I'm going to help you inside. I can almost feel your friend Miri burning me in effigy already, and we'd best let her see to you if their healer hasn't shown up yet."

Calder shook his head. "I don't want her to see to me." It was a whisper, small and humiliated.

"Well, I've been thinking." Dallin kept his voice low and near affable as he retrieved his sidearm, checked the safety, and deliberately holstered it, securing it in its straps. "Your right hand needs setting and wrapping, and we can't very well have you shackled for that, can we?" He set his jaw when Calder shot a hopeful glance from beneath his fringe. "I'm not letting you go. And if you make me go through this sort of set-to again, you'll be a lot worse off than you are now, I promise you. If you try to run, I *will* catch you and make you regret it." Dallin shrugged, a small concession. "But I need my right hand free and can't have you attached to it"—he patted the holster—"and your right hand needs seeing to, so I can't cuff myself to you. If you can behave yourself until I get us safely upstairs, we'll take those shackles off."

Calder's face fell, but he didn't protest, only dropped his gaze with a slow nod. "I'll... behave." Dallin didn't miss how it had been spoken as though it tasted sour.

It was only the work of a few seconds to get Calder on his feet—amazing how light and thin he felt when he wasn't trying to kill a person. He turned with no resistance when Dallin prodded him, stood still and quiet, waiting patiently for Dallin to fish the key out of his pocket. Dallin had seen this slumped posture before, this submissive-seeming compliance, so he remained chary as the shackles came off, one hand clamped to Calder's elbow as Dallin resecured them on the back of his belt. But Calder only swayed a little on his feet and didn't tense or try to jerk out of Dallin's grip, only brought his right arm around, cradled it to his chest, and waited for Dallin to turn him again.

"All right," Dallin said, "calm and quiet, now. Lean into me if you have to, but if you try to get away from me, I'm going to have to hurt you."

Calder's jaw twitched. "I *said* I wouldn't." Tight and resentful.

It confirmed Dallin's initial assessment—Calder was never going to admit defeat, no matter what the situation. He'd mimic defeat, say all the right words to convince his antagonist, but underneath it all, Dallin had no doubt there was scheming and calculation and the patience to wait for the next opening. Calder would cooperate meekly and politely, right up until he was cutting your throat. Or his own. And Dallin was a little pissed off to realize he was grudgingly impressed. If nothing else, Calder had stones of pure, solid brass... or maybe it was more like a head full of rocks. Unfortunately, there would likely be several more opportunities to decide which.

Calder did lean into Dallin as they made their slow way around to the back porch, and Dallin didn't think there was any sham in the unsteady gait or the occasional stumble. Calder had been through the wringer—several wringers, by the look of him—and it wasn't a wonder the effects were catching up with him. Nonetheless, Dallin kept a good hold on Calder's arm, alert for a sudden move toward any of the weapons secured about Dallin's person. There were many dangers involved in his line of work, but the most embarrassing among them was getting shot with one's own sidearm. Dallin had no intention of finding out how that one felt.

The small crowd Dallin had ordered away before had merely migrated around the corner and to the porch. And grown. Likely bollixing and skewing any evidence Dallin had hoped to find once Calder was seen to. Who knew what sort of mess they'd made out of the scene in the common room? Damn it, it needed a bloody regiment to wring some order out of this cock-up, and Dallin was only one person.

Calder shrank back as he caught sight of everyone staring at him, some of them almost hostile, some of them merely curious—only one of them willing to break from the security of the crowd and approach them. Dallin was not in the least surprised when Miri strode over to them with shoulders thrown back and

Tom, as always, at her back, a frustrated scowl of reprimand and resignation darkening his thin features.

"Are you all right?" Miri asked Calder as she shot an accusing glance up at Dallin.

"My head hurts" was all Calder said, eyes nailed to the ground and hair hanging to cover his face.

It seemed Miri couldn't decide between sympathy for Calder and irritation with Dallin. She settled for grudging practicality.

"The sheriff's arrived," she told Dallin, maneuvering over to Calder's side and gingerly taking his elbow. "And she en't happy."

Dallin couldn't imagine she would be.

"We found the others," Tom offered from behind. "I thought you said you'd only done away with two of 'em?"

Dallin paused with his foot on the bottom step of the porch. He'd actually forgotten about the men out in the yard. He turned to Tom. "What d'you mean?"

"They were all dead." Tom was eyeing Dallin with more suspicion than before. "One of 'em had his throat cut, and the other three—"

"Poisoned." Dallin shook his head and clenched his teeth. "*Damn* it." He should damn well have gone back and checked the first two, once he'd seen what the last had done. Still, who would have guessed...? "What the deuce *are* these people?"

"True Believers," Calder muttered, then blinked up at Dallin as though he'd had no intention of speaking and was worried about the repercussions now that he had. His mouth worked for a moment before he shut it and looked down.

"Mm." Dallin glared at the people blocking the porch.

"*Come* on, then, out of the way." He didn't wait for them to move, merely began shoving his way through them and dragging Calder—and, perforce, Miri—along with him. "Clear out, I tell you, move along." He peered over Calder's head at Miri. "Where is this sheriff of yours, then?"

"Right behind you" came the laconic response. "Move along, you heard the man, out of the way."

The crowd parted this time, making way for a woman, broad and tall and keen-edged, with sharp, intelligent eyes set wide in a face ruddied with sun and wind. A spiderwork of smile lines stretched from the corners of her eyes and swept up toward her graying temples, the only silver in an otherwise deep chestnut mane that was tied back in a tail at her nape. More than just fit, the woman was the very definition of *rough and ready* and could probably give Dallin a run for his money, should she so choose. She could have been anywhere between thirty-five and seventy—and Dallin had no intention of having a guess, at least not out loud.

The sheriff took her time mounting the steps—moving slowly for no other purpose, Dallin guessed, than to have herself a good long look. She said nothing yet, but tipped Dallin a businesslike nod in greeting and then peered down at Calder. She stared for so long that Calder started to twitch before she took pity and turned her gaze back to Dallin. She lifted one expressive eyebrow.

"Quite the mess you boys've made here."

Dallin liked her immediately.

She jerked her chin over her shoulder. "That your arsenal up yonder in the trees?"

Dallin would hardly call it an *arsenal*, but he nodded. "Still as I left them, I trust." That eyebrow went up again, and Dallin gave the sheriff a little shrug. "I'm told some of the other detritus I left up there didn't fare as well."

"Six dead," she said flatly. "We've not had something like this in the province in...." She shook her head. "We've *never* had something like this in the province, and I'll tell you true—I *don't* appreciate you coming into my jurisdiction and wreaking holy hell without so much as a *Mother, may I*. Even the lowest bounty hunter stops by and checks in with the local law before wading in."

"I appreciate that, and I do apologize, Miss...?"

"*Sheriff* Locke."

Dallin had the presence of mind to flush. "Right, sorry. And I would've done, but by the time I tracked Mister Calder here—"

"Wil."

Dallin paused, then peered down at Calder in surprise. When Calder did nothing but hang his head, Dallin went on, "By the time I tracked *Wil* here, things had already progressed to the point where immediate intervention was necessary."

"Mm, by way of shoot-to-kill, I see." Locke looked like she'd bitten something sour.

Dallin really needed to work on his first impressions. "Actually, no. Look, might we...?" He cast a quick, pointed glance at the crowd still gathered behind Locke.

"Oh, we shall," she retorted. "I've two cells down the office, both of 'em empty and ready for... guests."

Dallin blinked, bridled. Oh, for pity's sake, this woman didn't seriously think Dallin was going to allow her to appropriate Calder or even arrest *both* of them, did she? Dallin made a concerted effort to make his voice calm but firm. "Surely you don't mean—"

"Surely not." Locke smirked. "But as the local law, it would be impolitic if I failed to offer aid and comfort to a fellow officer." She leaned in and lowered her voice. "And we can talk without an eager audience."

"Ah." Dallin snorted. He *really* liked this woman.

Locke jerked her chin at Calder. "Is this man under arrest?"

Calder's head came up, eyes shooting a sideways glance at Dallin, gaze finding something other than the toes of his boots for the first time since they'd left the side yard. Apparently he was just as interested in the answer to that question as Locke was.

"I don't know yet," Dallin answered honestly, looking first to Calder and then to Miri. He deftly changed the subject. "Will you help me get him ready to travel?"

Sheriff Locke arranged for Tom to saddle horses for "the visiting constable and his... friend" while Dallin kept an eye on Calder as Miri fussed and bandaged—the healer had yet to show up. Tom dragooned one of the bar lads to hitch the inn's only draft pony to the inn's only cart, also on Locke's orders, for the purpose of carrying the bodies to the local healing house, the cellar of which apparently doubled as the local morgue. And then Locke commandeered Tom to drive it. Garson nattered at Locke the whole while that all property—animals, cart, *and* hostler—had best be returned within a night cycle and in no worse shape than they'd been when they'd left, and furthermore, how did one go about submitting a voucher for damages and services rendered?

Dallin didn't really blame him—the common room was a mess, bloodstains already darkening the wood floors to an ominous reddish black. On the other hand, once the tale spread, patronage would increase tenfold for at least a week, so Garson would likely profit at least a little.

Someone had retrieved Dallin's kit and weapons from the wood. Tom saw to securing it in the cart along with a ratty pack Calder had dredged from underneath a chair.

Watching all of the activity while he stood about and made sure Calder didn't bolt again made Dallin feel a bit silly and useless, but he chuckled to himself as he watched Locke directing while at the same time examining evidence, taking careful notes, and wringing semicoherent statements out of those who at least hazily remembered the course of events. He'd wished earlier for a regiment to bring order to the chaos; he'd apparently got one in the form of Sheriff Locke and was well pleased.

Bruised but no longer bloody, hand beneath so many bandages it looked like a great lump of linen on the end of his arm, Calder stood carefully and quietly offered what appeared to be very sincere thanks to Miri. Dallin was tempted to step in closer and listen in but refrained. Miri answered just as quietly and then, to Dallin's surprise, leaned in and embraced Calder, hugging him like a long lost brother. It was odd—not only did Calder bring out the animal in people, he seemed to bring out the mother hen in them too. Even Dallin, trained in such matters and resistant to most manipulation, wasn't immune to it. He frowned when he saw Calder's good hand go to Miri's apron pocket before pulling away from the embrace, then frowned even more when he saw the flash of coins in the lamplight.

"How much did you drop in her apron?" he asked Calder on the way to the horses.

Calder hitched a weary shrug. "Whatever was left in my pocket."

Dallin stopped them both in midstride. "You gave her *all* of your money?"

"What use will it be to me? Dead men don't need money, and neither do prisoners." Calder shot a quick glance over his shoulder, eyes glittering in the light still spilling from the windows of the inn. "She was kind to me. And she's to be married." He made it sound so... simple.

Dallin only stared for a moment before he shook his head, gave Calder's elbow a tug, and got moving again.

Calder balked when he saw the horses, and then nearly went into hysterics when he was told he was expected to ride one of them.

"I'd rather ride in the cart with the dead," he insisted anxiously, digging in his heels and eyeing the animals with wary suspicion.

Dallin probably could have forced him, but somehow he couldn't find it in him. He felt as exhausted as Calder looked. Anyway, the horse Tom had saddled was little more than a cranky plow horse, indignant at being dragged out in the cold, and Dallin really didn't fancy fighting the reins for however long the ride to Locke's office would take. And this way would save Tom a trip; perhaps that would win Dallin some points with Miri.

Sighing, Dallin handed the reins back to Tom, shoved Calder into the box of the cart, and drove it himself.

By the time they got to the sheriff's office, set in the center of the small town between a shabby little hostel and an apothecary, Dallin was having a continuous argument with his eyelids and Calder kept slumping into his shoulder, relaxing for a moment and then careening back off again when he realized what he was doing. Calder had been in a semidoze for most of the ride but had blinked out of his stupor when he'd watched sleep-addled gofers unload the cart's gruesome cargo at the healing house. It seemed to have sapped the last of what was holding him together.

Locke silently led them inside, lit some lamps, and immediately guided Calder to the cell in the western corner. He stood remarkably quiet and compliant while she confiscated his shabby coat and moldy boots, only closed his eyes, lifting his arms while she patted him down. When she found nothing, she jerked her chin, gesturing him into the cell. An iron-framed cot, a bucket, and a basin were its only furnishings. Calder stared, owl-eyed, on the threshold for a moment, then lurched to the cot, fell to the clean linens, and didn't stir again. Dallin doubted he even heard the barred door close behind him or the key grinding the lock into place.

The sheriff blew out a great, deep sigh and turned to Dallin. "Tea?" She didn't wait for him to answer, just stepped to the stove, retrieved a kettle left simmering, and began to make a pot of tea.

"Coffee?" Dallin asked hopefully.

"Tea," Locke replied, smirking and without pity. She waved him to a seat opposite her desk, brought the teapot and two cups, then flopped into her padded chair, leaned back, and propped her boots on the edge of the desk. "Now," she said with a bone-cracking stretch of her spine. "Talk."

CHAPTER 4

"...Strangest damn thing I ever saw. Not a single one can give an account from start to finish."

A heavy sigh and the creak of a wooden chair.

"I'm not surprised. I saw their eyes. From what I understand from witness reports, it was the same in Putnam."

A long pause, the *clink* of porcelain, then:

"Tell me about Putnam."

Wil tried not to gasp and groan as he adjusted his head on the lumpy pillow and stopped listening. He'd seen and heard all he wanted to of Putnam, and listening to a repeat would likely just make his slight nausea turn into acute nausea.

He turned his mind instead to his present circumstance, trying to get a better idea of his new prison without letting on that he wasn't unconscious. Not that he cared if they knew he was listening—he just wasn't up to questions or penetrating looks at the moment, and as soon as Brayden thought Wil could sit up without falling over, Wil was more than certain he'd find himself on the receiving end of both. With an added dose of that sheriff in the bargain. Wil had no idea what to think of her yet. She'd taken an instant dislike to him, he'd felt it the moment she showed up at the inn, but that was nothing new. He made her uncomfortable. Someone like Sheriff Locke—practical, down-to-earth, direct—was not the sort to appreciate odd feelings she couldn't explain.

Wil didn't much care what Locke thought about him, when he considered it seriously. If he was reading the situation correctly, Brayden ranked Locke and had claim to Wil, so Locke wasn't likely to have much influence on what was left of Wil's future, dislike and discomfort notwithstanding. Though she could probably make things unpleasant while they were here, so Wil had best not antagonize.

He slitted his eyes and cast a blurry glance as far as it would go. The cell was nothing more than two brick walls and two made of heavy iron bars. Meant for the temporary detention of drunks, vagrants, and petty criminals, Wil guessed, and those being held before transfer to the nearest courthouse internment center for trial. It was cleaner and more comfortable than several others in which he'd been a "guest," though the pillow had seen better days. Not that it mattered much, the way his head was throbbing.

"...know what either one of them was doing there, but it may well be they came after Calder. Orman was likely involved in the talks somehow, but he appears to be a minion and not someone of note, so the Dominion wasn't concerned with...."

A little free with information, Wil thought at first, but when he paid attention, he could tell Brayden was holding back.

Details, mostly, but there was no mention whatsoever of Wil's own interrogation, nor any hint that Wil had presented false papers. As far as Locke had been informed, Wil was a witness and Putnam wanted him for questioning. Brayden did everything but flat-out lie to give the impression that Wil was innocent of any knowledge of the men or their intentions before they'd shown up and tried to kidnap him. Brayden told Locke that when he'd arrived in Dudley, he'd stumbled upon what seemed to him at the time to have started out as some kind of bar fight, and since Wil seemed to be the unwitting and unwilling center of the storm, Brayden had decided to extend the province's protection to him until he could get them both back to Putnam. Which he would like to do as soon as Wil was fit to travel.

The altercation between Brayden and Wil was explained as Wil having been somewhat in shock, a stranger to the village and not knowing who to trust, and probably afraid he was going to be arrested and sent to a workhouse or perhaps conscripted into the military. It *could* have been true, if either one of them had been someone else, but Wil was surprised at the forethought behind the intentional sidestep.

"Mm," Locke grunted. "Someone like him wouldn't last long in either."

Someone like him. Wil clenched his teeth, then winced at the pain that pounded through his jaw and deliberately relaxed it.

"Did he give you that black eye?" Wil could hear a smirk in Locke's voice.

"Is it blackening?" Movement again, and heavy footsteps traveling over the squeaky floorboards, before Brayden's voice came from across the room: "Bloody hell, that's a good one, innit? Have you got ice?"

"Not until the morning. I'll fetch some from the hostel next door before I go down the mortuary. I want to send a healer over to have a look at your friend there too."

"Mm." It sounded like agreement but could have merely been a displeased grunt. "Have you got any plaster? I didn't realize these scratches had bled."

Huh. Wil didn't remember landing any blows, but apparently he'd marked Brayden—and Brayden didn't seem too terribly upset about it. Seemed, in fact, rather amused. Odd.

Wil loosed a quiet sigh, wincing when his ribs twinged. *Fuck*, he hurt. His head and hand, especially, but when he mentally probed the rest of his body, there wasn't an inch of it that didn't at least whimper a little. He was going to have a bugger of a time even getting up to piss, so he put it off for now and concentrated on ignoring the sick thump in his head and how it inexplicably kept wanting to throb down into his stomach. It was a battle he'd probably lose eventually, but he'd had a very nice supper before everything had gone to hell, and he intended to hold on to it if he could. Anyway, throwing up would probably make his head explode.

"...three or four days, I expect. I'll send on to my superior in the morning by fast courier and let him know to expect reports and vouchers from you to cover the expenses of the... unfortunate incident."

"Incident." Wil could hear the skepticism in Locke's tone. "Tell me—if these men had nothing to do with what happened in Putnam, how was it that you decided to accost them before you even knew there *was* an altercation?"

Wil perked his ears. This should be interesting.

"I'm afraid," Brayden began, cautious, "that I have reached the end of the information I can share with you until I'm able to contact the constabulary." His voice took on a somber tone. "I'm sorry." He sounded sincere. "I am fully aware of the position this puts you in, and you've every right, but... I can't tell you more."

Wil frowned. Huh.

"Anyway, I've too many unanswered questions myself, and all of this looks to be a lot bigger than what I'd thought it was when I left Putnam. P'raps, after I've had a chance to question Mister Calder, things will be clearer and I can be more forthcoming. But as it stands, I've no idea. I mean, one of the men last night alluded to hundreds of others, and if they're as dangerous as—"

"Which is *exactly* why I need all of the information you have!" Locke's voice was harsh and impatient. "I've concerns of my own, and if you're right in thinking those men were responsible for the destruction in Kenley—"

"I know, I do, and I'm sorry, but...." An uncomfortable pause and the scrape of a chair, then bootsteps on the wood floorboards. When Brayden spoke again, Wil was startled to realize the voice was coming from mere feet away. "You must understand, this is no longer the assignment for which I was sent. There's something going on here, something very big, and I don't know how much of it's political and how much of it's some kind of religious dementia. Either one could present serious problems between Cynewísan and Ríocht, problems that could queer the talks and perhaps even result in another all-out war. Those men were willing to kill and die for something, and it appears that something is our Mister Calder, or what he represents to them."

"And what does he represent?"

"I can't tell you that either." Brayden really didn't like keeping a fellow law enforcement officer in the dark like this—Wil could tell by the remorse in the tone. "But until I know why they're so eager to have him, I've a responsibility to see that no harm comes to him *or* my country, and in view of all that, I'm afraid that's all the information I can share."

He was looking into the cell, Wil could feel it, staring through the bars, calculating, *watching*. Wil tried to look as natural as possible, breathed evenly, and allowed a small twitch and stir, relieved when the sound of Brayden's boots finally shuffled and then moved farther into the office.

Locke was silent for another long moment. There was a *clink* of metal against porcelain before she asked, "And what are we to do if those hundreds the man spoke of show up and try here what six of them succeeded in doing at Kenley?"

Another weighted sigh, and the creak and groan of wood as Brayden dropped heavily into his chair. "Have you got a militia?"

Locke huffed a derisive chuckle. "As much as any other village, which means one-legged veterans and any farmer who can afford a rifle."

"Then I suggest you put them on alert for now. I expect Chief Jagger will send along what I ask for, and I intend to ask for ten men to accompany us back to Putnam. Until then, we rely on Dudley's resources."

"Such as they are," Locke muttered.

"Just so."

Well, that was good news—perhaps if the Brethren did send more, Miri and the others at the inn might be protected. If the citizens were watching for them, Wil doubted the Brethren would break cover and attack. Their strength lay in their invisibility, and they rarely risked it unless absolutely necessary and unless they were sure they would leave no witnesses.

"...said 'tranced,' so why haven't you got this man in shackles? Don't you think it would be wise? What's to keep him from doing the same to us?"

Wil's heart picked up pace, panic thumping in his chest and blooming down into his roiling belly. Bars he could take, but shackles would likely send him over the edge again.

Brayden paused for a long time before replying thoughtfully, "I've been thinking about that. I don't think he was responsible for it." Sheriff Locke must have opened her mouth to protest, because Brayden quickly went on, "No, I was there, I saw it—Calder was unconscious on the floor long before the spell or whatever it was seemed to break. It wasn't until the man I shot died that the others began to show some life again. That Miri was the only one who seemed aware of what was going on, so perhaps we should talk to her again in the morning with that in mind. She might be able to tell us some of what went on before I got there and when exactly the gaps in her memory begin and end."

"You think it was these men, then?"

"I think... maybe. But again, I'll need to talk to Calder."

Wil pondered that one. He hadn't been aware that the inn patrons had been tranced, and Brayden's explanation surprised him—not only the lack of suspicion directed at Wil himself, but Brayden's near defense of Wil to Locke.

It was possible, Wil supposed. Whatever sway he seemed to have over others was wild and unpredictable, and even tonight, when he'd actually tried to use it on purpose, the results were varied and not something he could understand or foresee. He'd succeeded in reaching Eyebrows, but the other had been unaffected enough to start using Wil's head as a tether ball. It was not unreasonable to think that Eyebrows had been the only one affected. And it hadn't worked at all on Brayden.

Except there had been Old Bridge....

"Either way," Brayden continued, "I don't think we're in any danger of magicking from him. At least, not unless he thinks he's in danger from us."

Wil almost snorted. Probably true enough.

"And even if that's the case, I think I'd worry more about him doing himself in than anyone else." There was a pause. "Should've thought to take his belt." Wil could feel Brayden's gaze right between his shoulder blades.

He'd like to snipe that he had no intention of hanging himself, so Brayden could just stop his righteous fretting. If Wil got that desperate again, he'd go for a gun—quicker and likely less painful.

"Anyway, shackles seem to have an ill effect on him. I'd prefer to keep things as calm as possible."

Wil tuned them out again and sank deeper into the bedding. He frowned.

All right, so Brayden didn't seem to want Wil dead; in fact, Brayden seemed intent on keeping Wil alive. Then again, so did the Brethren. Except Brayden wasn't with the Brethren, as Wil had first assumed last night. A stupid assumption, he realized after his mind had semicleared and he'd thought about it. The

Brethren denied the existence of the Guardian and worked to expunge all doctrine that even mentioned the legend. Brayden's very existence neatly negated almost half their beliefs, so they probably wanted Brayden dead just as much as they wanted Wil alive.

So the fact that Brayden had eliminated those men *could* mean he was now working for the Guild. But that made no sense, either—Brayden could have killed Wil several times over tonight and explained it easily, if he had to. After all, Wil hadn't exactly been cooperative, and who would question a constable of Putnam about the apparently necessary death of some drifter nobody?

And yet, here Wil was—caged and battered, certainly, but very definitely and undeniably alive.

And unshackled. Brayden had actually argued *against* restraining him.

It made no sense.

Perhaps it was another cruel game. Brayden was too good at playing with people.

Wil rolled slowly to his side to face the wall and breathed out a sleepy half snore in case anyone was paying attention.

So it seemed he was under the "protection" of a man born and sworn to stamp him from the skin of the world like a filthy disease. If nothing else, Wil decided as he adjusted the pillow and shut his eyes, the irony was pretty amusing.

Always faceless before, but now he knows the eyes that watch him, and he doesn't know what that means, but it's different and

he doesn't think that's good. Father sleeps on, won't answer his questions, and sometimes it seems like he's been asking them forever, over and over again, but he can't make himself stop.

"What am I?" he begs. "Why am I here? Why can't I just... stop?"

Father doesn't answer him, and then Father isn't there anymore. He is alone, always alone, friendless and defenseless, heart as raw as his abraded fingertips, with only the silent, brooding Watcher at his back.

"Go away," he says over his shoulder, fingers flying, and he tries to concentrate on what he's doing, but he's afraid and he can't think. "I don't want you here, go away*!"*

He closes his eyes, tries not to weep, but he's so tired. "I want Mother," he whispers, though he has no idea why he says it—it's stupid and childish and his cheeks darken with humiliation. He shakes his head, confused, and says, "No. I have no mother."

A wide, heavy hand lands on his shoulder, and he jolts, peers up into deep, dark eyes and stumbles back.

Sucks in a ragged breath and screams—

"Bloody *hell*!" Brayden lurched back and nearly staggered, only just saving the contents of the tray he was holding from crashing to the stone floor.

Wil jerked up, heart thumping wildly, and scuttled back over the tiny cot until his shoulders hit the wall, immediately regretting every single move as stars exploded behind his eyes and every bone, joint, and muscle screamed in agony. He gasped, slumped, and probably would have toppled over if Brayden hadn't held him up. Wil wanted to scream again at the touch, but he hadn't the breath.

"Easy, now." Calm, smooth, and soothing.

Brayden wouldn't move his hand, just kept holding on, keeping Wil upright—not hard, not threatening, not cruel.

Wil made himself take several deep breaths, ignoring the way the muscles in his chest and belly protested as he drew his knees up, planted his elbows atop them, and cradled his pounding head in his hands. The bandaging around the right one reminded him his hand was hurt too, and he followed that thread until he remembered how it had got so, and how he'd got to where he was now.

He groaned.

Right. Dudley. Gaol.

Mouth tight, Wil probed gingerly at his forehead, fingertips carefully marking the scabs and swelling. He groaned again.

A semiurgent need to piss was knocking at his groin, but the thought of standing up made his stomach turn over.

It took him another several moments to work up the courage to open his eyes, and when he did, bright afternoon sun stabbed into them, slanting in through the barred windows of the doors and the window above the sheriff's desk. He winced, blinking eyes gone gummy as he tried to focus and couldn't quite make it.

"All right, then?" Brayden sounded... cautious. "Didn't mean to startle you, but you've been sleeping a long time."

Wil almost nodded, thought better of it, and merely closed his eyes again. "Sorry." It came out a hoarse whisper. His throat was *killing* him.

"Here." Brayden took up Wil's hand and pressed a warm mug into it.

Wil didn't even have the energy to flinch at the touch that time. Brayden's hand was over his, guiding something hot and fragrant to Wil's lips—some kind of spiced cider with a very strong liquor that gave its mild taste an impressive kick. Wil took several cautious sips, relieved when it soothed the dry burning in his throat.

"Can you hold it yourself?"

Wil wanted to say *Yes, get your great paw off me*, wanted to fling that great paw away and be rid of the unsettling touch, but found himself mumbling "Dunno" instead. He pried open his eyes again, squinting at the cup, his hand wrapped around it and Brayden's around his. "I... what...?" He paused, confused, not at all sure of what he'd meant to say, then he blinked up at Brayden and peered a question at him with a slight tilt of his head.

"You've been dead to the world since last night." This time Brayden sounded amused. "And it's now early afternoon. I'm sorry I startled you—I imagine your injuries have set into the muscle while you slept, and all that jumping about couldn't have felt good. Are you in much pain?"

Wil just kept blinking stupidly.

"The healer was by, but I told her I'd call for her again when you woke. I didn't think you'd appreciate someone prodding at you while you slept. Considering the way you woke, I'm thinking I was too right." Wil couldn't see anything but a big dark smudge fringed with gold, so he couldn't tell for sure, but it sounded like the constable might be smiling. "D'you always wake as if someone's trying to kill you?"

Wil didn't know if he was more surprised by the question or by the fact that Brayden was actually making an attempt at a light tease. Wil shrugged with a muttered "Someone usually is" and flushed at the truculent bent to his tone. He ducked his head and took another sip of cider.

"Right." Brayden cleared his throat and changed the subject. "Anyway, the healer left some mæting for you, if the pain's bad. You took rather a beating, y'know."

"Ya think?" It was a little less sarcastic than Wil had been trying for, but Brayden's hand was still there, *touching*, and the fact that it was no longer unnerving was unnerving. Wil gingerly pushed the cup away until Brayden took it and released Wil's hand.

Wil frowned, still trying to catch up. "What's mæting?"

Brayden bent and placed the cup on the floor, then retrieved the tray he'd apparently laid on the far end of the cot when Wil was having his little spasm. "Reverie." Brayden jerked his chin and waited for Wil to straighten out his legs before placing the tray over Wil's lap. Apparently noting Wil's questioning look, Brayden shrugged and clarified, "The more common name for it is dreamleaf."

Wil stiffened, panic flaring again in his chest.

"I don't want it." Wil only realized when the great smeary blob that was Brayden only kept standing there, being a very *silent* great smeary blob, that it had come out rather harsh and heated. He uncurled the snarl that had unconsciously pulled at his sore mouth and instead looked down at the smudge on his lap that was the tray. He willed the banging of his heart to slow and didn't dare release his grip on the edge of the tray. His hand was shaking, and if he moved it, he'd likely wind up with whatever was in the bowl all over his lap, and then Brayden would want to know *why*.

Brayden remained silent for a long moment. Wil could feel those eyes on him, digging away, and only just held back another resentful snarl. What *right* did the man have, after all?

"No need to be brave." Brayden's tone was measured and careful. "You've enough injuries to justify a painkiller, I should think. You've more bones in your hand broken than not, and that head can't be feeling good. The healer was quite reproachful that we hadn't given you something last night."

And why did Wil have the impression it was said more to gauge his reaction than out of concern?

"I don't want it," Wil said, more calmly than before, then tried to focus on the bowl—some kind of beefy soup, he guessed by the smell, but his vision was horribly blurry and all he could see was something brownish and sloshing slightly as he shook. He'd thought the smell would make him nauseous, but instead, despite the rabbiting of his heart, the rich, hearty aroma made his mouth water. He'd like nothing better than to dive in and take a swim in it.

Except—

Wil peered up sharply with narrowed eyes. "You didn't put it in anything, did you? That dreamleaf, it wasn't in that drink, or in—"

"Of course not!" Brayden snapped, indignant. "You think I'd drug someone all unsuspecting? What d'you think I am?"

I know exactly what you are, Wil thought, *and a lot better than you do*, but said, "I wasn't...." He cleared his throat. "I'm sorry. I didn't mean to imply... anything. I only... well, the problem is that I *don't* know."

Brayden stared, wordless, while Wil just sat there, mutely enduring it and trying not to twitch, until Brayden finally pushed out a long, heavy sigh. "Right. Hold on a moment." He turned and walked out of the cell. Wil didn't even have time to wonder where he was going—the big blur that was Brayden was back almost immediately, dragging what was likely a wooden chair behind him, because he set it in front of the cot and dropped himself into it. "We need to talk." He gestured at the tray. "You should eat, get some of your strength back. Or would you rather wash up first?"

Warm water on his sticky eyes did sound rather good, and there was also the matter of needing to piss.... Wil weighed the all-encompassing ache that was his body against the other two prospects and decided moving still came out on the bottom. He looked back down at the tray, determinedly blinking and squinting, but it wouldn't come into focus. "I can't see," he said quietly. "Is there a spoon?"

"What d'you mean, you can't *see*?" It sounded like real alarm rattling through the question.

"It's blurry." Wil shrugged. "I can see a big brown spot that I assume is soup, but...." He almost shook his head before he remembered not to. "And I smell eggs." He frowned. "They're not *in* the soup, are they?"

"No." Brayden's tone was relieved now, and he leaned in to pluck up a spoon and put it in Wil's hand. "There're some boiled eggs in the office. I'll get you some if you want, and if you hold down the soup. The blurriness should be gone in a little while. Sometimes, I'm told, it can last for a few weeks, but it mostly clears up when the headache starts to go away. Are you left-handed?"

Wil blinked. "Why does that matter?"

"Well... it doesn't, not in that way, at least. Except that you've not started eating yet, so I'm wondering if your left hand is clumsy and you don't want to risk eating soup with it, or if you're nauseous too."

"I'm not nauseous. And I'll manage." To prove his point, Wil aimed the spoon for the brown blob, pleased when it hit its mark. He ladled up a spoonful, managed to get it to his mouth without spilling it down his chin, and sighed when the lush, meaty flavor of the broth hit his tongue. His mouth was incredibly sore, and his bottom lip felt like it was a three-foot-wide bees' nest, but eating was a pleasure he never rebuffed. Anyway, he hadn't realized until now how foul his mouth tasted.

"The hostel next door sent over a late lunch before their kitchen got busy for supper," Brayden told him. "I don't think I'd want to sleep in the place, but their food is surprisingly good."

Wil would have agreed, but he was keeping his mouth busy with slurping the soup.

"They've a small room off the kitchen with a tub. Miss Jillian says if we let her know an hour before, she can have a bath ready for you. The healer said a good soak would likely loosen you up some."

That seemed... unusually generous. Either Locke was owed several very large favors by the hostel owner, or Brayden was a lot more charming than Wil would have given him credit for.

Apparently an awful lot had gone on today while Wil slept.

"Locke stood the watch overnight, so she's gone home for a bit," Brayden continued. "She's arranged for a few of the local militia to stand post outside, so we've got a bit of time to talk."

"Talk?" Wil ignored the little frisson of nerves that skittered up his spine, concentrating instead on the dip and lift of the spoon.

Brayden, in his turn, ignored the mock innocence in Wil's

tone, keeping his own even and conversational. "It seems to me we've been working at cross purposes. More cider?"

Wil gave a careful shake of his head. He kept his murky gaze on the bowl and dipped the spoon.

"So." Brayden leaned back in his chair. "I've been wondering what I should call you."

Wil paused. "Sorry?"

"Well, it occurred to me when I was sending off my report this morning that I'm still calling you Wilfred Calder when it's obviously not your name. So I'm wondering what your real name is."

A queasy bubble rose in the back of Wil's throat, but he stubbornly swallowed it down along with another spoonful of soup. He pushed the spoon back into the bowl and swirled it slowly. "How d'you know it's not my name?"

Brayden sighed. "We've been through this. And by the time we get back to Putnam, we'll have confirmation from Lind. Anyway, in case you'd forgotten, you admitted you were Ríocht's Chosen last night—that makes you a Dominionite, and *not* Wilfred Calder. Let's put away at least one game between us, shall we?"

Wil *had* forgotten, actually. Damn. And even though he'd more or less been expecting... well, something clever, anyway, the question caught him too much by surprise. He didn't like that he couldn't see Brayden's face, didn't like guessing at the expressions by the carefully controlled tone of voice.

"I doubt you want me to go about calling you 'Chosen,' do you?"

Wil tried to shovel another spoonful into his mouth but couldn't quite manage it. He let the spoon drop to the tray. "I'd rather you didn't," he answered, annoyed when it came out a raspy little croak. He cleared his throat. "I like 'Wil.'"

Brayden hummed, noncommittal, and shifted forward in his chair. "But it isn't *your* name, is it?"

They might as well be back in the interrogation room in Putnam. This was Constable Brayden now. The real concern Wil had felt from Brayden only a few moments ago was gone, buried beneath whatever Brayden saw as his duty and his righteous loyalty to what *he* thought was right. There was no table between them this time, no chains on Wil's wrists, but Wil just as trapped with a man who knew how to draw secrets from a person, how to drag things out your mouth you didn't want to tell.

Wil wanted to balk at the snare, mulishly refuse to give even an inch, but there was no real point in dodging this time. Brayden had known the second he'd laid eyes on Wil that Wil wasn't from Lind, so it followed that he wasn't Wilfred Calder. And there was the matter of whatever confession Wil had made last night, so what was the point? Except the truth wasn't any more believable.

"I have no name." It came out a whisper, and Wil couldn't help but be incensed by the tears that rose at the bald reality of the statement, the lump of genuine *ache* in his chest—and even more incensed at the man who forced it from him.

"No?"

It wasn't a real question—it was some kind of setup, and Wil had opened his mouth and walked right into whatever little trap hid beneath it. And would *keep on* walking into them, because he didn't know how not to.

Brayden leaned in farther, until the dark blur of him blocked the hard autumn light from the window. "Not *Aisling*?"

Wil jolted so hard the tray went over, a rush of warm broth spraying over his throat and chest. He didn't know where he thought he was going—he couldn't even see, and Brayden was between him and... well, everything—but he lurched anyway, threw himself sideways, but Brayden's wide, solid hands were grabbing Wil by the shoulders, pushing him back against the wall.

"*Listen* to me." Brayden's voice was even and unruffled. "I'm not going to hurt you, but you're going to hurt yourself if you don't calm down."

Wil didn't have much choice—he was pinned. Brayden had been ready for him and had got them both into a position that would make it easy to keep Wil still. Wil had no leverage, he had no open path to escape, and he had no strength. And even if those three things had converged in his favor, he still couldn't *see*. If he tried to run, he'd likely sail headlong into a wall of bars or bricks and knock himself cold.

Which might not be so bad, he reflected morosely.

There should have been terror roiling in his gut, and there was, but it was overwhelmed by a smothering wash of pure, unadulterated rage. How *dare* Brayden toy with him like that? How *dare* he play at sympathy, slip hope into Wil's heart, the insidious trickle of it so small and subtle that Wil hadn't even known it was there and growing until it was suddenly and cruelly snatched away. Every time Brayden had a chance to kill Wil and didn't, every time Brayden had spoken a small defense, every time he was kind when he didn't have to be... it had been a game, all of it, culminating in this one moment of trickery and revelation. Wil could've wept—which only enraged him further.

And how *dare* Brayden do it all when Wil was weak and beaten and vulnerable?

"So that's it, then, is it?" Brayden went on softly. "Aisling?"

Wil lifted his head and glared up into what he hoped was Brayden's face. "That is *not* my name!"

"It's certainly *something*. You can't tell me you had a reaction like that to something you've never heard before. You know the name—it's what you've been running away from all this time. If it's not *your* name, then what is it to you?"

"It's a command!" Wil was immediately sorry that he'd said it, but what difference did it make now?

"It means 'dream,' doesn't it?" Brayden's hands on Wil's shoulders tightened. "Is that what the Guild commanded you to do—dream? D'you dream true?"

They weren't questions—Brayden *knew*. He was the Guardian—of *course* he knew. Everything else had been some kind of cruel sport.

Wil shut his eyes, bowed his head. The anger deserted him in one great searing rush, the empty chasm in its wake wider than he'd ever thought possible, and so choking that breathing became all at once painful. It was humiliating, Wil decided as he sucked in a shaky breath and shook his head, because he was *trying* to hold back the defeated tears, but they burned at the backs of his eyes and fell down his cheeks in fat scorching drops.

Over and done, and not in the middle of a brawl and with guns blazing, but trapped in a cell, cowering against the wall, his last meal dripping down his chest. Wil was going to die quietly and with his last shameful tears drying on his cheeks.

"It... I tried not to let them, but I couldn't stop them." He sounded utterly pathetic, but he couldn't feel the mortification that should have come with the shaky tone of the words—just a swelling sense of cold, empty nothing. "I couldn't *ever* stop them. I didn't want it—you have to believe I didn't want it, and I don't... I don't even think I care anymore, but you... I'll ask you not to make it... hurt."

He lifted his head, tried to find Brayden's gaze and couldn't —he was even more blind now, the tears queering even the small focus he'd managed before. After all this time, all the desperate damned *running*, and now he was begging pity in his last moment from someone who was made not to have it. Some part of him lamented at the pathetic thing he'd become. The greater part of him was bone-tired and more than done. What good had pride ever done him, anyway?

Wil dragged in a long breath and stubbornly firmed his aching jaw. "I just don't want to *hurt* anymore. You know how... you could do that... right?"

The silence stretched forever, the weight of Brayden's hands on Wil's shoulders pulling Wil down and down, expecting any moment for those hands to twitch, shift, then slide in, close around his throat. It was better this way. No long, inescapable torture in whatever hovel the Brethren chose, no last chuckle from Síofra echoing off the cavernous walls of the Guild and following Wil into darkness. Wil would die the way he was meant to die, at the hands of the man who was meant to kill him. It was oddly fitting, in a way he'd refused to look at before.

It was, beyond all sense, a relief.

But Brayden let go, backing away until he was hovering on the edge of the little cot. "Mother's *tits*," he breathed. "What *happened* to you?" His hand, warm and broad, closed over Wil's left wrist, fingertips pressing into the lumpy scar. "How did you get this?" Brayden asked softly. "Was it the Guild?"

Wil closed his eyes and shook his head slowly. It was as though he'd become an entirely different person—he didn't care what he told Brayden anymore, didn't care about the wrong words or the right lies. He didn't even feel the need to tug his hand from the surprisingly gentle grip.

"All right." Brayden blew out a deep breath in a long, noisy hiss. "All right." He set Wil's hand in his lap and pulled away. "I'm somehow 'meant' to kill you, is that what you think?"

Something like a weary chuckle trickled out from Wil's throat, and he closed his eyes, let his head fall back to the wall. He wondered abstractly if he was deliberately exposing his throat or if it was just an unthinking accident. More games, perhaps, but the question didn't have the feel of it. Wil could play along, prolong the inevitable, or he could give in to the exhaustion, the pain, the relief, and direct his own suicide. Because how many times could a person be forced to stare his own mortality in the eye before he finally blinked?

"You still don't know what you are, do you?" Wil said it quietly, but still there was a rebuke beneath it he wasn't sure he cared enough anymore to intend.

"Why don't you tell me?"

"Guardian." Wil smiled. "Watcher, Hunter, Sentinel, Spy. Righteous Protector; Remorseless Avenger." Eyes slitted, he peered up through his lashes. "How many more names would you like?" His lip curled back in a small, resentful snarl. "You've so many names and I haven't a one." He leveled a fuzzy glare in what he hoped was Brayden's general direction. "I've always thought that terribly unfair."

Brayden didn't answer at first, only sat where he was, a great dark blur on the edge of the cot. The blur shifted with the sound of a rough hand scraping over a stubbled chin.

"And what am I meant to guard against?"

"Me, of course."

The silence this time wasn't tense or weighted—merely long. Brayden broke it with a small growl. The cot shifted abruptly as he stood.

"Right." Brayden made a business of retrieving the spilled tray and empty bowl. "You've been reading the wrong fairy tales, I think." He sounded angry. "Get out of those wet clothes, I've got a change here for you. Might as well leave your shirt off. I'm going to send for the healer and order your bath."

And then he was gone, closing the door of the cell brusquely behind him, before barreling out the office without another word. Wil blinked into the stillness, trying to understand how he'd gone from an almost eagerness to have an end, to an unexpected and not wholly welcome reprieve.

And why did the fact that he wasn't dead make him so all-fired *furious*?

"I've been reading the wrong fairy tales." He laughed. "That might have been terribly clever *if I could read*!" he shouted at the door, then slumped back and rubbed lightly at his forehead. Annoyed, he flipped an obscene gesture at the door for good measure. It was... decidedly unsatisfying. And the knot in his chest was just... odd. It was *odd*. Mostly because it felt strangely like loss.

Wil ran his fingers carefully over his blurry eyes. "Maybe I do have a death wish."

He didn't know how long Brayden left him sitting there alone, pondering this newest turn and trying to wrap his mind around what it might mean. The wrong fairy tales—except they weren't fairy tales, they were Doctrine, Canon, passed down from the Hand of the Father and directly to the Guild. If anyone had got it wrong, it had to be Brayden, a man who'd been torn from his people before he'd been ordained, before he'd been told what he was and what his purpose was—a man who'd made his purpose the law, protecting the weak and victimized. Should it be a wonder that, when Fate finally showed Brayden his purpose, he'd be conflicted?

Except Fate was Fate, Destiny was Destiny—you couldn't escape it, you couldn't outrun it. It was possible that every kind gesture, every expression of concern from Brayden had been sincere, possible that he really did have the best of intentions, but none of that could stand against Fate. Perhaps when Destiny finally did take over, Wil would end up dead by Brayden's hand purely accidentally, and Brayden might even feel bad about it, might even mourn a little... but it couldn't change the inevitable outcome.

Wil shook his head—cautiously, because fucking *ow*—and unlaced the soggy strings of his tunic. The fabric was cold and heavy against his chest, and he carefully peeled it off and over his head with a grimace of both disgust and mild pain. He had to wrestle the sleeve over the lump of linen that was his right hand. After several bouts of cursing interspersed with wincing and hissing, he got loose of the shirt. There was cold soup all over his lap, but he left his trousers on though he removed his stockings, the cool of the stone floor against his bare feet sending a pleasant shock from toes to soles to calves to thighs. He stumbled about for a bit, aiming for the gray blob he was pretty sure was the bucket, and finally had his piss, thinking how mundane and ordinary his actions were considering he'd been staring at death with a welcoming smile only a short while ago.

He wasn't sure how to feel about that. After all, could a person totter on the edge his whole life, fighting the inevitable with every breath, kicking and spitting defiance, and then go back to that angry rebellion after it had finally been beaten out of him? Once he'd let it go, gone so far as to embrace his end, was there such a thing as will left?

Although... perhaps that wasn't such a bad thing. He'd been thinking before that dying by Brayden's hand, however it might happen, was the better alternative—the kinder alternative, perhaps. Nothing since then had changed his mind.

He refastened his trousers, noting with a bit of wry amusement that his belt was missing, vaguely disturbed that someone —likely Brayden—had removed it and Wil had slept right through it. He'd been on a hair trigger for so long and had got used to jumping awake at the chirp of a cricket—he must have really been out.

The cup of cider still sat on the floor next to the cot where Brayden had left it. Thankfully, it hadn't spilled in the scuffle. Wil retrieved it and gulped the rest of it down, the warmth of the spice and liquor soothing his raw throat and blooming in his belly. He wondered if there was enough in it to get him drunk—

perhaps he could sleep away the rest of the headache, and the muddled confusion in the bargain.

The sun had lost its brighter edges by the time Brayden returned, the light more sullen than hard and slanting a wider swath across the stretch of floor Wil could see in front of Locke's desk. He stood at the bars as Brayden approached, his vision slightly less blurry, enough that he could see the relaxed set of the shoulders, the lack of tension in the set of the spine—Brayden must be the sort who walked off anger.

Brayden stood in front of Wil on the other side of the bars for a moment, just looking. Wil looked back, didn't try to put on any face or mask. He had no real idea what he was feeling, so he didn't know what his expression was revealing. And didn't necessarily care.

"Are you hungry?"

Wil thought about it, decided he was, and nodded.

"We've still the eggs and some bread." Remarkably, there was no apparent hostility in Brayden's tone. "D'you want it now, or would you like your bath first?"

Wil thought about that too, answered, "Bath," then paused, asked, "Why are you being so nice to me? Why are you... why *aren't* you...?" He brought his good hand up to grip one of the bars, leaned in until his brow was pressed to the cool metal, and blinked furiously, trying to clear his focus so he could see the expression on Brayden's face.

Brayden merely reached out and opened the cell's door. "Because I'm not what you think I am."

It wasn't until he'd been guided out of the sheriff's office and over to the kitchen door of the hostel that Wil realized he hadn't heard a rattle of keys when Brayden had let him out. The cell hadn't been locked.

Huh.

"Turn your head to the left now."

Wil obeyed and allowed the woman to prod at his throat until a bony finger pressed too hard at an especially tender spot. He hissed, reflexively pulling back. The bath had made him feel worlds better, and a full belly hadn't hurt. His head was starting to feel less like a giant lump of "ow," and he'd even been able to chew the bread and eggs Brayden had given him after they'd returned from the hostel.

"All right, then." The healer leaned back and helped Wil get his shirt back on and laced. "Besides the hand, there's plenty bruised, but nothing broken. I don't like that big one across your middle, but there's no swelling, so you've not ruptured anything. Likely bruised a kidney. Have ye been pissing blood?"

Wil flushed, but answered, "I don't know. I can't see very well right now."

"Hm," said the healer. "Has it got worse or better since you've been up?"

"Better."

It had. Wil could actually tell that the healer's hair was a light mousey-brown and her eyes were blue. He could even vaguely make out the angles of her face.

"Good. Then it'll keep getting better. Should clear up tomorrow or the next day. Everything else will just take a little time to heal. You're lucky you got away with no sutures, so infection won't be a worry." She peered over her shoulder at Brayden, who was leaning back into the bars by the cell door, arms crossed over his chest. "He's to rest for a few days. If I'm called back here to tend to any more injuries, I'll be filing a complaint with Sheriff Locke."

Brayden's wide form shifted, but didn't move toward them. "Mistress Slade," he said slowly, "I didn't do this, and I'd appreciate it if you'd stop looking at me as though I'm some kind of fiend."

Ah. That explained the coldness Wil had been feeling from the healer toward Brayden since she'd arrived. Quite a different sort of feeling than Wil had got from Miss Jillian at the hostel, who'd seemed like all she needed was one encouraging word from Brayden and she'd start disrobing in the yard. The healer must've had a look at Wil while he'd been sleeping, and since he didn't think Brayden would have been forthcoming with explanations, she'd probably formed her own opinions—after all, Brayden was huge, and Wil probably looked like hell. It wouldn't be a colossal leap of speculation. Big giant lawman versus skinny little criminal—typical, really.

"He didn't," Wil volunteered quietly, not at all sure why he'd even opened his mouth. "It happened before."

"Hm," the healer said again, then didn't say anything else. She patted at the fresh bandaging around Wil's hand, checking her work, then stood, a whiff of antiseptic and hazel flowing from her like a cloud of perfume. "Keep on with the boneset and willow bark as ye've been," she told Wil. "Take the mæting at night to help you sleep, but watch the dose—too much can be dangerous, and I've only left enough for two days. I don't want you taking it longer than that. The stuff's made slaves of many a good man."

Wil gave shudder but otherwise kept still and silent.

"He doesn't want the mæting." Brayden's voice held only calm fact, with no judgment Wil could detect. "Have you got anything else? Something, perhaps, less likely to... enslave?"

The tone was direct, too understanding. Wil's cheeks flamed beneath it, hot resentment flaring in his chest. Damn it, Brayden was bulky and handsome and looked like he should have muscle where his brain belonged—why did he have to be so bloody *shrewd*?

"All right, then," the healer said finally. "I'll send Mal over with some meadowsweet and skullcap. You can mix it into a tea in the evening. Give him half and leave the other half in case he wakes in the night."

Just that quick, she'd gone from speaking directly to Wil like he was a normal person, to speaking over him like he wouldn't be able to understand the simplest instructions. He would've clenched his teeth, but his jaw was more sore now than it had been when he'd woken up.

He listened while Brayden offered thanks, listened as Brayden led the healer to the door, listened as she murmured things Wil couldn't hear, and then listened as Brayden murmured back and shut the door behind her. Heavy footsteps crossed the floor again, and Wil continued to listen as the chair was once again plopped to the side of the cot and Brayden once again lowered himself into it. He even listened to the silence as Brayden sat and stared at him.

"D'you need anything?" Brayden finally asked. "There's more of that cider in the kettle keeping warm."

Wil shook his head, abstractly pleased it didn't thump when he did it.

"All right, then," Brayden continued. "We've a little more time before Locke gets back, and I intend to use it to get a few things straight. I need you to listen to me, and I really need you to *hear* me. I am not your enemy."

Sure, Wil thought. *Not as far as you know, anyway. Yet.*

"All right" was all he said.

"No, I won't have you pulling that meek-and-agreeable routine on me. You don't believe me, then have the brass to *say* you don't believe me, tell me *why* you don't believe me. But I won't have you putting on faces for me anymore—we can't afford it. There's too much going on and too many ways it can all go very wrong."

Slowly Wil opened his eyes, lifted his head, and focused as best he could until Brayden's face shimmered into something close to clarity. There was what looked like a bruise around the right eye, and if Wil stared long enough, he could make out how a hank of wispy gold strayed down to curl over the left eyebrow, how shadows darkened Brayden's face around the chin and upper lip as though he'd not shaved lately. How the look in the eyes was hard and determined but sincere.

"All right," Wil said again, firmer this time. "I believe that you believe what you're saying. I believe you intend nothing but good and right... or at least what you think is right. I believe that if you... hurt me, it will be because it's something you cannot prevent or to which you can see no other alternative."

"But you've been told you should fear me, and you think I've not killed you yet because I've no idea what you are. You think as soon as I find out what you are, I'll change my mind and do you in."

Wil shrugged. "Or perhaps because you don't know what *you* are."

"Right. The Guardian." Brayden paused with a tilt of his head. "Tell me what that means to you."

A wild little laugh burbled at the back of Wil's throat, and he choked it off. It *was* pretty funny, though, in a dark-mad-paradox sort of way. Brayden was serious. He really was serious. And he really did expect an answer. He might as well have said *Give me another reason to kill you.* It would have been no less merciless.

Interesting. Apparently Wil didn't have a death wish after all. He wished he could make up his mind.

He made himself take a deep breath, made himself blow it out slowly. Made himself ignore the question.

"How did you get your eye blacked?" he asked instead.

Brayden sighed. "You've a mean left hook." It was curt.

Wil blinked in surprise. "*I* did that?"

"And the scratches." Incredibly, there was a hint of amusement beneath the tone. "That make you feel better, does it?"

"I...." Wil frowned and leaned back against the wall. He thought about it. He didn't remember doing that. Although... he did seem to remember hearing Locke point it out last night, now that he thought about it. He also remembered Brayden having plenty of opportunity—and plenty of excuse—to increase the count of Wil's own injuries and refraining. Wil shook his head. "No, I.... Sorry."

"Accepted." Brayden shifted in his chair with a light

chuckle. "You're very good at changing the subject. But I'm very good at getting answers."

Wil slumped. "I know." That was what he was afraid of. "I can't answer you. I mean... I can, but I'm afr—" Wil shook his head, frustrated. "I don't want to. You ask me to betray myself."

"You were willing to kill yourself last night. You sat here this afternoon ready to die by my hand. How much bigger of a betrayal could the truth possibly be?"

It sounded so reasonable.

"I didn't care this afternoon. I wasn't... afraid."

"And now?"

"Oh yes."

"What if I told you," Brayden said slowly, "that I know exactly what I am?—or what legend says I'm supposed to be. What if I told you I know the story of the Aisling and the Guardian, and that it doesn't quite suit the one you've obviously heard?" He leaned in. "What if I told you I don't believe in legend or fate or any of those things zealots twist about to prove their madness is a righteous means to everyone else's end?"

"Then...." Wil pulled in a heavy breath. "Then I would say you are a very lucky man." He managed a weary smile. "And you must sleep very well at night."

"Oh, I do. Mostly because I don't allow anyone else to tell me what I am."

"How very fortunate for you."

"Aisling means 'dream,' doesn't it?"

Wil started at the sudden turn, then set his sore jaw when he realized the purpose of it. Trying to catch him off guard. More games. And Brayden had been rebuking *him* for "wearing faces."

"We've been through this already." Wil's tone, though soft, was deliberately insolent. "If you already know all the answers, why d'you keep asking questions?"

"Because you keep not answering me."

"Because you keep asking questions I can't answer!"

"You can't tell me what 'aisling' means?"

Wil rolled his eyes. "All right. Fine. Yes, it means dream."

There. Brayden already knew anyway, so what difference did it make?

"And the Guild holds the Aisling as some sort of figurehead?"

Wil couldn't help the derisive snort. "I suppose some might look at it that way." Then he shook his head. "No. The Chosen is the figurehead."

"They're not one and the same?"

"They're meant to be."

Brayden propped a booted foot across his knee, tapping at the leather with long, callused fingers. "What did you do at the Guild?"

"I...." Even had Wil wanted to voice it, the answer grew weight and sharp edges to clog in his throat.

The raw shock of violation, so deep and profound it makes his soul scream. Too many tears, too many pleas, and pain *and need and craving, and he can't tell what's his and what isn't, until it doesn't matter anymore, it all flows to him, from him, and he can't stop it, so he opens himself up, swallows emptiness....*

He'd been calm a moment ago, but now his gut roiled and his heart thumped about behind his ribs. Bile burned at the back of Wil's throat, sour and bitter. He was going to be sick. He was going to lean over and retch all over Brayden's boots.

"You said Aisling isn't a name, it's a command," Brayden persisted. "Did you dream for them? Is that what this is about?"

Wil shook his head. "There's... I can't...." It was getting harder and harder to breathe.

"Are you a prophet? Some kind of oracle?"

"Wait." It ground out of Wil's throat on a whisper. He clenched his eyes shut tight. "I'll tell you, just... just *wait*, let me... just...."

A moment, he needed just a moment to slow his pulse, calm his breathing—

"Are the Brethren part of the Guild?"

"No—*no*, just... stop for just a moment, all right, let me—"

"What did they tell you about the Guardian? Why are you so afraid of me?"

Wil snapped his head up, blurted, "Because you're a *bloody* terrifying man!" He tried to shove his hair out of his eyes before he realized he was using the bandaged hand and was doing nothing more than pawing stupidly at his head. "Look at you—d'you have any idea what it's like to... to... I mean, if you were me, wouldn't *you* be afraid?"

Brayden's boot hit the floor with a *thump* so hard it made Wil jump. "*Damn* it. If you'd just—" He scrubbed a hand over his face and took a long, calming breath. "All right." It seemed like he was deliberately trying to even out his tone into something less snarly. "Fine. Then let me tell you the little fairy tale *I've* heard." He reached into his coat pocket and withdrew a dark shape that, as Wil squinted at it, resolved itself into a small, slender book.

It was so surreal that Wil huffed a shaky little snort. "Are you going to read me a bedtime story?"

"Shut it," Brayden snapped, the rein he'd obviously been keeping on his patience now stretched nearly beyond its strength. Wil sometimes had that effect on people when he stayed around them for too long. "You had your chance, you didn't take it, so you'll shut your mouth and listen to *me* now."

Constable Brayden was back again. And he wasn't happy.

It was strange—the first time Wil had been on the receiving end of that tone of voice, that hard stare, he'd nearly wet himself in his terror. Now he didn't even twitch. The steady *rat-a-tat* of the questions had nearly had him on his knees begging for reprieve, but these overt near-threats didn't even faze him. In fact they were almost a relief. Odd. For all Brayden's size, Wil was more afraid of the mind beneath it than he was of the obvious strength.

"According to this," Brayden was saying, "the Father created the Aisling as a gift for the Mother, gave him... hold on...." He turned a few pages, scanning. "Right, 'gave him hair as black as the bower of the Stars, skin as fair as the Moon's face, and eyes the green of the Mother's Womb—'" He shook his head. Wil's eyesight must have been getting better, because he was sure he saw Brayden's eyebrow rise up into the hairline. "Now, I'll give you that the description matches pretty well, but is there such a thing as a green womb?" Brayden didn't wait for an answer. "'—and then he taught the Aisling to dream, taught him to sing the songs of the Stars and to weave the songs of Man.'" He paused again. "D'you know how to weave songs?"

He said it as though it was the most absurd thing he'd ever heard, but Wil's heart had lurched into his throat with the first sentence. *One cannot be reborn without returning to the Womb....* For the first time since... since *ever*, Wil wondered if it meant something other than a cruel riddle. His mouth worked, but nothing came out of it.

"Are you all right?" Brayden was leaning in again.

Wil flinched. No, he wasn't all right, but he needed to hear this. "Go on."

Brayden stared at him for a long moment, skeptical, before finding his place and continuing: "'The Mother was well pleased with her Gift, and loved the Dreamer well, but soon saw that Man would covet the Aisling, that the Father had taught him too well in the ways of dreams, but not enough in the ways of Men's hearts.'" He paused again, with some no doubt sarcastic retort on his tongue, but stopped and peered keenly at Wil. Wil didn't know what was on his face, but whatever it was, it seemed to make Brayden think better of whatever he'd been about to say. He merely read on. "'And so the Mother gave to the Father the Guardian, made of the hearts of mountains and the living rays of the Sun, gave him eyes as dark as the Father's mantle, and taught him to Watch. And when the Mother was well satisfied, she took the hand of the Father and led him to their bower, covered him with the veil of her hair and kissed him —' And it goes on from there about begetting rivers and meadows and rocks—apparently they were randy as teenagers—and there's something in there about banishing the old gods of the Four Corners to the boles of evergreens and other such nonsense.

"Now." He sat back, jammed the little book into his coat and folded thick arms across a wide chest. "Tell me what about *any* of that is worth killing for."

Wil could only stare blankly for a moment before he managed a shaky little "Sorry, what?" He was still trying to make sense of this version of the tale. And wondering how it could be almost exactly the same and yet entirely different.

Brayden either didn't see Wil's bewilderment or dismissed it in his growing impatience to get to the point. "I have never seen anyone in my life who had so many people on his arse, and I've been a constable for nearly a bloody *decade.* I've enlisted bleeding *posses*, for pity's sake!

"Six men died last night—three by their own hands—every one of them in the attempt to get those hands on *you.* And that's not even counting Palmer—*plus* Orman, who, unless there's been some miraculous recovery while I've been gone, has been turned to a bloody drooling potato. The highest authority of a bloody *country* wants you, is stopping just short of declaring war if I don't find you and hand you over, and I somehow can't make myself believe it's because their pet prophet ran away from home."

Brayden leaned forward, too obviously trying to squelch rising anger, real entreaty in his voice and in what Wil could make out of his face. "You say the Guild wants you dead. Fine—from them, I can believe anything. I can even believe that the Chosen they're supposed to revere and protect is actually a prisoner, and that they would lie to him and tell him anything to keep him one. In fact, it doesn't even surprise me.

"If you want to believe me this Guardian, then believe it, but at least *consider* that the people who you say are trying to kill you have also lied to you, and that what I'm meant to guard is *you*—I'm the only one trying to keep you alive right now!" He held his hands out, palms up. "I *have* to take you back, understand? I've no choice. So I need you to tell me why I can't."

Wil kept staring, a little bit stunned by the display of anxiety. He shook his head. "Why would...?" Was Brayden saying what Wil thought he was saying? Was this an offer, or...? "What would happen to you if you didn't?" He had to ask it, even if his voice did emerge too raspy and small.

"Then a warrant would likely be issued for my arrest, and I'd be just as wanted as you are." It was said in matter-of-fact tones, no self-pity or guile Wil could detect. "And Ríocht would likely use it as an excuse to stop the talks and withdraw the treaty. I imagine it wouldn't take long after that before war was declared—they've been looking for an excuse for the last five years."

"War...." Wil sat back, closed his eyes. He had no idea whether or not he should believe that—he didn't know politics. But he knew the Guild, and he knew how badly they wanted him gone, and he knew why. He shook his head. "They won't declare war, not yet."

Brayden was silent for a long time, breath coming heavier than normal, hands fisted. It took a while before he finally asked, "Why?"

"Because they can't—they need their Aisling."

That made Brayden's eyes narrow. "You'd best tell me what that means."

As near to real hostility as Wil had heard thus far. Not surprising, he supposed—he'd already pushed Brayden close to some kind of edge, and Wil had just more or less confessed to being a weapon against Brayden's country.

Anyway, Brayden was right—this was far too big, and Wil couldn't pretend to know all the repercussions. Brayden seemed to, and seemed also to sincerely think he could figure out a way around them. *If* Wil told him the things he needed to know. Except the things Brayden needed to know were also the things that would likely turn him from potential protector into the true Guardian.

Then again... what difference did it make? It was going to happen eventually anyway. Wil had seen it, couldn't stop it, could only put it off. And when it got right down to it, wouldn't he rather see it coming? Wouldn't he rather his last truths to be *truths*, instead of puling lies?

Wil lifted his chin.

"I was... six, I think, when they found out what I could do. I don't really remember. I was very young, and it was... forever ago." He curled his hand into a sweaty fist. Fuck, he was really going to do this. "There was a fever. It swept through the Guild, cut their numbers in half—that's when Síofra was officially indoctrinated to the Guild, and things—"

"Wait, *Dúthomhas* Síofra?"

Wil jolted. "You know him?

"No," Brayden replied slowly. "He was in Putnam when I left, but I didn't meet him. Came flying from the talks in Penley when our reports about Orman and Palmer reached the ambassador." He narrowed his eyes. "I was told he was merely a lackey to the ambassador."

A low snort gusted from Wil's throat, and he rubbed carefully at his temple. "Think about it. If someone wanted to get close to the opposition, have the most influence possible, without having to go through the bother of spying or the constrictions of state formalities, what profession do you think would be most convenient?" Wil lifted a somber stare to Brayden, a bitter smile. "As an ambassador's 'lackey,' he has functional invisibility and complete immunity. He doesn't even have to show his papers when he crosses the border."

Brayden was silent for a long time, assimilating this revelation before he sucked in a long breath between his teeth. "He came for you."

There was no real surprise in Wil. Still, a shudder skittered up his backbone. "Right." He licked dry lips. "Anyway, it was him who found me several years previous, before I was even born. The Chosen wasn't... it was meant to be one and the same, that's what they'd wanted since the Guild began, but the Aisling—it had become legend, and no one... I'm not even sure they believed it anymore themselves when Síofra came along. They'd been searching for hundreds of years, *thousands*, even before Ríocht became its own state, but they didn't actually find one until Síofra."

"You," Brayden said.

Wil nodded. "And so he could do no wrong as far as the Guild was concerned. They allowed him complete discretion, and when he found out what... the things that... I was only *six*—how was I supposed to...?" Wil made himself breathe evenly, then started again. "I was sick, I caught the fever. There was no treatment—they could only give the normal remedies, make a person as comfortable as possible, and hope they got well on their own." His heart was racing, and a trickle of sweat ran down between his shoulder blades. "The usual drug of choice was dreamleaf."

He peered up at Brayden, saw no judgment yet, only patient encouragement.

"And...?"

Wil looked down. "And... well, it's called such for a reason.

For normal people, it helps one sleep and... enhances one's dreams, makes them more vivid and real. For me, it...."

Why couldn't he just get it *out*? He could feel it, locked in a painful lump in his chest, and he wanted it *gone*, but he couldn't make his mouth speak the words that would expel it.

"Tell me what you did at the Guild before you got sick," Brayden said softly.

Another skillful turn in conversation. For some reason, this one made Wil able to breathe again. He latched onto the calm tone, steadied himself with it.

"I dreamed." It sounded so... simple, so insignificant when he said it out loud like that. "Minded the patterns, guided them into their proper... weave, I suppose you'd say, laced the new threads into the world and plucked the old—"

"All right, hold." Brayden was frowning and shaking his head. "The patterns of what?"

"Men."

"Men." Brayden lifted his eyebrows. "And you say these... threads—they're what? The patterns of men?" He tilted his head. "All men, or only certain ones?"

Wil almost smiled but couldn't quite make it. "Well, there's the trick. It isn't really our design, is it? We're not meant to meddle and change, only to guide the threads to where they should be."

"We?"

"Right." Wil sighed. "Fine. Me. The Aisling." He couldn't suppress a shudder. He hadn't said that word in reference to himself for longer than he could remember. "And when you do meddle and change, it... it *hurts*."

"Hurts how?"

Wil looked away. "I can't explain it—it hurts your *mind*, like a bruise inside your Self, like... like a tear in your soul...." He closed his eyes, pressed his fingers into them, realized too late that it was a mistake and pulled them back with a hiss. "Síofra—he discovered that he could...." Wil peered up at Brayden, pleading. "I was too young and I was *sick*, and, and *drugged*, I didn't... *couldn't*—"

"You were six years old, you were sick and full of dream-leaf," Brayden offered evenly. "Don't apologize before you've even confessed—it wasn't your fault. Just go on, get it done."

Wil laughed, bitter and small. "You may want to save your sympathy, Guardian. And you may want to rethink my status as friend or enemy before I'm through." He took a deep breath. "He can follow me."

"Follow you. Síofra?"

Wil nodded.

"How?"

"I don't know. There was talk that he was a magician, that he rose to his position through witchcraft, but it was only ever whispers, and I was—"

"No, I mean—follow you *how*? Where?" Brayden had gone tense, leaning in with a narrow frown. "Does he know where you are now?"

"Ah." Wil shook his head. "No, I mean I would dream and he would... follow somehow."

"*In* your dream?" The tone was incredulous now.

"Not... precisely."

"Then what, *precisely*?"

"The dreams, they...." Wil chewed his lip. "When I dream, they're not really *my* dreams."

An impatient bit of a growl. "All right—whose *are* they?"

"Sort of... everyone else's." Wil looked up, mouth turning down into a small grimace. "You don't believe it."

Brayden seemed to be thinking it over. "Well, I don't know." He sat back and folded his arms across his chest. "As you said, you were young and drugged, and—"

"It didn't stop when I was *six*," Wil snapped, whatever wire he'd been walking now twanging out from under his feet. "And it was no delusion. When he realized what he could do, that he could make me do *anything* in that state and I couldn't fight him, he.... It started with just maybe once a month or so, but then it got to be more and more and more, and I knew it was wrong, it wasn't what I was meant to do, it was *wrong*, and it *hurt*, but when he followed me, when he was there and telling me to do something, I couldn't *not* do it.

"So I finally refused to take the leaf, but they'd slip it into meals and teas—I was afraid to eat, so I stopped that too—and then I tried to run away, but there's *no way out* of that place, and there was no one to turn to, nowhere to go, and they got tired of trying to keep me under control, it was just easier after a while to keep me on the leaf all the time, except... except...."

It had been like chewing glass to get it started, and now Wil couldn't stop it—neither the flow of the words nor the flow of the tears.

"Except they had to take me to the Turning Festival—they *had* to, I had to be seen by the people, and I had to say my lines and give my blessings and aver my support of the Guild, but they couldn't take me out like a walking corpse, so they'd have to... have to take it away for a while." He couldn't look at Brayden, afraid of what he might see looking back at him. Shame set fire to Wil's cheeks, but he couldn't stop talking. "I *begged* for it." Low and shaky. "I promised things, *did* things that.... It *hurt* when they took it away, almost as much as when Síofra followed me, and they'd only take it away long enough for me to be able to put on some weight and stand up on my own and speak the lines they gave me without slurring and drooling—and then... and then they'd take me right back and it would start again for another year, until eventually even that got to be too much of a bother.

"They started a search for someone who looked like me, someone who could *behave*. They weren't going to take me out anymore, not even that, and when I realized...." Wil's voice was rising to a high-pitched tremor, so he stopped and drew a shaky breath.

"I tried to jump off the parapet at the Turning."

It sounded so stark, spoken in a lone sentence like that, with nothing of the despair and agony that came with it. A dark little chuckle rose through the cragged chunk of helpless rage in Wil's throat.

"The crowd was... well, *horrified* isn't quite right, and there was quite an outcry—never did know if it was against me or the Guild—so they couldn't take any more chances. The people had *seen* and I was too much of a risk, so when they found another, they took him out instead, and after that...." Wil couldn't help the impotent growling whimper. "I don't know for how long, they just... they kept me... sotted and stupid. And the worst part about it was that the only time I minded it was when Síofra was there. The rest of the time, I just...." A shamed, tearful little gurgle of a sob was all Wil could muster. "The rest of the time, I dreamed and didn't... didn't hurt, and it was enough." His hand clenched around the fabric of the bedding in a feeble fist. "Understand—I didn't know what... I didn't remember enough of life to know that wasn't it."

He stared into his lap, trying to staunch the humiliated tears, unable to lift his gaze, only watched the teardrops fall and wet the weave of his trousers, unable to even care what Brayden might think of him. There was no such thing as pride in Wil's world anymore—he wasn't even so sure there ever had been. He felt like an open wound leaking infection. Brayden had wanted the truth, he'd wanted answers. And now that he'd forced the key and thrown the door wide, Wil couldn't stop the avalanche of rot that came spilling out to bury him beneath it. Raw and unguarded and exposed—Brayden could ask anything now and Wil would answer it, wouldn't be able to *stop* himself from answering.

Except Brayden wasn't asking any questions—he was just sitting there, peering at Wil with a look that made Wil's gut roil and his head dip down. Pity, perhaps, or disgust or disbelief or maybe even shock—Wil couldn't tell, and the suspense was clogging his throat, driving a spike behind his eyes.

The silence was maddening, the gaze heavy. Wil couldn't take another second of it. He gathered the scraps of the wits still left to him and rasped, "What else d'you want to know?"

It took a moment for Brayden to answer; he just kept *staring*. Finally he rubbed at his chin with a deep, thoughtful frown. "How long?"

Wil shook his head. "How long what?"

"It started when you were six. How long did it go on?"

Wil puffed out a hoarse, sullen little chuckle. "*I* don't know. The last clear memory I have of any value is a Festival during which someone happened to mention that it was my sixteenth year. The trick on the parapet came sometime after, but I don't know how long. After that...." He bit his lip. "Before that, even —it's all rather murky. I don't remember much of anything but images and... and things I don't want to remember, until the Brethren stormed the Guild a little more than three years ago and took me."

Wil laughed—a real laugh this time, wild and a bit crazed. "When the leaf started to wear off and I could think a bit, I thought it was a rescue. Before the pain came, anyway, and then I thought—" The laughter stopped as abruptly as it had hit, turning the hollow echo of it even more demented. Exhaustion was sucking at Wil, and he blinked eyes gone once again blurry and heavy. "I don't know how long I was there. I don't even know how old I am. But there's something I do remember, something you should know, before you decide to take any risks for my sake."

Brayden merely raised his eyebrows. "All right."

Calm and detached. Simple encouragement, no emotion Wil could detect inside of it—no suspicion, no sympathy—just a cool, professional interest in what Wil might say next. It was oddly comforting.

Wil licked his lips, drew his knees up, and tried not to look so much like he was balling in on himself when he too obviously was.

"I said he could make me do anything when he followed me —I meant *anything*. The man could tell me to put my own eyes out and I'd do it."

Brayden leaned forward at that, peering at Wil closely. Wil lifted his head, let him look.

"You're serious," Brayden said after a moment.

Wil turned his fuzzy gaze to the floor. "There can be only one of us—one Aisling, and one Guardian to Watch. Another won't be born until I'm dead. And since I was too much trouble...." He looked straight at Brayden, wearing no face but his own. "He's their main strategist now, you know. Síofra, I mean. He's not only implicit Elder of the Guild, but he's also the tacit head of the military. They talk about him like he's a sorcerer, because he always seems to know who's going to do what and when they're going to do it."

"Because he 'followed' you into others' heads."

Wil nodded. "Except he couldn't follow me all the time—he couldn't control what I did when he *didn't* follow me. So every time he had me spy inside someone's head or influence someone through their dreams, I found someone of the opposite number and did the same."

That got a surprised gust of a laugh out of Brayden. "You *sabotaged* the *Dominion*?"

Wil dipped his head. "You need to understand—I didn't do it to help Cynewísan or hurt Ríocht. I knew they'd get tired of dealing with me eventually. I knew what would come—I think I knew it before it occurred to anyone else. That 'sabotage,' as you call it, was the only rebellion I had left. It was the only way I could hurt him back."

Brayden hissed out a low whistle. "They found out?"

"Of course." Wil shrugged. "Once Síofra twigged and knew what to look for, all he had to do was ask and I had to spill my guts." It hadn't been as cut and dry as all that—it had been more like spilling his mind and his soul, then splitting both down the center and gutting them. Wil shuddered. "That's when they decided they needed a new Aisling."

"And that's why they want you dead?"

"Yes. That was to be my last task—to find the next one so they could be rid of me."

Brayden pondered that for a moment. "Why didn't Síofra do it and save everyone the trouble?"

"I've thought about that," Wil replied softly. "I still don't really know for sure, but I imagine it's for one of two reasons. Either he lucked into finding me and didn't think he could do it again, or he wanted to make sure I knew I was signing my own death warrant. He hates me, so I tend to lean toward the latter. From what I understand, the only reason I was still alive when the Brethren attacked was because Síofra was away on Ambassador's business and wanted to do the deed himself after I'd found the next for him. Of course I had that from the Brethren, so who knows, really."

Wil knocked out a heavy sigh and set his jaw.

"But I've got away from what I was trying to...." *Damn* it, this was hard, and he hadn't even got to the worst part yet. His teeth all but rattled, the way he was shaking. "A Guardian is meant to Watch and ensure the Aisling doesn't do exactly the kinds of things Síofra had me doing." Wil looked up. "You're not meant to guard me—you're meant to guard *against* me."

If Brayden had come to any conclusion or judgment, his face didn't show it. "Keep going" was all he said.

Wil nodded slowly, braced himself. He'd live or die by what he said next. And he wasn't sure which one he was hoping for.

"You must have been about ten or so."

Brayden narrowed his eyes at that, tilted his head. Wil realized that, for the first time since he'd opened his eyes, he could see perfectly clearly—could see the hot spark of suspicion in Brayden's dark gaze, the swell of doubt and distrust.

Wil didn't buckle beneath it, didn't allow it to stop this last confession. He lifted his chin. "Síofra—he had me look for you." He kept his gaze steady on Brayden's face, watching for reaction, but there wasn't one. Shaking harder now, Wil swallowed, steadied his voice, said, "I showed him Lind. The raid, when you were a boy... they weren't really trying to annex Lind—they were looking for *you*. And I told them how to find you."

CHAPTER 5

Dallin went blank. Completely and utterly blank. Which was probably a good thing, because otherwise there was no telling what he might've done. What was a person supposed to do in a case like this? Had there ever *been* a case like this?

So he sat, stared, mind racing, heart pounding. Trying not to give the memories purchase. Trying not to let his hands close into fists. Trying not to launch himself at Calder and....

And do what?

Throttle him because he'd been used and exploited his entire life? Close his hands around the skinny throat and *squeezesqueezesqueeze* because a six-year-old boy had been made an addict? Watch as those damnable eyes bugged out their sockets, petechiae blooming and spider-walking the whites, because—

Because he killed your mother.

Dallin rubbed at his temple, slowly, because if he made Calder flinch, Dallin really might snap. He already couldn't look at Calder; the fear in Calder's face was doing things inside Dallin that made his chest burn and his gut clench itself into a hard fist. Dallin was *this close* to giving Calder a bloody *reason* to fear him.

He needed to get out of here, he needed to walk away, except he couldn't. He wasn't done yet. There was an open door in front of him, long-awaited information finally flowing through it, and if he walked away now, it might close, and close for good. This... whatever it was—problem, cock-up, big gigantic bloody political swamp—it was too big now, beyond anything Dallin had imagined, and he couldn't pitch the best chance he'd had thus far to get a grip on it.

Except the big gigantic bloody political swamp had just got personal.

Right up until that last revelation, he'd been perfectly willing to believe Calder delusional. After all, the functionally insane made it their business to dream up fantastic scenarios that fit lock and key with reality—it was how they could keep themselves believing they were the sane ones and everyone else was crazy. But, even as Dallin was talking himself into believing this comforting theory, he knew too well it was its own form of self-delusion. There might well have been lies and half-truths scattered through Calder's account, but the bulk of it felt like more truth than Dallin wanted to face.

And yet he couldn't look away. He couldn't *let* it be personal.

"How old?" he asked quietly.

Calder was sitting in a little ball on the cot, shaking, and staring at Dallin with eyes like a rabbit in a hawk's shadow. "S-sorry?"

Dallin's jaw tightened. "*How old* were you when this happened?"

Calder seemed to think about that one carefully. "I don't know. It was after the parapet." He looked down, brow creased, sweaty fingers picking nervously at the wrappings on his hand. "I... I *think*."

Dallin thought about it, doing the math in his head. He'd been twelve when his mother had shoved him onto that cart, and that had been more than twenty years ago, almost twenty-five. Calder said the parapet had happened after he was sixteen —by the sound of it, probably at least a few years after.

Dallin gave Calder a good look. "If your reckoning is even close to correct, that would make you at least forty years old." He shook his head. "You look *maybe* twenty-five, if that."

That wasn't *entirely* true. One of the first things Dallin remembered remarking about Calder was that he looked young and old at the same time, the face hardly more than a lad's, but the eyes....

Calder only shrugged and kept his eyes on the fraying linen on his hand. "I could be a hundred, for all I know." It was low, diffident. "It felt like forever. Sometimes there *was* no time, at least nothing to mark it by, and if I could be more precise, I would, but...." He trailed off with another shrug.

He was too good at lying, but Dallin was oddly certain that Calder at least thought he was telling the truth. Still, something about the timing tugged at Dallin's skepticism. "I thought a Guardian was born to Watch the Aisling. If I am what you think I am, why would I have come so late? What good could I have done against a grown or near-grown young man?" That tumbled a few more suspicions. "For that matter, why would I have been born on the opposite side of the border? If all of this is 'meant' and planned, why wasn't I, say, your elder brother, or even an uncle or something?"

"How would *I* know?" Calder's fear was slowly giving way to that familiar anxious anger that seemed to leak from him constantly in a peculiar, near-tangible aura. "You ask *me*, like I'm supposed to know, like it was all my doing." His shoulders hunched in, and impossibly, he curled into himself even tighter. "Believe me, if *I* were running things...." He paused, seemingly surprised that he was still talking, then shut his mouth tight.

Dallin stood and deliberately stepped away before he gave Calder a chance to cringe and ramp up the strange removed rage that was driving through Dallin's veins. He paced over to the bars, leaned into them, took a long, deep breath, and tried to think about it all logically.

Setting aside the question of Calder's age, and assuming the rest of the story was at least half-true, the raid on Lind would have happened when he was well into his addiction and more of a tool than a person. Regardless of Dallin's innate shock and anger at the revelation, and his real and sudden drive to exact some sort of belated vengeance, he'd known in his gut that Calder wasn't really where those emotions should be directed. A pawn. A helpless instrument. Someone to be pitied.

Except Calder seemed to deflect even the smallest show of sympathy like he was wearing some kind of repelling armor. Every time Dallin found himself feeling some small bit of compassion, every time he looked for reasons to forgive the constant biting and scratching, or even halfway admire it, Calder would look at him with that expectant fear in his eyes, and Dallin's blood would boil.

He'd stood on the other side of these bars only a few hours ago—looking over Calder's shirtless form, eyes dubiously roving the piebald chest, belly, back, sides, face... marking every bruise and wondering which of them had come from Dallin's own hand, watching Calder trying to blink his blurry eyes into focus —and feeling about two inches tall for those knocks to the head Dallin himself had administered. And telling himself yet again that he'd been doing his job, that any force he'd used had been entirely necessary and completely unavoidable.

And then Calder had looked at him in fuzzy confusion. *Why are you being so nice to me?*

I wasn't aware I was *being "nice." This is* nice *to you?*

It had been all Dallin could do not to start stomping about and snarling, proving himself the animal Calder kept expecting him to be.

Why was he being *nice* to him?

Because I'm a decent man, and I don't go about hurting people just because I can. I've never had to prove that so many times to the same person in my entire life, and if I have to do it one more time, I might snap.

Because I don't believe in beating confessions out of people, but every time I ask you even the simplest question, you keep making me wonder if a simple thrashing might not be kinder.

Because I have never in my life met someone who could make me want to put my hands around his throat and just keep squeezing, at the same time as I want to let him lay his head on my shoulder and tell him to weep until it all goes away.

He'd bloody *apologized* to Dallin for blacking his eye, when it was very likely Dallin's rough treatment that had resulted in Calder's near blindness—thank the Mother it only seemed temporary. And that apology.... Dallin wished he knew why it made his teeth clench. Nearly as much as Calder's confused, halfhearted defense of Dallin to the healer. *I didn't do this*, Dallin had told her, and he hadn't, really, at least not the worst of it, but Calder's odd vindication had hit Dallin right in the conscience.

"I'm tired," Calder murmured from across the small cell. "I want to...." He swallowed, head still ducked down and shoulders still hunched. He looked like a bloody weevil trying to hide up his own arse. "May I sleep?"

For the love of the Mother, I'm not your bloody keeper! Dallin wanted to shout—except he was. What was he, if not Calder's gaoler? Protector? *Guardian*? Ha. Dallin had put at least several of those bruises on Calder, and now he was standing here thinking about how good it would feel to wrap his hands about that throat and start squeezing.

Dallin sucked back a growl and beat back the fury that wanted to wrench at his chest, inexplicably rising because the simple request for some sleep had been exactly that—a request and not a statement, not a demand. Damn it, he didn't want to break the man, he only wanted....

Well. Dallin didn't really know. The truth. A truth he could believe and could do something about. A definition of what his job was going to be when he found that truth. A surety that he would be able to do what was right if it turned out that "right" conflicted with his duty to Jagger and the constabulary and bloody Cynewísan, for all that. Because it was looking more and more as though what the laws of his country required of him was going to be in direct contrast to what his instincts were telling him.

"All right." Dallin pointedly looked down at his boots and not at Calder. "A few more questions, and then we'll let it go for a bit." Calder sagged but didn't protest, just sat there waiting. "You said you found me." Dallin went back to his chair, and lowered himself into it. "How? Can you... whatever it is you do —go inside my head?"

Calder shook his head, frowning as though the question troubled him. "No." His voice was quiet but steady. "I found...." He paused, took a wobbly breath, and with obvious effort lifted his chin and looked Dallin in the eye. He looked as if he'd rather swallow broken glass than finish the sentence. "I found your mother."

Dallin refused to let it hit like a sucker punch, refused to even *feel*. "So you've tried to look inside my head and couldn't?"

Calder paled but willfully kept his gaze locked to Dallin's. Nodded.

Even though Dallin wasn't sure he even believed any of this story yet, that admission relieved him.

"And that's why you were so surprised when you saw me in Putnam? You thought I was dead?"

Calder opened his mouth at that, then closed it before he broke the stare and looked down. Something was there, something he didn't want to say. Dallin wasn't so sure he wanted to know it, considering, but after all, how much worse could it possibly be?

"*What?*" Dallin snapped.

Calder jumped and flashed Dallin a quick, uneasy glance. "I knew."

It was so quiet that Dallin wasn't even sure he heard it. "Knew *what*?"

There was a pause, heavy and filled with so much tension it was like a static charge in the air. Calder nearly crackled with it.

Dallin resisted the driving need to launch himself at Calder and shake the answer out of him. "Knew. *What?*" It was a snarl this time. Dallin didn't even chide himself for it.

The tears came again, sliding fat and slow down pale, bruised cheeks. Dallin watched them, knew he could ease them with a word, knew how to take an overwhelmed suspect and soothe him, calm him, gently pry the confession that wanted to come. He couldn't make himself do it, half-sick with the low rumble of satisfaction that purred in his heart at the sight of those miserable tears.

Then, finally: "I knew they hadn't got you," Calder whispered. "I knew you got away." He looked up at Dallin. "Síofra didn't bother... he ordered them to kill all the boys, all the young men, and they told him they did, no one saw you escape, he only asked me if the Guardian was gone, and... well, you were. He didn't ask me if you were dead, and you *were* gone from Lind, so I said... I told him yes, that you were gone, and he only told me to keep watching Lind for... well, for...."

The next Guardian, he didn't say. Dallin took this in with keen interest. "And you found...?"

Calder flinched as though Dallin had just hit him. "She didn't...." He swallowed heavily, like he had a boulder in his throat. Dallin had never had a telepathic encounter in his life, but he *knew* somehow who the "she" was to whom Calder referred. "She loved you very—"

"*Don't—*" Dallin's teeth were clenched so tight he thought they might shatter. He was closer than he'd ever been to reaching out and snapping Calder's neck. "Do not presume to tell me *anything* about my mother." Dallin allowed every bit of anger and threat to show plainly in his face, his voice. "I want nothing from you but an answer to my question."

Calder resisted cringing with a very conscious and obvious effort. "I knew you were alive."

"And why didn't you tell?"

A look of real bewilderment and anger crossed Calder's face, and for the first time since this latest confession, he looked away.

Dallin's hands curled into fists again, and he leaned forward in his chair, crowding in and making Calder instinctively press his back farther into the wall. "*Why*," he said through his teeth, "didn't you *tell*?"

"I don't *know*." It was helpless, bewildered, said in a whisper as Calder drew his arms across his middle and his knees closer to his chest.

"Not good enough," Dallin growled. "I'll have an answer, damn it—I want to know *why* you didn't—"

"Because he never asked!" Calder shouted. "Because my whole bloody *life* was *have to* and I didn't *have to*! Because it was a little bit of mutiny that was *mine*. Because if you lived, it meant you might one day hunt me down and put me out of my misery. Because—" He choked, closed his eyes, as close to actual broken whimpering as Dallin had ever seen him. "Because I told her I wouldn't."

The tone was heavy with decimated remorse and ruin, but the words were sharp enough to drive into Dallin's chest like knives. All the air went out of him, and he sat there, staring and shaking his head slowly back and forth, trying to deny the faltering confession, but somehow unable to dismiss it as he wanted to.

"I'd never been there when… when someone died before," Calder went on, halting, like he wanted to stop but couldn't. "I didn't even know I *could.* I mean, it isn't dreaming, that space between life and death, but it almost is, it's so *close* but nothing like it at the same time, and I hardly even had to *try*, and there I was. It was so real and solid, I was actually standing in *grass*, right in front of her, it was like I was *free*, and she… she *smiled* at me, touched my cheek." A small sob warbled its way from his throat. "She said… she said you were a good boy, that you'd be a good man, that you'd come, told me I mustn't tell, mustn't let them know—she *asked* me, looked right at me and *asked* me, and…." He seemed to collapse into himself, shoulders drooping, head sinking down to his knees. "How could I say no," he asked, toneless now and quiet enough to be almost without sound, "when I didn't even really want to?"

Dallin… stared. He couldn't do anything else. Mind caroming back and forth between *he was only six* and *but… my* mother.

The boys didn't occur to him, all those boys who hadn't been smuggled out in the back of a tinker's cart, not until he realized he was holding back a jagged little moan. He'd known of the deaths, the destruction—had deliberately lived the scenes in his head, time and again, until he could look at it without vomiting—but he hadn't even speculated it might have been because of *him.*

He tried to tell himself it wasn't. Calder was lying or insane, and Dallin couldn't rearrange every conviction he'd ever held because of some wild tale told by a delusional maniac.

So why couldn't Dallin make himself stop considering the possibilities?

He didn't know how long he sat there staring, scenes long put away playing once again behind his eyes, voices he hadn't heard in over twenty years now clear and vivid in his head. It was like he was that child all over again, that twelve-year-old boy who wasn't allowed to feel the things he felt out loud and in the open, so he felt them down deep where no one could see them, scrutinize them, judge him weak because he *did* feel them, and felt them hard. He was no boy now. No tears came to threaten at the corners of Constable Brayden's eyes; no cries of loss weltered at the bottom of Constable Brayden's throat.

Constable Brayden merely stood slowly, picked up the chair, and left the cell, closing and locking the door behind him. And then Constable Brayden let himself out of the office, tipped a calm nod and half a counterfeit smile to the man standing post, directed his gaze straight ahead, and started walking.

He went steadily south, with no real purpose to his course besides the nebulous awareness that it was the opposite direction of the Dominion. And that it would take him away from Calder.

Except he no longer felt comfortable calling him that. It seemed… improper. It wasn't his name, it was stolen, and perhaps it was silly, but Dallin had a problem with a stolen surname. A given name was just that—given—with only a small history attached, if it was inherited, and in more cases than not, no history at all besides the fact that someone's mother and father had liked the sound of it in conjunction with the surname. But a surname *was* history, inherited by son after son after son, all the way back to the Clans, and using one that didn't belong to you just seemed wrong.

He was the twelfth Brayden, and considering his preferences, likely the last, the name coming down the centuries to him through a line of men who had made it a tradition—no, an expectation—to serve their people with honor in both peace and war, to carry the name proudly and never do anything to shame it. His father had died when Dallin was only eight, before he'd had the chance to teach Dallin everything the name meant, hand down the songs of Lind's history with that name inside them, but he'd instilled in his son the respect of lineage.

He couldn't imagine the Calders had done less.

Dallin have to get used to calling Calder "Wil," he supposed, though it seemed... familiar. Which made Dallin uncomfortable. But less uncomfortable than the alternative.

So, all right. Wil it was. One problem down. Now Dallin supposed he had no choice but to think about the important ones he was busy not letting himself think about.

He pressed his mouth into a hard line and took a long breath of chill autumn air.

Fine. He could do that. He was good at thinking problems through, applying logic, finding the flaws, poking holes. Logic. Find one truth and follow its thread....

All right, start with the most obvious: he didn't kill her.

True.

He was a pawn, used since birth, weaned on betrayal and cruelty.

If the tale Wil had told could be believed, also true.

He thinks I'm some mythical creature, born solely to make sure he behaves himself, and apparently, since he hasn't, I'm to take him out.

Oddly true.

My village was raided when I was a boy, a third of its population decimated, most of them boys and young men, and among them... my mother.

Very sadly true.

He told them.

Dallin looked down, watched his boots eat the ground, frowned.

...*True?*

It had the feel of it. Dallin had learned to trust his gut, heed his instincts, and they were telling him he'd seen the truth of that raid even as it happened. He'd seen young men dragged out from their homes and shot, hacked, seen boys chased down and run through—fathers only being put to sword if they got in the way. They hadn't been out to take the village, annex a tiny border town that meant nothing in the greater map of geographic strategy. They'd been out to wipe out an entire generation of males. It had clicked into place like some long-lost puzzle piece the moment it stuttered from Wil's mouth, as though Dallin had known it all along and had simply never thought about it with his head before—he'd been so busy burying the pain in his heart that he'd buried everything else too.

It *felt* like truth.

Except, if he believed that, he had to more or less believe everything else. And what was he supposed to do, supposed to feel, about that?

His country's traditional enemy was trying to hunt down a man who supposedly invaded the dreams of others to gain the advantage in combat. All right, if Dallin took that as fact, what was he supposed to do about it? There were no laws for this, no rules, not even a vague guideline, and whatever he did would likely end up going *against* some law or rule or guideline.

He shook his head and flung his glance around the leaf-strewn lane on which he found himself, tried to pay attention to the scenery and couldn't.

He was going about this all wrong, chasing his own tail. He needed to approach it from different angles, weigh the evidence of each, and then formulate his theories. Right now Dallin was just trying to catch smoke in his hands.

So, what if everything Wil had said was the truth?

All right, that would mean they were talking about a man who could alter the course of a war just by falling asleep. He didn't just muck about in other people's heads when he was ordered to—he went against orders to do it, and he had to have been pretty damned motivated, because he talked about it like it was some kind of soul-flaying ordeal, and that Dallin could definitely believe. He could almost see the memories of the pain in Wil's eyes, could almost touch the shadows behind them.

So this was a man who could spy inside people's heads, and the only reason he had not to do it was the pain—which, according to him, he had already withstood for the "greater purpose" of getting even with Síofra.

There was also the matter of what Jagger had told Dallin about Síofra and Orman. Someone who could drive another man mad with a single look sounded like someone who would be capable of just about anything. That kind of man with *any* power was bad enough, but that kind of man with the power to direct the courses of others' lives through dreams? And what better way to do it? Men were at their most vulnerable, most open and unguarded, in dreams.

Dallin stopped where he was and sighed out a low whistle. "He'd be a weapon in anyone's hands, regardless of his intentions," he muttered. "Regardless of *their* intentions." Because even putting someone like Síofra aside, what man would resist the temptation to use that weapon once it was in his hands? Dallin knew the answer to that one without even really thinking about it too hard.

If I tell you, you'll want it too.

Dallin wondered if that assertion had come from the heart of ruthless experience.

Some have begged for the opportunity to bind me. Others have threatened it, even tried it, with no regard for my wants or fears.

"How many?" Dallin looked down to the ground, scuffed the toe of his boot through dirt and leaves. "Did you tell them, try to get help, and they turned on you? Is that how you got that scar?"

It would certainly help explain the nearly pathological distrust. But then, nearly everything about the story would.

Dallin shook his head.

All right. So, if any of this was truth, there was no way in the world Dallin could turn Wil over to Ríocht. If he did, he might as well stroll up to the border and plant the white flag himself. And he couldn't try to get Wil asylum, or even take him into protective custody—not without telling his own government why, and Dallin didn't trust them any more than he trusted the Dominion. Not with a weapon like that.

And while Dallin was entertaining worst-case scenarios, what was to stop Wil from wreaking havoc all on his own just because he could?

Believe me, if I *were running things....*

Wil had said it like he'd thought about it—and why not? A life like he said he'd led would be enough to leave anyone unbalanced. What if Wil snapped and decided everyone needed to just go away, curl up, and die? Could he do that? *Would* he?

Dallin... didn't think so. It was as though it went against something in Wil's core. He'd been nearly as concerned about the fact that it was wrong when Síofra forced him as he was about the pain. And it *had* hurt, in ways Dallin probably couldn't fathom. Wil had been perfectly clear on that point—many times—and Dallin didn't doubt the truth or depth. But Wil had been just as insistent that it was *wrong*. He'd said it several times, and with the same strident insistence in each repetition.

Dallin remembered that night in Putnam, watching "Calder" dance sideways down the road of truth, stopping just short of lies until Dallin took away all other avenues. Dallin had mused at the time that it seemed like some kind of twisted personal tenet of principles. He couldn't make himself give it a name as pretty as *honor*; Wil couldn't possibly know what real honor was. If he'd led the life he said he'd led, where would he have learned it? Dallin kept thinking Wil was so very good at lying—but if all of the tales today were true, Wil hadn't really lied about everything else, as Dallin had been assuming all this time. Wil hadn't stolen from Ramsford when he'd run, he hadn't tried to run once he'd promised not to, and he'd seemed more stricken at the thought of having offended or upset that Miri girl than he'd been over his own injuries. He seemed to have his own ideas of right and wrong, seemed to have come up with his own personal morality code, and messing with the "designs" went against it.

Except when someone pissed him off and he decided to even up the tally.

Dallin growled and ran a hand roughly through tangled hair.

Maybe... maybe Wil was right, and it would be better for all if Dallin just... fulfilled his prophecy. Put him down. Quietly and painlessly. Dallin could even do it while Wil slept, make it easy on both of them.

He dismissed it with a sickened snarl and a bit of a shudder. As much as Dallin had almost frightened himself with the intensity with which he would have liked to throttle Wil several times over, outright murdering him... it was different. There was no honor in something like that, no righteous justification. No matter how one looked at it, it was execution. Dallin had killed for his country before, he'd killed for his job—just last night, in fact—but he wouldn't outright murder for anyone. Apparently not even for someone who bared his throat for him and asked politely.

He shook that one off, resolute.

All right, so if it was all true, Dallin couldn't kill Wil, he couldn't take Wil back to Putnam, and no one could know what Wil was. And Dallin was going to have to find a way to keep what Wil did when he dreamed under control.

Ha. How he was going to do *that*, Dallin hadn't even the smallest clue. But still.

One down.

Dallin started walking again and came about from the other angle.

So, if he assumed everything Wil said was a lie or delusion, Wil couldn't have told anyone about Dallin or Lind, and all that blabber about Dallin's mother was hallucinatory twaddle. Which solved one very personal problem. But in the scheme of things, it was rather a small one and didn't really have anything to do with the bulk of the larger dilemma.

All right, fine. If everything Wil said was a lie, then the Guild was just the Guild, Síofra was just an ordinary minor diplomat, and they were looking for Wil because he was their Chosen and he was missing. They might have even been worried about him. It wouldn't be unreasonable.

That would certainly be easy.

Except.

Except, if that were true, what about the Brethren?

Dallin fetched up short with that thought—found himself standing over a dry streambed, pondering the arid texture of the air, the busy animal sounds pattering around the underbrush, the familiar autumn scents of withering leaves and cooling soil. Thinking how difficult it had been to find water when he'd been tracking his fugitive across the wilderness. Thinking how he'd wondered fractiously more than once when this part of the country had last seen rain.

Thinking how quickly and easily the flames in Kenley must have caught.

The bodies were what had convinced him, even before he'd really thought about it consciously, that it had been the men from the Brethren who'd done whatever magic had been done at the inn and not Wil. None of the corpses had been scattered about as though trying to escape the flames; rather, they were huddled in clusters—entire families—scorched bones in strewn clumps in the middle of smoking holes that had once been homes, twenty of them in the broken carcass of what must have been the grange hall. No blackened buckets half-filled with sooty water, mute testament to having tried and failed to stop the blaze. No *survivors*.

None of them had been shot. No telltale hack marks had been evident on the bones of the remains. They hadn't been killed and piled to burn—they'd sat there in the middle of the dozen or so small conflagrations and waited to be roasted like compliant slabs of meat.

Dallin could imagine it all too well—a malevolent spell, herding people who walked in manufactured torpor and did as commanded with no protest or struggle, a match here, a smoking piece of tinder there.

He wondered which of those men had done the deed. The one he'd shot had been the one to set the spell at the inn; Dallin was more sure of that now than he'd been when he'd initially presented the theory to Locke. And even if he put aside the whole trancing business, that man had seemed to Dallin like the one in charge. But the fact that he hadn't been the only one with those clan marks tattooed on his cheek seemed to wobble that speculation, at least on a superficial level. And if Dallin couldn't peg the man as the only one with power by virtue of the marks, he had to consider that perhaps they were all capable of it. And if all of them could do something like that....

That would be... more than worrisome. If Dallin was up against hundreds of men who could do that, and with no compunction—

No, that didn't fit. If the rest of them could do that, at least the man Dallin had fought with in the yard would have tried it on him before offing himself in such a gruesome manner. In fact, if the rest of them could do that, there wouldn't be much need for those suicide capsules, would there?

Still, even without that sort of power, they'd turned out to be dangerous enough. For pity's sake, at least half those who'd died in Kenley had been *children.* What kind of men *were* they?

Wil was terrified of them, perhaps even more so than he was of the Guild. Certainly more than he was of Dallin. Terrified enough to put a rusty knife to his own throat with every intention of plunging it home. Dallin had seen that truth in Wil's eyes along with the hatred and the fear.

Eyes narrowed, Dallin stared down into the dead stream bed, not seeing the parched cracks of cemented silt, not seeing the brilliant colors of dying leaves. Seeing instead the fear, the knife, the eyes that tried to bore into him and couldn't. Feeling the sympathy that had rocked through him and the uncomfortable but very present desire to help. For all that whatever Wil had been trying to do to Dallin with his eyes last night hadn't worked, the things he'd done with the stark and very real fear in his face and in his voice as he'd pleaded—for release, for his life—most assuredly and unnervingly *had.*

I can't, it hurts too much, and it never stops, they just keep wanting more, and I can't.

"I never asked what that means," Dallin muttered to the

ground. "You've told me why you fear the Guild. I think it's past time I heard about the Brethren."

Compassion, Dallin mused darkly, was likely going to get him into an awful lot of trouble. His hand moved to stroke the smooth butt of his revolver; his other curled into a fist as he decided that whatever the Brethren were, they couldn't be allowed to get their hands on Wil any more than the Dominion. If they could do something like Kenley without that power, Dallin didn't even want to think about what they could do with it.

Anyway, there was also the fact that, regardless of any other truths or lies or powers—real or imagined or complete lack thereof—these were not good men, and Dallin was not in the habit of giving bad men what they wanted. Call it his contrary nature.

Funny. It appeared Dallin had already made his decision. He wondered if he'd done it just now or all the way back in that cell. Or perhaps, he reflected morosely, he'd made it back at the inn, watching a beaten man refuse to be beaten.

Fucking sentiment. It really would be the end of him one day.

It was dark by the time Dallin came back, the streets of the quiet village dim-lit with the sputtering glow of the too-occasional gas lamp and even more deserted than the small villages on the outskirts of Putnam at night. Dallin's boots crunched lightly over the hardpack of the road, the sporadic rattle of a pot or a low laugh and the splash of water coming from the back door of the hostel the only sounds to disturb the cold tranquility.

The glow of lamplight spilled from the sheriff's office, cutting little slices of warmth into the night, slivering across the porch and into the road through the barred windows. Locke must be back and wondering where Dallin had gone—likely also wondering why he'd hared off without leaving word and left his prisoner sitting in the cell alone and in the dark.

A scraggy little man came humping from the shadows as Dallin approached, the butt of his rifle tucked into the elbow of his right arm, barrel propped across his chest and buttressed to the stump of his left. Dallin's hand instinctively went to the holster at his thigh, but he didn't bother flicking loose the tether. Instead he nodded to the man.

"If there's a password, Sheriff Locke hasn't given it to me yet," Dallin said easily, deliberately adding a small friendly smile. "Though I've a badge, if you need to see it."

The man puffed a small liquid snort, horked a mass of snot through his nose, then his throat, and spat it into the dirt. "I seen ye last night." He wiped spit from the scruff of beard on his chin with the back of his hand, his manner that of a man who belonged right where he was and was more than happy to welcome one of his own kind. "I didn't stop ye farther out 'cause I figured it was you. Hard to mistake your shape in the dark."

Dallin extended his hand. "Dallin Brayden."

The man took it, awkwardly shifting the rifle. "Ogden Newell."

"A pleasure, Mister Newell. And I appreciate that you would use your no doubt valuable time to keep watch like this. You'll understand when I say I hope it will all be for naught."

"You and me both." Newell leaned in, face pensive. "You really from Putnam?"

"I am." Dallin tilted his head. "Been there?"

"Nah." Newell snuffled another load of gunk into his throat, leaned to the side and spat again. "Never really been anywhere but here and Kenley, 'cept when I was in the army"—he lifted the stump of his arm a bit—"and then you don't get to see much, 'cept things you don't really want to see."

Dallin nodded agreement, not really wanting to get into veterans' laments but unable yet to make himself go inside. "What unit?"

"Oswin's. First Lieutenant, Third Infantry. The Shaw Campaign."

"The northern border?" Dallin slid a low whistle through his teeth. "Some rough clashes on that one."

Newell's eyes narrowed. "You were there?"

"Cavalry. Captain. Fifth Regiment."

"Ah, one o' them horse toffs, then." There was a good-natured challenging smirk that went along with the comment, so Dallin didn't bristle when Newell grinned, sly. "Bet ye still got your warhorse, en't ye?"

That made Dallin snort. "I have, actually. Smug and spoilt, and not good for much anymore but the occasional stud and looking down his full-bred nose at all the other nags, but...." He waved his hand. "He's a veteran too, and has the scars to prove it."

They were silent for a few moments, companionable, merely watching the night, before Newell twitched so hard that Dallin's hand went without thought to his sidearm.

"*Brayden.*" Newell squinted a narrow look at Dallin

through the darkness. "Well, I'll be damned. You're the one...." He stared so hard, Dallin nearly wanted to swat him. "What's it mean?"

Dallin knew exactly what the man was referring to. That didn't mean he had to like it. Or cooperate. "What does what mean?" He made his tone deliberately cool.

Newell either didn't notice or chose to ignore it. "*Mhàthair Diabhal*—as if you didn't know."

He'd mangled the pronunciation, but even so, the old epithet gave Dallin the same twist it had always done. His jaw tightened. "Mother's Devil," he replied shortly. "And that's the last I want to hear it, if you don't mind."

Newell smiled, then nodded somberly. To Dallin's relief, Newell dropped it and didn't dip down into war stories. Instead he turned his gaze back into the darkness and gave it a practiced scrutiny. "Shame what happened there in Kenley, *damn* shame." He shook his shaggy head with a grimace. "Lousy bastards." He spat again, still eyeing the darkness with wary thoughtfulness.

Dallin couldn't help a bit of a jolt. He kept his expression neutral. "What have you heard about Kenley?"

"Enough," Newell returned roughly. "More 'n most. Sheriff told me 'cause I have what you might call a special interest." He peered up at Dallin, mouth in an angry twist. "Had a sister there. Two nieces and a nephew. All gone."

Dallin looked down, trying not to see the scorched corpses, trying not to wonder which of the small charred skeletons had been this man's kin. He shook his head. "I'm sorry."

"You didn't do it." It was said matter-of-factly, with no anger and no blame. "It en't something that's spread too far yet, but it's a small village. Kenley's only two days' walk or so, and I'm not the only one with a relation there. People will know soon enough. I figure they'll go one of two ways. They'll either blame your friend in there"—he jerked his head over his shoulder —"and start grumbling about why en't we hanging him yet, or they'll blame the ones as done it and dig in like me."

Dallin was silent for a moment, thinking, then: "And which way d'you think they'll go?"

He expected a snort or a glare, but Newell merely shrugged, keeping his gaze on the night. "They're good people. They'll tumble as good people ought."

Dallin hoped that meant they'd go the way of the latter speculation.

"There's two more at the hostel, and three again down the livery," Newell added. "And just about everyone who's gone down to Garson's has gone armed." He dipped a decisive, confident nod. "You can sleep with both eyes closed tonight, Constable Brayden."

Besides worrying about everyone down the inn accidentally shooting each other, Dallin likely would.

"Thank you, Lieutenant Newell." Dallin gave the man a grave smile and a casual salute.

Newell nodded, said, "Cap'n."

Dallin watched him melt into the dark again until he couldn't tell anymore where Newell ended and murky shadow began, then he turned and went inside.

Locke looked relaxed and at ease when Dallin opened the door, her boots propped up on the desk as usual and a small pile of papers at her elbow. But her eyes were bright and alert, shoulders tensed, and her right arm was crooked beneath the desk—

Dallin had no doubt at least one barrel of some likely very powerful weapon was aimed right at his chest.

Locke visibly unfurled when she saw it was him. "Wasn't sure when I should expect you back. Out on business or pleasure?"

Dallin couldn't imagine what kind of pleasure there was to be had in this little backwater—sans Miss Jillian, which... just... no—so he ignored the question. He glanced over into Wil's cell. Still sleeping, and still curled in as if he was trying to make himself disappear. That infuriating bit of compassion crept into Dallin's chest, roosting like it meant to stay, and he sighed.

"He been asleep the whole while?" Dallin walked slowly over to the stove and helped himself to tea. He held up the pot to Locke, questioning; Locke shook her head and nodded to the mug on her desk.

She waited until Dallin sat down across from her before answering him in low tones. "I fed him and gave him the draft Lara sent over about an hour ago, but I'm not even sure he's asleep now. That one...." She shook her head, flicking a glance toward the cell and then back again. "He's... quiet."

Dallin's eyebrows went up. Not an especially heinous offense, in his own opinion. And not entirely true.

He cocked his head to the side, eyeing Locke speculatively. "You don't like him."

"Say rather I don't trust him." Locke directed another narrow stare at the cell. "He's the look about him of a man who's sold his soul."

"He may have done. But he didn't sell it cheaply."

Locke rolled her eyes. "I imagine you had plenty of time to talk."

"Unfortunately." Dallin grimaced, then took a sip of thankfully strong tea beneath Locke's questioning regard. "I didn't find out much that will help. Sorry. Except I'm fairly certain it wasn't him who did… whatever it was that happened. I don't think he's capable."

"Hm." Locke nodded reluctant agreement. "In light of what you said last night, and after I talked again to Miri this morning, I think I agree with you. What she says fits with your theory. It's not even good as far as circumstantial evidence, but it makes a certain kind of sense. And I expect that if your friend could do that, he wouldn't still be locked in a cell."

"True." Dallin stared down into his tea. "Listen…." He slid his mug to the desk, abruptly uncomfortable. "The things I did find out, if what he told me today can be trusted as truth…." Another heavy sigh tendriled from him, and Dallin rubbed at his brow. "I may have to… miss whatever orders come from Putnam."

Locke looked him over shrewdly. "Because if you never get the orders, you won't have to disobey them."

Dallin liked Locke more every time he talked to her. Which made him feel like a complete shit for what he was going to have to do to her. Unaware of his internal fits of conscience, Locke sat back and massaged at her temples. Dallin had been right about the gun earlier—a mean-looking snubbed shotgun rested over her thick thighs.

"This," Locke said tiredly, "must be bloody *huge*."

"It is. And please believe me when I tell you that my lack of forthcoming on the matter is as much for your protection as it is for…." Dallin jerked his chin toward the cell. He looked at Locke with sober calm. "*And* the Commonwealth's."

Locke nodded, still obviously not happy with being kept in the dark, but apparently willing to trust a fellow officer. It made Dallin feel somewhat low and foul.

"When will you go?"

Dallin shrugged, relieved that Locke wasn't going to make this more difficult than it already was. "How much time can you give me?"

Locke waved toward the cell. "Your... friend needs at least another day or two before he'll be fit to travel. And I don't expect we'll hear from Putnam for another... say three days, at least." She eyed Dallin keenly.

"I'll take two," Dallin said. "Thank you."

"And where are you going to, then?"

Dallin leaned back in his chair and looked down at his lap. He couldn't look her in the eye and say what he meant to say next. "It seems the answers I need are all in Ríocht. I imagine I'll start there."

"You're going to cross the *border*?" Real alarm flashed over Locke's face. "And you plan to drag that... *him* with you?"

"Well, I can't leave him here, can I?"

Locke shook her head in too-obvious disapproval and sincere worry. "He's going to slow you down at the least, get you killed more likely."

"Maybe." Dallin kept his gaze on his tea as he stood. "But he's in trouble."

"He *is* trouble."

"No, not really. But trouble does follow him, no matter how fast he runs." For the first time since he'd broached the subject, Dallin lifted his gaze back to Locke's. "I can't kill him, and I can't leave him to his own devices. He's part of the answer. He might be all of it, for all I know. Until I have what I need, he stays where I can see him."

Locke wasn't convinced, Dallin could see it, but she wouldn't get in his way, and he truly had no more energy for it tonight. He let the silence sink in, let his mind push everything away until he could make more sense out of the nonsensical.

More exhausted than he could remember ever having been before, Dallin left it there, drained the mug, slouched into the open cell, and threw himself on the tiny cot. He thought about taking his boots off, hanging up his guns, but it seemed like too much work. "Wake me if you need me," he managed, then plunged headlong into a deep, dreamless sleep.

The light was just going from gray to a light, watery yellow when the shouting woke him. Dallin was asleep one second, wide awake the next, with his hand on the butt of his gun before he realized there was no real alarm. And when the initial surge of adrenaline wore off a little, his next task was to decide whether to growl or laugh.

"They were *mine*," Wil was shouting—none of the warbling fear from yesterday in his voice, but real anger and furious indignation. "You had no right, I didn't say you could, you never even *asked*!"

Locke's voice came next, even and hard, but with obvious bewilderment beneath it: "As I said, they were past repair. There was nothing else to be done with them, and now you've better to replace them with."

Dallin got up slowly, padding quietly to the open door of

the cell, and stretched his neck to get a look. Wil was standing just inside his cell, barefoot and bare-chested, a wad of what appeared to be the deerskin shirt Dallin had given him yesterday in his hand. Locke stood just outside the open door, a pair of soft leather boots held in her outstretched hand. Wil looked cautiously enraged; Locke looked... interested. She didn't seem angry at the insolence Dallin doubted she'd have taken from a normal prisoner—she seemed like someone poking at a wild animal just to see what it would do.

"I don't *want* 'better,'" Wil told her through his teeth. "I want *mine*."

"Yours," Locke answered, dropping the boots to the floor, "are gone."

Dallin ventured out into the office. "Um... hullo?" They both turned to look his way, Locke with a bemused lift of an eyebrow, Wil with a fierce, offended scowl. He lifted his bandaged hand and pointed at the sheriff, looking for all the world like a lad tattling on his sister.

"*She*," Wil said crossly, "took my *boots*!"

Dallin stared. Blinked slowly. Said, "Sorry?" It came out gruff and grainy, so he cleared his throat. "Boots?"

"She *took* them," Wil repeated, as if it was the highest form of insult imaginable and he couldn't get over the audacity.

"They were falling apart." Locke's tone was low and calm, speaking to Wil in a manner that suggested to Dallin that she'd repeated this argument several times over and was convinced that if she said it slowly and clearly enough, the sense of it would eventually sink in. "Afton was kind enough to bring you some things that her Esmond left behind, and I should *think* you might be grateful, instead of throwing a tantrum like a spoilt six-year-old."

It was the "spoilt" comment, had to be. The indignant outrage in Wil's eyes dropped directly into aggressive fury. He pulled himself up to his full height—Dallin was abstractly surprised to note that he had at least an inch on Locke; he kept forgetting how tall Wil was—squared his shoulders, and leaned in. Dallin almost stepped up, but Locke could certainly handle herself, and Dallin was intensely interested in how this was going to play out.

He never got the chance to find out. Wil had just opened his mouth for some no doubt cutting epithets when several gunshots rang out from the direction of the road. Locke spun and drew her gun in one motion; Dallin's own gun was already in his hand before he'd taken his first instinctive step. Then the shutters on the barred doors splintered inward with a concussion that rang Dallin's ears, and Locke's head disappeared in a spray of scarlet.

"*Get down!*" Dallin shouted, already sprinting in a crouch toward the door, seeing through acrid smoke and an adrenaline haze Locke's body with its ruined face slumping and falling as he passed, Wil's arms outstretched to catch her. The weight of her was taking Wil to the floor too.

Dallin dismissed them both. He vaulted to the wreckage of the doors and carefully peered out through the fragmented pieces of it in time to see a man he identified immediately as one of the Brethren go down in a hail of arrows and bullets coming from an upper story of the hostel. Shouts were coming from the direction of the livery. A bell was ringing somewhere. Sporadic gunfire punched holes in the gray dawn.

Dallin shot a glance over his shoulder. Wil was now trying to drag his legs out from under the dead weight of Locke. Blood covered his face and bare chest and dripped from his hair. His eyes were wide and shock-wild inside their mask of blood and gore.

"Is any of that yours?" Dallin snapped, sharp.

Wil looked up at him like he'd forgotten Dallin was even there. He gave his head a quick jerk back and forth.

"Stay here," Dallin ordered. "Find cover and stay down 'til I come back for you."

He didn't wait to see if Wil answered or obeyed. He kicked open the remains of the doors and rolled out onto the porch. Three concussions followed him, thumping into the wood and splintering it in little forests of matchstick slivers as he rolled. The sounds of the shots themselves reached him half a second later. *You never hear the one that gets you* was an oft-repeated adage by veterans of any profession that involved being a target. Dallin had experienced evidence enough in his life to know the truth of it without the solid proof of having actually been shot. Shot *at* lots of times, and it never got any more pleasant, but he intended to keep the *not shot* streak going.

Answering fire came from the hostel again and from around the far corner of the apothecary.

Dallin kept rolling. Shots followed him all the way, until he dumped himself off the edge of the porch and behind the bushes hedging it. He slithered in the dirt 'til he reached the corner of the building. Bullets were raining down where he'd been seconds ago, shredding the shrubbery. Concentrating on where they thought he was rather than paying attention to where he'd gone.

A grim little sneer pressed at Dallin's mouth, and he gritted his teeth. *Idiots*.

They had no idea what they were doing, likely relying on numbers and surprise and hoping to catch everyone lazy and stupid in the morning. Dallin should probably be thanking the Mother they didn't learn lessons very easily. Instead he cursed the fact that the small hand explosive that had taken out the doors was probably nothing more than a clumsy attempt to storm the office and the shrapnel that got Locke merely stray detritus. Dallin guessed the man who'd chucked the charge was the one now facedown in the street. Dallin allowed a brief, malicious little smile as he spat into the dirt.

The low chirp of a robin came from behind him, nearly forgotten code from his army days. Dallin dared a look around the corner at his back and down the end of the building. Newell was back there, crouched at the far corner, rifle laid across his thighs to hold up three fingers and then point over Dallin's shoulder toward the abandoned shack sitting obliquely aslant to the apothecary. By the faded sign hanging from rusty chains on its frontispiece, Dallin guessed it had once served as a mercantile.

Dallin had figured the direction, but not the number. He gave Newell a short nod in thanks, wishing he'd stopped to retrieve his own rifle as he'd abandoned the office. He'd put most of his weapons into Locke's armory. All he had on him were his two handguns and the knife in his boot, and he wouldn't even have those if he hadn't been too lazy to strip them last night.

Keeping low, Dallin pointed back at Newell and then to the office. Newell tipped a slight nod before disappearing around the corner, hopefully to make his way around the back and take up a guard post on the front. One shot came from the direction Newell had just gone. The robin's call followed immediately in its wake. Newell must have surprised one of them trying to sneak in through a backdoor that wasn't there.

Dallin shook his head. They hadn't even bothered to do proper recon. Bloody *idiots.* Which was a blessing in its way, but he couldn't get Locke's inauspicious end out of his head. A woman like that should not have gone out by way of unlucky accident, damn it. If these men had successfully stormed the Guild as Wil said they'd done, Dallin couldn't imagine how. The ineptitude of the Guild's defenses must be boggling.

He eyed the landscape with a grimace. To get around to the back of the mercantile, he was going to have to sprint out in the open between the sheriff's office and the apothecary, and he had no way to signal the men in the hostel to provide some covering fire. In fact, he had no way to signal that they shouldn't shoot *him.*

It turned out he'd worried for nothing—Newell had apparently got to his position on the other corner of the office and done Dallin's signaling for him. When Dallin finally broke cover and started his sprint, shots pelted the front of the mercantile from both the hostel and the livery until he was relatively safe behind the apothecary. Bless Newell and all veterans.

There were three men in the street crouching low and moving carefully. It looked like they were trying to make their way into the hostel itself and take the snipers out by surprise. Dallin wondered why Newell hadn't opened fire yet. They were well within his range and must be wide open. If Newell waited much longer, they'd be behind cover and a very real danger to the shooters upstairs. Dallin judged the range, and decided the new revolver could make the stretch. He stepped out between the buildings and took the creepers out himself. Fast and with no fuss. He checked to make sure they'd stopped moving before he sidled around the corner again.

From there it was a simple matter of finding a back door to the derelict mercantile. Dallin was almost impressed that it was guarded this time; they were learning. Dallin had surprise on his side, though, and better aim and speed. One shot clipped the man on the shoulder, and another took off the bottom half of his face. Dallin hoped the sound of the exchange was covered by the barrage still showering down on the front of the building. He took no chances, stepping over the gory body and easing open the door in a crouch. He peered to all points in the gloom of the interior before stepping quietly through it, reloading as he went. Both guns now in his hands, their familiar heft heartening and comfortable against his palms, Dallin made his slow, careful way from what he was pretty sure was once a back storeroom and into the main room of the dilapidated little store.

The volleys coming from the front were winding down to sporadic barrages. Still, Dallin really didn't fancy going down under friendly fire. He kept low and quiet, inching his way around a rotting chemist's bench until he could clearly see the backs of three men. All of them had their eyes and guns pointed out the gaps in the boarded windows toward the street. Two of them had taken up crouched positions at the west to cover the office and the hostel. That left one covering the livery.

Dallin took one man on either side. One of them flew halfway through what was left of the boarded window. The other simply slumped and slithered to the floor. It took a moment for the man who was left to realize what had happened, his gun blazing steadily until it clicked three times, the dull alert that he'd emptied his chambers. He turned, huddled down on his haunches with his back to the wall to reload—

"Calm and slow, now," Dallin said evenly. "Put it on the floor and lace your hands behind your head."

The man's glance shot to either side of him, finally taking in the fates of his compatriots with wondering eyes. Dallin watched him for a telltale shift of the jaw, saw it, and launched himself across the room, slamming the butt of his gun to the man's temple before he had a chance to complete his suicide. It was going to be interesting, Dallin thought as he laid the man on his back on the floor, finding a way to prevent him from chewing the capsule from inside his cheek in a way that would still allow him to talk, but he wanted at least *one* of these men alive, damn it. Provided Dallin hadn't just cracked the man's skull, that was.

Dallin stood, well away from the openings in the windows, thinking how ridiculous it would be for him to get shot now by one of the men at the hostel or livery, then made his way over to the door. He flattened himself to the jamb as he cracked it open.

"Hold your fire!" Dallin called into the street. "All is secure here, and I'm coming out."

He pushed the door the rest of the way slowly, spotting the barrels of two rifles pointing directly at him from the second story of the hostel and an archer on the roof. He didn't turn toward the livery, knowing there were at least another few poking from doors and windows in that direction. A moment of silence while he stood still, arms extended, and gave them whatever time they needed to recognize him. Then one of the men called down from the hostel.

"The office! Newell's down, and one of 'em got through!"

Dallin jerked his glance down the street to see a crumpled form to the side of the porch, half around the corner of the building. With a vile curse, he sprinted the distance, calling back over his shoulder to no one in particular for someone to secure the man still alive in the mercantile and for someone else to go for the healer *right now*. Somewhere in the back of his mind, Dallin hoped Mistress Slade wouldn't take as long as she had that night at the inn, which brought what might right now be happening at that inn to the front of his mind. He shoved it away, concentrating on getting across the street and giving Newell a quick once-over. Still alive, which was good, but bleeding foamy pink bubbles through a chest wound, which was bad. Dallin dragged Newell out fully on the ground and laid him flat on his back.

One of the men was hauling arse down the street from the livery. Dallin put a finger to his lips, gestured silently for the man to do what he could for Newell, then crept up onto the porch. He peered around the doorframe and into the office. He had to blink several times and shake his head before he could make his brain believe what his eyes were seeing.

Locke's body still lay where it had fallen, covered now with a blood-blotched sheet from Wil's cot. Farther into the office, the trail of destruction—a broken and upended chair, the cast iron kettle, shattered crockery, papers everywhere, even a desk drawer—told at least half the tale. The rest of it was lying in a crumpled heap just in front of the cell where Dallin had been sleeping, the body mostly intact and appearing unscathed—but from the neck up, Dallin wouldn't have known it had once been a man.

Wil crouched over him, bound right hand settled in a pool of spreading blood, linens soaked crimson, left hand methodically beating at the pulp that had once been the man's skull with the butt of Locke's gun. He was still shirtless and barefoot, still covered in Locke's blood. The effect was something like an archaic, cannibalistic savage. He was weeping, bruised mouth pulled up at the corners in what could either be a gentle smile or a delicately malicious snarl, tears cleaning stark tracks down his cheeks through Locke's drying blood. And all the while, his arm rose and fell rhythmically, like he was keeping the time of some darkling requiem, the dull, squelching *thunk* of it every time it hit home a perverse harmony.

Dallin had been a fool to think this man weak for even a second. Unbalanced, almost surely—the bleak look of beatific benediction in his eyes as he steadily beat away at a dead man's head was only the latest marker. But there was something hard and cold inside him that didn't allow weakness, and would bite and snap at any who mistook a momentary lapse for fragility. If Dallin had taken Wil up on any one of the desperate, tearful invitations yesterday or the night before, however sincere they'd been in the moment, he rather thought he'd've got his throat torn out for his trouble when that rabid survival instinct kicked back in again.

Slowly Dallin holstered both guns, approaching carefully and with just enough noise to alert Wil to his presence but not enough to startle him. Grim, Dallin prodded the kettle out of his path with the toe of his boot, watching Wil tense and turn, then took the last several steps just as slowly. Wil was watching him, eyes remarkably calm and sane as Dallin crouched down by the dead man's feet, eyeing Wil with an expression he hoped was impassive and free of unease or judgment. Dallin had no idea what to expect, and he didn't want to make a bad situation turn into a complete mental break by letting his disquiet show on his face. He didn't have the time for it.

But Wil merely blinked up at him, owlish, then stared down at the gory gun for a moment before lifting it and holding it out to Dallin in a shaking hand. "I didn't know how to work it." His voice was small but remarkably steady. "I kept squeezing, but I couldn't... it wouldn't shoot, so I...." He waved his bloody hand at the corpse. "Well, this worked well enough, I guess."

Dallin held out his hand and allowed Wil to place the gruesome thing across his palm. "You, um...." Dallin cleared his throat. "You didn't take the safety off." He ignored the feel of mashed brain and bone against his palm, ignored the impulse to chuck the thing under the desk and wipe his hand. Now that he had possession of the gun, Dallin couldn't fathom what he should do with it. "Are you all right?"

Wil only quirked a bemused frown. "Of course."

Dallin frowned. Was this a mental break already in progress, or was Wil even colder than Dallin had thought? "Have you, um... done this before?" He asked the question carefully, keeping his tone gentle but frank.

Blood-sticky black eyebrows rose this time. Wil stared for a moment, then looked down at what was left of the man. "This?"

"Have you ever killed someone before?" Dallin clarified.

That got a snort, and Wil shook his head slowly, wiping at his eyes with the crook of his elbow. "Don't you have other victims to see to?"

Dallin did. Anyway, he didn't have time for this.

It wasn't an escape, Dallin told himself as he stood and

made his way over to Locke's covered body, slipped the gun beneath the sheet, and wiped his hands on it. He walked out of the office without looking back.

It wasn't an escape.

Newell was conscious now, Mistress Slade already arrived and working to staunch the bleeding. She looked over her shoulder when Dallin approached. "It's hit a lung."

Dallin had known that just by the froth that burbled out from the wound.

"Did he get the lad?" Newell wheezed.

Dallin crouched down, gave Newell's shoulder a careful pat, and shook his head. Newell seemed to relax, and Dallin looked back at Mistress Slade. "Can you fix it?" Dallin hardly knew the man, but Newell seemed such a decent sort, and he was a comrade of circumstance, after all.

Mistress Slade nodded grimly but with confidence. "Hal, Edda, get a litter from the surgery and get him over there."

Hal, Dallin had seen milling about at the inn that night. Edda, he recognized as the archer on the hostel's roof.

"Anyone get a count?" Dallin asked.

A great bull of a man stepped forward, the right side of his face a mass of scar tissue, making the brilliant blue of his keen eyes even more startling. "Rylan's lad, Ryman, and his swain was out larking near the downs for a couple days." His speech was obviously practiced, emerging clear and unencumbered by the dead right side of his mouth. "They found a campsite looked like was just recently abandoned, so they followed the tracks. They didn't know about Garson's, understand. They was just curious and thinking maybe it was minstrels or a traveling show and they could get 'em to stop over in Dudley." He shook his head. "There was a score of men—from what the lads say, they was holed up out to Wayland's old place, hunkered in the old barn, cleaning and checking weapons. The boys saw the guns and came runnin' back quick-sweet. Rylan got here to warn us about a half hour afore the lot showed up and tried the trick with the sheriff's door." He frowned. "Where's the sheriff?"

Dallin winced. "I'm sorry. It appears she was the first casualty. And as far as the good citizens of Dudley, hopefully the only one." There were the expected gasps and outraged curses; a few of them forked the evil eye and spat. Dallin let it play out for a moment, allowing his glance to rove over the motley assembly. "I don't suppose there's a deputy?"

The big man dipped his head. "That'd be me," he said reluctantly. "Locke—she swore it was only for regulations, needed another name on the records. She *swore*...." His wide shoulders slumped. "I never thought...." His eyes were full of bereavement for his lost friend, but when he looked back at Dallin, the glance turned accusing. "Things like this don't *happen* here."

Dallin had nothing to say to that, so he turned his attention back to things he could do something about. "Twenty men. And how many are accounted for here?"

"Four down the livery." The woman who volunteered it looked like she might blow away in a strong breeze, but the rifle she carried was big as a cannon. "Another four here in the street."

"Two behind the hostel," someone else put in.

"And three in the mercantile," Dallin said, then shook his head—he'd forgotten about the one out back. "Four, actually. One in Locke's office, and I think Newell got one out back, but someone should check—that's sixteen. Were those lads sure they saw twenty? Exactly twenty?"

The big man shook his head. "I en't talked to them myself. I'll have to ask."

"Do that," Dallin told him. "In fact, have someone go find them and bring them to Locke's—your office." Belatedly, he held out his hand. There was dried blood in the crevices, but the man took it up with no hesitation. "Brayden," Dallin told him.

"Kenton," the man returned.

"Sheriff Kenton, with your permission, I should like to suggest that you have someone hunt down your local shaman—I assume you have one? Good—bring him or her along as soon as possible. I need to borrow Mistress Slade for a tick, so if you'd be so kind as to keep an eye on my...." What exactly was Wil now, and how was Dallin going to explain whatever Wil was to the new sheriff? "If you could keep an eye on the young man in the office, I'll explain what I can shortly, but get the shaman as quickly as possible. Get as many as you can to check their neighbors too, alert all to be on guard. And get a good lot over to Garson's—there are still possibly as many as four unaccounted for. I don't have to tell you how dangerous they are." Dallin didn't wait for an answer but looked at the small crowd of militia. "Did someone secure the man at the mercantile?"

Nothing but blank stares answered. Dallin reined in several curses and turned directly to Mistress Slade. "If you will?"

Hal and Edda had returned with the litter several minutes ago, and Newell was loaded and ready to be hauled to the surgery. Mistress Slade looked over the rest of the militia. "If no one needs seeing to?" They all shook their heads, and she shot a doubtful glance to Dallin. "I've only got a moment."

"That's all you'll need. Hurry, please. You'll need your kit."

Dallin waited impatiently for Mistress Slade to retrieve her bag, then led her quickly across the street and into the mercantile. A creeping sense of urgency all at once gnawed at his nerves, half-convinced he was too late and the man had already done himself in. Mistress Slade stared as they passed the man hanging half in and half out of the remains of the window, but she picked up her pace again when Dallin prodded her. He needn't have worried—his man was exactly as Dallin had left him, no pink froth dripping from slack lips. Mistress Slade started over toward the man lying next to him, but Dallin caught her elbow.

"Nothing you can do for that one. I need you to see to this one." He knelt by the man's head, took it between his hands, and tilted it back. "You saw the ones from the inn? The ones who weren't shot?"

Mistress Slade only nodded.

"I need you to prevent this man from doing the same."

He didn't need to explain—she'd done the autopsies and would have seen everything she needed to in order to understand what he was telling her now. She nodded again, knelt on the other side, took a long, soft leather wallet of instruments from her bag, and unrolled it on the floor. Several mean-looking sharp implements were lined up in their little sleeves inside. Mistress Slade chose a small scalpel and flicked a narrow glance up at Dallin.

"Try to make sure he doesn't bite me."

Nodding reassurance, Dallin hooked his fingers over the man's teeth and stretched his mouth wide. Mistress Slade took all of perhaps ten seconds to prod at the inside of the man's cheek with a long finger before she dipped the scalpel in. A quick slice and the plunge of pincers later, she was drawing the tiny tin capsule out of the man's mouth just as he began to moan and thrash weakly. Mistress Slade held the little thing out to Dallin with a questioning glance. "D'you need this? For... evidence or something?"

Dallin held out his hand and let her drop it into his palm. He held it up between his fingers for a moment, then shook his head with a disgusted grimace. "Thank you" was all he said as he dropped it into his breast pocket.

With more force than was probably necessary, Dallin turned his new prisoner to his side to keep him from choking on the blood no doubt pooling at the back of his throat. He didn't take any chances, drawing the man's hands behind his back and cuffing him securely before he regained semiconsciousness.

Mistress Slade rolled her instruments back into their little satchel, repacked her bag, then stood, one hand on her hip, and cast a dubious glance about. "You've made sure I'll have another few busy days, Constable," she said in mildly chastising tones. "You won't take it amiss when I ask you exactly how much longer you intend to stay in Dudley?"

Dallin didn't think snorting would be appropriate, so he only shook his head. "In fact, I hope to be off within hours. You really think Newell will be all right?"

"He en't the first to survive a sucking wound, and he's tough as wire. He'll live."

"Good. Now, if you'll—"

"The lad's got scars you en't seen." There was no hostility in Mistress Slade's voice this time, but her tone was forceful nonetheless. "Some of 'em in some very odd places, and not all of 'em on the outside." She shook her head, looking Dallin over with a critical eye. "Watch over him," she went on, softer this time. "But watch him too."

"I intend to," Dallin told her soberly. "On both counts."

She nodded as if this satisfied her, then without another word turned and left. Dallin stared after her for a moment before hauling his half-conscious prisoner to his feet and more or less carrying him to the sheriff's office.

When Dallin got back to the office, it was to an argument a little too similar to the one he'd woken to only a short while ago—which reminded him he hadn't even had a bleeding cup of *tea* yet—except this one didn't make him want to chuckle.

"—don't even know who you *are*," Wil was snarling. "You've no right—"

"Back off them bars, boy, or I'll *show* you what rights I've got."

Dallin stepped over the threshold, dragging his now less-limp cargo with him, to see Wil—face clean now, and dressed as though ready to take to the road, coat and all—glaring out through the closed cell door at Kenton. Kenton was glaring right back. Dallin shoved his man down through the office and to the opposite cell. Stopped. Frowned.

"Who did this?" He nodded to where Locke's body now lay on the cot where Dallin had slept. It was certainly more proper and respectful than having her laid out on the floor, but there were only two cells, after all. Speaking of which—"Why is he locked in there?" Dallin asked Kenton.

"Because he was all packed up and getting ready to fly when I walked in." It was curt and annoyed. Kenton nodded toward a ratty pack on the floor Dallin vaguely remembered being pried out of Wil's hands the other night at the inn. "You said keep an eye, and I figured that meant he ought not be let to hie off."

Dallin sighed—all right, more like growled—dragged his prisoner back through the office, and stopped in front of Wil's cell. He rolled his eyes. "You don't make anything bloody easy, do you?"

Wil wasn't biting back, wasn't saying anything, in fact, just staring at the man Dallin had by the arm, fear and hatred in his gaze. He backed up an instinctive step and flashed an unreadable glance up at Dallin before his eyes locked once again on the man. In his turn, the man had woken up fully now, muscles tensing under Dallin's hand and a tiny, arrogant smile beginning to curl at his mouth.

"Caught and caged after all, Aisling," he said through bloody lips. "One prophecy come to pass."

Before he'd even thought about it, Dallin grabbed the man by his hair and yanked his head back with a quick wrench. "No talking 'til I say so," he growled, then shoved, very nearly knocking the man's head against the bars, and refusing to admit he was almost disappointed he hadn't. Dallin needed the man able to talk, after all, and bashing his brains wouldn't go very far in accomplishing that goal. That, unfortunately, brought the other to mind, and Dallin flicked his glance down toward the end of the narrow room, where he spotted a bloody lump beneath a blanket tucked up against the far wall. Dallin sighed.

This had been one giant fuckup since he'd stepped foot out of Putnam.

He turned to Kenton. "I need these two exchanged. Let that one out so I can put this one in."

Kenton raised an eyebrow, then jerked his chin toward Wil. "He'll run."

"Then I'll just have to catch him." Dallin flashed a sharp smile, all teeth. "If you please."

Kenton shook his head dubiously but did as Dallin had ordered. Dallin hoped they'd be long gone before anyone realized Kenton was actually the one in charge here.

Wil stepped back as the door opened, eyes locked on the new prisoner, who stared back at him with that same smile as Dallin shoved him through the door. Wil gave them a wide berth as he stepped past, his stare hard and cold but with that ever-present coal of dread behind it. He had the look of a barefoot man trying to be brave in a room full of venomous snakes.

The prisoner leaned in, smirking as Wil sidled past him. "He is not your salvation, Aisling." Low and smooth, like he was attempting to woo. "Caught and caged you were born, caught and caged you will end."

Kenton rolled his eyes and took a step back. He'd only just met Wil, and even *he* knew it was only asking for trouble.

So Dallin was only slightly caught off his guard when, just as Wil got to the threshold of the cell, he spun back and drove himself at the prisoner with an undulating, wordless roar. He went in low with his shoulder, catching the man square in the midriff. They crashed to the floor with a hard *thud*, low animal grunts and snarls knocking loose as they fell. Wil already had the man on his back, straddling his chest, good hand tight around his throat, before Dallin managed to get behind him and jerk him back. Except Wil wouldn't let go. His hand, having apparently lost its grip around the man's throat when Dallin yanked him back, was now latched onto the man's shirt. Dallin wrapped one arm about Wil's chest and clamped his free hand over the knot of linen and fist.

Wil growled but didn't fight Dallin, though tension ran through him like a bound lightning storm. He turned his head over his shoulder until he could look at Dallin. "Let me." A whisper from between teeth clenched tight. Command and entreaty both.

Dallin shook his head and adjusted his grip. "He's shackled. Helpless. It's murder this way."

"So bloody *what*." Wil's eyes were blazing. "D'you know what they *want*? D'you know what they've *done*?"

"Some." Dallin gently pried Wil's hand open, mildly surprised when Wil simply let him. Dallin peered down at the man, who was no longer smiling but panting with a look of fear in which Dallin took a probably unhealthy amount of satisfaction. "I would know it all." Dallin let the statement take on the tone of a request.

He tugged at Wil's elbow, prodding until Wil backed off and allowed Dallin to help him stand. Once he was steady on his feet, Wil yanked his arm away and turned on Dallin. "If you think I'll go like a compliant little sheep back to Ríocht with you, you're a lot dumber than you look." There was still anger in the tone, but restrained panic flared beneath it.

Dallin only dragged Wil out of the cell, gesturing for Kenton to lock it, then shoved Wil down toward the office. When they were out of earshot, he wrenched Wil around to face him. "Is that why you were going to run? Have you been sitting in that cell going to pieces about this since *last night*?" Wil only stared at him, but he didn't really need to answer. Panic was simplifying things a bit, Dallin knew. Wil had been watching from behind that mask of meek defeat for his chance to run—if Kenton hadn't snagged him, Wil would already be miles away and Dallin would have to waste *more* time tracking him down again. Dallin pinched at the bridge of his nose. "For the love of—" A sharp growl, and he clenched his teeth. "You know, if you're going to eavesdrop, you could at least listen with your head as well as your ears. I told Locke we were going to Ríocht because they would have asked her, and I couldn't expect her to lie."

Wil shook his head. "That isn't an answer."

He said it like he deserved one. Dallin rolled his eyes, irritated with himself that he was going to capitulate and give him one. "Yes, Wil, I'm that idiotic, and I'm going to take the Dominion's most wanted straight to their capital city and hope no one hangs us before we get there. *No*, we're not going to Ríocht."

"Then what *do* you plan to do?"

"I haven't got a lot of options." Dallin willfully *did not* clench his fists. "We're going back to Putnam."

"Are you *insane*?" Wil backed up a small step. "I can't go there either. If you want me dead so badly, at least have the balls to do it your damned *self*!"

And that was just about enough for Dallin. He took hold of Wil's arms, dragged him in close. Wil twitched instinctively but otherwise stood his ground, such as it was, and maintained his fierce glower. Good. If there was a true self to this man, it was the vicious survivor glaring out from behind those bruises, and

Dallin was more than willing to accept it as proof of sanity, however dubious.

"That is the very *last* time I want to hear something like that from out your mouth," Dallin said through his teeth. "If I ever *do* want you dead, rest assured, you'll see me *and* my balls coming with both barrels. Until that time, you would do very well to keep in mind that I have as yet resisted every very good reason and excellent opportunity you've thus far presented me to choke the life out of your bony neck—if for no other reason than to get you to shut your damned mouth every once in a while!

"Now, we are going back to Putnam because I need help. If this is what you say it is—and it's looking more and more like it's at least close—I can't do it by myself. I need resources, allies, people I can trust, and I can't find any of that out here in the middle of bloody nowhere, not with men like this behind every bush and boulder."

Dallin had expected Wil to jerk back, but he didn't—he leaned closer until they were nose to nose and kept his voice just as low as Dallin's. "I've been doing just fine by *my*self." There was no small amount of venom and a strange bit of perverse pride in the retort. "If you need your friends in Putnam, then fine, go and get them, but you won't drag *me* back there so they can hand me right back to Síofra."

"Oh, you've been doing 'just fine,' all right." Dallin snorted, derisive. "When I got to the inn the other night, you were bleeding, broken-boned, and blue in the face."

Wil's lip twitched, and his eyes flared. "I'd've—"

"No you wouldn't've, and you know it. How many close calls have you had over the past few years? How many times have you been caught or almost caught? The Guild is so desperate to find you they've solicited bloody *Cynewisan* for help, and I thought they'd chew off their own tongues before *ever* admitting they didn't have complete control over every bleeding thing that goes on over there." Dallin jerked his chin toward the far cell. "I've seen more than enough evidence to suggest that at least these fanatics aren't about to give up, and they're serious enough about whatever it is they want out of you to raze entire villages and then off themselves in probably the most gruesome manner *I've* ever seen, and that's saying something. If I hadn't come along when I did, you'd right now be...." He let go, backing off a step, and dipped his voice even lower. "You'd be doing whatever it was those men had in mind for you. And somehow I doubt whatever it was would've involved arguing with your keepers."

Right up until that last comment, Wil's eyes had been on fire with anger and defiance. Now they dulled somewhat, and he swallowed, deflated. His mouth was working like he was trying to be outraged and couldn't find the ire necessary. "I never...." He looked away as he flushed bright red. "I never thanked you for... for *that*." His gaze shot over his shoulder, down toward the far cell, then back again to Dallin, moving quickly from hesitant and resentful to frank and open. "Thank you." His voice was low, and if there was deceit in it, Dallin didn't detect it. "You're right. I don't think I'd've got away this time. Perhaps it doesn't seem so, but I'm grateful."

Dallin's eyebrows shot up. He didn't really know what else to do, so he nodded.

"So... you would make me your prisoner?" Wil's voice was quiet but even. "Are *you* my keeper?" Dallin rolled his eyes, he couldn't help it, and sighed up at the ceiling. "I don't mean it like... like...." Wil waved the bandaged hand about. "There were shackles, and then there weren't. There was a locked door, and then it was open, and then it was locked again, and I don't.... It would be better if I knew."

All right. Fine. That was... fair. And annoyingly reasonable. Dallin hadn't exactly been consistent, after all, undecided himself as to whether he was detaining Wil or protecting him. Though it was more like a bit of each, so Dallin wasn't surprised he'd managed to confuse them both.

"I didn't lock the cell because I wanted to see what would happen." Dallin was careful to keep the admission matter-of-fact. "If you'd bolted, you wouldn't've got far. When I wasn't sitting on the porch myself, I had a guard on the door."

Wil's jaw twitched, a flare of anger spiking his gaze. "A *test*?"

Dallin merely shrugged. "You fight shackles like a wild animal, but you accept a cage like you belong in one. You didn't even try the door." He watched with interest as Wil frowned at the floor, thoughtful. "If we're going to do this," Dallin went on, "you're going to have to make up your mind about yourself. If you act like a kicked puppy, you can't be surprised when people go on kicking you. If you act like a vicious cur, they'll want to put you down. Find a place in the middle before you get us both killed.

"And you're right—we need to be clear about this." Dallin held Wil's suspicious gaze steadily. "However you've managed to stay ahead of these people for the last three years, it's done now—they've caught up with you and will keep on catching up with you until you're caged for good. I told you before I'm your best chance, and nothing has changed my mind. If you want me to be this Guardian, then fine, but it'll be on *my* terms, and I do not consent to being your execution—*or* your suicide, while we're at it. I *will* get you someplace safe and figure this out, you have my word, but if you fight me, if you run, you'll have the rest of the world *and* me on your arse, and I guarantee I'll catch you first. And what follows will *not* be pretty."

Wil was silent for a moment, considering, before he took a bracing breath. "What if...." His gaze traveled over the bloody lump of blanket, hung there. "What if you figure it out, and it turns out it's either me or Cynewísan? What if the only answer you find when we get to Putnam is that you have to hand me over to the Guild?"

He was still staring at the gruesome lump on the floor but very conspicuously didn't mention the Brethren. So. He'd already figured out that Dallin had no intention of letting them get what they were after. Good. At least that was one point of trust between them.

"Then," Dallin answered tiredly, "I shall have to figure something else out." Wil looked up sharply at that, gaze heavy with cynical doubt. Dallin opened his hand. "If what you told me about them is true, then—"

"*If?*"

Dallin ignored the way it emerged like the point of a dagger. "—then it's a matter for nations and not mere peons like us. And if an entire country can't manage to keep one peon in line, *I'm* hardly going to do their job for them." Dallin smirked. "Quite a coup for one Commonwealth peon, innit? Snatching away the Dominion's Chosen when I wouldn't've even known what you were unless they told me."

Wil shook his head—almost disbelieving but not quite—blinked a few times, then eyed Dallin soberly. He stared for a long time, searching, thoughtful, before he finally nodded. "All right. Fine. We'll do it your way."

Not exactly enthusiastic endorsement, but it was at least an accord, however halfhearted. *Finally*—an understanding. Which should make the trip to Putnam a lot less fraught with... everything it promised to be fraught with. Now Dallin would just have to keep on his toes and make sure it stuck.

There was more. Wil was still staring, working himself up to something. Dallin recognized the set of the mouth, the look of taking a bit in his teeth. "I should...." Wil lifted his chin, gaze set firm to Dallin's. "I'm sorry." Soft but steady. "For... for...." He lifted his right hand as though he meant to push his hair out of his eyes, noted the red stains on the wrappings quickly going to brown, then curled his lip and lowered it to his side again. "I don't expect you to believe me, but if I could've prevented what...." He paused, jaw set firm, but he couldn't stop it quivering. "If I could've prevented Lind, I would've done."

It made Dallin's stomach hollow out a bit, but he kept his face impassive. "Even knowing what you think I am and what you think I'm meant to do?"

If Wil hadn't stopped to think about it, Dallin likely wouldn't have believed him. But Wil did, staring down at the floor for a moment before lifting his eyes back to Dallin's.

"Yes. I don't think it would've been because of any kind of selfless sacrifice. In fact, it likely would've been out of selfishness. I just...." He shrugged uneasily and looked away. "I would choose not to have something like that on my conscience." He twitched a grimace. "Such as it is."

Dallin stared for a long time, thinking he should tell Wil it shouldn't be on his conscience, it wasn't his fault, he shouldn't be apologizing for having been a walking wounded casualty in a war he hadn't started and couldn't possibly even understand. In the end, Dallin couldn't quite get the words out his mouth yet.

He only nodded, once but firmly. "Then I believe you."

Wil took a long, deep breath, flicked another glance down to the other cell, then bowed his head, peering at the toes of his new boots—the ones Locke had given him. He nodded.

"Am I to understand that you mean to question that man?"

Dallin narrowed his eyes. "Yes. Why?"

Wil didn't answer the question. Instead he asked, "And should I assume that we can't leave until you do?"

Ah. Impatience to be gone. Dallin could certainly identify with that. "That would be a fair assumption, yes."

Wil was silent for a moment, scuffing the toe of his boot along a seam in the floorboards. "I think...." His sigh sounded like it was dragged from the depths of a very resentful and put-upon well. "I think I can help."

CHAPTER 6

Wil watched the steady parade of Dudley's citizens busily filtering in and out of the sheriff's office with something between sympathy and dark amusement. They wanted so badly to help, to *do*, and while it seemed there was plenty to be done, it also seemed there were too many helping hands to do it. The new sheriff and Brayden had all they could do to keep track of the comings and goings. Wil, on the other hand, had nothing to do but wait and watch.

Miss Jillian had been by earlier, trying not to chirp and smile coyly at Brayden as she proffered baskets of breads and boiled eggs. The not-so-subtle advances on Brayden did seem a little tasteless, Wil had to admit, what with Locke's body only feet away, but Wil couldn't help but like Miss Jillian. Probably due to the fact that she seemed to think being extra nice to Wil would win points with Brayden, and as a result Wil had ended up with one of the only two sausage rolls she'd brought. Brayden had accepted his like he was afraid it was going to detonate in his hand, but Wil made short work of his while Miss Jillian prattled about the lonely life of a prosperous hostel owner—she'd said "prosperous" three times—while handing Wil a couple of eggs and a small salt cellar and telling him what a good listener he was. Which was mostly because she was keeping his mouth full, and he hadn't much of a choice. Then again, he hadn't exactly complained.

Mistress Slade was dourly directing Mal and Hal in the grim business of preparing the bodies to be moved to the morgue. Someone had mopped up the lake of blood and brains that had leaked from Sheriff Locke's head, but the dark ghost of it still stretched across the floor only a hand's breadth from Wil's feet, which were clad in the boots Locke had been trying to give him when her head exploded. She'd been right—they were better than his, newer and better made, and a lot less likely to fall off his feet if he stumbled through a mud puddle. And he *was* grateful—he'd been grateful even as he was arguing with her. But the others had been *his*, and he still wanted his own back. He had so few things that *were* his, after all. Childish, perhaps, as Locke had accused. But still.

It took less than thirty minutes after the smoke cleared for people Wil hadn't seen before to begin poking their heads hesitantly through the door to stare—at Brayden, at the man in the cell, at their new sheriff, at the sticky pools of blood on the floor, at Wil. Wil watched them back with still-blurry eyes, impassively let them get a good long look, then watched them grow as uncomfortable beneath his stare as he was beneath theirs.

And while Wil was watching people, Brayden was watching Wil and trying to look like he wasn't. Kenton was too, but he didn't really care if Wil caught him at it. Which was fine.

Wil didn't much care if Kenton watched, so they were even. Despite his proximity to the door, Wil had no intention of running, at least not at the moment, so let them both watch.

He'd been planted behind Locke's desk earlier, out of the way of both the comings and goings and the darting glances from between the shattered doors, but when Mistress Slade had shown up to begin the business of preparing and moving the dead, Wil had moved to a spot on the floor by the doorway where he wouldn't have to watch. It was a good spot. He didn't mind the chill filtering in through the broken doors. He didn't even really mind the prisoner staring at him. In fact, Wil had to keep from smirking at the irony—him on the outside of those bars, free to walk about as he pleased, and the man on the inside, shackled and bruised. He wondered if the paradox had sunk in with the man yet. Likely not—they were all so bloody sure of their cause. The man was no doubt sitting in there praying and blissfully certain he'd be saved somehow, and if he wasn't saved, then martyred. Wil was more than willing to help out with the latter, but he'd gone and bollixed his chance.

"...how to do suppression spells?" Brayden was asking the shaman, a portly little man with a hangdog face that transformed into near-artistic serenity with his gentle smile.

Wil had never seen a shaman before and hadn't realized he'd even formed a notion on them until he'd seen Brother Millard. Wil expected a shaman to be tall and dour and robed in something like a dark, modest ulster. Brother Millard was short, round, clothed in local fashion, such as it was, and quick to smile, with bright hazel eyes that seemed to have never known judgment or bias.

"I assure you, Constable Brayden," Millard said kindly, "I was schooled at the Temple in Penley. I know what I'm doing."

"Glad someone does," Brayden muttered, then gave Millard a weary look. "Can you protect entire households? I've seen charms engraved into lintels and such for the purpose."

"But of course."

"And how many initiates have you got? I'm going to want every shack and farmstead protected. It would be helpful if you could cast individual spells too—you know, for when they're out and about."

That rippled Millard's smile into a disappointed grimace. "It's a small village, you understand. I've three novices but no initiates."

"*Shit.*" Brayden blinked as though just realizing what he'd said, then flushed a light pink and cleared his throat. "Um. Sorry."

Millard chuckled. "It's quite all right. And there's no need to agitate yourself. I understand the problem, and I'm aware of the danger. Be easy, Constable Brayden—it's a simple spell, really. It'll just take a little time. If I didn't think my apprentices and I could handle it, I assure you I'd let you know." He clapped his pudgy hands together. "Now, I think we'll all be a bit easier once this is done, and I'll want to get started twenty minutes ago. If you'll allow me...?"

"Of course." Brayden hopped up from where he'd been perched on the edge of the desk, waved the shaman to his feet, and led him to the door. "I'm sorry to have kept you, Brother Millard. It's only... I can't stay much longer, and I don't like going off and leaving people unprotected like this, and especially with Sheriff Locke.... Er. That is, if I had more men—"

"But you don't, so we shall all do as we can." Brother Millard was the very definition of cool tranquility and ease. He extended his hand. "We all appreciate what you've done for Dudley, Constable. Let Dudley do for itself now."

Brayden shook Millard's hand warmly. "I'm not sure I've done much for Dudley, but I appreciate—" He jolted like a shock had just sparked up his arm.

Millard was staring, clutching Brayden's hand in both of his own with eyes gone sharp and narrow. "Ah." It was soft. Millard tilted his head, turned... looked at Wil.

If Wil could've pushed his back through the wall and disappeared, he would've done. Millard's smile was there, serene as ever, and his eyes were kind, but the way he looked, *saw*....

Wil didn't even have time to twitch before Millard was crouched right in front of him. Wil's hand had been propped lazily on his upthrust knee; now he found it trapped in Millard's, the grip stronger than Wil would've thought—hard, in fact, and relentless.

"The Mother loves you." Brother Millard's tone was soft and earnest. "She fears for you, for your path has only just begun, and you refuse Her gift."

Wil tried to jerk his hand away, but Millard's grip was like a vise. The touch was fire against his skin, yet his hand was going numb and frozen. "She is not my mother," he whispered hoarsely, "and I want nothing from her." He hadn't known he was going to speak until the words were already out his mouth, couldn't help the clench of teeth and the flare of duped fury that writhed beneath his sternum. His lip curled back in a knee-jerk snarl, feral as the vicious cur Brayden had named him only a short while ago, but he couldn't help it—what animal didn't bite when it was cornered? White rage and a confused sense of having been duped all at once swarmed through Wil, and he couldn't stop it spilling from his mouth. "I have no mother." Betrayed. *Seething*. "And yours is *dead*."

He'd expected... he didn't know—shock, perhaps, or angry denial. He'd *hoped* for outraged recoil, at least, a jerk back and the release of his hand. He'd just blasphemed in a shaman's face, after all. But Brother Millard merely shook his head and squeezed Wil's hand.

"She gives you a choice." Millard's gaze was shrewder now. "But then, you know that, for it is Their most precious gift to Their children, and you are most favored." He leaned in. "*Their own*."

Wil shook his head slowly, mouth moving, but no angry denial would come. He was shaking, all the calm amusement from a moment ago gone and forgotten.

"Accept the gift, starless child," Millard went on kindly. "Let the warp bind to your weft. Your destiny is obscured by guile that is not yours and fear that is. Your true design remains hidden until you are ready to see it, and yet you persist in blindness."

He reached out, passed his hand over Wil's brow, and the last of the blurriness was gone. Just gone. Wil blinked perfectly clear eyes, almost hoping it was merely some strange illusion—he'd heard a shaman could convince a man to stop bleeding, if he was skilled enough, but he'd never really believed it—but his vision remained clear and sharp-edged.

By contrast, his whole arm had gone dead, a dull tingle working beneath the skin like vibrating wires. He brought the bandaged one up, tried to push Millard's hand away, and couldn't. Tried to drag his eyes away from the warm hazel, and couldn't do that either. He meant to call out to Brayden, tell him to get Millard off him, get him away before Wil tore out Millard's throat with his teeth, ripped him apart just to get him to stop *looking* at him like that, but when Wil opened his mouth, "Please... what am I?" wheezed out of it.

He hadn't wanted to ask the question, didn't even know where it came from—he knew what he was—and now that the question was out there, Wil thought he'd give just about anything to not have to hear the answer.

Millard's smile slipped into melancholy, and he peered at Wil with unhappy compassion. "You are the badger, fierce when cornered, snapping razor teeth, but you must mind where you strike." Wil gasped, a spangling little shudder rippling down his backbone. "You are the crow, flying too fast to see the dangers of clear panes of glass until you find yourself broken-winged and broken-necked in your haste to find the things you think you want but do not need. You are the chimera, the Father's Gift, and your time runs short." He reached out, touched Wil's cheek with a warm hand. "Reject the Mother's Gift and you deliver yourself into the hands of your enemies."

It was too much, *too much*, and it needed to stop *right now* before Wil jittered apart on the floor, dissolved by some strange alchemy into nothing more than another insubstantial stain, a companion to the one Locke had left behind. His arm was a dead thing, he couldn't tear it from Millard's grasp, so Wil jerked his whole body instead. He shot up against the wall, and *wrenched* until Millard finally let go. Panting, Wil shot a desperate glance up at Brayden.

"Make him *stop*."

Brayden was staring, something between vague horror and perplexed doubt. He was standing back and away, like he didn't want to get too near for fear the crazy might jump out and infect him too. It took a moment before Brayden finally looked at Wil, really looked at him. Wil didn't even want to guess what was on his face, but it made Brayden shake himself and take a step forward. He leaned down to take Millard by the elbow and prod him to his feet.

"Brother Millard." Brayden was apparently not happy with how his voice rasped, because he cleared his throat. "You, um... that is—"

"I shall be on my way." Millard's smile was once again placid. "I've much to do." He nodded sagely up at Brayden. "As do you, lad. Time is indeed short, and you mustn't linger. Accept your calling, for the Mother has laid Her blessing upon your path. If you choose to mire yourself in the quickmud of reason, you shall only squander it, and all gifts shall be lost."

And then he was gone, waddling out the door and into the chill morning, leaving Wil unsure if he wanted to chase Millard down and beg him to tell him more or snatch up Brayden's gun and shoot him in the back so he couldn't. Of course, then Wil would have to get Brayden to show him what a safety was and how to take it off, and it was doubtful Brayden would fancy allowing Wil even a sharp eggshell at the moment, but still.

Wil rubbed at his arm with his bandaged hand, not caring that the linen was stiff with dried blood and beginning to smell. He'd expected the dull ache of pins and needles, but his arm felt perfectly fine, as though it hadn't been a long slab of useless flesh and bone a moment ago. Wary, he slid his glance over to Brayden, almost afraid to look.

Brayden was shaking his head, staring out the ruined doors. "That," he said slowly, "was very...." He couldn't seem to come up with a word, just kept shaking his head 'til he finally turned back to Wil, eyes narrowed. "Are you all right?"

"The.... Did...?" It was absurd. The question made no sense at first. Wil's mind was moving too fast and in no particular order. Until the words clicked into place, reminded him they had meaning. He blinked, still shock-stupid, opened his mouth—

Wil didn't know he was going to laugh until the manic bark of it spilled out his throat. Brayden tilted his head, frowning in concern. Wil shoved his fist in his mouth, blinked again, but the raspy little chuckles kept bubbling up his throat.

"Sorry." Wil snorted, frayed nerves lacing him tight, making him lightheaded. "It's only... well, you ask me that a *lot*, y'know."

Brayden's eyebrows rose above a sophic little smile. "Well, *are* you? Not just...." He waved at the door. "Not just that, but how are you feeling? D'you need a draft or anything?"

Wil resisted the urge to be idiotically touched by the apparently genuine consideration in Brayden's gaze. Damn it, every time Wil decided what was what, Brayden would go and do something... *nice*. It was bloody disconcerting.

Wil rocked his shoulders inside his coat. "I'm all right."

Not really—he was still very sore, and the headache was still hanging on, though a lot less intensely than before. His hand was bloody *killing* him, even worse than yesterday, and trying to manhandle Millard hadn't helped. But if Wil admitted any of it, there was the chance Brayden might continue this new niceness... *thing*, whatever it was, and decide to wait another day, and Wil was growing increasingly restless to be gone.

Brayden eyed him speculatively, obviously disbelieving, but he didn't argue the point. He nodded over his shoulder. "Kenton's made tea, but I'm thinking some of that cider laced with the—Oh, hell, I have to take care of this."

Two youths had just ducked through the doorway. Wil guessed they were the young men Brayden and Kenton had been waiting for, the ones who'd seen the men of the Brethren before they'd attacked.

Brayden peered at Wil with subtle concern. "Later, all right? And then we'll see what to do about...." He didn't finish, just jerked his chin toward the cell with a scowl.

Wil didn't bother to follow his gaze. He sighed, the earlier laughter gone and forgotten.

"Can't we just kill him?" Because Wil was suddenly bone-weary and wanting nothing more than to curl up in a corner somewhere and sleep until everything just went away. And he knew right down to his core he was going to regret his earlier offer of "help" if Brayden decided he wanted it.

Brayden was shaking his head slowly, but Wil didn't think it was in answer to the question, though he hadn't exactly expected agreement. Brayden was watching Mistress Slade, now making her way through the small crowd gathered about Locke's desk, leading the little procession of litters.

Locke's body came first, covered respectfully with a clean sheet, little sachets of spices and herbs laid over her chest. The men who carried her were stone-faced and silent, Mistress Slade leaking tears as she led somberly. Kenton stood to private attention as the body passed, his ruined face working with emotion, intense eyes misted and blinking repeatedly. Even the boys stood and watched sadly and reverently as the litter carried Locke on her last trip out of her office, each of them whispering prayers or blessings—or superstitious charms, for all Wil knew.

Mistress Slade paused minutely as she passed Brayden and Wil, offering a soft, sad smile to Wil and a pointed look down to the bandaging around his hand. Wil was selfishly glad she'd noticed. He'd very much like to get the disgusting thing off before it started really unnerving him. He put it aside as Mistress Slade led the litter out onto the porch and down the steps. Wil watched with what he was surprised to realize was real sorrow and regret. Locke hadn't liked him, but she also hadn't pretended to, and she hadn't let it stop her from doing what she thought was right—even if "right" meant taking care of Wil, making sure he didn't starve, seeing that he had something to wear besides the bloodied rags he'd come in with. She'd been kind in her way, and honorable, and tough as steel. It wasn't right that she'd gone out as she had, and Wil hadn't missed the fact that her bulk had blocked the explosion from taking him out too.

He pulled his gaze away from the litter and pointed it down at his new boots. Offered silent apologies to a ghost.

The mood changed palpably as the second litter followed, grieving faces turning hard and vengeful in the wake of their regard for Locke. Wil flicked his glance to the prisoner in the cell, but he couldn't tell what the man was thinking. The man was staring like the rest of them, but his expression was blank, his eyes dry. Wil wondered if it was because he thought the dead man was already communing with the Father, or if he was simply trying not to give anything away. Or maybe he just didn't care. They weren't exactly reverent when it came to the lives of others.

"Why did you do that?"

Wil turned away from the prisoner, peering up at Brayden and then following his gaze to the bloody mass of body and blanket. They hadn't covered this one with a clean sheet as they'd done for Locke. Brayden was frowning at the litter as it passed, thoughtful, like he was trying to solve a difficult puzzle, but there had been no accusation or judgment in the question.

Wil's eyebrows went up. He thought the answer was pretty obvious, but he spoke it anyway, and with no irony or hostility: "It was him or me. I chose me."

Brayden shook his head, a grim little smile twitching. "No, I mean, why did you do *that*?" He nodded to the pulpy mess that had been a man's head this morning.

"Oh." Wil shrugged. "Sheriff Locke didn't have a face anymore. He did. I didn't think it was fair."

Perhaps it sounded a little demented, but it had made sense in Wil's head at the time, and it was the truth. All right, at least half the truth, but he didn't think Brayden wanted to hear about how it had made Wil feel better, how it had taken every bit of the terror of the previous moments, and with every hate-filled, rhythmic thud of wood and metal to flesh and bone, pushed it out from his chest, down his arm, and just... away. He'd had a blissful few minutes of utter inner peace after Brayden had taken the gun away from him, just staring down at the mash of red and gray, knowing that for the second time in a mere stretch of minutes, it hadn't been Wil. Three years' worth of stored-up hatred, throttled terror, impotent rage—Wil had taken it all out on the man, cleansed his own soul with the spilled blood. And he wasn't sorry he'd done it. Brayden probably wouldn't want to hear that either.

Wil looked back at Brayden, waiting for some kind of scowl or shocked recoil, but it didn't come. Brayden merely thought about it for a moment, nodded like it made perfect sense, then stepped to the doors and closed what was left of them. Wil hadn't noticed the last of the gawkers straggle out behind the corpses, but he was relieved now that the lack of bustle set in.

"The worst is done for now." Brayden jerked his head toward the office. "I need to take care of this, and then we'll take care of that."

Meaning the man in the cell. Wil tried to make his answering shrug careless and not twitchy. He waited 'til Brayden joined Kenton and the boys before letting his legs wobble out from under him and sliding down the wall to his previous seat on the floor. He pulled his knees in, let his head drop back, and closed his eyes, blocking out the low murmuring from the office and trying to sigh away the tension, but it wasn't done with him yet.

Too much had gone on this morning, and the sun was only just up. Wil hadn't known he'd even cared about Locke, but her death was having *some* kind of effect on him, though he wasn't sure what kind just yet. Perhaps it was simply because it had almost been him, very well *could* have been him, if she hadn't been built like she was and standing right in front of him. Standing right in front of him and arguing with him.

And damn it, why did that make Wil flush and want to bow his head?

He wasn't dead, and he was glad. She was, and he hadn't killed her. If it had been a choice between him or her, he would have chosen the same, so why did the fact that he *hadn't* chosen it feel like some kind of lame excuse? Why did he keep staring at the toes of his boots as though they held some kind of answer?

Maybe because he *was* a mutinous little badger. It appeared Síofra had got at least one thing right. Even Millard had named him so.

Wil peered up at the ceiling, blinking eyes that were still remarkably not blurry, and gave a little shudder. He looked down and picked at the stiff wrappings about his hand. Millard had thrown him, and thrown him good. Nerves were still running through Wil like tiny ropes of lightning, and his stomach wouldn't settle down. A dose of that laced cider really would have been good, and Wil was sorry Brayden's offer had been interrupted. Wil wanted to hate Millard, but those warm hazel eyes wouldn't let him.

Badger. Gift. *Mother*.

Wil clenched his teeth and plucked some more at the wrappings. They were getting more and more uncomfortable. He hoped Mistress Slade wouldn't forget, but he wasn't terribly optimistic—she was liable to be very busy for a while, and she was mourning, after all. Wil couldn't imagine what it must be like to have to autopsy a friend, and tending to the trouble-making transient who caused it probably wasn't on Mistress Slade's list of priorities. Wil shuddered again, wondering why old brown blood on a wad of bandages was making him so—

"Time *is* short, Aisling."

Wil controlled the flinch. He refused to let the man see that he'd even heard, let alone reacted. He kept his gaze nailed to his hand, kept picking, flecks of brown coming loose from the wide weave and embedding themselves beneath his fingernails. It wasn't the first blood on Wil's hands, but somehow it was the most visceral. Even if it wasn't Locke's, it felt as though it should have been.

"We only want to save you." The man kept talking, softly cajoling. "Help you fulfill your destiny. Why do you keep running?"

Wil shifted his gaze to the scar lumping around his wrist and scoring down the back of his hand, and remembered how four sets of greedy eyes had gone feral, the want and need slicing Wil to bone, overwhelming him, and so he'd screamed and flung it all back at them. Snarls and blood and the thick squelching sounds of violent death. Livid, searing pain as the metal had bitten into skin, flayed it right down to the bone as Wil had wrenched free like some kind of wild animal chewing itself out of a trap. The stench and the fear and the fever as Wil had stared around at the carnage and taken his first weak, wobbly steps away from captivity.

"You need us, Aisling." A whisper this time, smooth and seductive. "All will be forgiven, if you'll only—"

"Shut *up*." The hissed growl was louder than Wil had meant, and too shaky, but he couldn't help it.

"He is not your answer—he is only your path to destruction. He will dragoon you to the *Cliabhán*, make of you a sacrifice to feed the Mother's famine. The Guardian is no more, he is false, a trick, he will bind you and cage you, and all will—"

"*Shut up!*"

"—be lost, you will be shunned from the Father's sight, cast naked into dark dreams and left alone, forever alone, friendless—"

Wil was on his feet now, charging the cell, only remembering at the last second that he couldn't actually walk through walls, and instead pressing himself against the bars, an impotent snarl curling his mouth. "Shut up, shut *up*, shut the fuck *up*, you lying son of a whore, *shut your bloody mouth*!"

Unbelievably, the man did. Wil stood there, ears ringing with the silence, and watched helplessly as the man *smiled.* Looked at him, eyes roving like he could see Wil's end and it made his mouth water, like it pleased him, and *smiled.*

The subtle clearing of a throat made Wil jerk his glance to Brayden, peering back at him over the heads of the two boys. The boys were staring at Wil with wide eyes and too obviously trying not to smirk. Wil almost snapped at them too, but the near smirks were directed past his shoulder and into the cell, so he choked it back.

"Want help?" Brayden asked calmly.

Wil didn't know what to make of the offer, so he said the first thing that came to his tongue: "Please—can't we just kill him?"

He was dead serious, but Brayden's eyebrow went up like he was amused, and the boys snorted. Kenton reached over and smacked one of them on the back of the head, but that only made them both duck their heads and snigger into their collars.

Wil didn't know what to make of any of that either. He just stood there, staring, gripping the bars in a fist so tight his hand was going numb. If he could rip the bars off himself, he wouldn't have even asked the question, and he was pretty sure Brayden knew it. Damn it, why had Wil let himself be pulled off the man in the first place?

Brayden sighed. "Why don't you wait on the porch. We shouldn't be much longer."

Wil stared for a moment, wondering if Brayden meant to let him walk out the doors by himself unwatched, but then he remembered the militia. He shot the prisoner one last hateful glare, then spun about and pushed through the splintered doors.

The sun was thin and bright, the cold not so terribly noticeable beneath the protection of the new coat—wool-lined suede, a bit big in the shoulders, but the sleeves were long enough, and the fit otherwise good. Wil had slipped it on when he'd been readying for flight only a short while ago, and though the flight had been short-lived, he'd been loath to remove the coat. It still had the smell of another—something a little bit spicy and smoky —and he wondered if this was from the same Esmond of the boots, the same Esmond who had left behind Mistress Afton. Wil wondered if Edmond had been Mistress Afton's son or her husband or her father, and if he'd be pleased or dismayed to see the use to which his coat and boots had been put.

Shaking it off, Wil sucked in a great lungful of cold morning air, watching the thin plume of it mist from his mouth as he lowered himself to sit on the porch steps. One of the men who'd been helping Mistress Slade was out there—either Hal or Mal, Wil didn't know which was which—and he turned when he heard Wil's boots on the step, gave him a pleasant nod. Wil nodded back, and the man turned again to watch the street, rifle gripped in both hands, at the ready, across his middle. Several more made slow circuits around what Wil could see of the square—which, now that his vision was no longer fuzzy, was pretty much all of it. It was a very small village, now that he was getting a real look. People still milled around like it was market day, stopping in little clusters to natter about the recent goings-on, no doubt, once or twice turning to point surreptitiously at

Wil. He didn't pay attention, gaze instead wandering to the splintered holes in the wood of the porch. Bullet holes, of course. If he still had his knife, he could probably dig out the slugs.

Curious, he dipped a finger into one of the jagged little cavities until the tip butted up against solid metal. It couldn't really still be warm, but it felt like it.

He'd heard the reports when Brayden had barreled out the doors, heard them clearly even through his panic, and knew exactly what they were and at whom they were aimed. It took Wil quite a while to figure out why he'd been so anxious—besides the obvious reasons, like who was shooting and how long before they got to him—why he'd started to panic even further until he'd crept to the window behind Locke's desk and seen Brayden's shape sprint from one building to the other. It made more sense now. At least Wil was bound and determined to shove it into a shape that looked like sense.

He'd thought yesterday that if he made it through all his confessions, every last one, even the worst, he'd either end up dead or with Brayden as his misguided protector. And he hadn't woken up dead. Even if Brayden had intended to take Wil back to Ríocht—and Wil believed now that Brayden hadn't—it wouldn't have been to hand Wil over to the Guild. Beyond any sense or reason, Wil had an ally now, even if that ally was still somewhat uninformed, and until Brayden decided to start believing in his own religion, Wil thought he was probably safer with Brayden than out on his own. Brayden was right—they'd caught Wil's scent, all of them. They were catching up too quickly, their numbers were growing, and Brayden knew a lot more about reconnaissance and survival than Wil did. Except for the fact that Brayden was dead set on Putnam, Wil was probably a lot better off with him than he would be with Brayden joining the hunt.

Anyway, there was the whole matter of shamans and gifts and things Wil didn't understand and was afraid to believe, but if any one of them offered even the smallest chance of him getting out of this alive and with his freedom, he'd embrace it without thought or hesitation. If the morning had held no other lessons, it had shown him that Brayden was a killer, but he wasn't a murderer. Wil still might find himself dead at Brayden's hand one day, but it wouldn't be because he'd been knifed in the dark or strangled in his sleep. A death by Brayden's hand would be an honorable one. Still, honor meant nothing to the dead, and Wil had no use for it—he'd run from it if he saw it coming in time, take it standing in his boots if he didn't.

Although if it got to the point where he did have to run again, escape from the man who now thought to redefine the Guardian's purpose, Wil was going to have to make damned sure he got away clean. Brayden was too good at this sort of thing. Then again, there was always the possibility that Wil wouldn't want to run. A death by Brayden's hand wouldn't just be honorable—it would be clean. No Síofra, no Brethren. There might come a day, Wil reflected darkly, when he'd beg the Guardian to fulfill his purpose. And Wil had already proven he wasn't above begging.

"Well, Mother," he murmured to the ground, "whoever you are, *if* you are, it appears I am accepting your gift, such as it is. You've not exactly left me much of a choice." He blinked up into the thin early winter sunlight. "And if I've just somehow endorsed my own grisly end, I'm going to be *really pissed*."

He was still sitting there, scrunched down in his warm coat, staring at his comfortable boots, musing how strange it was that hope could be so depressing, when Kenton and the young men emerged from the office. The boys each gave Wil a small smile and a wave, sauntering down the steps hand in hand as Wil squinted up at them and returned a bemused wave of his own. He supposed he'd probably seemed a bit bloodthirsty to them, and he couldn't help but wonder if they'd be disgusted or titillated if they knew Wil had spent a good chunk of his morning up to his elbows in a man's brains. Young men were strangely impressed by gore.

"...can likely hand him over to the contingent from Putnam when they arrive," Brayden was telling Kenton. "I don't expect to get much out of him, but I'll leave a report with you to pass on to them."

"And I'll repeat my opinion that you should wait for your men." Kenton's tone was deferential but still chiding. "You don't know how many more there are out there, and you're only one man."

Wil deliberately ignored the way Kenton was deliberately ignoring Wil.

Brayden blew out a heavy sigh. "We can't wait for them—the longer we're here, the more danger we bring to Dudley. Perhaps if we're gone, the danger will follow us."

"I can't say I wouldn't prefer that, considering, but...." Kenton hesitated.

Brayden took advantage of the pause. "I acknowledge the wisdom of your concern, and I appreciate it." And then he changed the subject. "How long will you be, d'you think?"

Kenton thought about it. "I want to see the lads home, and

I'll need to arrange a few things." He scowled. "I've not even told my wife yet that she's married to the new sheriff of Dudley. If she doesn't kill me, I ought to be... say an hour, maybe two."

"We'll be finished with our business by then and ready to go."

Wil's stomach dropped. He really wasn't looking forward to that "business."

"And you'll wait 'til I get back?" Kenton sounded fretful.

"We will," Brayden replied. "Wil?"

Wil jumped. He'd deliberately kept himself turned away, as though they didn't know he could hear every word, and being addressed directly like that startled him for some absurd reason. Slowly, he peered over his shoulder.

Brayden gave him a curt nod. "Ready?"

Wil looked from Brayden to Kenton but found no help there. With a subdued sigh and the renewed curling of his gut, Wil stood, nodded a polite good-bye to Kenton, then walked past Brayden and into the office.

He'd sort of expected to be bustled into the man's cell with Brayden pushing him from behind saying, "All right, *go*." Instead Brayden silently stepped past Wil, past the cell, and on down to the stove.

"You've no idea what I'd do for a cup of coffee," Brayden muttered as he poured two mugs of what Wil was pretty sure was the spiced cider he'd wished for before. "What kind of forsaken hole doesn't have *coffee*?" Brayden went on ranting quietly, mostly to himself, before he looked up, saw Wil still standing by the door, and gestured him over.

Wil shot one quick glance at the prisoner as he passed but snatched it away again just as quickly. He accepted a mug from Brayden gratefully, took a cautious sip of the steaming cider, and leaked a happy sigh. Heavily laced, the familiar heat blossomed through him and damped some of the jitters, calming them beneath a warm, cinnamon-scented haze. He leaned closer to the stove. Locke had kept it stoked high so its heat reached every corner, even down to the cells, but Wil had noticed that Brayden often forgot about feeding it unless he wanted tea. It was burning high and hot now, and though he wasn't cold, Wil soaked in its heat like a cat on a hearthstone.

"Now." Brayden leaned back against the desk. "We haven't much time, and I've seen this man's sort before—it would take days to break him, and we've got less than two hours. Have you got something to tell me?"

Wil's eyebrows shot up. "Tell you?"

"Well, I assumed by 'help,' you meant you had some information that would make prying something out of him a bit easier."

Wil frowned. "And I would assume that he knows a lot more about all this than I do." He saw Brayden's teeth clench, so Wil shook his head. "Look, I'll tell you what I know—I'm not trying to be difficult—but... well, I don't know a whole lot. You probably know as much as I do by now."

Brayden sighed and set his cup on the desk. "All right. You said you could help. How? And bear in mind, I'm not much for pulling fingernails, but if you've got a brilliant idea, I could certainly use one."

Wil took another gulp from his mug, mostly to stall, and shrugged. "I said I *think* I can help. And I'm not sure how. I mean, I know how, but I don't know *how*, and it's... well, it's rather difficult to explain." He tried to look sane and reasonable, but thought he was probably lucky if he managed slightly twitchy. "It doesn't involve any fingernails." Wil grimaced, subdued. "Except maybe my own."

Brayden's expression was vaguely disappointed but not at all surprised. He heaved out something between a tired snort and a growl. "Don't know why I was expecting a straight answer."

Miffed, Wil scowled. "There *is* no straight answer. Or if there is, I don't know what it is. Sometimes I can... I don't know how to explain it, and I doubt I'd want to if I could. I can't tell you—I'd have to show you."

"Does it involve anything sharp or explosive?"

Wil rolled his eyes. "It involves you opening the cell door and letting me in, then not leaving me in there alone. I don't know how it works, I don't know *if* it'll work, but you want answers and you don't want to pull fingernails, and I want to get out of here, so I'll try."

Wil paused, blinking. Shit, had he just argued his way *into* this?

Brayden stared, calculating as usual. Wil stared back, no expression except perhaps a small bit of challenge and a touch of impatience. He didn't want to do this—would probably sacrifice a vital body part *not* to do this—but he did want to get out of this little death trap of a village, he did want to see the very last of that man in the cell and all others like him, and the sooner this was over, the sooner Wil could walk out those shattered doors and never look back. It had occurred to him only a little while ago to ask Brayden if they couldn't perhaps leave by way of Garson's so Wil could see Miri one last time, see if maybe he could catch a glint of blame or absolution in her open gaze so he'd know how he was supposed to be feeling about everything that had happened, but he didn't even want to do that anymore. He just wanted to be done and *gone*.

This quest of Brayden's for answers—it was bewildering and infuriating. Who bloody *cared* who they were, why they did what they did? They were a bunch of lunatics who thought the Father spoke directly in their ears, thought He'd enlisted them to imprison His Dreamer and take away his dreams. They were a band of blackguards who had no hesitation over wiping out dozens of people at a time, and all so that their secret brotherhood would remain secret. They were a gang of thugs who wanted *him*, and they wanted him willing—but if they couldn't get him willing, they had no reservations about force, any more than Síofra did.

It was more than enough for Wil to know he had to keep several steps ahead of them. What more did he need to know?

"All right." Brayden finally straightened and waved toward the cell. "Let's have at it, then."

Wil merely blinked, watching Brayden take the keys from inside Locke's desk then make his way down the narrow room. Wil knew he was supposed to follow, but his feet suddenly felt like they'd taken root in the floor. Brayden didn't rush him, just stood there, one hand resting on the door's lock, eyebrows slightly raised expectantly, but the overall stance was one of patience. Wil looked down into his cup, took a long, deep breath, then gulped what was left, slid the cup onto the sideboard behind him, and followed.

He waited for Brayden to turn the key and swing the door open before he peered up, caught Brayden's gaze, and held it.

"Don't leave me in there alone."

Brayden's face didn't give anything away; he merely nodded confirmation. Wil wiped his sweaty palm on his trousers and stepped across the threshold, Brayden a looming and surprisingly comforting presence at his back.

The prisoner was staring at them, that little smirk twitching at his mouth, but his eyes betrayed alert trepidation and his posture distinct unease. Which was also comforting, Wil reflected darkly. There was no chair this time—Wil seemed to vaguely recall having hurled it at that other man earlier as he was being chased down the length of the office—just the little cot Wil had woken up in this morning, the bucket that had not yet been emptied of his morning piss, and the basin he'd used to wash away the blood.

The man sat cross-legged on the cot, dried blood turning to rusty brown on his chin, dark hair askew and stuck to his brow with a thin film of nervous sweat. He was still shackled, both hands behind his back. Wil thought without sympathy that the man's arms must be really hurting by now. The thickening rope of bruises around the man's neck probably should not have made Wil want to smile smugly, but it did. Though he doubted a smile would've come now anyway.

"This is Constable Brayden." Wil said it evenly and with a calm he didn't feel. "You can answer his questions on your own, or I can make you answer them. The choice is yours. Make it now. You won't get another chance."

The man's eyes darted from one of them to the other before locking onto Wil, then narrowing. "You can't." It was cocky, but the confidence behind the smirk faltered.

Wil merely looked up at Brayden, questioning.

"What are you going to do?" Doubt and caution colored Brayden's tone.

Wil shrugged, trying to make it look indifferent, but he couldn't quite find the courage to pull it off. "We'll both find out, I think."

A long, deep breath pushed away some of the jitters. Wil squared his shoulders, told himself it hadn't killed him before, told himself it would get them out of here that much quicker... made himself believe it. Then he turned and locked his gaze to the prisoner's.

The man was already watching him—wary now, unconsciously pushing back into the wall as Wil came closer, slid a knee up onto the cot, and leaned over him. Wil tilted down and in, so close he could smell the fear pulsating from the man's skin. He took the man's head between his hands.

The man tried to wrest away. "What—?"

"You made your choice." Wil tipped closer. "*This* is what you want now."

Reached out. Let it in.

It was different than the last time, sharper and more primitive, the sensations deeper, leaching through mind and body both instead of one and then the other. Wil flinched back, hissing as a bright white blade of throbbing *want* laced through him, so hot and alive he nearly swayed. A grinding wave of nausea washed up his throat, gripped his gut, and he clenched his teeth tight.

"It's working." It was choked and unsteady, so Wil didn't know if Brayden heard him, but it didn't really matter.

He didn't even need to reach this time, grope around to find the threads—they were right there, right within Wil's grasp, and all he had to do was open himself wide, take hold. The craving was almost all-encompassing, strangling him. Vertigo clenched him in a tight fist, rocked him, and he gasped and tried not to sag.

"Too much," Wil whispered, or thought he did. "Shitshit-shit, it's too much and *right there*." It was like he was touching bolts of emotion, streaks of cognizance, colors ripping through him in the shapes of thoughts. He was *too* open, too deep, and it was all winding into the crevices, pushing him out. A strangled little whimper spattered up his throat and he clenched his teeth, shook his head. "Too much." A wheeze this time, breathless and strained.

The man was too strong, that's what it was, and the only reason Wil had got as far as this was because he'd taken the man by surprise. The man hadn't had a chance to build a guard against it—hadn't known he should. Wil might have laughed—the irony just wouldn't stop coming—but he couldn't spare the energy or the concentration. The man was insane, a zealot in the worst sense, he wanted too profoundly, and now that Wil had it in his hands, he didn't know if he could take it all in. Hot, spangling pressure built at the backs of Wil's eyes, tears crowding, gathering like sparks of Self and leaking away. He was going to drown inside his own soul.

Then a wide, heavy hand landed on his shoulder, holding him up. Wil gathered his resolve in his heart like he gathered threads in his hands—*pushed.*

The sick ease of the give was at once enthralling and revolting. The sense of alienness, of *other*, inside his own skin sapped him. Wil pulled back, shifting aside and letting himself slump. There was a storm inside him, muted and thick and viscous. He throttled the nausea, pushing away all but the most basic attention to the physical, and kept his concentration on controlling the blitz.

Woozy, Wil blinked and found himself sitting on the mattress, his knee touching the man's thigh, so he jerked back and away. Brayden's hand was still on Wil's shoulder. Somehow Wil didn't mind.

"Ask him what you want." Wil shot a glance at the prisoner, staring at Wil now with rapt hunger, and couldn't help the mild shiver that slipped over his skin. "He wants to answer now."

Brayden was still for a long moment before his hand fell away from Wil's shoulder. He stepped to the side, crouching in front of the cot. He looked from Wil to the prisoner and back to Wil again. His expression was intensely interested but also deeply troubled.

"What did you do?"

Wil only breathed a hollow little snort. "I don't really know." He rubbed at his brow, then shot a quick glance to the man still staring at him, vacantly ravenous. Wil's lip curled and a slight shudder rippled down his spine. "But getting in was easier this time." Holding on and then getting out again were going to be the hard parts.

Brayden narrowed his eyes at that, but didn't pursue it. "Can you keep him like that for a while?"

Wil shrugged, still trying to control the shaking, and looked broodingly at the prisoner. "I don't know." He peered over at

Brayden, noted the frown, and shook his head. "I really don't. I don't even know how... I mean, I've no idea—"

"Never mind," Brayden cut in. "We'll just have to be quick. Let's get this done."

Bless the man and his stiff practicality. Wil tried his legs, found they wouldn't hold him yet, so he shuffled as far to the edge of the cot and away from the prisoner as he could get. The nausea was still churning, and his head was beginning to pound, but Wil kept his grip steady, kept pushing.

"Tell me your name," Brayden said.

The man's eyes never left Wil, but he snarled, as though Brayden were some kind of annoyance he couldn't be bothered to swat away. Brayden stared at him for a moment, thoughtful, then looked at Wil with a lift of his eyebrows.

"Oh fucking *hell*." Wil closed his eyes with a sigh and then shifted his gaze to the prisoner's, resisting the persistent urge to swipe at his skin like he had ants crawling over him. "Tell me your name."

"Fírinne." The man answered promptly and with no guile.

Brayden's eyebrows went up again, but he only paused for a second. "Ask him what he wants with you."

"*I* could tell you that," Wil snapped. Most of it, anyway, and he didn't want to waste time on answers he already knew. His strength was stretched too thin as it was.

Brayden gave him a steady look and a nod. "Ask him."

Wil rubbed at his temple as he turned back to the man and swallowed back bile. "What do you want with me?"

The man smiled, soft and revoltingly amorous. Another shudder spider-walked up Wil's spine, but he ignored it, clammy sweat beginning to sheen his brow and nape.

"To save you," the man breathed. "Execute the calling of the heretic Guardian, take the dreams from the wayward Dreamer, carve his place anew in the Father's Book, prize the songs from out his soul—"

"*Stop.*" Wil was panting, shaking harder now.

The man shut his mouth, obedient as a well-trained dog. Wil bowed his head, swallowing against the surge and curl in his gut, his throat. His skin was bloody *crawling*, inside and out, like razor-clawed little animals skittering along his bones, inside his mind. His head was pulsing, *hammering*, a steady *thudthudthud* like an alien heartbeat that knocked behind his eyes. Thoughts, feelings, wants, needs, and none of them his, pounding at his senses from all angles.

Wil peered dizzily at Brayden and sucked in a quivering breath. "Sorry. I can't... couldn't—"

"It's fine." Brayden was still crouched in front of the cot. Now he shifted over and looked at Wil closely. "Are you all right?"

If Wil wasn't having such a hard time holding back tears of pain and revulsion, he might've laughed. Instead he shook his head—carefully, so it wouldn't wobble off his neck.

"Don't ask me that. Just get this done. What else d'you want to know?"

The answer was immediate this time, like Brayden was aware that Wil was in the process of drowning. "Ask him how they take away the dreams."

Wil flinched. Another answer he could give himself. He could describe everything he remembered, and he didn't know which would be worse—speaking it himself or hearing it spoken in the prisoner's dreamy voice while he stared at Wil with lustful desire.

"How...?" Wil licked dry lips. "How do you take the dreams away?"

"The Cleric must commune with the Aisling," the man answered. "Unite his mind and soul to the Dreamer, then annex him, drive him back and supplant—"

"Wait, something's wrong." Brayden's voice was somewhat gruff and unsteady, and he reached over to grab Wil's arm. "Stop it. Shit, no, wait—ask him who the Cleric is."

"—wrest the songs to his own design and cast the Aisling—"

"Who is the Cleric?" Wil was hoarse, the question holding hardly any sound to it at all. Everything was muffled and distant. He saw the man's mouth move but couldn't hear what was said.

It had never happened like this before, never been so raw, never lasted so long. Wil realized from the bottom of a deep dark well that this had been a mistake, a *big* mistake, because he couldn't stop pushing, couldn't fling it back, and it was crawling all over him, taking him under.

"That's enough now." Brayden's voice came to Wil from a distance, weak and muffled.

Wil tried to listen, to hear, but it was all getting away, slipping from out his fingers. He smelled copper, far away and faint, tasted it, and he reached up to touch his lip. His fingertips came back shiny with bright red blood. A nosebleed. Huh. That was new too.

He must have started to topple, because Brayden's hand was on Wil's shoulder again, by turns holding him up and shaking him lightly. The prisoner was snarling, all at once gone from well-trained dog to rabid wolf, eyes wild and greedy and burning into Brayden. The prisoner tried to lunge, but only fell clumsily into Wil, awkwardly pinning him sideways on the cot. He growled and spat out curses at Brayden in his own language, guttural and ugly. Wil tried to get out from under the man, but didn't have the strength, didn't have the balance, didn't even have the presence of mind. He could only cry out feebly, pushing weakly and waiting for Brayden to rescue him.

And then Brayden did. Strong hands on Wil's shoulders, pulling him, supporting him. Wil let himself slump. He had no room for pride or self-respect, just let Brayden hold him up, and drag him away from the snarling creature flinging himself about on the narrow mattress.

"Stop it." Brayden shook Wil cautiously by the shoulders. "Whatever you're doing, stop it *now*. You're bleeding."

Wil snuffled out a weak laugh. "I can't. It's never been like this before, I don't know how. I can't stop *pushing*."

Fuck, it was *hurting*, eating Wil up from the inside, and no matter how wide he opened himself, ate the emptiness, it kept filling itself back in with the *need*, the *want*, gnawing at his guts and slicking through his mind. His head was going to explode, his whole body was going to wrench itself apart—

"Look at me." Brayden was grimly stern. He shook Wil again until Wil thought his eyeballs would burst. "*Look* at me, Wil, c'mon, right now."

Wil dragged his gaze up, found eyes dark as night, latched on.

"Stop it," Brayden demanded. "Whatever it is, stop pushing." Wil's eyes started to close, and Brayden shook him again. "You're meaner than this. You're a vicious little shit who never bloody quits. Take it by the throat. If you can't stop pushing, then *pull*."

There was uncommon practical sense to that, compelling reason, and it wended through the muddle in Wil's mind and lit like a beacon. He wondered dazedly why he'd never thought of it before. Perhaps because he'd never got this far before. He'd never *had* to end it—it had always ended with its own bang, everything snapping back at him like a slingshot, that otherness depleting, slipping away in physical mortality.

The pull… it was *easy*—astoundingly so, easier than it had been to open up. Wil latched onto the threads of his own Self and pulled it in, filling the emptiness with it until it crowded out everything else.

And then it was over. Just gone. Wil didn't thump back into himself but alit gently, like a feather floating to ground on a windless day.

Darkness and vertigo closed in, and Wil let it—just closed his eyes and… let go.

He blinked open heavy eyelids to Brayden calling to him, voice and expression both fraught with concern and maybe even a little bit of fear. Brayden was shaking Wil by the shoulders, and Wil shrugged weakly to make it stop, found himself on his knees with Brayden kneeling across from him, holding him up. Wil was panting, still dizzy but alone inside his skin, mind and spirit blessedly intact.

"Are you in there?" Brayden had stopped the shaking but looked like he was more than willing to start up again if Wil didn't answer him.

Wil's head was still pounding, so he decided he'd best answer or Brayden might shake it off his shoulders. "'M all right." He swiped at his nose, grimacing when he realized he'd done it with the bandaged hand and made the linens even more gory.

"You don't look all right." Brayden eyed Wil doubtfully. "You're white as paper. Here." He dug into his pocket and dragged out a handkerchief, shoving it at Wil's nose. "Tip your head back. Has this ever happened before?"

Wil blinked up at the ceiling. "I've only done it the once on purpose," he said through the wad of cotton. "The other times —" He caught himself and shut his mouth.

Useless, of course. "Other times?"

Wil sighed, looking past the tip of his nose to meet the suspicion on Brayden's face with blunt candor. "It happens sometimes. Not on purpose." He took the handkerchief away, sniffed experimentally, then stuffed it back in place when he felt the blood still trickling.

The prisoner was slumped over on his side, eyes wide open. He looked very still.

"Is he dead?" Not that Wil cared much—in fact, he sort of hoped he was—but it likely wouldn't sit well with Brayden.

"No." There was new anger creeping beneath Brayden's tone. "But I'm thinking now I should've just let you have at him when you had the chance." He glared at the man over Wil's shoulder, a distinct curl to his lip. "He was talking about bloody *possession*, for fuck's sake, taking a person's own *mind* away." He shook his head, fiercely indignant, as though the very idea offended him down to his core. "Bloody *ghouls*." He spat it like it burned his tongue and left a bad taste behind.

Wil's eyebrows went up, but he didn't have anything to say

to that. Not that it mattered—Brayden shook off his bit of a rant with deliberate temperance. His gaze shot back to Wil, sharp.

"What other times? *Was* it you that did... whatever at the inn?"

"No." Wil tipped his head back down, dabbing at his nose. He sniffed. The bleeding seemed to have slowed now, at least. "It's too hard to explain, but no, it wasn't me."

"How d'you know for sure? You said it's happened accidentally. And your *eyes*...." Brayden shook his head. "You should've seen your bloody eyes."

Constable Brayden, Wil reflected, bleakly amused, was not the sort of man who appreciated being plunged headlong into the surreal.

Wil sighed. "Because I've thought about it, and if it was me, they would've been at each other's throats. Like Palmer and Orman. It seems to happen when... well, when there's no way out." Wil shuddered, then blinked it away. He thought about expanding, if only just to appease Brayden, but he couldn't make himself do it.

"I want to get out of here."

Wil got to his feet slowly, pausing for a moment as a wave of dizziness hit him and momentarily blackened his vision. Brayden was there again, taking Wil's elbow so he didn't fall over, leading him out of the cell and down to the office. Slightly woozy, Wil found himself plopped in Locke's padded chair, a fresh cup of cider pressed into his hand—his around the cup and Brayden's around his. It was like that first morning, even down to the headache. Shit, had that only been yesterday?

"I've got it," Wil mumbled.

Brayden backed off, watching Wil for a moment, presumably to make sure he didn't keel over, then slid his thigh onto the desk and leaned back. He crossed his arms over his chest, eyeing Wil with a keen edge.

"I begin to see why you're so in demand. Not even shamans can do what you did back there."

Wil snorted, small and bitter. "And the irony of it is, they don't even know I can do it. *I* didn't even know I could do it, not 'til Old Bridge, and even then—" He bit his tongue, slid the cup to the desk, and dropped his head into his hands. Damn it, why couldn't he keep his bleeding mouth *shut*?

The all too predictable question didn't even take two seconds to voice itself: "What happened in Old Bridge?"

Wil shook his head. "Look, I'll tell you anything you want to know, all right? I'll even tell you things you probably don't want to know. Just...." He peered up, unashamed by whatever pleas might be showing on his face. "Right now, I'm holding onto my breakfast by sheer force of will, and my head feels like it's going to explode if I so much as sneeze. I want to get out of here—it's like an itch in my brain. I don't know if it's because of the shaman or that man, but I can feel something closing in on me, and I want to be gone when it gets here. Please—can we do this after we've shown Dudley our backs?"

Brayden was silent for a moment, gaze roaming to the barred window over Wil's head. He sighed, ran a hand through his hair, and scratched at the stubble on his chin that was steadily growing into a substantial beard. "I've been feeling it too." It was low and quiet, like it bothered Brayden to admit it. He grimaced unhappily, then nodded. "All right. If you think you'll be able to travel, let's get our arses out of here.

Although...." He slid his glance sideways. "D'you know who *Bráthair Coimirceoir* is?"

Wil wanted to bang his head against the wall. "Is that the name he gave you?" He rubbed at his brow. "Terrific." He peered up at Brayden with a sour grimace and pitched the bloody handkerchief to the desk in disgust. "I *told* you, but you had to waste time on questions I could've answered myself, and now you've got *nothing*."

"And how was I...?" Brayden looked like he couldn't decide between indignant defense and apologetic capitulation. "I'm sorry, but you don't always tell me the truth, and I had to—"

"I haven't lied to you! I have *never*—"

"Maybe not. But you hardly ever give me a straight or complete answer, and you deliberately don't answer more times than you do. I took a chance. I was wrong. I'm sorry, I had no idea...." Brayden hand vaguely at Wil's face. "Now, what do you mean we've got nothing? D'you know the name or not?"

Wil slumped and kneaded at his temple. He wasn't even really angry with Brayden in particular—he was just angry. *Furious*.

"It isn't a name. It isn't anything. It means 'Brother Guardian.' Generic and worthless. It could be anyone. It could be *me*, for all you know." Wil almost pounded his fist on the desk, caught the blotched bandaging out the corner of his eye just in time, and snarled instead. "In other words," Wil said through his teeth, "it means absolutely nothing."

It took all of thirty seconds for Wil to get ready to leave. All he had to do, after all, was reclaim his pack. While he waited for Brayden, he amused himself by poking around the office, seeing the little bits of Locke in the severe, stark surroundings, touched every now and then by a spatter of personality. A small statuette of an eagle on a shelf above the stove. A heavy pewter medal tethered to a bright blue silk ribbon, but Wil couldn't read the engraving, though it had a tiny little rifle etched into it, so he assumed it was for sharpshooting. There were about ten little tins Wil thought probably held teas, each of them with a different sort of flower or herb painted on.

He avoided the far cell completely while Brayden sat at the desk and scribbled... whatever he was scribbling. When Brayden finally put away pen and paper, Wil confiscated the now vacant chair and spent the rest of the time waiting and kipping lightly with his head on the desk while Brayden rammed around the office disassembling, sorting, checking, counting, and reassembling his kit. It was kind of funny, actually, watching Brayden fuss like an old woman, rolling up clothes in neat little balls and managing to stuff what appeared to be an entire clothespress into his admittedly gigantic pack. It looked nearly half as big as Wil and probably weighed as much.

There was a small mountain of food tins and sacks of dried something-or-others, plus a huge bag of salt, presumably for preserving whatever wild game Brayden managed to hunt down along the way. Three small graduated pans nested neatly inside a slightly larger pot, a tin plate fastened over the top with clever little clasps to hold the kit together. Wil remembered all the times he'd huddled over a spark of a fire, roasting a scrap of squirrel on a stick, and wondered why he'd never even guessed there was such a thing as that ingenious little cook set.

A small shovel and hatchet hung on either side of the pack, snugged in narrow little sleeves apparently made for the purpose. And what in the world did Brayden think he'd need all those candles for? For pity's sake, he carried what seemed like the equivalent of two entire households on his back. Three extra pairs of stockings made Wil slightly jealous, though the ones that had come with the new clothes from Mistress Afton were heavy and warm and not likely to wear out soon. But still.

Brayden's bedroll was thick, double-lined, and shiny like it had been waterproofed—that one almost made Wil's mouth water. He hated the cold the worst. Hunger he could take, even the constant ache and weariness of continuous travel, but the cold was sometimes enough to make him want to weep pitifully through chattering teeth. Perhaps, if they weren't who they were, and if Wil made an offer at just the right moment and in just the right way, he could carve himself a space inside that divinely warm-looking cocoon. It wouldn't exactly be a hardship, he reflected as he watched Brayden move purposefully about—Brayden was a good-looking man, after all, extraordinarily fit, and he was no longer as frightening as Wil had found him before, so maybe—

That line of thought woke Wil *right* up. He blinked and slapped his mind away from its ludicrous wanderings. What the *hell*? A slight growl wended at the back of his throat, and he swallowed it, wondering, absurdly discomfited, exactly when he'd become a sixteen-year-old girl.

Annoyed, he adjusted his head on his arms, arching his back up a bit and giving his shoulders a light stretch. Two more days of a relatively soft mattress would have done him a lot better, but he was eager to get moving, so he'd make the sacrifice. He wondered bemusedly what his face looked like. There had to be a mirror around here somewhere. Not that he really wanted to know. It was enough to know that everything still hurt.

Brayden finished with his pack, then went and retrieved the shackles from the prisoner—who was still, Wil noted with a dark, not wholly pleasant satisfaction, staring blankly at the wall of his cell—and moved on to a locked cupboard to the side of Locke's desk that turned out to be a small armory. With practiced ease and something akin to fluid, frugal grace, surprising in a man of his bulk, Brayden began checking, cleaning, and readying his weapons. There were a *lot* of weapons. Wil was caught between snorting quiet derision and sighing enviously.

A long, fierce-looking rifle was laid out then checked thoroughly, rubbed with an oily cloth, and loaded with large, lethal-looking shells. Wil watched attentively as a little metal catch was flipped from one position to another behind the trigger and checked twice before the gun was laid aside. Had to be the safety. Wil filed the information away in case he needed it later. A sheathed short sword came next, quickly unsheathed and swiped with the cloth, then resheathed before being belted at an angle about Brayden's hips. Wil's interest perked even more when a crossbow made an appearance. He was pretty good with a longbow. He'd never actually shot a crossbow, but he'd seen others use them and had thought he'd like to have one. Depending on the archer, they were more accurate and covered more distance, in Wil's admittedly spare observation. A bolt from one of those would likely drive through three men and have some punch leftover.

The weapons on Brayden's person came next, each one removed from a holster—or in the case of the long malignant dagger, a boot—then emptied, cleaned, checked, reloaded, and reholstered. By the time Brayden finally finished, Wil was very nearly writhing with envy and resentment. Brayden carried a bloody arsenal, for pity's sake, and Wil didn't even have his rusty little dirk anymore. It wasn't fair. The ammunition alone took up its own good-sized carryall.

Wil was drifting in and out of a light, hazy doze, pleasantly warm inside his coat, half watching and half ignoring Brayden's labors, when Wil's own pack was snatched up from the floor beside the desk then dropped onto it mere feet away from Wil's nose. Wil sat up, blinking and rubbing carefully at his still bruised eyes. He frowned. Without even a glance at Wil, Brayden upended the pack, apples and potatoes rolling out first, then everything else following in an unruly heap.

"Hey!" Wil caught two apples before they rolled to the floor, and made a grab for the pack. Brayden merely scowled at the messy mound on the desk that was, to Wil's very sincere indignation, everything he owned in the world. "That's *mine*." Wil was completely awake now and already seething. "You must have already searched it, I haven't got any weapons, give it back."

He was on his feet, trying to gather his meager belongings into some semblance of order, but Brayden ignored him, long fingers poking through *everything*, damn it, and rearranging it all into nonsensical piles. Wil stalked around the desk, tried to roughly shoulder Brayden out of the way, but he might as well have been trying to move a boulder.

"Leave off," Wil snarled. "These are *my* things, you've no right, I didn't go through *your* things, *get off*!"

But Brayden just shook his head and kept on. "You can't

carry all this rubbish." His tone was that of a parent chastising a child—and how *dare* he? "I mean, what the fuck, with the potatoes? How long have you been carrying—?"

"It's called *food.* And I intend to carry it until I've eaten every last bit of it."

"You can't carry this much weight. Did you pick this up in Kenley? No wonder your tracks were so easy to follow—they were nearly half an inch deeper than they'd been before."

"I *have* carried this much weight, and never you mind where I—" The fury dimmed a bit as that last comment sank in. "Wait, what?"

"Your trail was difficult to find after the fens." Brayden looked like he was trying for patience. "I was cursing your light step for days, until I picked up the tracks of those men. And they'd trampled your trail under theirs so badly that for a while I had to follow their tracks and hope I'd find one or two of yours along the way to confirm I wasn't following the wrong ones. After Kenley, though, it was easier to spot yours because you weighed more. I assumed you'd resupplied there, but potatoes and apples?" He shook his head, waving at the mess on the desk. "Who taught you how to—?" He paused as though struck, then nodded with a rueful little shrug. "Right, no one taught you. My mistake."

"*Don't,*" Wil seethed quietly, "patronize me. I've been doing all right, y'know, I'm not slow, and I'm not completely uneducated—I've managed to figure out quite a lot on my own."

"I don't think you're slow." Brayden fixed Wil with a steady, sober gaze. "And I'm amazed by what you've been able to do, and especially seeing as how you've been running for your life the whole while you've been doing it."

The little hairs on Wil's nape were smoothing despite himself. Brayden looked like he really meant it. And the strangest thing about it was that Wil actually believed him.

"I don't mean to belittle what you've done," Brayden went on, "and I'm sorry if it came out that way, but...." He picked up Wil's now empty pack. "Haven't you even got a bedroll?"

Wil looked down, found an apple in his hand, and rubbed his thumb over a bruise on the skin. "I used to. It got stolen."

"How have you been keeping warm when you slept? I only found the bones of one fire."

That made Wil shift uncomfortably, and the hackles came back to half attention. He didn't like Brayden going on about tracking him, examining the remains of paltry little campsites and finding Wil's footprints among the muddle of the Brethren's. He didn't like knowing everything he did had left some kind of shadow behind for Brayden to follow, some little piece of Wil himself that had betrayed him. It gave Wil a prickle between his shoulder blades, like someone was watching him even now, and he had to really try to suppress a shiver.

"I wasn't keeping warm while I slept." The resentment bristled in Wil anew. "I was freezing my arse off, and I was starving nearly to death until I bought those potatoes and apples—with my *own* money that I'd *earned*—so that's 'what the fuck.' And I don't have a pack the size of a small cart or enough food to feed an entire regiment to fill it—*or* anything to hunt food *with,* now that I think about it—so I'd appreciate it if you'd get your great paws off of what I *do* have."

He snatched the pack from Brayden's hands, feeling a flush to his cheeks that bloody *infuriated* him, and began chucking everything back into it, not caring what went where. A small clutch of flat colored-glass Tables stones had bounced about and scattered. Wil didn't have a board, and he'd never actually played the game, *and* he'd lost several of the pieces through a hole in a previous discarded pack, but the stones were nice to look at, especially when he held them up to the sun, and they didn't take up much room. And why the *hell* why was he justifying it, even to himself? He reached for the stones and had started to count them to make sure none had bounced off the desk and onto the floor when Brayden's hand reached too, closing over Wil's. Wil jerked his hand away, stones scattering everywhere, and backed up a few steps with a ready snarl. Damn it, why did Brayden have to *touch* all the time?

Brayden held up his hand, his expression calm and... sympathetic.

The snarl curling at Wil's mouth stretched wider, indignant now and profoundly offended.

"Just leave off, will you? You don't need to—"

"Listen." Brayden's voice was even but pointed. "I'm not trying to take what's yours. I'm trying to tell you that what you've got here...." He ran a hand through his hair, like he was having a hard time finding the right words. "It's just not going to work, all right? I can—"

"It's been working just *fine*. D'you think I've been living in some squire's country estate all this time? D'you think I've never done this before? What I've got here is *all I've got*—I've bought or found everything here, I've stolen *none* of it—and you're not taking *any* of it."

"I'm not trying to *take* it! I'm trying to get you to pitch it!" Brayden winced as Wil's mouth dropped open, and he held up his hands to forestall the imminent wrath. "That didn't come out right," Brayden said quickly. "I didn't mean it like... like however you think I meant it. I only...." He waved his hands around, then turned to the desk, snatching up half of a broken marble carving of a rose. "What the bloody *hell* d'you need *this* for?"

Wil scowled. "I *like* it."

"All right, very pretty, or at least I'm sure it used to be, but... honestly, when I picked up that pack the other day, I thought it was loaded with explosives or something, it was so heavy. And you haven't even got a change of clothes! You've been carrying around *stones*, for pity's sake, and—and—and *leaves*, and scraps of tin—you've even got... well, I'm not sure what this is, but it looks like a bit of carpet."

"It *is* a bit of carpet." Wil snatched it, balled it clumsily, and stuffed it into the pack. "When the ground is wet, it keeps me dry."

"It's too small to keep even your *head* dry."

Wil ignored him. "And the 'scraps of tin' are nice and sharp and can bend about my knuckles—comes in handy when you're bedding in a common room, fighting with fifteen others for a spot next to the fire, or making sure they keep their trousers buttoned. And the leaves are just nice, I liked them, they had nice shapes, and just, just—" He was sputtering. He was actually *sputtering*. "Why am I even *explaining* this to you? I don't owe you anything. You don't get to say what's worth keeping and what isn't."

That shut Brayden up for a moment. He only stared at Wil, mouth hanging open—annoyingly, *infuriatingly* perplexed—then sighed and slumped. "You're right. I, um... I should apologize. I wasn't trying to... I'm actually trying to help, y'know."

He cautiously took the pack from Wil's hands. Wil was abstractly surprised when he just blinked at Brayden and let him. "You've nothing in here that'll help you," Brayden said, tone and expression kind but not the least condescending. "Nothing to keep you warm, nothing to eat besides potatoes and apples that weigh far too much. You haven't even got a blanket. I know you've managed, and likely with even less, but you don't have to manage this time—I can help you, if you'll let me."

Wil stared. And then he blinked. "Um."

"I've enough to feed an entire regiment," Brayden went on, "because I didn't know what to expect when I finally caught up with you, and I decided to prepare in case there was no place to find provisions. I didn't want to get stuck trying to feed two of us on twigs and berries. I've more than enough for the both of us—you don't have to carry the potatoes and whatnot. You can—I won't stop you—but I've seen you without a shirt, and you can't tell me you're not still feeling those bruises."

Wil's eyebrows went up this time. He couldn't think of a single thing to say.

"You're also going to need a change of clothes, at *least* one, and a bedroll. Can't *believe* you've been going without, I'm amazed you've not—" Brayden stopped, shook his head. "Never mind, it doesn't matter now." Another sigh, heavier this time, and he rubbed at his brow. "I suppose, if you want to take all this"—he waved at the mess on the desk—"it won't make much of a difference, since the horse will be doing most of the work anyway, but I'm going to have to insist that you let me help you kit yourself a bit better."

Well... when he put it like that.... Wait.

"Horse?" Wil frowned suspiciously. "You're not expecting me to ride one of those beasts, are you?"

Brayden stopped short. "Oh *hell.*" He actually groaned. "I'm afraid so, yes."

Wil gaped. "And when were you planning on telling me *that*?"

"Right about when I was shoving you into the saddle." Brayden pinched at the bridge of his nose. "We're not tracking anyone this time, and time is short—riding just makes more sense. I've bought two sturdy mares from Rayburn, who runs the livery. Both very tame and good-natured. I've seen them—there's nothing to be afraid of."

"I'm not *afraid.* I just don't like them. They try to eat your hair and butt at you with their great heads and knock you over. The ones at Ramsford's wouldn't ever leave me be. I'd try to cross the paddock with a barrow full of horseshit, and they'd all jog over and—What's so bleeding *funny*?"

Brayden had his head bowed, hand over his face, but his shoulders were quivering, and Wil was sure he'd just heard a very distinct snort.

"No, no, it's not...." Brayden shook his head and too obviously held back real laughter. He slid his glance up with a sideways grin. "It's only... well, you do realize that all of those things —it means they like you."

Wil wasn't sure he'd ever seen Brayden with a real smile on his face before. It was somewhat transforming—opened him up, lit his whole face, and made his eyes spark warm and easy. Wil caught himself wondering how he'd ever believed this man had meant to harm him. Even the weapons strung about him looked completely incongruous with that smile.

Disconcerted, Wil pushed it away, dismayed by the sharp discomfort. If he kept thinking like that, he'd never see the bullet coming.

"That's what Ramsford and Mistress Sunny said." Wil shrugged awkwardly. "That the horses liked me, I mean. And it's all well and good, but I don't appreciate horse breath down my neck all the time, and they're... well, they're very tall, and you have to sit rather high off the ground, and I've never actually saddled one, just curried and bridled them, and I don't know—"

"I'll show you everything you need to know."

"And they'll want all the apples."

Still grinning, Brayden rolled his eyes and dipped a little half bow in acquiescence. "If I must, I shall protect your apples with my life," he said, affably resigned. "Fine. I won't argue about all of your... stuff, if you won't argue about the horses."

He said it like he wasn't getting exactly what he wanted anyway. Still, Brayden had been right—Wil was still horribly sore, and carrying his heavy pack on a cross-country trip would likely sap him for at least the first few days. And this way he wouldn't have to fear that the pack would just disappear or "accidentally" get kicked over a cliff or something. It's what he'd've done.

"Fine." Wil sighed, long-suffering. "But if it does one of those things where it rears up on its hind legs and throws me off it, that's it, and I get to shoot it. *If* I live." He tried a sour grimace but only ended up with an annoyed twitch. "Now, where am I supposed to get a change of clothes?" He held up the bandaged hand. "And if I don't get this disgusting thing off soon, I'm going to steal one of your five hundred extra shirts and shred it for new bandages."

Brayden chuckled. Likely because he didn't think Wil was serious. *Ha.*

They were both kitted and ready by the time Kenton came back, Wil's pack stuffed with what he'd arrived with plus clothes—Mistress Afton had been even more generous than he'd thought—soap, some of the food tins, and dried fruits from Brayden's pack. "In case we get separated," Brayden had said. Wil decided he couldn't decide if that thought made him hopeful or apprehensive. There was also a bedroll made up of three of the blankets from the cupboard in the bathroom behind Locke's office. Wil had been working himself up to a healthy snit that Brayden and Locke had had indoor plumbing all this time, and there he'd been with his bucket, but Brayden had distracted him with the discovery of two pairs of clean wool stockings, stuffing them into Wil's pack and saying Locke would have approved.

Brayden did end up changing the bandage for Wil, saying he doubted Mistress Slade had forgotten, but that she was likely just very busy, as he went about nicking more provisions from Locke's cupboard. He'd had a bit of a happy seizure when he found the stash of medical supplies, and spent a few minutes shoving some things he said they might need into his pack before he sat himself in Locke's chair to rewrap Wil's hand.

Wil was sort of wincing preemptively before he realized Brayden's touch was surprisingly deft and gentle. Wil only hissed once when Brayden had to spread Wil's first two fingers to get the linen between them. They looked... really bad. Fat as sausages and mottled a disgusting black-blue-green. Even the ones that weren't broken made him curl his lip, and the way the wrist was swollen made it look misshapen and crooked. Well, Wil supposed he had at least some idea now what his face must look like.

They were both sort of pacing around impatiently, trying not to accidentally knock into each other, Wil trying not to look in the cell, when Kenton finally got back.

"What's happened to this one?" he asked immediately, staring into the cell with a dubious frown. He turned to Brayden, twitching a short nod over to Wil. "Ye didn't let that one at him, did you?"

And Wil had had just about enough. *That one.* Honestly.

"My name's *Wil.*" He rather barked it, and he hadn't really meant to, but... well, Kenton had been treating him like he was some kind of mangy mutt, and it was grating on him. Wil shot a quick glance to Brayden, looking for reaction, squaring his shoulders and setting his jaw against it.

But Brayden merely tipped him a nod. Wil wasn't sure, but he thought he even caught the faint tic of a smile.

He was absurdly encouraged. He looked straight at Kenton. "I'm sorry," he said in a tone that was not the least apologetic, "but you keep talking over me like I can't understand what you're saying, and it...." He shrugged, floundering. "Well, it's *rude.*"

There. No kicked puppy and no vicious cur—he'd chosen something in the middle, and now he intended to stick with it. Unless it didn't work, and then all bets were off, and Brayden could take his supercilious advice and shove it.

Kenton turned those intense blue eyes on Wil, really looking at him for probably the first time since Wil had run headlong into Kenton's chest on his way out the door.

Kenton gave a slight nod. "All right, Wil. What happened to him?"

Wil blinked. *Damn.* It appeared the consequence of demanding to be addressed like an actual person was that you were then expected to provide half of an actual conversation.

"We don't know what happened to him." Brayden was apparently perfectly comfortable this time with lying through his teeth. "I was attempting to question him when he threw some kind of fit, and...." He shrugged. "Well, you can see. Mistress Slade was supposed to come by anyway, so you may want to have her give him a look, and Brother Millard when he's through. He's going to have to be fed and watered at least, eventually. It's all in the report I've left for you. You can ink yourself a copy, if you like—sorry, I didn't have time to do it—but the men from Putnam are going to need the original with my signature. I've left all of my reports, plus a letter addressed to my superior, Chief Jagger, detailing my plans and the reasons for them." He stuck out his hand. "I thank you, Sheriff Kenton, for all of your assistance."

Wil wondered if Kenton's head was spinning with all the information like Wil's was.

But Kenton merely took up Brayden's offered hand with obvious reluctance. "And you really mean to head to Ríocht?"

"I'm afraid our options are limited." Brayden let go of Kenton's hand, shrugged into his pack, and shouldered the rifle, slinging the crossbow to fit over the pack. "You've seen what these men can do."

"I have, but.... Well, you know my objections." Kenton turned his scarred face toward Wil. "The Mother's blessings upon your path." He pointedly said it to both of them. "You'll surely need it."

He saw them politely to the ruined doors. Wil shot one more look over his shoulder at the man slumped on the cot in the cell, staring vacantly at the wall. He spared a tiny shudder and then, with one last curl of his lip, let Brayden push him out the door.

Despite the fact that he was actually walking willingly to the livery with the intention of riding a horse, and despite what waited at the end of this journey, Wil couldn't remember the last time he'd been so glad to cross a threshold.

CHAPTER 7

Lesson One was simple: *Do not, under any circumstances, attempt to remove a personal possession from Wil.*

It was Dallin's fault, really. He'd handled it badly, bungled a sincere attempt to help into what could easily have been—and very definitely was—interpreted as an attempt to bully and demean. A man who owned so little would of course defend what was his with rabid insistence, and Dallin should have thought of that before he'd opened his mouth. If nothing else, the truncated row over the boots should have clued him in. Nevertheless, when Locke had snorted over the pack that first night when she'd searched it, told Dallin he ought to have a look, he'd had no idea. And when he'd actually seen the... possessions inside it, he'd... well, he'd boggled.

Even now, it was hard for him to believe Wil had survived all this time carrying that sort of... all right, Dallin might as well think it if he couldn't actually say it—that sort of rubbish. Dallin wasn't even sure *he* could survive with those kinds of "provisions," and to think Wil had been doing it for *years*... truly—it boggled the mind. Dallin was caught between a sad sort of horror and profound respect.

Wil *was* a vicious little shit who never bloody quit, and that pack was proof all by itself. And the way he held on to it, defended it, defended himself for demanding to keep it—it only drove Dallin's respect up a couple of notches. Before he'd seen the proof of how much the meager possessions meant to Wil, Dallin might have acquiesced and then made sure the thing got lost somewhere along the way, or even "accidentally" kicked it off a cliff or something. Now he thought he'd likely defend it as intensely as Wil would, if it came to it.

The content itself was interesting and worthy of thought and study. The bits of tin, a little bit of nonlethal self-defense for someone who probably needed to practice it daily, nestled right next to leaves selected and stored because they were "pretty." If there was a starker contrast to lay bare what a man lived as opposed to what a man was, Dallin didn't know of it.

He'd guessed it fairly quickly and early on, but those two items put it in plain terms in a tangible way. This was a man who took hold of every bit of life that passed within his desperate grasp, and if you left him to it, you'd likely get a timid smile and a polite nod of the head before he harmlessly skirted around you and scuttled off. But if you fucked with him, he'd tear your throat out for it.

He'd shown no remorse or discomfort at having turned a man's head into porridge, but Dallin believed it when Wil said he would have prevented Lind. Wil had nearly wept relieved tears when Dallin had told him they would stop at Garson's for lunch so he could see Miri, that she was fine, no attacks out this way, yet he *knew* Wil had used those scraps of tin before, could easily see the metal wound around those long fingers, curled into a tight fist.

There was a line somewhere between using brutality to survive and just brutality, and Wil walked it according to his own moral compass—stepped back and forth across that line easily and without so much as blinking.

Dallin shook his head and leaned back against the paddock's fence.

Lesson Two, he thought as he watched Miri straighten Wil's collar and lay a light kiss to his cheek, *you get more flies with honey than a threatening look and a stern command.*

In truth, this last visit to the inn had been twofold, but Dallin didn't see any reason to fill Wil in on the ulterior motive. Let him think Dallin was doing something nice just to do it. Wil didn't need to know that Dallin hadn't been talking to Tom about the care of horses when he'd dallied at the little stable, and he didn't need to know that Dallin had been planting the story of their supposed destination and pumping Tom for information on what had gone on at the inn over the last two days. Dallin had known, of course, that nothing had gone on, save for better-than-usual business last night and plenty of talk about the doings in town this morning—he'd had it from Rayburn before they'd even left the village proper—but hearing it from Tom and seeing it for himself was still a relief.

It had been frustrating this morning, not having the power to be two places at once. The two lads he'd spoken with back at the sheriff's office had been unable to say exactly what the Brethren's numbers were—"a score" could have been just as much an exaggeration as an underestimate—and Dallin didn't like to think there were still some of them skulking about. Everyone in the entire village was now alert to strangers, and Dallin didn't think those men would dare another attack, but he also didn't think they'd give up.

And he'd *very* much like to know how those men this morning had known to find them in Dudley, and more specifically in the sheriff's office itself. He was sure there had only been six of them at the inn the other night and none of them had escaped, and the men from this morning hadn't been following Wil's trail from Putnam—Dallin would have had to be blind as well as brainless to have missed *that* trail. So how had they known to head to Dudley from wherever they'd been before, and how had they known to center their attack on the gaol?

Dallin pondered it all through the hearty lunch Garson himself had served them, but no promising theory presented itself. For the moment it was going to have to remain a mystery. Dallin *hated* mysteries.

"The quickmud of reason," he muttered to himself, then let a heavy sigh slough from his chest as he spotted Tom leading the horses out to the yard. Dallin straightened from his slouch against the fence, whistled to get Wil's attention, and nodded at the horses when Wil flicked a look over his shoulder. He was standing on the back porch with Miri—right beneath the new charms engraved on the lintel, Dallin was pleased to note—carrying on a conversation on which Dallin was dying to eavesdrop. But it couldn't be anything terribly informative, so he didn't. *Honey*, he told himself and waited patiently.

Wil tipped him nod then turned back to Miri. Miri shot Dallin an inexplicable little smirk around Wil's shoulder, then leaned up and said something low—and likely coy, judging by her expression—into Wil's ear, and Dallin was treated to the surprising occurrence of witnessing Wil grin, hearing him laugh. He'd smiled almost all the way through lunch—couldn't seem to stop, once they'd ridden up into the yard and Miri had greeted them warmly from the front porch—but Dallin hadn't ever heard an actual laugh from Wil before. He'd heard its semblance—manic little giggles and derisive snorts—but this was a *real* laugh, winding up from the belly and flowing through the chest. It made Wil... almost handsome. In a gawky sort of way. Nearly fetching, actually. Even with the bruises.

Dallin shook his head with an uncomfortable frown. *Fetching*. What the fuck?

Still chuckling, Wil leaned in, gave Miri a tight hug about the shoulders with his good arm, then clattered down the two steps and into the yard, his gait lighter than Dallin had yet seen it and the smile still lingering. It didn't even falter when Wil spied the horses.

"Ready?" Dallin asked him.

Wil dipped a pleasant nod, thanked Tom as he reclaimed the reins of his roan, and swung up into the saddle without even a slight grimace. Rayburn had been a lot more useful in basic instruction than Dallin had been, teaching Wil in ten minutes what it likely would have taken Dallin two hours of grinding his teeth to knock into Wil's head. As a result Wil had taken only a mile or so, once they were on the road, to catch on to the rhythm of the mare's dip and roll as she jogged. Dallin had expected at least several days of steady complaints and balking from Wil, but it looked like the stop at the inn had been one of Dallin's more productive intuitions.

Anyway, distance wasn't crucial today. Getting on the road and out of Dudley was the only real goal, and though it was already going on early afternoon, Dallin had high hopes of hitting the next inn on the road in time for a late supper. Now that Wil knew basically what he was doing in the saddle, and he was in a good mood for having seen his friend, Dallin hoped he could push more than he might've been able to do before. Honey had its uses. Dallin mounted his own horse, flipped a quick wave around the yard to whomever was about—and there were several; they'd been stared at all throughout lunch, and once Wil had vacated the porch, some of the patrons had leaked out onto it to stare some more.

"Thank you, Tom." Dallin spotted Garson mingling with those on the porch and gave him a nod as well. He looked back at Tom. "I've no doubt you'll be on your guard. I know I don't need to tell you, but these men are formidable in numbers, if not in skill. A delegation from Putnam should be here tomorrow or the next day, and Kenton means to arrest anyone who doesn't belong until then, but...." He shrugged. "Just have a look over your shoulder now and then."

Tom nodded soberly. "We've one of Millard's apprentices bunking here for a couple of days, and Garson's set up a target range around back of the paddock for anyone who's gone rusty. We're watching." He gave Dallin's chestnut a light pat on the rump and stood back. "Have a care on the road, Constable. Ríocht en't where I'd choose, but I expect ye know what you're doing. The Mother's blessing."

"Same to you." Dallin gave Wil a bit of a nod, satisfied when Wil nudged the roan lightly with his heels and led her out onto the road. Dallin followed, settling into the horse's cadence and allowing himself to relax.

Though he likely wouldn't relax much until he'd put some distance between Wil and anything but a long stretch of wilderness. Not that it would necessarily stop Wil if he decided to take off, and especially since Dallin had gone out of his way to make sure Wil could survive alone better than he'd been doing. Still, Wil wasn't nearly skilled enough in the saddle yet, and even if he was, Dallin had made sure he himself had gotten the faster of the two horses—and his saddlebags carried the packs with all the supplies, while Wil's carried the horses' oats. If there was any running, Dallin would catch up quickly enough. He didn't think it was a real risk, at least not yet, but it was an ever-present vibration beneath every move Wil made, like it lived under his skin and he had to willfully keep it tamed and quiet when he wasn't in immediate danger. Wil was *very* good at survival. If it came right to it, Dallin thought he could probably hand Wil a gun and set him loose, and he'd disappear and survive more effectively than Dallin himself could do. He'd been doing awfully damn well thus far, and with very little.

That man back at the office this morning had been almost twice Wil's breadth, and yet Wil had managed to somehow get the man down and then eliminate the threat in probably one of the more gruesome ways possible. And Dallin believed with his whole heart that if he'd left Wil alone with the second one, Wil would've found some way to get into that cell and take that one out too. Even now Dallin wasn't sure if the man's catatonic state had been purposeful on Wil's part, or if Wil really hadn't known it would happen.

Then again, Dallin didn't think it really mattered, and as

disturbing as that thought was—it *should* matter; it was his job to care about things like that—Dallin couldn't make himself feel corrupt for it. What these men planned, what they wanted... it made Dallin's stomach turn. There was something deeply, profoundly disquieting in even thinking about it, let alone thinking there were hundreds of men who thought it was not only their right to do it, but their calling, and were willing to wipe out anyone who got in their way, covering their tracks by killing and destroying—

Dallin paused... frowned.

No, they weren't covering their tracks. That hadn't really made sense from the beginning, but Dallin had been too disturbed by the deaths in Kenley to think about it clearly at first, and then too many other things had left him little time to scrutinize his reasoning. Now the clarity of it hit him like a pebble between the eyes.

There had been no need to burn Kenley, and doing it held far more risk than allowing it to leak about that a stranger had come by asking questions and looking for another stranger. If they had wanted to keep their presence a secret, all they had to do was snatch and question one person, get the answers they needed, then kill that informant and skulk away. These men might be inept, but if they were that stupid, they wouldn't have even made it across the border with their heads still on their shoulders. The most any remaining witnesses would be able to relay was that a dark-haired stranger had passed through looking for another dark-haired stranger. A dark-haired stranger who was no more remarkable than any other lone drifter, except for a pair of *extremely* remarkable and very distinctive green eyes. Anyone who knew what kinds of questions to ask would know immediately who fit that description.

They hadn't been covering their own tracks—they'd been wiping out Wil's. They'd been covering up the fact that he even existed.

Dallin sucked in a thin breath. "Oh... *shit*."

But that was insane. *Why* would—?

No. He couldn't think about this like a constable. Millard had been right in at least this one thing—reason wasn't going to help Dallin deconstruct the unreasonable. He was going to have to come at this from inside the psychosis of a believer.

All right, then. He could do that.

The Aisling was legend in the Dominion, not reality, the Chosen more a symbol, like Cynewísan's Planting Plays, chanting raucous songs around bonfires to symbolically wake the "Mother," a woman chosen each year by something as ordinary and unmagical as a lottery. The people of the Dominion didn't even know they'd been seeing an impostor at their Turning for however many years, so it was reasonable to suspect that, before Wil had been removed altogether from the public eye, they hadn't known they'd been looking at a real Aisling. And there had been no outcry when he'd disappeared—no national hunt, no Guild Elders coming forth to plead for his return. Once it was known Wil was in Cynewísan, there had been no outraged demands made at the Council in Penley, no accusations of kidnapping or threats of revenge. Except for the Guild, it seemed no one in Ríocht knew their Chosen really was the Aisling. And Síofra had kept it that way.

And then along came the Brethren, trying to rearrange an entire religion to suit their own interpretations. Perhaps they'd begun as priests or initiates within the Guild itself, learned the secret, and decided the Aisling had been corrupted and needed to be set onto a path of their choosing. They'd kidnapped him, run across the border, and kept his existence secret, because....

Dallin stared down at his hand, fist clenched tight around the reins. Why would they—?

Because if the people of Ríocht knew how badly they'd been duped, the hunt would be on, they'd be out for blood, and the first throats they'd go for would be the Brethren—first for keeping the Aisling's authenticity to themselves, and then for stealing him. As it stood now, only a few people knew of their existence, and most of those were on the wrong side of the border. But if the people of Ríocht knew, there'd be massive hunts, perhaps even treaties with the Commonwealth, a cooperative effort on a larger scale than just Dallin and Jagger. The Brethren would be wiped out and the Aisling put back into the hands of the Guild. Síofra would also likely suffer the same fate as the Brethren, because there would be no way his role—his sickening abuse—could stay secret.

The bottom line, Dallin thought, a cold little knot forming somewhere in his chest, was that keeping the existence of the Aisling a secret benefited both the Brethren and Síofra. The Brethren were willing to kill as many as they had to in order to ensure secrecy. Did Dallin think Síofra would do less? If Dallin did drag Wil back to Putnam, hand him over like he was supposed to, would Dallin then be marked—wind up dead shortly after? And Jagger?

Dallin had set out on this particular little ruse as a mere precaution, hoping to throw the Brethren off and avoid anyone of authority on his own side until he could get Wil safely back to Putnam and lay out what he knew to Jagger. Let Jagger handle it from there. He was a good, intelligent man and knew more about politics than Dallin did, after all. Now Dallin thought perhaps the subterfuge was the most brilliant stroke of intuition he'd ever had. Because if he was right, who knew how many ambushes lay in wait along the way? And there was no telling from which direction they might be coming. For the Mother's sake, Dallin might end up in a shootout with his own men.

Although....

Keeping what Wil was—or was supposed to be—a secret had seemed good strategy when Jagger had relayed the order, but now Dallin wondered if it wasn't playing right into the hands of... well, everyone else. Letting it be known the Aisling existed would cut at least the Brethren's power in half, but letting it be known the Aisling was in the Commonwealth might very well bring about those hostilities between Cynewísan and Ríocht that Jagger had been trying so hard to prevent when he'd given Dallin his orders.

Dallin eyed Wil—from the side and slightly behind, so he couldn't see Wil's entire face. But Dallin caught a partial profile, noting the pleasant, oblivious set of Wil's expression, the way he flicked his gaze around constantly in what could have been mistaken for that ingrained survival instinct, if one didn't look closely, but Dallin thought it was more that Wil was just sincerely interested in his surroundings. The past two days had been more violent and confusing than Dallin had seen since his tour in the army, and he'd needed almost a year after his discharge before he could walk down a street without doing constant and unconscious recon. Wil was actually sightseeing.

The thought of dimming this small contentment lumped a guilty little weight in Dallin's chest, but he still had a badge in his pocket, and it tethered him to his duty. And until he could get back to the constabulary and do some real investigating, Wil was the only one who could give Dallin even the smallest indication that his speculation was at least close to reality.

He sucked back a regretful sigh and bit the bullet. "Tell me about Old Bridge."

It was amazing to watch, now that Dallin knew what to look for—Wil's expression snapped shut, going from mildly congenial to hard and closed in under a second. His relaxed posture curled in on itself, shoulders hunching in and back stooping so he was nearly curved down over the saddlebow.

"What d'you want to know?"

"I want to know everything." Dallin nudged his horse, pulling up even with Wil's so he could see his face. "I know it's difficult. I know you don't want to talk about it. But I need to know. Something has just occurred to me, and I think whatever happened in Old Bridge may either confirm or negate the theory."

He'd found that Wil was much more apt to accept the wisdom of a chosen course if Dallin explained the reasoning to him. If Dallin had thought of it yesterday, or even all the way back in Putnam, he might be richer in information than he was now. It had taken him nearly all day to get the tale of the Guild out of Wil, and that had been with a steady barrage of questioning and cajoling, but the matter of where they were going and why they were going there had taken only five minutes of straightforward arguing.

Dallin was going to have to get used to it. He'd spent too

many years giving orders and expecting them to be carried out. Asking nicely was usually a formality he could choose to eschew according to circumstance. With Wil, it was going to have to be habit. Dallin hoped it was a habit he wouldn't forget about in the heat of... whatever.

"Old Bridge...." Wil took a long breath and set his shoulders. "Old Bridge was where the Brethren took me after they'd snatched me from the Guild." He looked down and rested both hands on the saddlebow. "It isn't there anymore."

The reins were slack in his hand, allowing his horse to simply take her cues from Dallin's. Dallin had rather guessed that Old Bridge had suffered the same fate as Kenley, so he didn't prod, just waited patiently while Wil girded himself to speak what was obviously a difficult thing to even think about.

"There were four of them. They killed each other, and I got away. I was very sick, coming off the leaf, and when I got loose, I stumbled into an old woman—quite literally, in fact. She was mad, thought I was her son who'd died in the war, so she took me home with her and took care of me. I was just starting to be able to get around by myself, and I made the mistake of going outside her hut in the middle of the day...." Wil shook his head. "That doesn't matter, except they figured me for a witch and ran me out. I found a stand of bushes up on a ridge about a mile out of the village, and I laid up there for a couple of days until I felt like I could walk. I saw the flames... I think it was two nights later."

He looked up at Dallin, brow quirked in baffled disquiet. "There were no screams. I could see everything clearly, and no one was running away, no silhouettes against the flames —nothing."

Dallin had to look away for a moment, unclench his jaw and cast his glance about, before he could turn back again. "It was the same in Kenley."

Wil only nodded. He must have overheard everything Dallin had discussed with Locke, because there was no surprise in his expression—no reaction at all. Dallin peered at him closely, frowning.

"The men who took you—you said they killed each other?"

Wil looked at Dallin straight, jaw set, but the muscles twitched and jumped beneath the bruises. "Do you need to know the details in order to confirm or negate your theory?" His voice was quiet, the question sincere.

Honor and duty did disconcerted battle in Dallin's conscience. If he said yes, he needed the details, Wil would give them to him. All Dallin had to do was push the tiniest bit. Except his theory had been confirmed without those details, Dallin was sure now—even the more insubstantial speculations felt like too much truth—and Wil very obviously would rather slice off an arm than relay those details. But here Dallin was, yet again being told half the story, when he knew in his gut that only the whole of it would complete another missing puzzle piece. And he *needed* the damned puzzle pieces.

Honey, Dallin told himself morosely. He shook his head with a sigh and adjusted his seat in the saddle.

"I want to know it all, and I have a feeling I need it all, in order to fulfill my word to you. Maybe tonight, yeah? Everyone keeps telling us that time is running short, and I don't know about you, but I feel it."

Dallin dropped it there. He merely nodded, made a business of getting himself a drink from his water skin, and turned his eyes straight ahead. When he next dared a glance sideways, Wil was once again admiring the scenery.

Lesson Three. Dallin sighed, very consciously resisting rolling his eyes. *Don't spring things on him.*

It was actually tangential to Lesson Two, when Dallin thought about it, but it was important enough to rate its own category.

"We're headed north," Dallin said patiently, "for the same reason we're traveling on the road. We need witnesses. We need people who can be questioned and answer honestly that they saw us on the road and we were heading toward Ríocht. Now, please—get back on the horse."

Wil shook his head, mouth set in a stubborn line. "Everyone in Dudley will tell them that. *You're* the one who keeps saying time is short, and if we're really going to Putnam, this is a waste of time."

Throwing himself on the ground kicking and cursing, Dallin reflected, would likely not achieve the results he wanted here. Neither would shooting Wil.

Dallin dismounted slowly, and just as slowly led his horse off the road and into the trees. He tossed her lead over the first low branch he came to. Leaned against a nice, thick pine. Waited.

It only took a moment. Wil stared at Dallin with a quirk of eyebrows and shoved at his horse—who had her nose buried in the nape of Wil's neck, nuzzling—then stalked across the road, dragging the roan behind him.

Dallin only watched him come, trying very hard to suppress the smirk that was twitching at the corners of his mouth. "Don't yank so hard. You'll hurt her, and she'd likely follow you off a cliff anyway."

It was actually true of both horses. Dallin had never seen horses act so much like adoring puppies as these two did with Wil. And Wil gave no indication of anything but constant annoyance with them. It went against every animal instinct Dallin had ever witnessed—well, except maybe cats, but cats were odd and temperamental and didn't really count—made him shake his head and snort every time Wil shrugged away their slobbering affection.

Wil tried to look as though he was ignoring the advice, but Dallin noted an obvious slackening in the lead as Wil stomped the last few steps then stopped in front of Dallin, the mare halting obediently behind and picking up right where she'd left off with the nuzzling. Wil shrugged at her absently, peering down at Dallin with a scowl that was somewhere between suspicious and perplexed.

Dallin decided to head him off before he got started. "We're *not* going to Ríocht. I didn't lie to you."

Wil's mouth opened, then closed again. He slumped down. "I didn't think—"

"Yes, you did. You thought I'd told you we were going to Putnam to shut you up and get you to come along quietly."

"The thought of going back to Putnam doesn't exactly inspire coming along quietly."

Dallin had to concede the point, muttered caustically though it might have been.

"Likely not. But getting you to go to Ríocht would have

been a lot harder, and don't think I don't know it. And don't think I'm unaware that you trust me about as far as you can throw me."

Wil flipped an unconscious glance over the length of Dallin, caught his gaze, and flushed.

"It's all right," Dallin told him. "I'd worry more about you if you did trust me. But I've not lied to you, and I've told you at least as much of the truth as you've told me."

There. Let him chew on that one for a while.

He did, staring down at his boots with a grimace that wanted to be outraged but couldn't seem to find the rationalization.

"Now, I need you to think about this." Dallin kept his tone even. "Do I look like I don't know what I'm doing?"

That made Wil look up with a puzzled frown.

Dallin opened a hand, palm up. "You can withhold your trust in disclosing things you find painful or personal. You can withhold your trust in what I am and what you think I should be. But you *need* to trust me when it comes to strategy and tactics, because I promise you—I *do* know what I'm doing."

He had Wil's full attention now, even if that attention was cautious and skeptical.

"I've trained probably half of those who will be coming from Putnam. I know what the procedures are, and the first thing they'll do is send at least two men after us to either try to talk me out of what I wrote in that letter or arrest me for absconding with a prisoner and deserting. Depending on the men, it's more likely to be the former—I've been with the constabulary for quite a while, and I can't imagine the thought of me turning traitor will sit easy with most of them. But facts are facts, and the letter I left is commensurate to a confession. It's quite possible that by this time tomorrow or the next day, I'll be branded an enemy spy, and they'll be hunting me even more avidly than you."

A confused scowl twisted Wil's face, like he was angry and couldn't figure out why. "But why would you—?"

"Because it's what I think is right, at the moment, and until I have all the pieces to this puzzle, I have to play it close. Do you know that Chief Jagger and I are the only two who know who you are, and that I was sent to retrieve you for the Guild?" Dallin waved his hand when Wil snapped a wary glance at him. "I was told in no uncertain terms that no one else was to know. I'm not so sure now that was the best idea in the world, but as far as any one of those men coming from Putnam knows, you're a fugitive, a suspect in a grisly murder. And after they read my letter, they're going to have no choice but to think I'm aiding and abetting you, or disbelieve both their superior and what's written in black and white in my own hand. If they catch up to us, they'll arrest us both, and I'll have no control over what happens from there.

"Now, I told you that I'm doing this because I think it's right, and that's true. Not just because I don't like the idea of handing you over to Síofra, but because I'm hoping this bit of misdirection will mislead not only those from Putnam, but any of the Brethren who I've no doubt will try to follow as well. We travel north—on the road, in plain sight—and we stop at the first inn we come to, make ourselves seen. Then we head back on the road north and disappear at the first opportunity. We'll turn west for a while, maybe double back once or twice, and then angle south before we head east. That's the plan, and it's our best chance of getting back intact. Now—will you *please* get back on your horse?"

Lesson Three, Dallin reflected as he watched Wil scowl, slump, and then remount reluctantly, was going to come in awfully handy on this trip.

They came upon the inn, as Dallin had hoped, just before the kitchen closed, so they were able to manage a hot supper of ham and boiled potatoes along with stale black bread and something they said was split pea soup but looked and smelled more like congealed pond scum. Dallin pushed his aside with a dubious pinch of his lips, but Wil slurped up all of his, sopped up the leavings with the bread, and then asked Dallin for his portion. The man could definitely eat, and apparently he wasn't picky. Anyway, Wil could certainly use any little bit of bulk he could get. Dallin slid the bowl over without expression or comment.

The inn was bigger than Garson's but not as busy. Shabbier and without even the barest hint of hominess. Not surprising—it was set on the road between New Bridgeford and Penley, more frequently traveled, so the patronage was transient, not a majority of locals like the more secluded Garson's. There were at least two dozen customers in the common room when Wil and Dallin arrived. Dallin made sure they sat in the middle of the room, made his voice louder than usual, and when anyone glanced their way, he met their eyes and made sure they got a good look.

No coffee here either. In fact, by the way the innkeep had looked at him when he'd asked, Dallin was beginning to wonder if coffee was just a figment of his imagination. How could an inn that, if it wasn't precisely *in* civilization, was at least on the road to it, not have *coffee*? Honestly.

Despite the inn's faults, it did boast indoor plumbing, and for an extra two gilders, they'd fill a small tub with hot water in your room. Dallin noted the spark of interest in Wil's eye, decided he could use a warm wash himself, and so handed over four gilders and ordered two beers while they waited for their room to be prepared and the tubs filled. The innkeep eyed them speculatively and with a knowing little smirk. Dallin merely rolled his eyes and took the beers back to the table. If he only knew. Dallin could just imagine the skewed tale the innkeep was going to tell the men who came asking after them.

It took him 'til halfway through his beer to notice how quiet Wil had gone. Silence from Wil wasn't exactly remarkable, but he'd at least been somewhat amiable all afternoon and downright contented through supper. Dallin was in the process of toying with making the guideline—*If you want a pleasant Wil, keep his stomach full*—an actual Lesson, when Lesson Four just about dropped on his head: *Think about how what you're saying might sound to a man who takes almost every word literally, and never*—ever—*assume you've not said anything that could have been taken very, very wrong.*

They'd been shown to their room, their packs already brought up and laid on the bed, two tubs—larger than Dallin had assumed—steaming away in front of the fire and taking up almost every bit of space in the room not occupied by the bed and rickety little cupboard, when the Lesson started to tap lightly at Dallin's consciousness, but in small ways he only saw in hindsight. He had to actually push Wil, who stood stiff and pinched-lipped on the threshold, through the door. Dallin tried not to be obvious about locking it and pocketing the key, but there was only so much activity in the room, and none of it coming from Wil.

Considering the way Wil had been living, Dallin couldn't imagine he was put out with the shabbiness of the place. Maybe he was one of those who disliked baths, but Dallin didn't think so. Wil had been tidy and kempt the first time Dallin had seen him back in Putnam, and when Dallin caught up to him in Dudley, Wil had been scrubbed beneath the blood and bruises, and that was after a hard journey.

Perhaps he was worried Dallin was going to hammer him with questions about Old Bridge. Perhaps Dallin had said something thoughtless. Perhaps Wil was just tired. Perhaps the saddle-soreness Dallin had deliberately not mentioned was kicking in before morning, as Dallin anticipated.

Perhaps Wil was just a moody little pain in the arse.

It could have been any one of those things, or something else entirely—who could tell? Dallin decided he didn't care. He was tired, he was sore, and he wanted his bath, and he couldn't climb into his and leave Wil wandering around the room with Dallin's weapons lying about. He'd checked the crossbow with the innkeep—it was rather awkward to tote indoors—but that still left the handguns, the rifle, the sword, and the knife, none of which Dallin could exactly take into the tub with him. So Dallin tried to chivvy Wil into his bath first. Which was right about when Lesson Four dropped on Dallin's head like a load of bricks.

He piled his weapons beside the tub nearest the door, turned to Wil—innocently enough, Dallin was convinced, even in retrospect—told him, "All right, why don't you get undressed and hop in that one, while I dig out some clean clothes?" He stepped back, intending to make a path for Wil between the tub and the foot of the bed.

Wil didn't move. He looked from the bed, to the tub, back to the bed again, then slid a slow, narrow glare up to Dallin. And *still* didn't move.

"Is this part of the 'plan' too?" Wil's voice was quiet but with a dangerous edge beneath it. His whole body was rigid—shoulders thrown back, chin set, and jaw clamped tight. Challenging. Tensed for battle.

Except Dallin had no idea where the battle line was. "Um...." His eyebrows beetled in wary confusion. "Sorry?"

Wil's lip twitched. Dallin didn't know why, even when he thought about it later, but that little tic nudged the tumble—right down a slippery slope and into a canyon.

I do not sleep with men for money*!*

I am no doxy.

...comes in handy when you're bedding in a common room, fighting with fifteen others for a spot next to the fire, or making sure they keep their trousers buttoned.

Dallin, once again, for probably the fiftieth time that day, boggled.

"Oh, for *fuck's* sake." Now *he* looked from the bed, to the tub, back to the bed... the *one* bed, behind a locked door, in a room with a six-inch slit for a window, with two steaming tubs. "Well, *shit*." He rolled his eyes to the ceiling, couldn't help the growl. "You think I'd—? Of all the—" He was caught between absurd embarrassment, sincere contrition, and profound, indignant outrage. What sort of person *did* that kind of thing, and what had Dallin ever done to make Wil think he was one of them? And what sorts of people had Wil been exposed to that the idea had come so easily, and with no apparent surprise? "I *cannot* believe you would think—" Dallin couldn't seem to finish a sentence. The offense was so acute it was blocking the path from his brain to his mouth.

Wil seemed to twig to his mistake with a bit of a jerk and a whole lot of blinking. He deflated, expression going all at once apologetic, posture once again curling in on itself. Dallin didn't know if he was more angry about the insulting assumptions or seeing that timidity leach back into Wil's stance.

"I'm... sorry." Wil's eyes were wide, and his voice was just a touch uneven. "I didn't mean to—"

"*Oh* yes you did. And if it's all the same to you, I'd really like to pretend this never happened."

Wil's mouth flapped for a moment. He really did look sorry, Dallin had to give him that, but sorry wasn't the point. The *point* was.... The point *was*....

Well, if Dallin knew what the point was, perhaps he wouldn't be so damned angry, but he thought perhaps it was either the experience that must have been behind the implied accusation, or the ensuing cringing when it proved unjust.

"Look." Wil held his hands up, placating. "I really am sorry. I shouldn't've—"

"Did you *not* hear the part where we pretend it never happened?"

"*Yes*, but...." Wil huffed, then waved toward the bed.

Dallin's mouth set in a grim line. "I intended to bed down on the floor in front of the door—to keep others *out* and you *in*."

"So I *am* a prisoner."

Something inside Dallin's brain... popped. He actually heard it. He took a step toward Wil, made himself stop, and then just stood there, hands clenched into fists so tight his palms were tingling.

"You are un-*bloody*-believable." Livid, shoved out from between clenched teeth. "I have a pretty nice life, y'know. I've got a brilliant house that I love, with a nice comfortable chair by the fire I like to sit in to read at night, a job I'm damned good at, friends who think I'm a fairly good person and who like my company. Have I got *any* of that here? *No!* Instead I've got the images of burned-up little children behind my eyelids every time I close my eyes, bullets flying at my head from every point of the bloody compass, and a traveling companion who spends his time whinging and griping when he's not busy dreaming up all the ways I might kill him.

"And *now*, after I've just spent the last two weeks of my life tracking you down, then risking it trying to save yours, risking my job, the regard of my men, my friends, my *country*, everything about my life I love—yes, we monsters *are* capable of love—after all that, you just *assume*—" Dallin couldn't even say it. He sputtered. "Did you think I did all that to impress you? Did you think that when you didn't throw yourself at me, I just decided to make you? Believe me—you're not that bloody special! And—and—*and*... you know, you know—" He was pointing at the ceiling like some indignant old woman. "In case you'd forgotten, you've made several rather crude offers, so now's a *hell* of a time to come over all frightened rabbit and prudish!"

He shouldn't have said that last, but he was angry—really bloody *angry*—and anyway, Wil didn't seem ready to go to pieces because of it. He only dropped his gaze to the floor and sucked in a long, shaky breath.

"Yes." His tone was soft, disconcerted. "I did think... you're right, I'm sorry." Wil lifted his gaze. No anger, no defeat, just a steady contrition, unfeigned. "I think... I think perhaps you're a good man—a truly *good man*—and... well, I don't...." He dipped an awkward shrug. "I know what to do with monsters. This is new."

That....

Dallin blinked.

That had rather taken the wind out of his sails. The heat and rage from two seconds ago left him in one long confused rush. And then he didn't know what to do with himself. He just shook his head, ran a hand through his hair, and then waved toward the tubs. He thought he muttered "Bath," and he must've done, because Wil sidled slowly past him and over to the tub.

Dallin made it a point to keep his eyes on the floor, on his own buttons, on his feet, on the bottom of the tub, on the soap—anywhere but Wil. Wil probably needed help, what with his bandaged hand and all, but there didn't seem to be any helpless splashing coming from the other tub, so Dallin didn't offer. The bathing was carried out in tense silence and as quickly as possible. They were both dressed in clean shirts and linens, Wil settled stiffly on the bed—*alone*—less than thirty minutes later, waiting in complete and utter silence for someone to come empty the tubs and haul them away.

When they finally did, Dallin arranged his bedroll in front of the threshold, lining his weapons to either side so he could reach them quickly. He'd known this moment would come; he'd been pawing at it all day and had known there was no real alternative. And he'd known that broaching the subject would be uncomfortable at best—downright traumatic at worst. But he hadn't guessed there would already be so much *tension* between them when it came to the point. A penitent sigh ground out his throat, and Dallin closed his eyes, rubbed at his brow.

"Tomorrow, all right?" Wil said softly, as though he'd read Dallin's mind. "I'll tell you all about Old Bridge tomorrow."

Dallin nodded, surprised to realize he was actually relieved, then lay down on his bedroll and closed his eyes. "Blow out the lamp, will you?" When he heard Wil comply, Dallin allowed himself to drift into a light, erratic doze.

He smells the smoke first. Then he hears the cries, the screams, the clash of steel on steel and the thunk and squelch of steel on bone, the heavy, gritty grind of cart wheels on hardpack. He can't see, and he knows it's only because his eyes are closed, but he doesn't want to open them, so he doesn't.

He's left her behind, allowed her to force him into the cart, he hadn't fought hard enough, and now he's running away, and she's staying behind.

"I love you—remember that always. I'll find you."

Her last words to him, and he'd wept and shouted at her—

"You can't make me, I can shoot, don't send me away!"

—and he hates her just a little bit, because he is supposed to be the man now, she had no right, and yet she'd all but carried him onto the cart, locked him in the little compartment beneath the boards, the tinker growling anxiously—

"Nownownow, hurry, they're coming!"

—and him weeping like a child, closed up in his little coffin, out of the danger he's leaving her behind to face alone.

A cool hand touches his brow, and a soft voice calls to him, "Come now, brave lad, open your eyes."

He doesn't feel brave, but he hasn't heard her voice in so very long, wouldn't hear it, refused to hear it, and he's missed her so. He opens his eyes, blinks slowly.

She is not his mother, though she looks something like her, enough so that his heart gives a great wrench in his chest and an embarrassing little sob leaks out from his throat. Her hair is the gold of the setting sun, eyes blue and clear as mountain lakes, and she smiles at him, strokes his cheek. His eyes water, and he blinks, watching the curve of small, circular tattoos—no, scars—etch themselves along her cheekbone, lifting and stretching minutely with her soft smile.

Dallin frowns, reaches out, but doesn't dare touch. "I've seen those marks," he tells her. "But I can't remember where."

"And you will not until you acknowledge your calling."

It has the tone of light chastisement, but she still smiles, and he doesn't really understand, but he can't care about anything else but that smile. She is young and old, ageless, and it's odd because her features are rather plain but somehow perfect, and she's the most beautiful woman he's ever seen.

She is not his mother—she is All Mothers, she is the *Mother. Dallin thinks at first he should be kneeling, but decides it wouldn't please Her, so he doesn't.*

"Is this a dream?" he whispers.

Her smile turns melancholy. "How could it be so," She asks him kindly, "when you refuse such comforts?"

He means to answer, tell Her his dreams have never been a comfort and he doesn't miss them, but he tries to wake up and can't, and She smiles knowingly at him, so he doesn't say anything. He peers around, realizing it's utter darkness, and yet he can see everything, like it has its own inner light. He can see himself, so much younger, leaning his back to the rough boards of the barn behind what will be the Kymberly in only another several years, but he doesn't know it in this-when, this moment when he'd worn a fake smile and lied understanding.

"I love her," Ramsford tells him, eyes to the ground, like he's ashamed, and that by itself is enough to break Dallin's heart, but he keeps anything that's real behind his teeth.

"It's time and past time," he tells his friend. "Don't look so glum. I understand."

Ramsford shakes his head, leaning up to lay a single chaste kiss to Dallin's mouth. "You've half of my heart," he says, almost angry and trying not to be. "But I need half of one who'll give it."

Dallin swallows hard and keeps his false smile. "She's perfect," he tells the man who is kissing him good-bye because he's found someone who can give him what Dallin can't. "She's a brilliant girl. You'd be a fool not to snatch her before she twigs to your more unattractive habits."

Ramsford snorts and peers up at Dallin, soft asking in his eyes. "Will you stand Second?"

"Of course." Dallin consciously controls the wince, keeping the tiny little flare of anger from leaking into his eyes. "You're my best friend," he manages, proud that it sounds even and sincere. "Did you think I wouldn't?"

"Did you love him?" She asks Dallin.

He stares, watching two young men whisper brave good-byes, each speaking sweet, comforting lies, keeping truths where the other won't see so they can find their friendship again when their hearts stop breaking. He shakes his head.

"Not enough."

He hadn't. He'd always known it. He'd spent three years waiting for Ramsford to understand that what Dallin could give would never be enough, that Ramsford deserved so much more, and in all that time and all the time since, Dallin had never been able to understand why he couldn't love someone so near perfect the way he wanted to—the way he should've done.

"He was not the Weft to your Warp," She murmurs.

Dallin nods, not really listening, instead watching himself kiss his lover a smiling good-bye in another when. "Yes" is all he says.

"Have you ever loved?" She asks him gently.

Dallin only shakes his head, turns away.

"Show me those hands now, little man," his father says, gruff voice not as loud as it used to be before he'd gone off to the war, not as... present.

Dallin ignores the little bit of discomfort he doesn't understand, puts out his grubby hands, and wriggles a bit as his father takes them up in both his great palms and turns them over.

"Some lovely calluses you've here, lad," his father tells him seriously. "You've been taking care of your mum good and proper while I've been away, then." He nods with satisfaction.

Dallin's proud smile near cracks his face. "Will you tell me about the war?" he begs. "Tell me how you got that scar, pleeeeeease?"

He points to a long, jagged twist of flesh that ropes from the corner of his father's eye and down to the crook of his mouth, cutting right through and hopelessly distorting the proud indigo Mark on his cheek. He's writhing to hear the story of how his dad had scragged the scum who'd done it, for surely the bastard hadn't got out from under Ailen Brayden's sword after he'd left a mark like that.

But his father shakes his head, says, "Another time, lad." And then he hugs his son, whispers into his hair, "The Old Ones have spoken. Great things wait for you, and dark times. Carry your name and your land in your heart always, lad. Never forget your name."

Dallin snorts as he pulls back. "How could I forget my own name?"

His father smiles, but it's sad and doesn't touch his eyes. "What does Brayden mean?" He brushes Dallin's hair from out his eyes.

"Brave," Dallin answers promptly.

"And what does Dallin mean?"

"Um...." Dallin smirks, puts a finger to his chin and squints up at the sky, pretending to think about it. His father skims a narrow look at him, but Dallin can tell there's a smile beneath it. He laughs again. "Pride's people," he finally answers.

"And...?"

Dallin tries not to sigh. He's played this game so many times—it's a baby game, and he's bored with it—but it's almost like it used to be before his dad had gone away for so long, and it makes his father happy. "From the valley."

"And what valley?"

"Cildtrog."

"Which is...?"

"Lind's Cradle."

His father grins—a real grin that touches his eyes this time—and he runs a rough hand through Dallin's tangled mop of hair. "You're a good boy, Dallin," he tells him. "And as long as you never forget your name, you'll always know your way home."

Dallin grins back, bouncing impatiently. "Now will you tell me about your scar?"

"I will," his father replies. "But not today." He cuffs Dallin lightly on the chin when a sulk begins to bloom. "None of that, now. Another time, lad."

There will be no other time to hear the tale, no other time to learn the songs of his name, no other time to play the stupid baby game and make his father smile. Ailen Brayden came home to die, and Dallin Brayden has very little else to remember him by.

Dallin swallows, trying again to wake himself up, but it seems he has no control over anything here.

"You have forgotten your name," She tells him sadly.

Dallin frowns, offended, and turns a scowl on Her. "Never."

"No?" She slips Her shoulder up in an elegant shrug, runs a finger over the Marks on Her high cheekbone, then does the same to his. "Where is home?"

His scowl deepens, truly insulted now, and despite the sincere indignation, he almost says Putnam, but She's laughing now, so he doesn't say anything.

"Where did you get that scar?"

Dallin sits across the table from a dark-haired stranger who pretends to be a man named Wilfred Calder from Lind. The man doesn't answer him, doesn't answer anything, until:

"What did you do to merit shackling?"

The man chuckles—a bleak, tired little thing. Tells him, "I had the audacity to exist."

Dallin reaches across the small cot, runs his fingertips over the lumpy thing, tremors vibrating beneath the man's skin and right up Dallin's arm. "Was it the Guild?" Dallin asks.

Wil shakes his head, turns his hand in Dallin's grip, takes hold. "I'll tell you all about Old Bridge tomorrow."

Pain shoots up Dallin's arm and he gasps, tries to jerk himself away, but he can't move. He closes his eyes, clenches his teeth; there's a pull inside him, and he doesn't have time to fight it, to even think about fighting it, before he's jostled, thrown.

"You wanted to know it all," She whispers in his ear, takes hold of his hands, and guides him gently. "Take your feet from out the quickmud and look." Her tone is more stern than it had been. "Guardian. You have been called."

He's not himself, he doesn't feel like himself, and he can see a shape that looks like him over his shoulder, blank-faced and Watching, and it's as though he can see out of two sets of eyes. The vertigo is nauseating, so he tries to swallow around it, but he can't. Her hands still hold him, direct him, gentle but implacable. She guides him and he lets Her, lets go of one Self and slips into another.

It isn't him, this other Self, but he sinks into it smoothly with Her to guide him. Another language enwraps his thoughts, his mind, his everything, and it's strange because he can understand, he can understand all languages, and it shouldn't make sense, but it does. He's learned a lot in dreams—too much and not enough. He's learned what people want from him, and that he's helpless to stop them from taking it.

He's confused, dazed, but there are other walls here besides the towering stone of the Guild, and he almost weeps in relief. He thinks maybe he's dreaming—it's been so long since he wasn't—but it has the feel of life to it, solid and real.

"You're safe," someone whispers to him.

He doesn't know the man's name—there are four of them, all with the Old Ones' Marks on their cheeks, but they're off somehow, they're wrong. It's all horribly confusing and no one's told him a name, so he hazily notes the way this one's hair and beard curl crazily, and he names this one Curly.

"The Guild will never find us here," Curly tells him, patting his arm awkwardly. "Síofra can't hurt you anymore."

He wants to kiss Curly's hand, wants to weep on his shoulder and tell him how grateful he is, but he can't seem to make his mouth work or keep his eyes open, and everything's spinning. A light shiver runs from the top of his head right down his spine, and he shudders weakly.

"What's wrong with him?" one of them wants to know. He's tall and skinny, with a nose like a hooked beak, so this one becomes Hawk. "You don't suppose they've addled him, do you?"

Curly frowns and shakes his head. "I don't know. It shouldn't matter."

He wants to take serious exception to that, but he can't find the energy to be offended. "Not addled," he whispers, or at least he thinks he does, but they don't listen to him.

"C'mon, then." Curly lifts him up by the shoulders and half drags, half leads him over to a plain wooden chair in the middle of the room. He lets Curly push him down to sit in the chair, blinks woozily at him as Curly leans down to peer suspiciously into his eyes. "I can't tell if he's in there. Let's see if it makes a difference."

And then fingertips are digging into his scalp, pressing hard, but he doesn't flinch away, doesn't complain. These men have rescued him—he's free, beyond all hope, beyond anything—and he'll do whatever they ask, whatever they want, so he tries to sit obediently still as the fingers press in harder. Curly's eyes are closed, and he's sweating now, thin trickles running slowly down his temples.

He can almost feel it on his own skin, like an itch on the inside of his head. He tries to sit still, tries to be good—they've rescued him, he's safe, and he's oh so grateful—but now that he's noticed it, it won't go away, and it's driving him insane. Itchitchitch, and now he's starting to sweat too. His stomach is flopping slowly around in his gut. So, he reaches up—just a small movement, a quick scratch and then he'll sit still again—but when he touches his head, all his hair is gone.

He can't help the little gasp.

Did he have lice? Did he misbehave and they've punished him?

"Why have you cut off my hair?" His voice sounds funny—scratchy and weak, like he's not used it in a long time—and Curly either doesn't hear him or ignores him, fingers bearing a steady pressure, making his eyes throb.

He skims his fingers up and over, feels something warm and sticky sliding from beneath Curly's fingers and tickling behind his ear. He draws his hand back, lifts it close, blinks until it comes into focus. He's bleeding. They've cut off his hair, and he's bleeding.

He can't make sense of it. He stares at his fingertips, turning his hand in front of his bleary eyes.

The itch is driving him mad, spiking splinters into his head, into his mind, pushing at him, digging and prying, and he stares at the blood and realizes the itch is inside*, Curly's trying to get in, pushing, just like Síofra. He can't get his mind around it at first, he just keeps staring at his hand like it's going to speak an answer.*

They haven't come to save him at all. They've only brought him to a new nightmare.

The betrayal is... bottomless. Shattering.

"C'mon, then, Aisling," Curly whispers. "Give it to me, lad."

"I can't," he tries to answer, but his voice cracks and breaks apart in his throat.

He really can't. It's what he is, a part of him, inextricable, and he can't let it go without letting go of everything.

"We are the new Guardians," Curly tells him, angry now, like he's got the right. "We come to arrest the corruption. The Vessel is weak and unworthy. Let it go and it can all stop."

Guardians. Ah. That explains it. He should have known. The Marks, after all.

He wonders vaguely where the other Guardian went, and if he'll be angry that these men have stolen his task from him. He thinks he snorts.

The pain comes then, hard and wrenching, all-encompassing and all at once, and he leans over and retches on Curly's boots.

Curly jumps back, cursing. The pushing stops, the prying stops, and he slumps in relief, weeping and shaking. There's blood all over Curly's fingers, and he thinks for a moment that Curly has dug right into his skull. He reaches up, feels bare skin where his hair used to be and shapes carved into his head, right into his skin—eight of them, right where Curly's fingers had been—and he's all over blood, dripping everywhere, and how has he not noticed this before?

He screams, tries to lurch up. He doesn't even know where the door is, but he has to run, he has to, except he can't, his legs won't hold him up, and he thinks Oh, right, the leaf *as he watches the floor rise up to meet him. Hands on him, pulling at him, and he screams some more, kicks and bites, and then he's vomiting again, abstractly pleased that he gets Curly again and another he hadn't seen yet, but he knows right away this one will be Brute, because the man lifts him up, shakes him 'til his teeth rattle, then throws him back to the floor when the vomit hits him too.*

Crawling now, trying to find a door, a way out. He thinks he's still screaming, but he doesn't have a voice, just low animal whimpers leaking from his throat and sobs that shake right down his spine. More hands on him, and he can't see this one, but he names him Brute II, because his hands are hard, he wants to hurt, and he does.

His wrist is gripped tight and his arm twisted, pulled up between his shoulder blades. Cramps lock a tight fist inside his belly, and he tries to double over, but Brute II holds him arched. It's all too much, there's too much pain coming at him from too many different directions, he can't hold beneath it—his eyes roll back, and merciful darkness encloses him.

He drifts, he doesn't know for how long, snatches of conversation coming to him from out of the darkness. He hears just enough, clings to the sense of it, makes his mind turn it into shapes he can understand through the pain and the fever and the odd spasms that jerk through his body like it belongs to someone else.

They don't know what's wrong with him, they think he's insane and sick, and they fret because they don't know what to do. He lies on a hard mattress, bare and cold, damp sheets beneath him crumpled as though he's been writhing. He can smell his own sickness, and it makes him gag, but there's nothing left to vomit, so he only chokes a little before he slumps in on himself, exhausted.

It takes him a while to understand why he can't move his left arm, why it's gone numb and cold, but he catches the glint of steel about his wrist in a fleeting moment of clear vision, the other end clamped around the iron bedpost, and then it makes sense. He thinks he should care, but he's occupied with the pain, the cramping, the nausea, and every bit of him that isn't busy trying to breathe through it is concentrating on not telling them about the leaf. He wants to, wants it more than he wants them to let him go, more than he wants the pain to stop—he just wants*—and if he tells them, they'll give it to him, and it'll all go away.*

But he doesn't—if he tells them, they'll know, and they'll get in, and they don't just want to get in, they want to push him out*. He could feel it when Curly was prying and digging, that push, could feel the greed and want inside it, and they've taken everything else from him, damn it, they won't take his Self.*

He comes to awareness in the middle of an argument, Brute II shouting at Curly, "We followed you because you said you knew, you said you could do it, but all you've done is sent him mad, and now he's dying!"

He thinks that should make him sad, but it doesn't.

Curly looks angry and thwarted, shakes his head. "Perhaps you're right," he tells Brute II, "but I will not go back to the Cleric and tell him I've failed."

He shrinks back as Curly moves toward him, blue eyes hard and intent. Fear grips him, as tight as the fingers about his head pressing into the wounds, and he feels the itch. He screams, flails, flings his free fist up, and connects with Curly's jaw. Four sets of hands are on him then, holding him down, and Curly digs down into his mind, pushes.

He knows this is it—they'll either get in or kill him—so he gathers his desperation in a mental fist. Pushes back.

He hadn't known he could do it, wonders if it's new or if it's been there all along and he just hadn't known it. Wonders if Síofra had somehow throttled it, or maybe the leaf did. He doesn't even know how *he's doing it, but he's doing something, and it's stopped all four of them cold in their tracks.*

It's forever inside, and he's crawling with the want, overwhelmed with it. They're a greedy lot, they want it badly, they're rabid with it, and he doesn't know what to do with it all, so he does the only thing he can—he flings it back at them.

Thunder rolls from somewhere, and the flash of lightning spatters four faces set in feral masks.

Huh, *he thinks through the haze,* I think I made it rain.

Somehow it's much less important than the fact that he is no longer helpless. He has taken action, done *something to save himself, and the wondering pride is stunning and sublime.*

He doesn't watch everything that happens next, but he hears it all. Two of them turn their guns on the others before they're brought down. One goes down with another's teeth in his throat. The last two standing spend their dying breaths snarling and spitting death at the other.

Silence but for the raging storm. Long silence and bad sleep, thrashing about on stiff, cold sheets, moaning through the pain until he fights to consciousness. The rain has stopped, he notes, but he doesn't know why he cares or why it matters.

He stares at the blood congealing on the bodies, on the floor, on the walls. Lets his gaze drift up to his left hand. If he'd been just a little more coherent, known he could do what he'd done, he might have had the presence of mind to get one of them to unlock him before allowing them to have at each other like animals. But he hadn't, and now he's going to die anyway—he's going to die of dehydration or starve to death, or just die of the pain, alone in this perdition made of blood and gore and the smell of piss and vomit.

For days he lies there, lurching back and forth between waking and dreaming, in and out of sanity. The corpses speak to him sometimes, but he knows that's only part of the madness. The knowing doesn't help, though, and he screams his throat raw, screams 'til he spits weak little sprays of blood, and still they whisper to him of slow death and long torture, and they laugh.

He doesn't know when he decided to do it. One moment he was lying there, trying to accept a protracted end—it wouldn't hurt anymore, he kept telling himself; a few days of misery and then it wouldn't ever hurt again—and the next he was dragging himself up, lubricating the cuff around his wrist with his own blood—

She pulls Dallin back into himself with a gentle tug. He gasps, thinks he should feel embarrassed by the tears on his cheeks, but his horror is too acute, and he can't make himself care.

"Why did you show me that?" he demands, breathless and nauseated.

"I would spare him the ordeal." She turns to Dallin, Her blue gaze earnest and somber. "Take the veil from your eyes, Guardian. You have heard the call; now you must heed it."

She raises Her arm, points.

Dallin turns his gaze slowly, almost afraid of what She means to show him this time. He looks to where She points and sees... Wil.

A soft brume of mist broods around him, stretching from one end of eternity to the other. Scintillating sparks of iridescence flare through it, inside it, like millions of infinitesimal stars birthing, then exploding in brilliant death. Wil's hands whisk through it with unthinking grace, fingers flying, plucking out a rhythm Dallin can't ken, but his whole body vibrates to the cadence, like it's a song so fine and high he can't hear it, yet he could sing it if he concentrated hard enough.

"What is he doing?" he asks.

She looks at Dallin closely, so intense Dallin feels naked beneath Her regard. "Tending the Threads."

"I can't see them. I see stars inside of clouds."

"All see it differently."

Dallin thinks about that for a moment. "Why does he weep?" he whispers.

The melancholy slant to Her smile has never left, but now it turns to anguish. She sighs, looks at Wil with a poignancy that slides a slender blade of grief through Dallin's own heart. "Betrayal is a harsh teacher," She tells Dallin sadly, "and its lessons are steeped in deceit."

"I don't know what that means." Dallin looks at Her expectantly, but She only keeps gazing at Wil with that doleful melancholy. Dallin scowls, annoyed. "Why aren't you helping him?" he demands.

She turns to him with an elegant lift of Her perfectly sculpted eyebrow. "But I already have."

And then She's gone. Dallin blinks into the darkness, rubs at his eyes, tries to wake up, but he can't.

He walks slowly over to Wil, musing, somewhat unsettled that his feet touch nothing—no ground, no floor, only emptiness—and yet he doesn't fall. He wonders a little dazedly if he spread his arms wide, would he be able to fly? The thought seems so trivial as he draws closer to Wil, who is moving steadily, finding patterns with his fingertips and weeping quietly, tears slipping slowly to spatter down on....

Dallin frowns now, angry, and he reaches out, gently takes up Wil's hand in one of his own. "Your fingers are bleeding."

*Wil jumps, spins; Dallin thinks he's going to scream, but then Wil chokes it back. He stares, face twitching between misery and confusion, eyes half-lidded and pulsing out something that nearly hums with betrayed resignation—*burning, *Dallin thinks dazedly,* doesn't half cover it. *There is nothing so mundane as radiance coming from Wil's eyes, but* power. *Dallin can almost see it in physical form just below his corporeal vision, green irises swirling that fluid malachite and glistening jade he'd seen the first time he'd laid eyes on Wil and again in a cell in Dudley.*

Somehow it doesn't matter now—it's as it should be, and it's of less concern than those bleeding fingers. He turns Wil's hand palm up, touches lightly at a fingertip. "Why d'you do this to yourself?"

Wil doesn't answer the question, instead says, "You're... here."

Dallin shrugs, a small smile quirking the corner of his mouth. "I'm here."

"You're always here," Wil mutters unhappily, pulls his hand away, and looks at Dallin, eyebrows coming together in consternation. "What d'you want?"

His voice is dull, weary. He looks so much like he's expecting Dallin to say he'd like his soul, thanks, and his mind and heart while he's at, that Dallin has to smile.

"That's a very big question," he answers. "What do you *want?"*

Wil doesn't even think about it, just looks up at Dallin, drained. "I want to not be afraid anymore."

Dallin nods slowly, reaching out to lay his hand to Wil's shoulder. Wil doesn't shrug it off.

"Are you still afraid of me?"

A slight frown crinkles Wil's forehead. "Not... mostly," he answers slowly. "But I can't tell yet. I have to know first."

"Know what?"

Wil rolls his eyes with an impatient growl. "What do you want *from me?"*

"Ah." Dallin wants to laugh, and he doesn't think he should, but the question seems too simple to have been voiced so seriously. "I don't want anything from you. I want to help you." He runs a hand roughly through his hair and looks around at the bizarre surroundings. "But most of all, I really *want to wake up."*

Dallin was already sitting up, body still vibrating from its lurch into wakefulness. His chest was heaving—hard, shallow breaths sucking in and out like he'd just run five miles in his sleep—and his hands were shaking. He drew up his knees and lowered his face into his hands.

"Fuck." His voice trembled. He was being absurd.

He'd never had such a vivid dream in all his life. In fact, he couldn't remember the last time he *had* dreamed. And the things he'd seen, *felt*—

He shook his head. "Don't even think about it. It wasn't real, you're just spooked by all the... everything."

Except.

No. *No.* Shamans weaving little spells was one thing, but... but.... Well, and there had been Wil and that man in the cell....

A bit of a shudder he couldn't suppress, and Dallin rubbed at his face, peered around in the low, uncertain light from the dying fire, rubbed sleep-blurry eyes, and blinked 'til his vision cleared. He shot his gaze to the bed. Wil was still sleeping, thank the—

Dallin cut it off, jaw clenched. "You didn't see Her. You didn't see anything. It was a dream. You *need* your quickmud, damn it. Don't get all wonky now, for pity's sake."

Easier said than done. It *still* felt real. And the bit about Old Bridge—if it turned out it was even close to what really happened—

No. It wasn't. It was just Dallin's own imagination filling in too many blanks because he didn't have any facts to fill them with. It wasn't any more real than a man controlling other people's dreams. Just because everyone in Ríocht had gone insane with the wilder aspects of their religion didn't mean Dallin had to let them drag him along with them.

Still.

The lad's got scars you en't seen.

All Dallin had to do was slide his fingers into Wil's hair, feel about for scarred shapes beneath his fingertips. Their lack would prove that Dallin was just playing into everyone else's madness; their presence would prove.... He closed his eyes.

Their presence would confirm—at least circumstantially—that the Aisling was real. Which would, in turn, prove that the Guardian was real.

The thought turned Dallin's stomach, ever so slightly.

He growled. "All right, Dreamer," he muttered, low and quiet. "Why don't you do something useful and dream me up some coffee?"

A low snort knocked at the bottom of his throat, but it felt a little wild and crazed, so he kept it in. He ran a hand through his hair and peered up at the tiny window. It was going pinkish outside, dawn just breaking up the night. Maybe he could walk off the remnants of the dream, pick up some tea from the kitchen while he was at it. Do something nice for Wil, why not? Even if the dream hadn't been real, Wil had obviously been through some difficult times, and Dallin would bet no one had ever brought him tea in bed before. It would be a nice gesture. Wake him up in the right mood. Make him more cooperative.

There. It was decided. He'd go get tea. For Wil. Because it would serve Dallin's purposes. Lesson Two: Honey. He'd bring some of that, too—*hahaha*. Right.

He dressed quickly, throwing on clothes, strapping on his weapons with as little clanging as possible. His hands were still shaking, so it was hard going, but if he made too much noise he'd wake Wil, and then Dallin would have to explain why he was locking him in the room by himself so Dallin could get out somewhere he could breathe and pump some adrenaline through his veins to crowd out the ridiculous... whatever it was. And he didn't think he *could* explain.

Securely buttoned, tied, and strapped, Dallin slipped out the door and into the narrow hallway, locking the door behind him. *So, I am a prisoner* wanted to echo through his head, poke guilty little pins at him, but there was already too much racing around in there, so it couldn't get a handhold.

He sucked in a long breath, cleared his mind—or tried to—and clomped down the stairs to the empty common room. It was quiet and dark, no lamps lit yet, so Dallin followed the din of pots and a slice of dim light to the kitchen. The innkeep who'd served them supper last night—Dallin had neglected to ask his name—was already in there, baggy-eyed and sour-looking, along with two women busy with the morning baking. The innkeep looked up when Dallin reached the doorway.

"Ah, at least one person'll be happy for the bloody-awful-in-the-morning delivery."

Dallin blinked and lifted an eyebrow. After the night he'd had, he wasn't surprised that nothing was making sense. "Sorry?"

The man waved a hand tiredly. "Eh, not your fault. I'm up late to close up, and I'm not pleasant when I don't sleep 'til midday."

One of the women snorted and smirked at the other. The innkeep flashed them both a sour grimace, then turned back to Dallin. "One of our deliveries came early," he said. "Woke me up. I was going on back up, but I figured to tell Elli here to start brewing, 'cause I remembered you asking after coffee yesterday."

Dallin's stomach did a lazy little roll as the woman who must be Elli turned to pour the contents of a steaming pot into a good-sized mug. The aroma was undeniable and unmistakable. Dallin's head felt light.

"You...." Shit, that had come out rather high and thin. Dallin cleared his throat. "You've coffee?"

The innkeep spared Dallin a bit of a smile and gestured to the cup. "And more for you to take on the road, if you like."

Elli came at Dallin, proffering the mug. Dallin took a step back—he couldn't help it. He only just kept himself from turning tail and running. Considering the way his mind was reeling, Elli was probably lucky Dallin hadn't knocked the mug out of her hand and decked her.

"Just... I...." Dallin looked from the cup to Elli and over to the innkeep. He shook his head. "Hold just a moment," he managed. "I'll be right back."

And then he turned, bolted back out through the common room, and pounded up the steps. Hands juddering with that annoying tremor again, Dallin inserted the key into the lock as quietly as he could, turned it, and let himself inside.

Wil was still sleeping, curled up on his side but not scrunched in like he was trying to hide. He looked relaxed, in fact—deeply asleep, cheeks with some color beneath the bruises, not as hollow as only a few days ago, and brow smooth. One hand lay on the pillow beside his head, swaddled in its bandages, the other hanging over the edge of the mattress, fingers twitching slightly. He looked perfectly peaceful, sound asleep, nothing out of the ordinary.

Except for the tiny trickle of blood dripping slowly from his left nostril and onto the beige pillow slip.

"What the... shit." Dallin took a small step closer, reached out, then drew his hand back quickly. "No, no, no, don't do this to me." His voice was shaky and small. And he couldn't bloody care. He stared, watching the small trickle pool on the pillow slip, then blotch and spread like ink drops on paper. His hand slipped up over his mouth, holding back whatever little noises were trying to leak from it—demented laughter or ragged whimpers, he had no idea and *really* didn't want to find out. Slowly, like he was still dreaming, Dallin dragged his gaze away and peered up at the tiny little window, then back down at Wil. "Make it rain."

The low rumble of thunder growled immediately in the distance, the pink-yellow light through the little window darkening to gray in the space of only a minute or two while Dallin stood there and watched it. Wil stirred, groaning and shifting restlessly. A new freshet dribbled from his nose, heavier this time, and a thin little rivulet seeped from his ear, tracing along his jawbone.

"Oh no." Dallin shook his head slowly, and... stared. He couldn't do anything else, nailed to the spot. "I remember where I've seen those Marks now," he heard himself say, then barked out a harsh laugh and turned dazedly to look at the window as the first smattering drops of rain pelted the glass.

Lesson Five, his mind nattered at him, a wild little cackle hovering beneath its calm, chastising tone. *Everything he told you was the truth, and you have just spent the night being educated by the Mother Herself. You are the Guardian, and here before you lies the Aisling. You have been called. The Mother help you both.*

Boneless, bloodless, Dallin let his legs give, sat heavily on the bed, just missed plopping clumsily atop Wil, then bent over his knees and dropped his head into his hands.

"Oh no." A rusty little laugh shivered up his throat, shocky and hollow, and he closed his eyes, fisted his hands. "Fucking *shit*!"

ABOUT THE AUTHOR

Carole lives with her husband and family in Pennsylvania, USA, where she spends her time trying to find time to write. The recipient of various amateur and professional writing awards, several of her short stories have been translated into Spanish, German, Chinese and Polish. Free shorts, sneak peeks at WIPs, and other miscellany can be found on her website.

Website: www.carolecummings.com

Join the Rocky Ridge Books newsletter to find out when the Aisling trilogy and more of Carole's work will be available.

ALSO BY CAROLE CUMMINGS

The Aisling Trilogy

Guardian

Dream

Beloved Son

The Wolf's Own Series

Ghost

Weregild

Koan

Incendiary

The Queen's Librarian

Blue and Black

Don't Fear the (Not Really) Grim Reaper

ALSO FROM ROCKY RIDGE BOOKS

The Diversion Series from Eden Winters

Diversion

Collusion

Corruption

Manipulation

Redemption

Reunion

Suspicion

Decision

The Mountains from P.D. Singer

Fire on the Mountain

Snow on the Mountain

Fall Down the Mountain

Blood on the Mountain

Return to the Mountain

The Wrestling Series from D.H. Starr

Wrestling With Desire

Wrestling with Love

Wrestling With Passion

Wrestling with Hope

www.ingramcontent.com/pod-product-compliance
Lightning Source LLC
LaVergne TN
LVHW041108080826
845145LV00007B/1723

* 9 7 8 1 6 2 6 2 2 0 9 0 4 *